NAMELESS

ΠΑΜΕLΕSS

KYLE CHAIS

GALLERY BOOKS / KAREN HUNTER PUBLISHING

New York   London   Toronto   Sydney   New Delhi

G

Gallery Books
A Division of Simon & Schuster, Inc.
1230 Avenue of the Americas
New York, NY 10020

HUNTER

Karen Hunter Publishing,
A Division of Suitt-Hunter
Enterprises, LLC
598 Broadway, 3rd Floor
New York, NY 10012

First Karen Hunter Publishing/Gallery Books trade paperback edition January 2012

GALLERY BOOKS and colophon are registered trademarks of Simon & Schuster, Inc.

For information about special discounts for bulk purchases, please contact Simon & Schuster Special Sales at 1-866-506-1949 or business@ simonandschuster.com.

The Simon & Schuster Speakers Bureau can bring authors to your live event. For more information or to book an event contact the Simon & Schuster Speakers Bureau at 1-866-248-3049 or visit our website at www .simonspeakers.com.

Designed by Akasha Archer

Manufactured in the United States of America

10 9 8 7 6 5 4 3 2 1

Library of Congress Cataloging-in-Publication Data is available.

Chais, Kyle.
    Nameless / by Kyle Chais — 1st Karen Hunter Publishing/ Gallery Books trade paperback ed.
        p.   cm.
    1. Angels — Fiction i. Titls
PS3603.H33354N36 2011
813'.6 — dc22

2010035439

ISBN 978-1-4391-8725-8
ISBN 978-1-4391-8729-6 (ebook)

For the Abuela

I

HOST OF THE MILLENNIA

I am nameless. Names are for those with masters. Therefore, we have no name. The day of the demon is coming to an end. We await our pending execution. Many of us look forward to this imminent judgment. Others pathetically cower in their deserving of death. I have wandered the earth for millennia trying to find a way out. I realize now that it is hopeless. It can be quite boring when you're immortal and waiting at the same time. So I watch humans. From the Nameless realm I watch, analyzing their behaviors, motives, climaxes, recessions, and, most important, their power of choice.

From the beginning of man, I have witnessed the blackest crimes they have committed. Witnessed the crops of the earth watered with black blood spilled by men, women, and children all over the world. But one thing still torments me and my kind. It's the one simple thing that grips us in the back of our throats and won't let go. The one thing that has turned the most civilized ones among us into vengeful, raging lunatic monsters. That no matter how much we beg, no matter how much time we are given, no matter how much we pray, we will die, but humans . . . will remain. Irony's judgment is . . . ticklish.

Angels were given a perfect start, a perfect body, mind, and world with no problems. We were given the capabilities to serve our Father perfectly without fault. This was our great ability. Humans once had this ability but it was lost. Their ancestor parents traded it for a fruit and a snake. As for us angels, we traded it for our own fruits and snakes. We were at the pinnacle of perfection when we turned our backs on Father. Adam and Eve's offspring weren't. They were slaves to their selves. *Thoughts* . . . were my downfall. Thoughts. *Damn that woman*.

You are probably pondering, "What do demons do with their spare time?"

Well, first, don't ever use that term *demon* with us. It's extremely derogatory. We prefer to be called Fallen.

And I can't speak for my brethren, but I spend most of my time counting stars. It may be tedious, but it passes the time nicely. I enjoy taking long strolls through the park. I like going on carnival rides. I like going to operas. I like watching ballets. I also enjoy watching movies at theaters. That was one great addition to mankind—although I feel that the quality of movies is going down the toilet with these new special effects. I haven't seen a film that was truly original in years. The better the special effects, the worse the quality of the movie. How ironic. Yummy steak sauce with no steak.

This evening was particularly boring. I wish I could pass the time by sleeping, but beings such as me don't. Humans don't understand how valuable sleep is. They can kill eight hours or so just by shutting their skinny little eyelids and being still. So instead I decided to watch *The Wizard of Oz* on Broadway. This would be my 203rd time seeing it. I've memorized every single line from beginning to end. This is the only play I never grow tired of. Like Dorothy, I've searched the corners of a fantasy world trying get back home. With perseverance she made it back. How beautiful. How lovely. Such a good example to live by. What a crock of crap.

I'll never make it home. I am still here. In this fantasy world. Dreams really don't come true. For *my* kind. Funny. With all our power, that's one thing we can't do.

After drifting through the city slums of Manhattan, a human

male stumbled through an alleyway. He was drunk, so drunk he had to lean on walls to walk. He was looking so bad that even the harlots didn't want to get near him.

I watched, and I could see he was headed for a bar. I had actually been studying this human for a few months. His name is Aurick Pantera. He is one of the lowlifes of society; Aurick is always in debt, gambling his checks away, lying, cheating, and stealing. The money that was left was spent on women and booze.

It used to be worse. Before he was on meds, Aurick had bad hallucinations, imagining himself to be other people, some who didn't even exist. Poor pathetic creature.

Lately, Aurick had been hit with a certain . . . troubling issue. This problem is the most feared issue in the world. An excruciating evil. One of the biggest manslayers of this planet. Cancer. Not only that but it's one of cancer's most sinister villains, pancreatic cancer. The silent killer. Only about 5 percent diagnosed survive after three to five years. What a true villain indeed. You only have a chance of surviving this murderer if you treat it as early as it devours your flesh, bones, and soul. Foolishly, Aurick was too scared to follow through with more tests and treatment. He has the sense that if he ignores it, it'll go away. And if it doesn't go away, he will be too busy enjoying his life to care. Bury your skull in the dirt.

That's right, Aurick, live on to the bitter end. He was doing the right thing. People should not struggle against their demise. They should not think of the pain. They should just lie down and be at peace as I have. It is what has been keeping me separate from the others. My sanity is my reward.

I followed him into Dead Man's Pub. It's a bar where all the dregs of the city go to escape their problems and morals. It even has the saying "What happens in Dead Man's Pub stays in Dead Man's Pub." Original, eh?

Aurick climbed up the stairwell and knocked on the back exit of the bar.

The doorman answered and said in a gruff voice, "You can't enter this way. Go through the front."

"It's okay," Aurick said, flipping up the collar on his black jacket and combing back his soaked jet-black hair with his fingers. "It's me, Ben."

The guard opened the door and allowed him in. The bar was crowded with drunken thugs and goons. The lights were dim, which made the ugliest individual look attractive. One of my abilities as a spirit creature allows me to see germs clearly as bright green globs. Humans are covered in them, disgusting swine that they are—dancing and bumping into each other, touching and spreading impurities to each other. I watched them eat the green that covered their salted peanuts and Chex Mix.

The toxic odor of alcohol was immense. The packed bar had an almost overwhelmingly putrid stench of liquor and tobacco smoke. Tension hovered in the air.

Yet I was safe since I reside in the spirit realm. Spirit creatures such as me dwell in the Nameless realm, which is a separate dimension intertwined with humans' material realm.

Nameless is intangible to beings of the material realm. Only certain creatures, such as some cats, snakes, weasels, skunks, owls, and dogs can sense those of Nameless. In other words, I can see beings from the material realm but they can't see or affect me.

Aurick sat down at a barstool and ordered his drinks. He dove into his liquor and spoke to the female bartender about things the bartender didn't care about. Anytime a new female sat down at the bar, Aurick would stumble over to her and try to pick her up. His sour breath, slurred speech, and bloodshot, disoriented eyes were enough to make any female flee.

It was funny how he started out trying to court the most attractive females at the beginning of the night, only to wind up going after the most unattractive by the end. It was like going down from ten to one. Well, I guess the more you drink, the more attractive people appear. He whispered something atrocious into one blonde female's ear, which offended her so much that she slapped him across his face and treaded heavily away. He finally gave up and went back to his drinking.

The bartender asked him to stop drinking, but Aurick just got upset and started a drunken rant. Downing one drink after the next, he finally fell asleep (or passed out) at the bar. A group of four thugs approached him and tapped his shoulder with great force. Aurick didn't wake up, so a tall, brutish-looking white man with a ginger-colored beard picked up a drink and splashed it over Aurick's head and down his shirt.

He woke up in a daze, looking around, disoriented. "Hey, why would you waste a perfectly good drink? There are less fortunate people than us that would die for a drink, ya know."

"Cut the crap, Dwayne!" said the one with the ginger beard, using the fake name Aurick had given him. "You've been holdin' out on me. Where's my money?"

"Oh, Samson, fancy meeting you here!" Fear sobered Aurick and his voice trembled. "How'd you find me?"

"You know why I'm here. Where's my money?" Samson said with rising irritation.

"Look, Samson, I don't have the money right now. I-I need another week to get the cash up."

"You said that four months ago, Dwayne. I've been real patient. So are you saying you don't have my money?"

Aurick sank down into the barstool and stayed quiet.

"That's it. Get up, Dwayne. . . . I said get up!" Samson grabbed Aurick's collar, lifting him with ease.

Two of Samson's goons grabbed each of Aurick's arms and escorted him to the back exit of the bar. I followed to watch the entertainment. They stepped down the steel steps of the bar outside into the alleyway. Aurick tumbled down. He drunkenly got up, revealing a bloody cut on his forehead.

"Look, Samson, I'm sorry," Aurick whimpered. "I just need some time."

Samson delivered a hard, quick blow to Aurick's stomach. Aurick collapsed on his knees and coughed up spit and mucus. The other goons cheered.

"Yeah! Give it to him good, Sam, give it to him good," one of the goons said. "Teach that lowlife to learn to keep his promises!"

As Aurick was on his knees gagging, Samson kneed him in his face, flipping him onto his back. Samson lifted Aurick to his feet with ease and delivered blow after blow to his face, spilling blood from the open wound on his head. Samson then lifted Aurick over his head and threw him into nearby trash cans and bags, causing a great crash and commotion. Aurick rolled over the dirty, wet garbage bags. He pleaded, crying for mercy. Samson didn't want to hear it. The other thugs kicked Aurick repeatedly in his sides while he was curled on the ground.

I thought maybe these barbarians could give Aurick an escape by ending his miserable life, providing him with a shortcut.

"Okay, that's enough," Samson said to his goons. "We need to get out of here. Lift him up." His goons obeyed and lifted Aurick to his feet and stepped away. Aurick seemed to be gasping for air as if he were drowning.

"You're . . ." Aurick stopped to fill some more air into his shaky lungs. "You're letting me go?" His eyes widened in great surprise.

"Yeah, I'm letting you go."

"Oh, thank you, Samson!" Aurick placed his shaking, scraped palms on Samson's shoulders. "I'll get you the money tomorrow. I swear." Aurick's voice sounded as if he had been locked in a freezer for hours and was desperately trying to keep warm.

Samson reached into his jacket's inner pocket and pulled out a black object. He lifted the black object and pointed it toward Aurick's face. The object was an instrument of death. A gun.

"I'm setting you free, Dwayne. This is the most mercy that anyone could ever give you."

"No, please, Samson, don't do it! Please! Oh, God, please don't kill me!" Aurick eyes squirted tears that flooded his face.

"Yeah, do it, Sammy. Take him out for good," one of the goons said. Another advised Samson not to do it. Samson told him to shut up. Aurick squeezed his eyes tight and started praying to God for help. What a riot. Aurick's life would end before the cancer ate him. How lucky indeed.

I contemplated whether I should help Aurick. At least it had been entertaining and helped me pass some of my time. This poor man's life was pitiful. This would put him out of his misery and give him a shortcut to salvation. And I could just watch another human for fun.

Nonetheless, for some reason, I decided to save Aurick.

If we spirit creatures are strong enough, we can interact with the human realm. Using my abilities to accurately read Samson's muscle exertion in his arm and read his blood pressure to tell when he was going to pull the trigger, I diverted the trajectory of the bullet by bending the surrounding air. The bullet grazed Aurick's arm. Samson and his goons stood there confused.

Aurick peeked with one eye at the group.

"It was a blank! Shoot him again!" one of the thugs said. Samson pointed the gun again and Aurick shut his eyes again. The gun let off another bang but I deflected the bullet again, saving Aurick's pathetic life once more.

"What the hell, another blank?" Samson said with confusion. Samson squeezed the trigger again but I caused the gun to backfire. Shards scattered and sliced through everything around.

Samson gazed down at his hand, his once manly hand he'd used to torment his foes. He clenched his water fountain of a hand and screamed, like a woman giving birth. Two of Samson's fingers were blown off, and shards from the gun were sticking through his skin.

"Let's get out of here!" one of the goons said as the others ran off.

"I swear, you'll pay for this, Dwayne," Samson cried, following his crew, holding his hand in pain.

Aurick wiped the tears from his face and ran off, muttering, "Thank you, God."

There goes God taking underserved credit again. *My* credit. I laughed and then followed him down the alleyway until a voice called to me.

"You're walking on thin ice, Jackie-sama."

I looked around to see who it was. A dark figure was standing on the rooftop of a three-floored building nearby. He wore a long, black trench coat. The collar was up reaching ear level.

"Oh, it's you," I said. "Didn't I tell you to stop calling me Jackie, you nosy barn owl?"

"Oh, I'm sorry. What would you like me to call you?"

"Don't call me anything. I'm as nameless as the realm where I dwell."

"All right, 'Nameless.' I saw what you did just now."

"So? What of it?"

"It's my job to remind you not to break the rules. If you had gone any further, I would have had to take you in."

"I know what the rules are. I know that my destiny is sealed in Father's forearm. I don't need babysitting, so stop stalking me."

"Stalking? You're the one following people around for no apparent reason."

"I have reasons. What are you doing here anyway? Don't you have better things to do?"

"Nope, just patrolling through this shameless city. Levels of violence have been rising dramatically recently."

"Well, what do you expect? It's the last days. Not only that, but this is New York City. The modern-day Babylon."

"You're right. Though much of the violence is caused by Fallen. In fact, I haven't seen so much Fallen influence since the last War of the Flies. Not only that, but some have been searching for you."

"Me?" I laughed. "Well, I'm flattered."

"It was your old faction. It seems some want you back."

"I haven't spoken to them in centuries. I never had any time for them."

The figure smiled. "The way I remember it, you were *kicked* out," he said smugly.

This was getting much too uncomfortable. I wanted to change the subject.

"How are the other fairies holding up?" I said, using a word as derogatory to him as *demon* was to us. Angels hated to be called fairies.

"They're a little stressed-out but they'll hold up."

"Good to hear."

"Well, I'll be on my way, Mr. *Nameless*. Be careful and don't get too attached to these sinners."

"Understood, old friend," I said.

The figure phased out of sight. He was an old friend from the days before human existence. He was still my friend, occasionally popping by to visit me, even though he's one of the high-ranking maroon angels. Maroon angels were stationed on earth seven thousand years ago, ever since the Eden incident, to keep Fallen from going too far in harming humans with the command to stay on earth in the Nameless realm until Father orders them to return home when He commences the Great War. The Great War to end all wars.

Even for the maroons, living an immortal life in Nameless can be tiresome. Some through the ages have gone postal, and a few others AWOL. Some have even crossed over and become Fallen themselves.

Maroons that become Fallen have it the worst. They are caught in between—shunned by the angels and bullied by those who have been Fallen longer.

As I thought about my friend and the life I used to lead before the fall, I continued in my current life—watching Aurick. I followed him drag his way home to his cruddy, old apartment building. It was a six-story walk-up. Well, it wasn't supposed to be, but the elevator never worked. The walls and the floors were always filthy and garbage- and glass-strewn.

The floors were stained with bloody footprints of children who played in the hallways. The walls were marked by handprints, profanity, fingerprints, and even a few footprints.

Aurick drunkenly walked up six flights of steps to his apartment. He stumbled to his room, collapsed on his bed, and went to sleep.

I believe I am going to go insane watching people live their lives while I wait for mine to end. I left and went to sit on top of the roof, looking over the insects of Manhattan going about their daily lives, unaware of the cataclysm that will one day befall them all. I lay flat on my back and returned to my routine of counting the stars of this galaxy. Counting the endless quantity soothes the mind. It helps organize my thoughts. Thoughts of how I was going to bear living a boring day like this over and over soaked my mind. Thoughts of how I used to have a purpose. The days of purpose were long gone. I wondered if anyone was watching me live my life as I had watched Aurick's. How would they think of me? Would they think of me as a great person who temporarily fell short of the mark, who bravely took the consequences? Or would they feel that I'm just a fool who's going to get what he deserves? After a few hours, a pitter-patter sound made me mess up my count.

I ignored it for a while but the sound wouldn't stop, which

annoyed me, so I sat up and looked around. The perpetrator was a young kitten chasing after pigeons. It was small and feeble, brown, with a reddish calico.

It would only have a few days of life left before it starved to death. But this kitten chased and chased, never giving up. It breathed hard and wouldn't stop. It had a slim chance of survival, yet it wouldn't lie down and die. Suddenly, he ran after one pigeon at the edge of the roof. At least the kitten will soon end his lonely pain, I thought to myself.

The pigeon flew off the roof with the kitten leaping after it. The kitten missed and fell to his doom with a loud screech bursting from its tiny lungs. I caught it at the last moment and placed him back on the roof.

"I'm giving you a second chance," I said to the kitten as if I were going to get a reply. This was becoming a habit, it seemed. "Now fight on and live, you pathetic low-life organism that no one cares about. Live tonight, but know that you will die one day."

The kitten briefly looked up at me and ran off. Then, as I resumed my counting, the creature came back. It stared, purred, and sat next to me. The few species that can sense spirit beings still have a limited sense of our presence, but this creature seemed to fully see me. Not only that, but he was calm.

"What's the matter? Are you lonely like me? Do you have a heavy burden as well?" It felt wonderful having something know of my existence. And I suppose the kitten felt the same way. I felt in my heart I wanted more. I wanted someone to know that I was alive. I knew what I wanted to do.

"I give thanks to you, kitty! By the way, I know that you exist, right? Well, everything that has been noticed to exist should have a name, right? Obviously, you can't give yourself a name so I'll give you one. I'll give you the most important name in the universe. I'll name you Sephirot."

I grabbed a pigeon and killed it instantly with crushing air pressure and let Sephirot feast on it.

"You can thank me later," I said. "I'm going to find a name of my own. Sit tight, Sephirot."

Watching Sephirot fight so hard to stay alive reminded me about how little fight Aurick had. That kitty had more heart than he did. Aurick was a loser and a scoundrel. No one will miss him when he's gone.

I went to watch him. He was dead asleep on his bed. Sleep. Oh, how wonderful his sleep must feel. Oh, how I missed those wonderful nights of rest. Oh, how unfair this is that such an ungrateful man should enjoy delightful slumber while a mighty being such as I have to suffer the constant awareness of myself.

His guard was down. I wanted sleep and I wanted it now. What about the risks? I wasn't really adept in body possession, so what if an accident occurred? And Aurick has that vile disease in him. Oh, it will only be for one night, I thought. And even if it were to suddenly try to kill him, I would be more than enough to restrain it. It would be just one night of blissful slumber. In the morning, I would leave Aurick's body and lock the door. Nothing bad would happen from just a few hours of sleep, right?

I sighed. Is this how I was going to act for the rest of my life? Indecisiveness was how I landed in this position in the first place. Leaning on two opinions had gotten me nowhere. To hell with the risks. I wanted . . . I needed to take action and I needed to do it now.

Then, just as I was about to synchronize with Aurick's body, he abruptly woke up and went to the bathroom. He fell asleep on the toilet, which was an annoyance because I didn't want to fuse with his body in such an indignant position. Three hours passed and he was still asleep on the toilet. I didn't feel like waiting until the next day, so I fused with him anyway.

When I came into consciousness, I could smell the vile alcoholic odor of this body's sweat and fecal matter. All of my senses—especially my sense of smell—were forced into immediate action, and I began to gag.

Things were not totally in sync as my spirit body was still making the adjustments. I wasn't fully able to manipulate his body yet and had to sit on that toilet in that stench for about two more hours.

When I developed the ability to move well enough, I stood up and slowly walked into the bedroom. I reached for the bed but the body's legs gave out and I collapsed to the floor on my stomach with my pants and boxer shorts down.

The rest of my senses caught up and I began to feel the intoxication still having its effect, which forced me to fall asleep right there on the floor, facedown, with my pants around the ankles. How indignant.

The next morning, I awoke. Every muscle in this body was aching something terrible. The powerful Samson really did give this body a beating. I didn't think I would be synchronized this well enough to feel the pain yet.

I took a shower to wash the impurities from this body. (Aurick never did wash frequently.) I still wasn't in full control of the body, so I had to be careful not to fall and break my neck.

The shower stung every cut and bruise on this body. After a few painful minutes, however, it felt good. Through endurance comes virtue. I started to drink the steaming-hot water that was coming from the showerhead. It felt so . . . delightful. Just as my hunger pains were manifold so was my sense of touch. I could feel each and every one of the thousands of warm droplets fill every microscopic pore on the moist flesh. I spent another two hours in the shower. It killed me having to have to step out of such an oasis.

Afterward, as I was drying off, Aurick's stomach organ gripped me. I guessed it was because I was feeling hunger.

There I was, standing in front of the bathroom mirror. Cuts

and bruises were all over this body. The side of my left eye socket was swollen and red. A cut was right over the brow of the right eye socket. It wasn't bleeding. The hands were badly scraped. It hurt when I clenched them closed. This was my identity. There I was and now I must leave. Suddenly there was a growl. Was that a dog? No. I looked down. It was Aurick's stomach organ. I was so hungry. I remembered that eating food was . . . delicious, delightful. Oh, but it was time to go. I wouldn't feel hunger anymore in my spirit form. Oh, but what was that dish I once loved? Was it . . . tomatoes? I adored tomatoes. Perhaps I could stay longer in this body than for just one night, to experience the pleasures of taste. Oh, but this would be dangerous.

I looked into the refrigerator and saw only a bottle of milk and a bologna-and-cheese sandwich. The bread had a greenish color and foul smell. I was hungry but this seemed unappetizing.

I got dressed in a black suit and decided to go out to get something to digest. As I was walking down the stairs, caught up in absorbing my surroundings in this body, I walked into a young woman in her early twenties carrying bags of groceries. Our collision caused her to drop her groceries down the stairs.

"Oh, I deeply apologize, miss," I said, and started to retrieve her items and put them in one of her plastic bags.

As I picked up a can of coffee, I paused. I stared at the mess and back at the woman with amazement. My amazement turned into excitement, and my excitement soon turned into glee.

"I bumped into you?" I asked.

"Yeah," she said, looking at me oddly.

"You can feel me?"

"Yeah." She started to back away from me.

I finished putting away all of her groceries and handed them over.

"Thank you," she said.

"No, thank you!" I said with a giddy smile. I had not made

physical contact with a human in centuries. I felt . . . I didn't know how I felt.

"Are you high or something, dude?"

"I am high on existence," I said.

"What happened to your face, man? That looks terrible." The woman reached out slightly without actually intending to touch me. I didn't want to explain so I pressed on with something else to talk about.

"My name is Aurick. What is your name, ma'am?"

"I know your name is Aurick," she said with a puzzled expression. "I've known you since you moved in here. Here, this will sober you up." She handed me a can of coffee and then told me her name was Jamie.

While I was walking down the stairs, the landlord opened his door and started yelling at me. "Aurick, where's my goddamn rent?"

"I'll get you the rent."

"You've been saying that for three months now. If I don't get my rent, your ass is going to be on the street!"

I ignored him and continued walking.

I went to the vegetable store and bought tomatoes. I walked through Manhattan for hours, savoring the sounds, the smells, the people. I walked past human after human, watching them go to their miserable places of work.

I could sense flashes of thoughts bubbling to the surface: "Why do I put up with my boss?" "I wonder how many calories I'm burning right now walking." "I hope Latisha doesn't find out I cheated." "God, I hate my job!" "I'm going to shoot everyone at work when I get there."

So much despair. So much emptiness. So tiresome.

I walked across the Brooklyn Bridge and walked back. I worked Aurick's body more during this one day than he probably had in three years. I couldn't exercise as a spirit, and this was wonderful.

I went to the beach to feel the cold, salty water seep into every pore of my human body. I used most of the money Aurick had to purchase different types of flowers so I could deeply inhale their odors.

I didn't want to leave the body. Weeks of my merrymaking continued. I inhaled an assortment of wonderful wild odors when I walked through the park. Sure I walked through the park as a spirit, but now I could actually experience all the sounds and smells that my spirit body could not have sensed as a human could. The movies were far more enjoyable, and I understood why humans were enthralled by the newest special effects.

I even found a special showing of *The Wizard of Oz* on the big screen. I could actually converse with my neighboring meatbags as we watched the screen. Some rudely told me to quiet down, but I was so merry that they could actually hear my sounds. I happily told them to shut up and they yelled back. This was fun. *The Wizard of Oz* was never so wonderful. The wonderful Wizard of Oz.

Sadly though, my steam was running out. I found that nothing much had changed. I was simply a Fallen with a human body. I was doing the same things I did in my spirit form. I wanted to do something that the Fallen don't do. I wanted some direction. I decided to go to support groups. There were all kinds of them. Support groups for drug addiction, sex addiction, gambling addiction, eating disorders, anxiety disorders, cancer, HIV, suicide prevention, abuse survivors, divorce.

I decided to go to a support group for testicular cancer. Cancer can be unstoppable. And you can't stop the unstoppable. I could identify. My own fate was sealed in Father's forehead. *He* was the true unstoppable object, and there was no unmovable force to shield me.

I would have been depressed if I hadn't already been sick of being depressed. The humiliation and agony of the support group members filled me with strength, though sometimes we would have to hug one another. One weepy man forced a hug onto me. I didn't want to blow my cover, so I cringed and accepted it. I soon stopped going (not just because of the hugging). I grew tired of their misery.

Still, I did begin to actually listen to their advice. One suggested that I needed to keep myself busy. Finding my purpose in life would keep my mind off my testicular cancer. Little did they know that I'd had a purpose in life.

What could be a grander purpose than directly serving the Creator of the cosmos? Nothing, that's what! Though I knew it was pointless, if I was going to be human for a while, as I realized I had no intention of leaving this body, then perhaps I should take up their advice. Hone my mind. Develop a career and new reputation of sorts. Give Aurick a new direction quickly and affordably. I needed a cheap education at a cheap price, at least for now.

Community college, here I come!

II

STALKER

Busy hands keep a man sane. Busy hands keep a man proud. Busy hands give a man hope. What happens when the busy man finishes his work? Will love be the thread that keeps those hands busy enough for more work to arrive? And how long will that thread hold?

It's been three years and I'm still in this body. Nice and neat, I might add. I cleaned up the apartment quite nice. I didn't add much decoration except for clocks in every single room, including the closets. A fellow has to keep track of time you know.

Over these three years, I have acquired careers that most humans view as desirable. I used my mass millennial experience to flash through college for a Ph.D. in literature studies and a Ph.D. in psychology. (Also with a little help of light hypnosis. Just a little.) Under the pseudonym Harry Baal, I have written several self-help books, which have sold millions of copies.

The landlord and I are best of friends. Well . . . he's friends with *me*. He's amazed about the change in personality. He's even commented, "Are you another person?" a few times. Rent is always on time and doubled. He invites me for dinner. I turn down the offer. He owns seven cats. Sephirot hates the smell of other cats.

Sephirot and I have a commitment to each other, and I wouldn't let a man get between us. He would never have bothered to ask me over if I didn't have money. He treated Aurick like trash before. What a change.

Are all relationships like this? Do we merely have social relationships to drain profit off them? And if it wasn't for profit, wouldn't it be true that we just hang out with people to drain some sort of entertainment? We didn't choose our husband or wife just for the sake of choosing. We did it for some sort of gain. Give-and-take. Did we all choose to accept Father for this sort of relationship? We give him worship in exchange for services and hope? What did he even do with his time before creation? Are we all just filler time for each other to get through the day? If this was about giving and taking for the sake of happiness, why should our actions be punished at all?

It's funny that I didn't have these thoughts before I was grounded. We enter the world single and leave the world single. Money can buy you anything: companionship, trust, lovers, etc. Well . . . almost anything. With all the riches in the world, I can't buy time.

I'd also formed a rock band called Nameless, which was quickly growing in popularity. The music is a blend of gothic, alternative, and progressive metal. The songs, written by me, are typically longer than most rock songs. I made the compositional structures as complex as a Beethoven piece, but the lyrics are short and simple. In addition to composing songs, I work mostly as the band's legal counsel, manager, and financial officer. I don't normally play, but when I do, I play rhythm guitar on certain songs. I play primarily because I didn't feel like finding another member, but I will admit . . . I do like some of the praise that comes from being onstage. Just a bit.

My stage name is the Guitarist with No Name. It's No-Name for short. I wear a masquerade mask. This prevents fans from recognizing me. I try to act as boring as possible by playing my instrument, sitting on a stool in the background, moving nothing but my fingers and wrists. The troubling thing is that the more melancholy I appear, the more *metal* I am to the fans.

We are getting more and more requests for interviews, but I don't do interviews. This gives me the freedom to do what I want and not be pestered by paparazzi and our mindless fans.

I donate most of the money I earn to my coworkers and charity. Still living in that same old, cruddy apartment, I haven't even changed a single piece of furniture, partly in anticipation of Aurick's somehow regaining control of his body.

The only things I actually pay for are food, rent, water, electricity, soap, clothes . . . and curtains. I love curtains. Their beautiful silky texture. Their infinite number of designs. Just like the stars. I love them so much.

Yet my boredom has returned. Even with all my careers and hobbies, I can't escape this dreaded melancholy.

I am currently waiting for my next patient at my downtown office, looking at the watches I wear on each arm. I have shelves filled with all sorts of books. I have fairy tales such as *Alice's Adventures in Wonderland*, *The Wonderful Wizard of Oz*, and *Aesop's Fables*. I have various essays by psychologists and philosophers such as Fredrick Nietzsche, Sigmund Freud, and Aristotle. I have religious texts, such as the Pāli Canon, Quran, and Bible. These books can be useful in sparking conversations with anyone of any sort of background. I also try to fit in the book *The Adventures of Huckleberry Finn*. Most times using that story isn't appropriate for the situation I'm dealing with, but, eh . . . I like talking about it. It's one of my favorite stories.

And just in case you were wondering, no, religious texts do not have holy energy that burn *unholy* beings such as myself. The only pain us Fallen get from reading them are paper cuts. What a ridiculous notion. In fact, I've read them all. No human knows religious text better than I do.

Admittedly, I try to put the Bible at the side where it's harder for my patients to see. The closer I come to my demise, the greater my intolerance for looking at the thing. I don't appreciate the constant reminder of my time running out.

But on to the positive side of things. This is my favorite gig. Nothing beats watching people's mental stability collapse in front of your eyes. Though that's fun, for a challenge I do what I can to fix their brains . . . sometimes. Lately, this also has grown dull. The man I just saw was suffering from depression and was having nightmares about killing people. Yawn!

My next patient entered the room. His name is Cullen Holdfield. He looked at my wrists in an odd fashion. "Can I ask you something? Why do you have a watch on each wrist?"

I raised my eyebrow. "So that I will know the time. Why else?" What a stupid question.

Cullen nodded and didn't ask more of it.

He comes every week without fail. He tells me about how his wife beats him. His wife burns him with cigarettes when he doesn't jump up to do what she tells him. And when he does jump up to do chores, he gets another lashing if it's not done right. He says he particularly fears her infamous talons. Every week there's a new crimson scratch on his body, especially on his neck. He doesn't feel like much of a man anymore. His friends and family don't help much. They tease him almost as badly as she does. As a result, he has low self-esteem. He stays with her for the sake of the kids. I keep telling him to leave her, that she's not good enough for him. He's too in love and too scared to do it. He says he contemplates suicide sometimes.

I was growing weary of this man. I have been for weeks. None of the conventional therapy approaches were working so I thought I might try another approach. I slammed my knife on the desk, pinning it deeply into the wood.

"What's with the knife?" Mr. Holdfield said.

"Why *do* I have a knife?" I said, shrugging my shoulders.

He stared at me quizzically for a few seconds. "Um, I don't know."

"Come on. I'm sure you can come up with something." He

shook his head and looked around the room as his brain tried to process everything for an answer. "To peel an apple?"

"No," I said flatly. He widened his eyes, staring. I stared back. "Go ahead."

He laughed shortly and smiled. "To stab me?" he said, and shrugged his shoulders.

My face didn't make an expression. I sighed. "We all have decisions to make. Whether the decision is productive or unproductive, we must make decisions. A man who doesn't make a decision might as well not exist. I've . . . learned this all too well."

"What are you getting at?"

"You have three options, Cullen Holdfield. Option number one: you leave her. Option number two: you work it out. Option number three: you take this knife here and kill yourself." I tossed some painkillers on the desk. "Slitting your wrists can hurt a bit so these should help."

"This is crazy. This is unlike you."

"I'm a complicated person."

He yanked the blade from the desk and held it in his hand, staring at it.

"This is where you're headed, so why wait any longer?" I said. "You told me you've thought of this. You told me this was the cleanest way to go, so go."

Cullen's eyes watered. He stared at the sharp blade for a good couple of minutes.

"What are you waiting for?" I urged. "I thought you wanted to separate from your wife. Do it!"

He held the cold blade to his left wrist. Tears ran down his face and dripped on the blade. He jerked back, gasped, and dropped the knife to the floor.

"Just as I thought," I said smugly. "You don't want to die. But you don't want to live the rest of your life like this, either.

So do us all a favor, leave this lady. Find some joy in your miserable existence. Stop wasting my time. It's as simple as that."

Cullen got up and quietly left. I was sure that he wasn't going to come back ever again.

My next patient soon came in. Her name is Helena Way. She is an American woman. She has pale skin. She was wearing long, black pants and a long, black shirt, her jogging clothes. She tells me she likes to appear as common as possible when off work. She tells me she can't stand her coworkers and being cookie-cut into their patterns. She weighs in at about 120 pounds. She's five feet nine inches tall. She's pretty, but not the most appealing woman on the planet. Maybe it's the lack of makeup during our sessions?

But what made up for all of that is her hair. Her beautiful long, sleek, jet-black hair. Her hair is so long that it reaches down to her knees. Her network loves it also because it helps distinguish their newscast from others.

I imagine her hair covering my entire body. It reminded me of . . . *her*.

She opened up her mouth to speak and uttered, "Why do you have two watches on?" What a wonderful question.

"It's to know what time it is," I said, tilting my head.

Helena speaks with a calm, gentle, but nonetheless pompous attitude, just like my own. She spoke to me about how her day was and what had been troubling her the past week. She's so good as a reporter that she usually works alongside lawyers and sometimes the FBI. She once went undercover at a slaughterhouse upstate. She discovered and exposed an underground sweatshop and single-handedly brought the company to ruin. During a bloody war, she dove into the danger of battle for news coverage. Her efforts proved fruitful with the incrimination of a certain leader using her bombshell coverage.

Her antics get her a lot of death threats and murder attempts. Being one of the noncorruptible symbols of the city gave Helena the nickname the Second Coming of the Muckrakers.

She tells me about what she does and a little about the cases she works on. For weeks, she vented about all of her boring problems and I gave her my divine advice, which she often rejected, annoying me greatly. Yet, that was also intriguing. Helena had a melancholic personality at first, but the more sessions we had together, the more exciting and open she became. She opened up almost every weird corner of her personality, which always kept me guessing.

She told me she had always wondered if she would ever have sex with her identical twin. She thought it wouldn't be considered gross since they're practically the same person.

Helena told me about her wild adventures as a field journalist back in the day. She told me that she never lets a great story slip through her fingers. She does whatever it takes to be the first to get it. She once pulled a gun on a teenager who wouldn't give his eyewitness account. The teen didn't know that it was a toy gun so he gave his story to her. She then blackmailed him and gave him some money to keep his mouth shut.

Another funny story was when she dressed up as a clown to infiltrate an independent circus ring. They were suspected of kidnapping people on their tours and selling them into slavery. When the suspects discovered her presence, she released all the wild animals on them to make her escape. It turned out that they weren't really human traffickers. It was just a false rumor.

Helena may be the first interesting person I've met in centuries. I could barely wait for her return. In between sessions, it felt like an eternity. She never missed her appointments, but one day she was late. I sat with my hands folded, tapping my pen on the desk speculating what could have happened to her. I started off thinking, "How unprofessional!" But as the minutes ticked by, I became concerned, wondering if she had finally been killed. Waiting for Helena's arrival was almost painful to endure. She finally arrived, which curiously caused me to become jittery. Imagine me, jittery!

It was a bright, sunny day when Helena came in late. She'd missed her jog so she wanted to have a quick session so that she could go to the park afterward. I offered to jog with her.

"Wouldn't that be going against doctor-patient policy?" Helena said quizzically. She was right on point. I had to think of something quickly.

"Oh, it is only to *continue* the session outdoors. I believe you will be more comfortable expressing yourself."

Helena smiled and raised her left eyebrow. "Are you sure you won't get in trouble?"

I laughed with a short burst. "It is fine, Ms. Way. This is for *your* health."

She was still a little unsure, but she agreed to go through with the session outdoors.

The funny thing was, when we got to the park, we didn't even jog. We just talked and made fun of the people who walked by the bench we were sitting on. Fat people, short people, ugly people, poor people, rich people, crying people. It was all just so much fun. Helena's laughter was adorable. It was a laugh of a child. The Helena that wore makeup is surely different from this Helena. I realized that makeup not only hides one's humanity on the outside, but the humanity of the soul as well. This was the real Helena.

A Frisbee hit Aurick in the forehead. Aurick's shoulder muscles tensed up. I jumped up and stomped Aurick's feet on the ground and scanned around to find the fool who threw it. It was a young boy. He was laughing hysterically with his two friends. This would not go unpunished. My eyes targeted the terrorist. Perfect accuracy is one of my specialties. Nice and precise. Vengeance was absolutely mine. I noticed Helena. She was giggling. This was different. This wasn't the fake laugh that she used to perform for my terrible jokes in the office or the kind she put on in front of the camera.

"You like . . . this game?"

Helena jumped up and took the Frisbee from me. She flung it to the terrorists.

"Would you like to play?" I said, shrugging my shoulders.

And there we were, hopping and dashing about across the field. This was terrible. Grass stains were attacking the bottoms of my lovely pants and shoes. Though I wanted to cry from the degrading of the fabric, the sight of Helena's enjoyment made it worth it. She's so . . . childlike. I bought the three little boys ice cream. They wanted to play with us more but it was time for us old folks to rest. As we departed, one of the boys reminded me to give him back the Frisbee, which I was holding. My thirst for vengeance still gnawed at my toes. I flung it at him, knocking the ice cream out of the little fool's hands. He cried. I smiled inside.

We plopped down on the bench and stretched our bones and aching muscle fibers.

"This is nice, Dr. Pantera. You make me feel . . . normal."

"Normal is boring."

"True." She laughed. She stared deeply into my eyes. I felt uncomfortable. It looked as if she was trying to figure something out.

"What?" I said.

"You're smiling."

I didn't think that was a big deal. I didn't even realize I was smiling in the first place.

"So? Don't all hum—I mean, people smile?"

"You know that's the first time I have ever seen you smile," Helena said, smiling herself. "It's a nice smile."

Her smile made me smile. And I felt . . . exceptional. We

spent the next moments admiring the bright, smoggy sky of New York City. I wanted to draw more out of Helena so I said, "Isn't the sky amazing? It's amazing that a single being designed all of this. Don't you think?"

"I didn't know you were a believer." Helena sighed. "Lucky you."

"What do you mean?"

She didn't turn to look at me. She kept her eyes to the blue sky. "I meant that you're lucky that you're a believer. People like you seem to be happier. Happy and full of hope and all. Usually the dumb ones though."

"You do not have hope?"

"I hope that when I die the doctors will find patients who'll be able to use my donated organs."

"That's your hope?"

At that, Helena finally focused her eyes on me. It seemed that she was getting upset. "I'm just saying it's hard to believe there's an all-knowing being who looks out for everyone."

"I could sort of believe that."

"Oh, yeah, well, let me tell you something," she said, raising her tone. "When I was seven, my priest touched me where his fingers didn't belong. All eleven of them. I cried to my parents about it, but they were proud, stern believers, so they didn't believe me much. But they did confront the priest about it. He admitted to what he did. And you know what?" Helena waited as if I were going to ask. "He apologized and confessed his sins. He went back to leading the congregation in a month."

This was the first time I was hearing this. She was opening up to me. She refused to before. The only reason she came to me was because her superiors, uncharacteristically concerned, ordered her to go to therapy because of her pathological urge to go toward crisis. Helena was the face of their industry. She was too valuable to lose.

This revelation was as I thought. Helena had so much in her

past that still gnawed at her. Mental chain mail was the only thing that kept her going.

"Your parents didn't tell the police?"

She laughed at what I said. "They were admonished to not tell. Didn't want to rattle the cages. Like I said, they were proud, stern believers, so they didn't dare tell on him. Right in the Lord's house. So let me ask you something?" Her voice and fingers stiffened. "Where was God when that freak was thrusting into me over and over again despite my cries of pain? Huh?" I didn't dare to respond. "Like I thought. Life's a bitch and then you die. That's my philosophy. Just hope that there's plant life around to feed on your carcass."

Helena was always intense, so this didn't bother me. What did bother me was that I was living proof of God's existence, but I couldn't dare tell her that. I would be in danger of getting even more punishment. All I could do was get close enough to talk to her about her life. After we had our session, I asked her out for dinner, deciding to do away completely with therapist-client boundaries. She declined, saying that she was in a relationship with another man.

"So what?"

"So I won't go out with you."

I treaded through the city for hours until the sun fell asleep. I was humiliated at being turned down by a mere human. It wasn't as if I wanted a romantic relationship. I just wanted someone deep to talk to, which is hard to find. Though she said that she didn't believe in God, she still held a code of honor. This fact boiled in me, but I was also gripped with curiosity as well. A human sticking by such trivial moralities *these* days was . . . intriguing.

I couldn't stand waiting for another appointment so I picked up my phone, canceled the rest of my sessions, and went to Helena's house to find out more of what she was about. She lived on the top of a thirty-two-story apartment building. The inside of the building was extravagantly decorated with sparkling chandeliers, marble floors and walls, and, best of all, embroidered silk curtains. I was surprised that she lived in such a place because she always wore cheap clothing. I didn't want to frighten her with the knowledge that I was following her, so I went up a building parallel to hers that was the same height. Security men questioned me, but with my hypnotic charm they let me pass. I took the elevator up to the highest floor. From there, I went up the steps to the rooftop. The gravel on the roof was messing up my shoes. I'd just gotten them polished too. I stood on the edge of the ledge, bracing myself against the chilly autumn wind. The smell of the crisp, brisk air of the night was most refreshing.

My extraordinary eyes allowed me to peer into her apartment. She took a shower for forty-five minutes and eight seconds. She brushed her teeth for two minutes and twenty-three seconds. She brushed her hair for five minutes and two seconds. A man knocked on her door. She opened the door for him and embraced him close to her chest. He had the chiseled face of a supermodel. He didn't look too deep. All muscle but no brains. They started kissing and then entered the bedroom. I looked on until an old, annoying friend appeared.

"Long time no see, buddy!"

He appeared upside down, suspended in midair in front of me, past the ledge. He chose to appear as a Caucasian human in his late teenage years. I've known him for a few thousand years since the Eden Incident. I actually knew him much longer than that, but I've never talked to him as much after that day.

"How long after have you been following me, Aisely?" I said.

"How long have ya been following this little hottie? More like stalking." He speaks with a childish, playful tone.

"I'm not stalking, I'm researching."

"Awww, don't tell me that ya fell in love. Kenny and Helena, sittin' in a tree. K-I-S-S-I-N-G. You're such a cute little Peeping Tom."

"Stop calling me random names, you foul heathen! My name is now Aurick."

"Oh, so your name is Aurick now. Can you ever decide on a stable name?"

"Why don't you mind your own damn . . ." Suddenly, both my arms went numb and the right side of my body started to feel pain.

"You okay, man?" Aisely said with a concerned expression while sustaining a smile.

I could no longer see out of my left eye and I started to get extremely dizzy. My legs collapsed and I fell over the edge of the rooftop. While I was falling, I lost consciousness so I couldn't leave Aurick's body. When I came to consciousness, I was on my back on the hard rooftop gravel. I was still dizzy, so I couldn't stand up. I sat up and rubbed my head.

"Hey, Aurick. You almost got your host killed. That wouldn't have been a good thing, ya know. Good thing you have a great friend like me to bail ya out," Aisely said, knocking on my head like a door.

"What happened?" I said, rubbing my eyes.

"Your body had a heart attack. If it weren't for me, you'd be dead. You've been in that body for too long. It's time to leave it."

"No, I'm not done with it. There're still things I have to do with this host."

"For what? Oooh, I get it. You want that woman to yourself, don't ya?"

"I asked her out, but she has a boyfriend."

"Well, why *should* she go out with you when she has that pretty boy over there taking good care of her?" Aisely looked into her apartment. "Wow, he sure knows how to handle a woman."

Aisely walked me home to my cruddy apartment. On the

way we spoke to each other, making other people think I was crazy because it looked as if I were talking to myself. Aisely was invisible to them. When we got home, he sat down on my couch, put his feet on my coffee table, and started to watch television.

"How'd you find me, Aisely?"

"How couldn't I find you, Aurick? You have one of the best bands in history. You're more famous than Jesus. You were bound to get attention. With all of that fortune, why do you live in such a dump?"

"This way of living is sufficient for me."

There was a knock on the door, so I answered it. It was Jamie. She lived in the apartment above me. Jamie had had a crush on Aurick ever since he'd moved in and had been asking me out constantly these past three years. At first, she was just an annoying pest. But after a while, I came to a liking of her. She's always cheerful even when she's depressed. She had a boyfriend whom she's with now. She genuinely liked him but they had fights because he was always cheating on her.

"Aurick, are you coming to my party? Me and Micky are throwing it. It's next week," Jamie said, holding her hands together and fidgeting around. I turned her down and lied that I had something else to do. She looked disappointed and said, "That's okay; I know you have more important things to do than be at a stupid party. Here, I made you these."

She handed me a plate of cookies. Jamie always made me cookies. They were just scrumptious, made with her secret family recipe. She's the sole owner since she's the only known member of her family still alive.

"Good night," Jamie said, scurrying away.

"Another hottie you pulled out?" Aisely said, dealing some more cards.

"No, just a pet."

"What's with the trouble with you asking out women? You

used to be the succubus of females back in the day. Hurry up and ace this one already."

"Mind your own business."

During our card games, I started to grow sick. I walked into the bathroom to release this body's waste. After I finished, I stared into the mirror. The mirror dripped water. I checked and the water came from no visible source. Suddenly images of random people flashed on and off in front of me. Objects all around me distorted and bent all over me. I suddenly couldn't breathe and felt intense fear. Clowns appeared, spraying me with acid and confetti. My stomach started to melt, showing all of my insides. Horrible birdlike beings with swords impaled inside their bodies slashed me. Water gushed up from the tub and swirled all around me, flooding the bathroom to my knees. Everything was so dark and distorted, I couldn't fight back.

I then saw the lovely Helena, strolling happily with her boyfriend. Helena's body got pale white. Blood started coming out of her eyes and her head started to swell up. That long, exquisite hair tangled up every part of my body. It felt as if I were drowning. Helena then called my name repeatedly: "Aurick, are you okay? Aurick! Aurick!"

"Aurick, Aurick, you dead in there?" Aisely said, shouting from the living room. I found myself back in the bathroom, still staring into the mirror. It was only a hallucination. I vomited into the sink chunks of food I had eaten earlier. "That's gross, dude; sick."

I was experiencing another side effect of possessing a human for this long. When a demon synchronizes with a human for a long time, both beings' minds fight for dominance over the body. The beginning effects are hallucinations, vomiting, and mild heart attacks. If a Fallen doesn't leave the body, things get much worse. This side effect keeps Fallen from mass-possessing mankind worldwide at the same time. If I were a weaker spirit being, I would've been totally mad by now. I was considering complying with Aisely's advice about leaving the body, but I knew I wanted to stay for a while longer.

Aisely and I sat down at a table and started playing Go Fish.

"What have you been doing with yourself for the past three years?" I said, dealing the cards.

"Glad you asked. I've been trying to find a way out."

"A way out? We all know that there's no way out."

"You've heard the news reports lately?"

"I don't watch television much."

"I've been protecting people, Aurick. I must've saved thirty human lives already. The news reports say that an invisible force has been looking after the city."

"That doesn't matter, Aisely. Once an angel loses favor with Grandfather, there's no going back. We can never receive redemption."

"I don't believe that bull crap. I don't believe there's anything in this universe that can't change. Not even Dad."

"Yeah, right! You know once Father says something, it has to stick, no matter what."

"There has to be a way. We all know that Papa obsessively believes that everything in existence has to be paid for equally and justly. Maybe if we pay for our crimes equally with good deeds before the execution, we can go home again. Maybe we can be more than equal. I want you to help me. We can both be saved."

"That's a waste of time, Aisely. Just be brave and embrace your eventual death. It was our fault for opposing a force greater than us. Now shut up and play."

I beat him thirty times straight without losing. I got bored and played with Sephirot instead. My lean feline had become a fat pig. He was so out of shape that he couldn't even jump for the string I was dangling. He used to play this game for hours. This is the destiny of all. Once you have all that you need, you simply stop moving. Once you gain everything, you lose everything. At least he keeps a nice coat of fur.

"Okay, let's make a deal," Aisely said. "Let's play a game of Rock, Paper, Scissors. If you win, I'll run two laps around the sun. If I win, you have to help me protect this city. Almost like superheroes."

At first I refused, but Aisely pestered me for hours, which forced me to agree. He could be very annoying. It was best two out of three. I won the first round and he won the second. We used both our abilities to form physical rock, paper, and scissors. It was down to the final round. "Rock, paper, scissors, shoot," we both called out. I chose rock. He chose scissors.

"Goddamm it!" Aisely said, slamming the table, breaking it in half. He opened the window and went on the fire escape.

"Well, a deal is a deal."

Aisely walked on air and eventually was out of sight. Good riddance.

I spent the next few days reading headlines in newspapers on the "invisible helpers" of Manhattan that Aisely was speaking about. While I was sitting on the ledge of the Empire State Building, I read an article by my client Helena Way about the "weird" overflow of miracles lately in New York City. In one incident some maniac threw her baby out a ten-floor window, but the child miraculously was caught by a tree. The article criticized the ignorance of people who believed that God and his angels were watching over the city. The article said the incidents were just because of luck. I wondered if saving lives was a good idea. It seemed good and all on the outside, but it logically seemed pointless to me.

Two days later, Helena was strolling through Central Park. I'd planned to bump into her. She sat down on a bench and enjoyed the view of a big water fountain. As I was walking in her direction to commence my plan, she got up and rushed to a man and embraced him. It was her boyfriend from the other night. I stamped my foot repeatedly in anger until a young boy holding an ice cream cone came over to my side.

"Are you okay, mister?" the boy said. I stood up and fixed my jacket. I used air pressure to splatter ice cream on the young lad's face, which caused him to cry like a wimp. I followed the couple around the park. Mr. Perfect told Helena jokes and stories, which she enjoyed. Their laughter made me sick.

They went boating in the pond. I considered sinking the boat to kill the guy, but I didn't want to kill Helena. When they were done, he bought her cotton candy. She smeared some of it on his nose and mouth. They laughed and played some more. In a fit of rage, I struck a man's bike while he was riding it down a hill, causing him to flip over into the pond. This backfired because Helena's boyfriend dived into the pond and pulled the man out. Mr. Perfect then took his shirt off, showing off his wet, glistening body, which excited all the ladies nearby. What a show-off. The biker thanked him and rode away. While Mr. Perfect was drying off, Helena caught sight of me. I pretended to be surprised to see her, but at the same time cool.

"Hi. It's nice seeing you here, Dr. Pantera."

"It's nice to see you here too, Ms. Way. And, please, call me Aurick."

"And please call me Helena."

Mr. Perfect finished drying off and came over to us. "Is this one of your friends, Helena?" he said, stroking back his hair, causing drops of water and hair gel to splash on my face. Some of the water got into my eyes, which burned. I didn't want to cause a scene so I withstood it.

"This is my psychologist, Dr. Aurick Pantera," Helena said.

"Oh, so you're her shrink? I'm going to need one too after dealing with this young lady," he said, grabbing Helena's waist.

"Oh, so this is the boyfriend you were speaking of?"

"Yes, this is Derek. I've been dating him for a few months now."

"It's only been a few months now but I feel like I've known her for a lifetime." Helena's cheeks turned red. "Let me get that cotton candy off your lips." He licked the blue candy off her lips, then started kissing her. I was uncomfortable and wanted to get away. I was forced to watch them drink each other's saliva.

"Well, it's time for me to take the old dusty road. I've got some psychos to treat."

"Oh, that's a shame. Can't you chat a bit?"

"No, no, Helena. We wouldn't want to stop the man from doing what he loves to do, especially when it involves helping people. I know I wouldn't like it if someone was keeping me from volunteer work at the homeless shelter."

No one asked you, I thought to myself. I didn't understand why Helena couldn't see past this *Derek's* phoniness. His phony lines and his phony lifestyle. Phony from head to toe. Phony from the lungs to the lips.

"Well, I hope that the rest of your date goes well. Good-bye."

Derek held his hand out to me. I didn't want to seem like a jerk in front of Helena so I forced myself to shake it.

"Good-bye, Aurick. I'll *pray* for you," Helena said.

I stormed out of the park angry. How could a mere human deny me what I wanted? I'm a spirit being for Christ's sake! I decided to buy a newspaper and get some fresh air on top of the Empire State Building. While I was reading the newspaper, Aisely popped out of nowhere and phased his head through the paper, which startled me and caused me to fall off the ledge. Aisely caught me and helped me to safety.

"Damn it, Aisely!" This falling-off-the-ledge business was getting tiresome. "You almost killed my host. You know what would happen if that were to occur, right?" He wasn't taking my words seriously . . . as always. "You couldn't have finished those laps around the sun this quickly."

"Are you kidding me? I always run around it in my spare time."

"Well, what do you want?" Aisely gave me pictures. "What is this, Aisely?"

"Just shut up and look." They were pictures of various women with Helena's boyfriend in a bed. "I took these last night."

"So Helena's boyfriend isn't such a perfect boyfriend after all."

"Oh, no, you're wrong. He is the perfect boyfriend. In fact, a fair fight over Helena or any other woman would result in him winning."

"Well, apparently he's not so good if he did this. Unless you did something that I hope you didn't." Aisely turned away from me. "Well, did you do anything you weren't supposed to, Aisely?"

"I followed him around and couldn't find any flaws so I possessed him and rounded up some women and hid a camera in his bedroom."

"You what?"

"What? What's wrong?"

"What's *wrong*? I want something legit. This is injustice! Why would you do such a thing? You're a stalker, you know that?"

"I wasn't stalking. I was just merely gathering evidence for you to use against that Mr. Goody Two-Shoes over there to score Helena; that's all. Now all you have to do is show her these and land her. I'll let you have the pictures if you help me with my cause."

"I told you before, I'm not helping you with such a redundant task. Meddling with other people's lives won't make me help you. Go ask someone else."

"Oh, come on, just think about it, Aurick. Look at yourself. You've sunk yourself into a low point. Watching how people live their lives and then living a human life and sneaking around after some human girl like a child. You've lost your pride, man. You've lost hope for the future. You try to cover it up, but I see that you've lost your pride. We can beat this thing, I know we can. You just need hope. We need hope. Our entire kind needs hope. Just think about it. I'll be back to get your final response."

Aisely left me on the roof alone, stunned with the language he'd used against me. How dare he speak to me in such a manner?! I sat there, staring at the pictures, contemplating what to do next. I hated Derek. But I also hated using such unfair tactics, especially against a human. It's like bullying a child.

I went home and burned the pictures over the stove. I fed Sephirot and went to bed.

III

BANDMATES

The need for companionship is the greatest weakness; no beings can live without it. It is not God but companionship that is the true giver of life. All of existence needs a companion, such as the sun and the moon, the stork and its mate, the wind and the ocean, the parent and its babe, the Father and the Son. Companionship will be savior or destroyer of all creation. No one is safe from companionship, not even the Father.

The night arrived when I had to perform with my band at a shabby nightclub. The club was painted dark with a deteriorating ceiling and walls. The corners had the carcasses of bugs entangled in cruel spiders' webs. The club could only pack about four hundred bodies in. Getting trampled was quite easy. My bandmates opposed the idea of performing in such a small club considering how famous the band had gotten. I didn't want to bother going too far to a bigger concert hall, so I didn't care. This caused the band members to be annoyed with me. I felt that was preposterous because I was the one who made them money and fame. I recruited each of my three band members, Angry Kid, Doughy, and Terra, when he was at the low point of his life.

I first met Angry Kid when he was living on the street near a train station. He was addicted to heroin and alcohol. Nothing has changed much with him since then. I thought for just a second maybe he would change with some money, but he's still a loser. He's also a bit superstitious. He always wears a rabbit foot around his neck. Anytime he has a show or does something exciting such as surfing on top of trains, he kisses it for good luck.

Doughy was a loser pushover who waited tables at a café for a living. People would always bully him around because of his weakling demeanor. Now that he's rich he's become a tyrant to others.

Terra didn't have such a great education and used to go from man to man, even dangerous ones, throughout much of life. The long scar on her cheek is the price she paid for it. She became a crack addict at one point. Even with all her past drama, she's still maintained a kind personality.

While we were performing, Angry Kid drowned out my part with an uncalled-for loud guitar solo. He's been trying to be the front man of the group lately. His arrogance has been annoying.

The club thundered with cheering from a starstruck audience. There was almost double the allowed maximum capacity in the audience.

Then suddenly, while performing, I felt disoriented to the point of almost falling off the stage. The mask also made it harder to breathe. I eventually retained full control and continued playing. I was relieved when we were done with the show.

I wanted to hurry up and leave so I wouldn't have to sign autographs, but just when we were about to leave the club, Kid decided to use the bathroom. We waited and waited but Kid didn't come back out. I couldn't stand waiting there anymore so I went into the bathroom after him to see if he was passed out on the toilet again. I systematically opened each booth until I heard snorting noises. I opened the door where the noise came from and, as expected, found Kid snorting cocaine off the toilet seat.

❖　❖　❖

After signing hundreds of autographs, the band and I walked together through the alleyway behind the club heading toward our cars. There was an awkward silence. "What is your problem, Kid?" I said.

"What do you mean what's my problem? I didn't do anything."

"You know what I mean! You're high out your mind and you drowned me out onstage. You've done that four times in a row."

"Mind your own damn business, Aurick. I don't gotta listen to you."

"I don't care about how you screw yourself up, but when you butt in to the rest of our performances, I get angry, especially with an attitude like yours." We both stopped and turned toward each other.

"I ain't messin' up nobody. I'm saving this band! We've all seen the reviews and sales lately. We're in the toilet now! All thanks to your tired lyrics. We need to start branching out."

"What are you complaining about? You got everything you wanted: money, women, and glory. Your arrogance is turning you into a spoiled brat."

"I'm tired of you thinking you're so superior to all of us. You don't control me!" Kid came close to me, poking me with his index finger. I held back my desire to break it off.

"All right, you guys can stop flexing your muscles now," Terra said, pulling us apart. "Let's head to the car. It's starting to get cold."

We went into two separate cars. Terra was driving with Angry Kid and I was with Doughy. I felt stupid getting into a car with the drunken Mr. Doughy driving. He gets drunk and high a lot to numb himself from the pressure of being a rock star, and because he thinks it will keep him from looking like a pushover. When he's not drinking, he's the old weakling Doughy we know and love.

Traffic was dense so we decided to take the highway, only to find that it also was jam-packed with cars bumper to bumper. News vans and police vehicles zoomed past us. Something major must've happened close by. We had to wait patiently for a while on the highway. It was awkwardly quiet, so Doughy kept pestering me with odd questions. Actually, they weren't that odd. They just weren't the type of questions that I would expect Doughy to ask.

"Do you believe in hell, Aurick?"

"Why do you ask? Did you do something naughty?" I said, opening the window, letting the draft blow through my hair.

"I just wondered if you believe it exists," he said, constantly switching his eyes between me and the road.

"No, I don't. Now can you keep your eyes on the road?"

After a few minutes of waiting, Doughy's face got red. Soon his eyes turned red and eventually got watery. He kept wiping his face and rubbing his eyes. After a while, Doughy let out short whimpers and mutters. He suddenly exploded into tears. I told Doughy to get a grip on himself, but he just cried more. "What's wrong, Doughy?" I said gruntingly.

"My mother's in the hospital, man. She's real sick." Traffic started to pick up at high speed, but Doughy had absolutely no attention for the road so I told him to pull over on the side so we wouldn't get killed. I was irritated because we were falling far behind Terra and Kid's car.

"Your mom's going to be fine."

"No way, man. The doctors don't know how long she's going to live." I wasn't sure what to say to comfort him. How could I anyway in his drunken state? I just wanted to tell him the truth, that when she dies, she won't feel any more pain and all that jazz, but I didn't think that would work.

"Doughy, it'll all be fine. You just need a little—"

There was a loud crash of thundering metal with car

screeches. The smashing steel knocked Doughy out of sulking into a full alert. Cars were colliding with one another up ahead on the highway. One collided so hard that the engine burst through the car hood. The engine smashed into the driver's seat of another vehicle, causing more pileups. Another car rolled over about six times and eventually smashed into a tree.

"Aurick! Where the hell's Terra and Kid?!" Doughy drove slowly along the side of the crash. There must've been nine wrecked cars. Others had veered off to the side while many more had collided into each other's rear. The white smoke was too thick to see through so I knew I had to get closer. Doughy tried to get me to stay in the car, but I shrugged his hand away from me and got out. The scene was like a death trap: I stepped over metal plates, tires, debris, and bloodstained glass shards. A few cars were caked together, which blocked almost all exits in the car. Most passengers were unconscious but some were dead. All I could do was move forward.

"Help me!" a loud voice called. The voice came from a disfigured news van that had cars pinned up against the doors of the vehicle so I continued forward, only to hear, "Please, my leg is stuck."

"Not my problem, miss," I said, walking away without missing a beat. I didn't have time to help other people; I just needed to help Terra and Kid to avoid the pain of replacing them. The voice cried out to me again and this time it sounded familiar. I backtracked and peered through the cracked window at the back of the van. It was Helena, pinned under an unconscious cameramen and camera equipment. "Ms. Way?" The woman stopped crying and looked in my direction.

"Aurick? Oh, thank God you're here!" I pulled the handles on the double doors but they didn't open. I started yanking but they still wouldn't budge. "Aurick!"

The door was jammed with some equipment on the inside. I

asked Helena if she could get up, but she just wound up hurting herself more. The van's white smoke soon turned into black.

"Helena, close your eyes!"

"Why?"

"Just do it. Quickly!" I pulled at the doors with almost my entire strength and yanked the doors from their hinges along with some mangled equipment and tossed them aside.

(It's not unusual for a possessed man to do this. A normal human can only use a small percentage of his/her muscles. God put this limiter on humans because if humans used the full potential of their muscles, they would overstrain and cripple themselves easily. Fallen are able to unlock the restraints the brain has over the muscles, nerves, and adrenal glands. With these limiters unlocked, even a 120-pound man could tip over a car.)

I jumped into the van and tossed the unconscious bodies of Helena's news crew off her. I carried her on my back and took her to safety onto a patch of grass on the side of the highway. Didn't want that long hair to get damaged. I checked to see if she had any broken bones, but she only had a sprained ankle. "Are you okay, Ms. Way?"

"Yes, but I need to go back there and get the cameras."

"Don't you want me to get your fellow reporters first?"

"Get the cameras first."

I got the cameras first as she said, then I started pulling the others out of the van. One of the cameramen woke up in a daze, walked over to the grass, and collapsed on his knees and started coughing up spit and mucus. "Get up, Timmy, and aim the damn camera!" Helena said, kicking him on the bottom and then pulling out a microphone.

"Yes, I'm sorry, Ms. Way," Timmy said, scrambling over to the camera. Timmy aimed the camera at the news van while I started pulling the rest of the crew of four out of the van. When

I'd carried the last man to safety, Helena shoved a microphone in my face and started asking me questions about the crash. Even after a close call from death, she moved on as if nothing had happened. She was the epitome of a field journalist. It's what made her famous. It's what allowed her to get away with being unkempt and reckless. She thanked me and said I was a hero for the camera. Without another word, she went off for more shots of the catastrophe.

I slipped off farther down the road. Those bandmates of mine still couldn't be found by Aurick's eyes. I walked and walked until I heard a familiar voice.

"What are you doing here Jackie-sama?" I looked around to see who it was but couldn't see well through the smoke. "I'm up here." I looked again and found an old nosy owl sitting on top of a wrecked Jeep roof.

"How did this mess happen?" I asked.

"A big fire nearby happened. Fire trucks, news vans, and police cars were rushing ahead and caused a big crash-up. I'm just here to see what's going on."

It was strange for that owl to be here just for that. I was trying to see through his deception when another angelic voice called out, "Morning Owl, why are you explaining yourself to the likes of him?" The being walked over and stared daggers into me.

"Hello, Condor. I haven't seen you in a couple millennia."

"That's *Shining* Condor to *you*, heathen!"

I've known Condor for ages. Oh, Condor. He was the spoiled brat of the heavens. I've never been friends with him. He's nothing but a pompous prick. He always kissed the rear ends of the higher ranks. He never had stable friends because he tossed them aside for his own social climbing. He was once a glorified cherub, but he let his ego blind him so he was demoted to a mere marooner angel. Not that a position of power means you're better than anyone else, but for someone such as Condor, it was the ultimate humiliation. Indeed, a satisfying punishment for a prick like him.

"If you ask me, that's too soon of a reunion with a shameless traitor like you. Don't you have a mansion to haunt?"

Condor's words evoked intense anger in me. I thrust out my arm and reached for his throat, but I forgot that I was in a human body so my hand just phased right through him. At that moment, six other angels appeared all around me with serious expressions on their faces. They were more than ready to do battle with me.

"I'll send you to the Null where you belong. Prepare, my brothers!"

"That's enough, my brothers. We are not here to battle," Owl said, looking over at us. The marooners backed off me but still continued to glare.

"Then why are you here, Owl?"

"That is none of your concern, monster. We are on official business," Condor said, taking a step closer to me.

"Aha, so you are up to something," I said in a playful tone.

"We're looking for someone," Owl said.

"Another of your brothers went renegade?"

"We are tracking Fallen. His followers caused the fire at a crowded mall ahead. On the pursuit he caused some humans to crash into each other somehow."

"You should've caught him by now."

"We caught some of his followers but not him."

"So just torture them and make them spill the beans. What's the problem?"

"Picking up human slang?" I ignored Owl's question. "I wanted to but Condor got them sent to the Null before I could interrogate them."

"Nice police work, nimrod. After billions of years of existence, you're still a royal nitwit."

Condor looked embarrassed. You didn't have to try hard to hurt his feelings because the smallest insult made him angry.

"I'll send you to the bowels of the Null, you dirty fly," Condor said with a flaring red face, causing air to flux around him. "I promise you. I'm going to make sure that *I'll* be the one to send you. And you're going to grovel at my royal feet for forgiveness. I don't break promises."

"I said enough, Condor! Take the rest of the unit to scout the area."

Condor objected but was put in place again by Morning Owl. He took the other marooners and went away. On their way they exchanged harsh glares with me.

"There've been a number of Fallen that have been causing a lot of trouble in this city recently. I don't know why. Some of them have been influencing a dangerous religious group."

"Religious group?" I asked.

"Yeah. People and their religions," Owl said, shaking his head. "They wear bunny masks and sometimes yellow raincoats. The police don't even know that they exist."

"Nope, haven't seen anything like that around here."

"Well, as long as you stay around your little girlfriend, Helena Way, you will." His words gave me a naked feeling inside. I didn't know what it was. I knew it felt quite awful though.

"Helena? But why her?"

"Her news van being caught in this crash-up was no coincidence. Her little muckraking escapades led her to be a target of the cult. She isn't a big target but she's still in danger. Enough for now. I have a trail to follow."

"Okay. I'll alert you if I see anything."

"Thank you. Let me know if you do see anything." On his way out of the scene I stopped him and said I was looking for two humans called Terra Hawkins and Angry Kid. Owl located them and said that their car wasn't in the accident. It annoyed me that I was so concerned about them, but at the same time it relieved me that I didn't need to bother replacing them.

I ran up the destroyed highway and found Terra and Kid pulled over at the side of the road at a ditch. Kid was vomiting up his drug-infested guts into a bush.

"You guys okay?" I said to Terra.

"Yeah, we're okay. Kid had to puke so I pulled over the car right before the accident."

"Thank you, Kid. Your drug habit saved your life."

"Shut up, Aurick!" Kid said. He gagged and then vomited on Terra's shoes.

IV

ΠAMELESS HERO

The sting of irony's judgment can be cruel. Cruel enough to make you question who your true friends and enemies are. In the hour of desperation, the first to answer is truth. When no one is looking, whom shall the desolate man accept first, the cherry-bearing demon or the fiery angel who brings judgment? The desolate man will say, "Breathe life into me, Dark Savior!"

"Liar!" a thundering, alarming voice cried out, awaking me from my slumber. I looked around in a daze but failed to find what it was. Suddenly, water stains appeared on the wall, starting to resemble a face with a thorny crown on its head.

"Aisely, that's disrespectful."

"Who cares? We're not part of the club, remember? And don't change the subject, you liar." He phased through the wall.

"What are you talking about?"

"I'm talking about last night. I saw what you were doing."

"Doing what?"

"Don't act like you don't know! I saw you going superhero and getting those people out of that burning van. I thought you told me that you didn't care about getting back into the gates?"

"I don't and I wasn't helping them. I was just doing a few humans a little favor, that's all."

"You are such a stereotype. Well, at least you changed your mind. Let's get to work."

"I'm not helping your cause. I told you I just did that as a favor."

But Aisely wouldn't take no for an answer. While taking a shower I heard, "Please." While brushing my teeth I heard, "Pretty please." While eating bacon and eggs I heard, "Please." While sitting on the toilet I heard, "Please." While at work counseling Helena I heard, *"Por favor."*

"Leave me the death alone," I said, forgetting that Helena was in the same room as me.

This continued through the whole day. Every time I responded, people thought I was crazy. "Who are you talking to?" That is what I got all day. While shopping at the supermarket, Aisely started knocking over cans and cereal boxes on the floor near me. People looked at me as if it were my fault, so I had to pick them up. This even continued into the night, literally keeping my eyelids from shutting. His begging continued for days, with him saying please in every language in existence and even a few dead languages. He then started to cry and moan. I knew he was faking because spirit beings can't literally produce tears, but it was still as annoying as the real thing. He continued this until one night in bed I couldn't take it anymore.

"All right, I'll help."

"Really?"

"Yes, really."

There was a long pause and deafening silence.

"Are you sure?"

"Oh, God, yes, I'm sure. Now leave me alone."

"Hurray," Aisely said, jumping on me.

We were finally on the sidewalk of Aisley's choosing. "All righty then, let's start our first act of heroics," Aisely said, standing next to me on the sidewalk. I couldn't use the vast amount of my abilities while possessing a human. I had put Aurick in a deep sleep when I left the body so that it would be ready to come back to easily. For some odd reason, my head was aching.

"You okay, buddy?"

"Yeah, I'm a little rusty ripping myself out of Aurick's body,"
I said, rubbing my head. Oh, boy! Rubbing my head? I've been
so comfortable being human that I forgot that I don't need to
rub my head, let alone have one. I did need a break from this
body. "Anyway, what are we waiting for?"

"We're waiting for a little situation to occur."

"What situation?"

"A little old lady will cross this street and get hit by a truck.
The driver, who will hit this woman, took too much medication
this morning. He will be too drowsy to stop in time and kill the
woman instantly. All we have to do is stop her from crossing the
street."

"Where is the old hag?"

"She'll be here in a few minutes." A few minutes passed with
no old hag and no drugged driver. I came to question Aisely's
resources.

"How do you even know this is going to happen?"

"I have a reliable source."

"Who is this *source*?"

"Our ticket off this big, blue dirtball."

"Yes, but who? How could we trust him?"

"I'm following my heart."

"My heart is what got me and many others in this situation in
the first place."

"Oh, please. You don't have a heart."

"*We* don't have hearts."

"*Whatever.*"

A few more seconds passed with no accident.

"What street is this supposed to happen on?"

"East Thirty-Seventh and Third Avenue." I looked at the
street signs and got irritated at Aisely.

"This is East Thirty-*Sixth* and Third Avenue, you idiot." We
hurried off to our true destination and in a few minutes spotted
the old hag crossing the street. A truck was speeding down the

street with the driver passed out at the wheel. I hurried off to the woman. I tried to push her but I forgot I didn't have a body anymore so I couldn't budge her. "Get out of the way," someone screamed. The woman couldn't hear so she kept on blissfully walking. The truck was a few seconds away so I tripped her with some air pressure. She collapsed to the ground while the truck passed over her unscathed body and drove through me. Someone rushed to her side and called an ambulance.

"You did it. See I told you this could w—" Suddenly, a loud screech and a crash drew everyone's attention. The truck that had missed the old lady had gone on and crashed into a bus.

"Aisely, what was going to happen if we had let the old lady get hit?" Aisely was quiet until I forced him to speak up. "Well?"

"It would've stopped right after and not crashed into anyone."

The ambulance came for the old lady, and once the EMTs saw the other crash, they called for backup.

"Oh, that's just great. We sacrificed a few lives on that bus for an old hag who was going to croak in a few years anyway."

"More like a few seconds," Aisely said, looking at the ambulance with a concerned look on his face. The old lady had had a heart attack in the ambulance and died.

Aisely took me to another place where another accident would occur. "All right, that one didn't count. This is our real first good deed." Aisely took me to a beach and we stood on the sand looking over the pier. "All right, see that man swimming? He has ignored that the beach is closed today thanks to the lifeguard strike. He will get sucked deep into the ocean and drown. Our job is obviously to help him to shore."

We both walked across the water to get close to the man swimming. He was a fat guy in his late forties. Sure enough, he started panting hard and the panting turned into struggling. The struggling turned into cramping, until cramping eventually turned into drowning. He swam desperately to the shore but the ocean kept dragging him deeper. He tried the dead-man's-float technique, but the waves kept splashing over him, causing him to go under.

"All right, let's help this fat bastard to shore."

We guided the waves to push the man to shore. "It's working, it's working; make the waves stronger."

I made the waves stronger as Aisely suggested and they pushed the chubster along nicely. The man felt relieved, Aisely seemed relieved, and I felt relieved. But then I realized that relief doesn't have to be reality. An immense shark came through the waves and chomped on the man's side. The shark's teeth sunk through his rib cage and pulled him under. Aisely and I exchanged looks and then looked for the man.

"Goddammit, why didn't you look out for him, Aurick?"

"How would I know that Moby-Dick would be here?" We looked for over an hour but all we could find was the shark. We managed to get it onshore. "There's not going to be much of him, Aisely. It's over."

"It's not over until it's over. Never give up, Aurick. Not even in the face of Armageddon."

"Cough it up, you stupid shark!" Aisely made the shark throw up all of its food. We saw some of the fat man's remains. "Aw, damn it."

We left and went back into the city for more patrolling. We tried rescuing a cat from a tree for a little girl.

"Come down, Tabby, don't you want to be with Mama?" the little girl said, raising her arms out to the cat.

"Here you go, little girl," Aisely said, knocking the cat off the branch. The girl caught the cat and embraced it against her chest. "Well, at least we made this girl happy." Aisely went closer and petted the girl's hair with the wind. The presence of Aisely must've spooked Tabby, which clawed her way out of the little girl's arms. Tabby then ran into the street and got run over by a school bus. The girl fell to the floor and wailed.

"Let's get the death out of here, Aurick." We went on for some more heroics, which all failed miserably. We tried to stop a ferry from sinking in the Bahamas. We managed to do that and it continued on its course only to be crushed by a cruise ship.

"That's it! I'm leaving. I told you this was stupid," I said to Aisely while quickly getting away from the scene to avoid any angels that might punish us for the accidents.

"Wait. Where're you going?"

"The band is picking me up at home. I'd rather deal with humans than an idiot like you."

"Hey, this never happened when I was by myself," Aisely said, hurrying behind me. I somehow doubted Aisely. How could such an idiot save thirty lives?

"'Cause you never aided any human in the first place!"

"Ya huh, I did."

"Tell the truth."

Aisely paused for a long time until he said, "All right, I never tried until you came along."

"Then what about the thirty lives that were saved? And about the media talking about invisible helpers?"

"It was another."

"Another Fallen one?"

"Yeah, he's the one I got the idea from. I watched him on his escapades."

"What happened?"

Aisely stayed quiet until I forced it out of him. "He made a little mistake and got himself and others sent to the Null."

"So you're telling me we're doing this idiotic plan that originates with a moron who failed to do it in the first place?" Aisely was quiet for a long time. "We were never meant to save anyone. Not even angels are. What made you think we were?"

Aisely stood there taking it. He knew I was speaking the truth. "You have to stop being in denial. You have to understand that someday you are going to die," I said firmly. "You are going to die. Say it!"

Aisely didn't repeat it. After a few minutes of scolding Aisely, I made him cry. Some of us still couldn't take the hard truth.

I traveled back to New York. It doesn't take long at all in my spirit form. It was now sundown. I went into my room where Aurick's unconscious body was on the bed. When I got closer to repossess him, he suddenly opened his eyes and sat up on the bed.

"What the hell happened?" Aurick said, rubbing his head in a daze. To avoid the consequences, I didn't want to possess him while he was awake, so I decided to wait for a better opportunity. He got up and walked into the bathroom. He peered into the mirror and was confused. "Why do I look so old? These wrinkles weren't there before." He started to recover small traces of his memory of his time being possessed. He walked in confusion all over the apartment. "Why do I have so many books?" He looked to all the walls of clocks. "Why do I have so many clocks?" He looked to his wrists. "Why do I have *two* wristwatches on?" Aurick checked his answering machine. To both our surprises, Helena had left a message.

"Hi, Aurick, this is Helena. I don't think I've properly thanked you yet for saving my life. I wanted to invite you to dinner with me and Derek tomorrow at seven o'clock. Thank you again, Aurick."

"I don't know any Helena. What did she mean by me saving her life? I need some fresh air." He walked over to the closet and opened the door. "Holy mother of God in heaven!" The thousands of dollars that I'd left in the closet hypnotized Aurick and drew him closer and closer. "Where did I get all of this money from?" Aurick held a stack of money. I didn't store money in a bank so that when I decided to leave the body, I could get rid of the money easily without leaving a trail of evidence behind. But I hadn't expected Aurick to wake up from the induced sleep I put him under. I decided that enough was enough and I couldn't take the chance of waiting any longer. I fused with Aurick's body. I closed the closet door and everything was fine for a few seconds, but then I started to not feel so good. My legs soon got wobbly and I started vomiting all over my feet. My control of Aurick's nervous system weakened and my vision blurred. I crashed into the walls and knocked over objects on the bureaus and tables. I collapsed on the floor and lost consciousness.

V

DR. DOCTOR

Death: the ultimate unknown, the ultimate contradiction, the ultimate liar and ultimate truth. The aggrieved embrace it and the triumphant fear it. No matter how powerful one will become, how one will evolve, there will always be one more step. Death is a second eternal God that one can experience even when one reaches it. When the final step is taken, one will find neither fear nor a closure, but the final evolution.

I awoke in a bed in a white room. Bright lights beamed into my eyes. I looked around and saw a familiar face from my apartment building.

"Aurick, you're awake!" Jamie said, hovering over my face.

"What happened?" I said, sitting up, rubbing my head.

"I found you in your apartment."

"How did you find me if the door was locked?"

"When I came over to give you a batch of cookies I made, no one answered. There was crashing and choking noises coming from inside the apartment. I kept calling out to you but you wouldn't answer."

"So that's when you called the ambulance?"

"Think again. I kicked the door down."

"Wow. You're a strong girl."

"When I stepped inside, you were unconscious on the floor violently shaking. The doctors say that you were having a heavy seizure."

"How long have I been here?"

"You've been asleep for four days now. Your medical records show no signs of epilepsy or head trauma, so they're still trying to find the cause."

Jamie kept me company for hours. She spoke to me about her boyfriend, Micky, who'd been giving her more trouble lately. I told her to dump him. As always, she didn't want to listen. Another hour passed, then Doughy and Terra arrived for a visit. Jamie shot hard glances at Terra, but Terra just smiled back. Anytime Terra spoke to me, Jamie would cut in and take over the conversation. They were irritated with each other. Jamie eventually decided to leave. She kissed me on my forehead and left me a plastic-wrapped plate of cookies.

"So how long have you two lovebirds been together?" Terra said.

"We're not together. She's just a friend."

"She's been at your side for hours every day. You must mean a lot to her."

"Jamie doesn't really have many people who care about her. Her parents died in a house fire and she doesn't have any known relatives. I'm like an older brother to her." A much older brother, I thought to myself. Doughy told me how they had had to cancel their show yesterday and how pissed off Kid was over it. "How did you find me?"

"I was visiting my mom in the hospital three days ago when I passed your room." Doughy said his mom wasn't doing too well. He tried holding in his distress and I didn't know what to do about it. Terra comforted him, telling him that everything was going to be okay. I thought I was the one who was supposed to be pampered here. "Oh, and by the way. You got a phone call from a Helena Way."

Helena Way?! My Helena called for me? I scurried to the cell phone. She didn't answer. Of course, she's a busy person. I left a message of where I was. At least I tried.

The next day, the doctors put me through an examination. They said that they couldn't find anything wrong, which was expected. They still forced me to stay another night for observation just in case.

I felt uneasy staying another night here. St. Peter's Hospital was one of the worst hospitals in New York City. It had an unusually high death rate. Countless investigations had been launched against the hospital for illegal euthanasia, but nothing solid was ever found. I wandered the hospital for hours, going from room to room on my floor, striking up conversations with the especially ill patients. I came across Shelia Connors, the mother of Doughy. She had a bald roommate who was asleep.

"Hello, Ms. Connors."

"Who are you?" Connors said, rubbing her eyes. Her skin was pale white. She had dark bags under her eyes, which were irritated red. She was missing about half of all her snow-white hair. I could see how a son could be so troubled by the deterioration of his mother.

"My name is Aurick Pantera; a friend of your son, Doug."

"Oh, I've heard about you. Doughy always talks about you, you and his other band friends." She coughed a lot, a deep, dry cough. I asked how she was feeling and about her condition. As an old hag who didn't get much company, she loved the conversation.

"Are you satisfied with your life, Ms. Connors?" She looked surprised by my question and was quiet for a while. "Oh, I apologize if I—"

"No, it's quite okay. It's just that no one ever gives me any deep conversation." She smiled. "The only time I get attention is when the nurses change me after I crap my diapers. To answer your question, no, I don't feel satisfied."

"Why?"

"I wish I could've given my son more. I wasn't really there for him like I would've liked. But friends like you at least keep him out of trouble."

Some trouble I kept him out of, I thought.

"The way I see it, no one truly feels satisfied with their lives. There's always something that's missing. But that's why I have Doughy to pass on my legacy. As long as I have someone to have me in their memory, I can leave this world happy."

Hearing Ms. Connor's words truly remedied my boredom. I felt a sense of inspiration. For the first time in centuries I felt . . . exceptional.

Connors's roommate started muttering things in her sleep. "What's wrong with her?"

"She just came in today wearing a bunny mask and a raincoat."

"A bunny mask and a raincoat?"

"All I know is that she was beaten up badly. She mutters, 'Adilah,' over and over. They're considering putting her in the psych ward. I have no idea why I was the one to be stuck with her. This hospital is so packed."

"Adilah?"

A doctor came in and asked me to leave so he could do Connors's daily checkup. The doctor was bald and had dark wrinkles under his eyes as if he was tired or unhealthy himself. He wore glasses that were clear as day. He was smiling with a big crescent-curved mouth. The room grew cold and made the hairs on the back of Aurick's neck stand up. The doctor went to the other side of the room and closed the window. There was more to this doctor than met the eye.

Nonetheless, I decided to take my leave. "Good-bye, Ms. Connors."

"Please, call me Shelia."

I stayed in my room for a few hours, desperately waiting for the sun to go down. Surprisingly, Helena walked past me without realizing it. I called to get her attention.

"What are you doing here?" I said. She replied that she came to visit me for her psychologist appointment that we'd missed. I thought she was a little insane to be that obsessed with our meetings. It was expected though; she'd never missed one.

"I got your message. I wanted to pay you a surprise visit. Thought I wouldn't show up, didn't ya?!"

I had a jolly feeling inside until her boyfriend, Derek, arrived. Derek said hello and shook my hand *without* my consent. I ripped open a smile and asked Helena what he was doing here. She said they were going out to dinner after visiting me. He asked me how the hospital food was while he rubbed Helena's behind. I wanted to kill him.

After asking me how I was feeling and hearing I would soon be discharged, she invited me over for dinner. Just when I was going to answer, Shelia's roommate came into the room with a crimson grin on her face. She was breathing hard and was sweating a lot. Her grin turned into an enraged frown. She launched herself at Helena. Helena ran, but she yanked Helena's long hair and stopped her dead in her tracks. She grabbed her throat.

"Are you happy now, Adilah? Are you happy now? Leave me alone!"

Derek grabbed her but was head-butted and ran off. Coward!

I charged in and tackled the maniac to the floor. Helena gasped for breath and called for help. The maniac grabbed my arm and bit my hand, drawing blood. I fell back and covered my hand in pain. She jumped on top of me and began to choke me. Finally, the nurses rushed in and pulled her away. The woman swung both nurses over the bed onto the floor and rushed past me into the hallway, screaming, "Don't let the angels get me." I ran after her to the stairs. Four male guards caught her by her arms and torso. She had seemingly stopped moving when suddenly she knocked all four to the ground.

I then realized this was no ordinary insane woman. She was much more. No woman (or man for that matter) could be that strong unless she was "influenced." She yelled, "Adilah," repeatedly until the guards got up and struggled with her some more. Their combined strength wasn't enough to take her down. I stepped in closer and stared into her eyes. I pierced deeply into her mind and saw madness, fear, and confusion. I then put her to sleep. A little hypnosis always comes in handy.

She fell to the ground and the guards put her arms behind her back and took her away. I walked back to my room. Nurses were all around Helena, tending to her, which filled me with relief. I wanted to follow "Ms. Hercules," but I was too fatigued after that hypnosis trick I used on her.

"Are you okay, Helena?" I said.

"Yeah. I guess we'll have to cancel the appointment this time." Helena left without my answering her invitation to dinner, which annoyed me.

A few hours later, I went to the psych ward of the hospital. I wanted to know why that "woman" attacked Helena. The area was as expected locked off. "Hey, you're not supposed to be here!" a security guard said, getting up from his desk. I wanted to get this done the quickest way I knew how.

"Yes, I am. Now give me your keys."

"Yes, you do belong here. Here are the keys."

"Now go back to your desk, put your head down, and go to sleep." He did just that. It took me a while, but I eventually found Ms. Hercules. She was wide-awake with her body, arms, and feet strapped down on a bed. I unlocked the door and stepped in and saw Helena inside.

She hastily turned around and said, "What are you doing here?"

"I should be asking you that."

"I'm a reporter. I'm reporting this."

"You're lying to me."

"No, I'm not."

"Just tell me what's going on."

"Just shut up and let me do my job." She stepped to the woman's side and said, "What's your name?"

She just kept repeating, "Adilah," and random things about angels over and over.

"I bet no one believes you right?"

The woman stopped speaking suddenly.

"No one believes you about the angels bothering you right?" Helena asked.

"Yes, no one believes me."

"Well, I believe you."

"You do?"

"Of course I do."

Ms. Hercules smiled with relief. "You're pretty."

Helena smiled. "Thank you. You are too. You can tell me anything. You can start with your name." She stepped over and leaned toward her.

The strange woman stared up at the ceiling. "M-m-my name is Brother."

"What's with the *Brother* part?"

"That's all of our first names." The more she spoke, the more I was mystified.

"Even if you're a girl?"

Vex nodded her head.

"Why did you want to kill me? Did this angel send you?"

"Yes. It won't leave me alone. I just want to be left alone!" she said loudly, still staring up at the ceiling.

"Shhh, I could help you. I could stop the angels from talking to you. You just have to tell me what I need to know."

"You can't help me. No one can help. Adilah's wrath will

arrive. It's only just a matter of time." Vex closed her eyes as if she were going to sleep.

"Who is Adilah? And tell me about your brothers. Tell me where your brothers meet."

Vex suddenly started shaking uncontrollably. She yelled, struggling to get loose from the straps. She screamed as loud as she could. The door slammed shut by itself. Helena tried opening the door but it wouldn't budge. Vex broke free of the straps and launched herself at me. I tried using my hypnosis again but was hit with the hardest punch I'd ever felt in my life. I fell to the ground with Vex falling down after me. After a few seconds of strangulation, things got blurry and I began to lose consciousness. Helena repeatedly hit Vex over the head with her bag. It had no effect so she held her in a choke hold, but it didn't even make her budge. Vex knocked Helena back a few feet. I tried leaving Aurick's body before it died, but for some reason it wasn't working. Suddenly, Vex started coughing. She started choking and coughing. She then rose and collapsed onto her bed and lay there motionless.

"Ah, are you okay, Vex?" There was no response. I went over to her and called to her again, "Vex?"

There was no response so Helena slapped her repeatedly to wake her up, but it didn't work.

"Oh, crap, this is bad." Just when Helena was getting somewhere, Vex just had to go ahead and die.

I thought it was weird that she'd died so suddenly. I knew she was heavily influenced by a Fallen, but she shouldn't have died like that. The question that stayed in my mind was *Who is Adilah?*

"What in the world did you do to her, Aurick?" Helena said, still shaky.

"I didn't do anything. She just started choking and then dropped dead."

Helena pulled the door and it wasn't jammed anymore. "Listen, you cannot tell anyone about this."

"Okay but—"

"Repeat it! *I will not tell anyone about this.*"

"I will not tell anyone about this. But—" Before I could get out my next word, Helena walked hastily ahead of me.

"Are we still up for that date?" I called after her. She said to bring a date and meet her next week at Neptune's Garden. It was a seafood restaurant in Times Square.

On my way down the hallway, I felt uneasy. The hallway seemed to get dark and blurry. It felt as if I were staring into a television that was showing static. It got cold. The hairs on the back of my neck stood up again.

"You shouldn't be here, Mr. Pantera."

I turned around to see Ms. Connors's doctor. He had that same creepy, ominous crescent smile. "We have to keep you under observation. Who knows what may happen to you while you're out of our sight."

I swiftly slammed him against the wall. I pinned him with my forearm across his throat.

"What are you doing?" He didn't struggle at all and still had that smile.

"Who are you?" I said, pressing against his throat harder.

"You're hurting me."

"No, I'm not." A sharp pain struck my abdomen. I looked down to see a hypodermic needle sticking into my stomach. I felt woozy. I felt dizzy. I fell asleep.

I awoke stretched out on a hard bed. I was still dizzy and groggy. I tried to get up and move but I was bound by straps. It was pitch-black. It was so cold. I called out for help but just got echoes in return. Then blinding lights pierced my eyes, forcing me to squint. A tall, blurry figure appeared before me. The figure got clearer as my eyes adjusted to the bright light. It was the doctor. He looked at me with that same damn smile.

"What are you doing? What did you inject me with?" I said, struggling to break free of the straps.

"Oh, you don't need to worry too much about that. The effects will die down in no time."

"Who are you?"

"You mean you don't recognize my presence? Wow, you have been in that body for a long time." I concentrated hard. "Come on Mr. Pantera, concentrate harder."

I did . . . and then it came to me, just like that. "Bashful Flycatcher? Is that you?"

The doctor burst into laughter. "Oh, goodness, I haven't heard that name in a long time. I almost forgot it."

"I knew you weren't normal. What are you doing here, Flycatcher?"

"Please, you know our names have long ago been revoked." Besides being given names by Father, we also get to choose code names in the line of duty. This particular Fallen used to be known as Bashful Flycatcher. "I am now Doctor." Angels usually give themselves new names after their descent.

"Doctor?"

"Yes. Nowadays I spend most of my time healing humans. It's a nice job when you get over the smell of death. What are you doing with your time, Mr. Pantera?"

"I spend most of my time healing human's brains. I also go to hospitals and get held hostage by psychopathic doctors."

"Oh, excuse my rudeness." Doctor untied my straps and helped me sit up. He put his wrist on my forehead and then rested his hand on my neck.

"Why did you kill Vex?"

"Heavens no! Why would I do such an awful thing?"

"Vex was babbling on about angels bothering her. You're telling me that was just a coincidence?"

"Now, Mr. Pantera, don't say such silly things. We both know if I truly killed her, I would be deported to the Null by now."

"I suppose you're right. But then who did?"

"Vex was a very sick person. To relieve the 'voices,' she was constantly hyped up on PCP. I guess it finally caught up to her." Doctor gave me a cup of water and asked how I was feeling.

"You seem to know a lot about Vex. Tell me who she is and why she tried to kill Helena Way."

Doctor laughed. "Mr. Pantera, we finally meet after centuries and all you can talk about is murder. You don't bother to ask me how I'm feeling. You never were the talkative type. What you really should be worrying about is your health. If you stay in that body too long, you'll be in deep trouble."

"I have it under control."

"Not for long, Mr. Pantera. That little cancer you have inside that pretty little body of yours is eating away at you."

"My spirit pressure has got that under control."

"Not for long. Although you can suppress it from eating your body, it aggravates the mental struggle between you and Aurick. The host's mind is already trying to synchronize and dispel the foreign object from the body at the same time. Your own conscience is doing the same thing. This constant fight for control always leads to one thing for both beings: permanent insanity."

"Enough with the small talk. Tell me what I want to know."

"Mr. Pantera, nothing is more important than your health. I am only looking after you."

"Stop playing games with me."

"Well, if you must know, Vex was simply a drugged-up schizophrenic psychopath. She was in a religious group for drug money for her addiction. People and their religions." Doctor sighed stridently. "With her mental condition, she always found her way here, my territory. And then Ms. Way happened to be here. She's been a thorn in that group's side for a while now. I guess when he saw Ms. Way, he saw it as an opportunity to put her out of the organization's misery. It's not like the courts are going to give a sick bastard like that life."

Doctor's explanation was a little too thin. It was a nice sensible explanation, but some elements were missing. Doctor was hiding truth from me. On my way out, I stopped and said, "Before he died, he kept saying a name."

"What was the name?"

"Vex called out for 'Adilah' and something about 'Adilah's wrath.' You wouldn't happen to know anything about it?"

Doctor laughed. "Vex did have a girlfriend. Her name was Adilah . . . I think. It was just mindless ramblings coming from a mindless human." As I walked away down the hall, Doctor yelled out. He ran and stopped before me.

"Good heavens! I almost forgot to give you your lollipop." He handed the lollipop to me, patted me on the head, and wished me good night.

VI

HELL DATE

There's a time you will be given a choice. A choice to live in reality for others or to pursue a dream. We all live or die for it. Stay in your zone of safety or chase down the corridors of the impossible shape. Whatever your choice is, what is real is a mirage to someone else. For the realest sanctuary can decay and the most sublime of dreams will be awoken from. As you age, you realize you will need more than present reality and dreams. Truth. I am certain that you, my dear, will make the right decision. Do not be misled by the scholarly knowledge of the world because you will decide whether my investment for you was perception or truth.

I had that naked feeling after learning that some religious faction really did want to kill Helena. This was the second time her life was almost ended by the hands of this cult. I'm sure it was no coincidence back on the night of the pileup and even back at the hospital. I knew some higher force was at work. Sure, Fallen organize religions and cults plenty of times, but why would a Fallen go through all the trouble of getting a mere single human killed?

I spent the week trying to come up with answers but failed. All of this thinking stressed me out so I put it out of my mind. I was ecstatic about my date with Helena today. But then I remembered that she told me to bring someone with me, which I guess I'd pushed out of my mind. Where was I going to find someone to go with me in just a few hours? I wanted to ask Aisely to take over someone's body and go with me, but

I remembered I yelled at him and made him cry. I paced back and forth until I heard yelling coming from Jamie's apartment above me.

I tried to ignore it but the noise broke my concentration. I went upstairs and knocked on Jamie's door. When Jamie opened the door, her eyes were red and her face was covered with tears. I asked her what happened. She told me that she'd gotten into an argument with Micky again. The argument had gotten heated and Micky had choked and slapped her.

"Where is he?" I said.

"He's having a party at his house." I asked her to drive me. "You're going over there?"

"Yes." She tried to get me to change my mind but it was futile. It was a thirty-minute drive over Micky's house. Jamie parked outside.

"What are you going to do?"

"He will never lay a hand on you again."

Music was coming from the backyard. There must've been about a hundred people. Micky was speaking with some women. He had the smug confidence that only the unintelligent fall for. He walked over to the grill and flipped hamburgers. Each step I took was powered by anxiousness. I walked over and slammed Micky's head onto the grill. Micky's guests looked on in shock. Some looked as if they wanted to help him out but they were too scared. Micky rolled on the ground, crying in pain. I kicked him repeatedly until Jamie called out to me to stop. I kicked him one more time and walked away. Seven of Micky's friends stepped in front of me, about to pounce.

"Don't let him get away," Micky said, still holding on to his face. I walked past them and continued on. "What are you waiting for? Get him."

"I can't move," one of the seven said. "I can't move my body. Someone help me."

Micky picked up a stone from the ground and threw it at me.

I easily caught it, walked over to him, and choked him with one hand.

Micky had black grill imprints on his face. He gasped for air and tried to yelp for help. I pulled his pants and boxer shorts down. To top it all off, I stuffed the stone Micky had tried to hit me with in his mouth. I forced him to his knees and grabbed his hair. Jamie was in shock the whole time.

"Ladies and gentlemen, this boy is guilty of laying his hand on a woman. Don't you think he should apologize? Now apologize to Ms. Jamie, Micky."

Micky muttered something.

"I'm sorry, Micky, I can't hear you with a stone in your mouth. Maybe you should project your voice more." He muttered more things. "All right, if you are sorry, clap your hands together seven times." Micky did just so. Many of Micky's guests laughed while others had their mouths open in dismay. Jamie just stood there smiling. Then we left and she drove us away.

"That was so cool, Aurick. Where did you learn those moves from, man?"

"My father taught me. By the way, do you have water to wash my hands?"

I soon looked at one of my watches and saw that I was running out of time. So I asked Jamie to accompany me on a double date later on. Jamie agreed without hesitation. We each went to our apartments and changed our clothes. Jamie drove us to Neptune's Garden. We got there a few minutes late. Helena and Derek hadn't gotten there yet, which annoyed me. We waited for what felt like an hour.

"Where are these people? Are you sure we're in the right place, Aurick?" Jamie said, fidgeting around and biting her fingernails. Just when I had enough of waiting for them, Helena and Derek waltzed right in.

"Oh my God, are we late?" Derek said, fixing his jacket.

Both Helena's and Derek's hair were messy. They were sweaty and breathing hard as if they'd run a mile. But I knew they didn't run anywhere since they drove here.

We all went on with small talk about the weather and such. Helena was wearing a nice slim black suit, the first time I'd seen her in elegant clothes. I was awed by her presence.

Derek moved in as if he were going to kiss her. So to stop him, I asked about her investigation on the cult that had been terrorizing the city recently. I wanted to tell her that the cult wanted her dead, but I didn't want to freak her out.

"Some freaky cult guy tried to kill me again, Derek," Helena said, pouring butter sauce on her lobster tail. Took the words right out of my mouth.

"Kill you?" Jamie said. "Good Lord! Why?"

"My investigation has led me to find the name of their group."

"What's the name?" Derek said with a peculiar focused look on his face.

"Adilah," she said.

"Adilah? What a weird name for a cult. How did they try to, um . . . hurt you?" Jamie asked.

"Strangling the life out of me. They would've succeeded too if dear Aurick here didn't help me."

"Aurick was there?" Jamie said, looking at me, her eyes the size of dining plates.

"Yeah. Sure," I said, looking away in discomfort.

"Yep. If Aurick hadn't been around, I probably wouldn't be here eating this delicious lobster tail," Helena said with her mouth full of food. "Nah. Nothing is going to take me down."

"Aren't you scared of being attacked again, Helena?" I felt Jamie groping my leg under the table. I pushed her hand away but she replaced it with the other hand.

"Nope. It wasn't the first time. I'm getting closer and closer, so this won't be the last."

"The Lord must really like you then," Jamie said.

"The Lord hasn't done squat. It is us humans who manipulate our destinies."

Or demons, I thought.

"You just have to have a little faith, that's all," Jamie said.

"To wait on a magical being for help is cowardice and ridiculous. What's the point of having free will if we cannot decide to follow our own path? We will never be our own person if we don't separate ourselves from *Him*."

Jamie looked bothered.

"Ha! Even if you follow your own path," I intervened, "there's still something you cannot defeat. Death. Your free will will amount to nothing. You will just be organic matter to feed the soil."

Helena laughed. "Then I hope the tree that I feed will grow big enough to crush death for me."

"Don't you think this investigation is way too dangerous for you to be involved in? Shouldn't you leave this to the authorities?"

"That's a funny idea. We haven't had competent officials in decades. I wouldn't have them investigate catnapping let alone terrorists. And besides, I live for the danger. I feel so . . . alive."

"Wow. You must be really brave to speak nonchalantly about people trying to murder you."

"In this world, the only thing that matters is keeping the people you love happy," Derek said, grabbing Helena's side. He moved in and started kissing her. I clenched my glass of water hard.

"Aurick, you're cracking your glass," Jamie said.

I immediately relaxed my grip. As I was gulping my glass of water, Aisely appeared, which startled me so much that I spit water all over Helena and Derek. I apologized to them as they wiped themselves. Aisely was pointing and laughing at me.

"How long have you two been together?" Derek said.

"Oh, we're not—"

"We've been going out for a while. I feel us falling in love and getting married," Jamie said, leaning closer to me. Jamie moved in and forced a kiss on me. I tried moving away but she moved with me and then shoved her tongue down my throat. Aisely laughed even harder. I did hand and face gestures to him, telling him to go away, but he wouldn't listen. Helena and Derek looked behind them to see whom I was gesturing to as I came up for air.

"Come on, Aurick. We have business to take care of," Aisely said, getting on the table.

I whispered, "I'm not helping you anymore. Get out of here, Aisely."

Derek asked if I said anything to him. I lied and said that I asked about the time.

"Come on, Aurick, you have to come. Something crazy is about to go down," Aisley said.

I whispered that I didn't care and to go away, but Aisely didn't listen. He got down from the table and walked behind Derek. Aisely began to manipulate Derek's hair, moving it to and fro. Helena told Derek to fix his hair, which he did, but Aisely kept messing it up again.

"It sure is windy in here," Derek said, combing his hair more firmly. Aisely walked over and did humping and spanking motions behind Helena.

"Aisely, stop!" I yelled. Helena, Jamie, and Derek looked at me as if I were crazy. I looked down at my plate and continued to eat.

Aisely grabbed Helena's rear with air pressure to make it feel as it were a human hand. Helena thought it was Derek and told him to stop. Derek didn't know what she was talking about so he just ignored her and continued to eat. I tried to stay calm but I could feel my face heating up. Jamie asked if I was feeling well, pointing out that my face was red. A waiter holding a platter of fish and drinks walked in the direction of our table. Aisely looked at him and smiled with a scheming expression on his face. As the waiter got near, Aisely knocked the fish and drinks all over Derek. Derek got up and yelled at the waiter. The waiter repeatedly apologized. Helena was in blissful melancholia and continued to eat. As a few more waiters came over to clean up Derek, I excused myself and went to the restroom to find out what Aisely was bugging me for.

"There's going to be another attack." Aisely's words blindsided me, as if a person were busy painting a masterpiece and suddenly punched in the face with brass knuckles worn by their little brother. It seemed as if anytime I tried to get away from the problems of the world, the more I got pulled into them.

I went back to the table and told everyone I was going outside to smoke a cigarette. Derek looked at his watch. He got sweaty all of a sudden. Helena said that Derek got gas easily when he ate spicy food. Derek excused himself and went to the restroom. Helena and Jamie continued to eat. Aisely and I left and went around the corner in an alleyway.

"What do you mean attack?" I said.

"It's that freaky cult again. They're about to execute another attack."

"I told you I don't care. I already helped you before with this idiotic hero stuff, which ended in calamity. I'm surprised that we weren't sent to the Null last time. Just get it through your thick skull that there is no salvation for us."

Aisely smiled and started cleaning his "fingernails." "Then I guess you don't want to save your precious girlfriend Helena." I asked him what he meant, but he kept smiling and said, "I thought you weren't going to help me with this hero stuff? I guess you don't care about Ms. Helena Way after all. You are so cold."

"Tell me."

"I'll tell you if you say, 'Sorry, Aisely, for making fun of your hero idea and making you cry.'"

"Go to death, Aisely!" I stood there glaring.

"Say it or I won't tell you." Aisely turned his back on me and crossed his arms as if he were a three-year-old human.

"I'm sorry, Aisely, for making fun of your hero idea and making you cry."

"Now say that you are absolutely nothing without me. I am the ink to your pen, the water to your well, the Coke to your cola."

"You are the pain to my ass."

"Oh, then I guess you don't need my information then. And I really thought you liked Helena. What a shame."

I sighed and rolled my tongue against my inner cheeks. "I am nothing without you. You are the ink to my pen, the water to my well, and . . . the Coke to my cola."

"Now that's better. That wasn't so bad was it? Okay, now tell me you love me."

"Aisely!"

"Okay, okay," Aisely said, chuckling. "I was just kidding." Aisely said that Adilah had placed some type of weapon in Neptune's Garden.

"What kind of weapon?"

"Does that really matter?"

"Do you want help or what?"

"I don't have time to explain. Just hurry up and get your girlfriend out of there." As we walked through the doorway, Derek passed us. I asked where he was going. He said he was late for something. I walked over to Helena and Jamie and said, "We need to get out of here." Helena and Jamie asked why and I said, "Me and Jamie are going to the movies after this. We're going to be late."

"You didn't tell me we were going the movies!" Jamie said, putting on a giddy smile.

"Have a nice time," Helena said. "You're probably gettin' lucky tonight. Just remember to leave your part of the bill behind before you leave." She broke a snow-crab leg in half. I left money for the entire bill and then Jamie grabbed my arm to pull me along. I brushed off Jamie's grip and insisted Helena leave with us.

"Fine, since you're so insistent, I'll go. I have to get back to work at the *Daily Universe* anyways." Helena wiped herself off and got up. The three of us left.

As I was walking with Jamie to her car, Aisely caught up to us and told me to come back and help him "save the day." I told him no under my breath, that I got Helena out of there and that's all that I wanted. Aisely said that if I didn't help, he would haunt me for the rest of my life.

I agreed but I also told him that this would be the last time I would help. I told Jamie to go on, that I had something to do.

"I thought we were going to the movies," Jamie said, putting on a disappointed expression. I told her to leave me behind and drive far away from here. "What's wrong? You're acting weird." I again demanded that she leave. She looked confused but eventually obeyed and left.

"All right, Aisely, let's get this crap over with."

Aisely led me into the restaurant's bathroom. I opened a bathroom booth's door and saw a brown cardboard box with a drawing of a cartoonish rabbit. The box had white smoke coming out of it with a pleasant fig smell. Aisely quickly told me that if I breathed too much of it, it would kill me. He pumped out of me the smoke that I'd already breathed in. I closed the bathroom booth door and said, "What kind of chemical is it?"

"I think it's some gas."

"No, really, moron? What *kind* of gas?"

"All I know is that this gas is going to kill a lot of people if we don't stop it from evaporating."

"How do you know this?"

"I told you, I have sources. Now shut up and get rid of it already." I asked him how I was supposed to get rid of a deadly toxin in the middle of Times Square. "If I knew, I would've done it by myself. Hurry. The gas is going to get more aggressive."

I told Aisely to keep me from breathing in the gas. I went into the booth and opened the box. A cloud of light yellow smoke rose up into my face. Inside were punctured bags of light yellow liquid. I opened the toilet lid but Aisely stopped me.

"This chemical is strong enough to get past the sewer system's filtration and get hundreds of people sick. If any of them get killed, you and I are getting a one-way deportation to the Null."

The yellow smoke got thicker and soon covered part of the bathroom. I had to think of something fast before the chemical reached the rest of the restaurant. "Standing there sucking this smoke isn't helping us any," Aisely said.

His words gave me an epiphany. "Aisely, you're a genius."

"What you talkin' 'bout, Aurick?"

"I want you to collect every particle of gas and put it inside my body."

"You want me to do what?!"

"I want you to put all the gas in this room inside my stomach. That'll allow me to transport the gas safely to the roof of this building. Just don't let my body absorb any of the toxins."

"But I was never good at air manipulation."

"We don't have a choice. You'll just have to concentrate. If I absorb any of the gas, my host will die and I'll be screwed. Don't screw this up."

Aisely looked nervous, and his nervousness made me nervous. He stretched his "body" and cracked his "fingers." He evaporated the rest of the yellow liquid and collected the smoke into a perfectly shaped ball. The sphere was no bigger than a golf ball. Aisely grasped it and said, "Open wide."

I did just so and swallowed the sphere. I ran up the stairs to the roof of the restaurant. "Wait, Aurick, you're going to make me lose my concentration," Aisely said, chasing after me.

"We're a few stories up. Up here, no one should get hurt by this chemical. All right, pump every single portion out and don't let any of it stay in my body."

Aisely concentrated and started drawing forth the toxins. About halfway through the process, I started to get dizzy. My chest started to spasm as if I were crying. My skin secreted ounces of sweat. Aisely was screwing up again and letting the gas get absorbed. I got cold and my body started to shiver uncontrollably. Eventually, everything faded to pitch-blackness.

Moments later, I felt air being poured into my throat. I opened my eyes to see Aisely performing CPR on me. I rapidly got up and spit up. I yelled at him for kissing me.

"What's wrong, Aurick? I was just trying to save your life."

"Bull, you're using that as an excuse to kiss me." I told Aisely that I was going home and never wanted to see him again.

He replied, "Um, we're not done here."

VII

LOFİE

You will learn that love is strong. It is strong, paradoxically, because it is weak. It is the force that drives us mad with possessive combustion. It will set you on fire and will not turn you into ash for as long as someone else doesn't put you out. It is the force that drives the cosmos itself. It is responsible yet it is treacherous and not trustworthy. Don't let your heart guide you because it is blind and selfish. And it is also pure without ulterior intention. Do not let the reins slip from your grasp as I have.

Lunch hour was about over. Aisely led me to the sidewalk. The area was busy. It was congested. It was claustrophobic. New York City was getting back to business and she didn't care who was in the way. It was about time she took a taste of her own medicine.

"What do you mean it's not over?"

"This is only one of the chemical weapons. We disposed of just one of four of those boxes. Three more of those boxes were placed throughout the area. There's one in a police station, one in the firehouse, and one—"

"I don't care, Aisely. I did enough today. I'm going to bed," I said, cutting him off and walking ahead of him.

"The third one is at the *Daily Universe.*"

That's where Helena worked. A naked feeling at the pit of my stomach gripped me. I couldn't explain the feeling. "I need a phone. Quick."

"Don't ask me. I don't have one."

"Just find me one."

Aisely went through the crowd looking about. He noticed a young man wearing a book-bag who was holding a skateboard while waiting to cross the street. Aisely tore a hole in the young skateboarder's bag. A device hit the ground—a cell phone. I scurried to it, not even worrying if the chap noticed me. I picked it up and dialed Helena's number as fast as I could.

"Not a 'Thank you, Aisely'?"

I ignored Aisely's question.

There was no signal to Helena's number. No automated message. No word. How could there not be a signal? *Peculiar.*

I turned around and ran. It was heavy-traffic hour. I dodged the speeding cars and barely made it safely through the streets. I got to the Daily Universe building and reached for the double door. The door was jammed. I pulled harder, but it wouldn't budge. I looked through the glass to see that both handles on the double door were chained together and locked. Some people who were trying to open it were confused. Some were getting out their cell phones while others were complaining that their cell phones weren't getting a signal. *Peculiar.* I went around to the emergency exit. It was also chained. Just what was going on here? Where were all the guards who were usually stationed up front? This was planned out.

I looked around to see if anyone was watching me. I didn't have enough time to find a way in so I gripped the door. I unleashed the limiters on Aurick's body and yanked the doors so hard that the chains broke. The lobby was crowded, as a news business should be, and especially on a weekday. I needed to find those bags of chemicals and dispose of them, but I didn't know where they could be. I had to make haste. Helena didn't have much time left. I decided to check the bathrooms first, as at Neptune's Garden. I got the directions and on my way to one of them, four men wearing yellow raincoats walked out of the elevator. One of them was wearing green lipstick and held a bunny mask in his hand. The one farthest to the right said, "You idiot, I told you to be careful." The one wearing green lipstick said, "I'm sorry. I didn't mean to set it off prematurely."

"Because of you, we lost one of our comrades," one on the left said.

"At least he died for a good cause."

As they walked toward me, I was ready to go into action and get some answers. But the closer they got, the more of that "naked feeling" I got inside. The moment they walked past me, the one wearing the green lipstick looked startled and stared at me. I stared back at him. The three walked around the corner and went through a side emergency exit. I didn't have time to follow. Just as I continued on, a loud, screeching fire alarm went off. Everyone in the lobby was startled, but they calmly walked over to the front door. They were calm until people from upstairs stampeded down the steps. More primal chaos ensued when they found the front door welded shut. They looked a little freaked but also stayed calm. They tried the back emergency exit but it too was welded shut. Someone yelled, "We can't get out!" which made everyone even more nervous.

Timmy, one of Helena's closest cameramen, along with dozens of other men, frantically ran down the stairs into the lobby. I called out to Timmy but he was too scared to hear me. As he ran past me, I grabbed his throat and forced him to stop running. I asked him where Helena was.

"Some psychos threw some type of chemicals inside." Others around us listened to Timmy as he spoke. "Some yellow gas went through the air. In just a few seconds, some people dropped down, one by one, like flies. They're all dead." Several spectators heard this and ran to the door, trying to yank it open to no avail.

"Why didn't you keep Helena with you?!"

"I tried to find her but everyone freaked out in there."

I stared at Timothy. A nasty smell hit my nose. I looked at his pants and saw he'd urinated on himself. I let him go. Dozens more people ran down the stairs, sending everyone in the now crowded lobby into a frenzy. Everyone had his or her cell phones out. No one could get a signal. My top priority was to keep Helena breathing, so I ran up the stairs to find her.

Thanks to my observations of Helena, I knew exactly which floor she worked on. The ascension felt as if it took an eternity. Thirty-three stories up, entranced by deliberation. Why did I feel this way? What was I going through all of this trouble for? Why was I risking my own safety for someone else? This was illogical. Whatever the reason, I felt the need to keep moving forward. When I got to Helena's floor, the elevator door opened. A light yellow smoke crept from the elevator, same kind of smoke as back at Neptune's Garden.

Aisely wasn't here to save me. I was alone. But I had to save Helena. I held my breath, covered my nose and mouth with my suit, and charged into the yellow smoke of death. As I ran, I tripped over an object on the floor. I looked back to see a body. It was a man with glasses wearing a black business suit. I looked forward and saw more people in business suits on the floor. Newspapers and white sheets of paper were scattered through the air and on the ground like snow on Christmas morning. It was quiet. It was motionless. I ran around the office. I looked down and spotted a woman. She was facedown. She had black hair and a black suit, just like Helena. My face got hot. Beads of sweat rolled down my forehead and stung my eyes. It felt like a sting from God. I rolled the woman over and saw that it was not Helena. I sighed in relief. My sides started to cramp as my lungs dried up from the lack of fresh air. Helena wasn't here. I was running out of time. I was running out of air. I had searched the room for about seven minutes with no success in finding Helena. It was strenuous keeping the limiters from making Aurick's lungs from taking a breath of air. Even through my intervention, Aurick's body could only last a few more minutes. I could feel the gas of death seeping into my skin trying to consume my insides. My skin and eyes burned and itched.

Then I heard a clank. After the clank, I heard a thump. After a clank and a thump, I heard a crack. It was coming from a room on the far right corner that I hadn't before noticed. I ran and stopped at the door. I heard a voice crying out for help. I didn't want to open the door and let the gas inside, but I could hold my breath no longer. I burst through the door and collapsed to the ground. Helena looked on and said, "You idiot. You're letting the gas in." She rushed and closed the door. She took the time and looked and saw it was me.

"Aurick! What are you doing here?" She helped me up and hugged me. I asked her what happened. She said some men in bunny masks set off gas explosions in the office.

Without warning, Helena picked up a chair and tossed it against the window. The window cracked, but didn't break as we'd hoped. She asked me to help her pick up the desk that was in the middle of the room. Together, we lugged it across the floor. In unison, we launched it. The desk broke through the already cracked glass and fell out the window and down thirty-three stories. The sounds of smashing metal and car alarms greeted us.

"Maybe throwing a desk out of the window wasn't such a good idea," Helena said, taking a look and seeing the desk had fallen on a car. I keeled over in pain from the effects of holding my breath and exerting myself with the table. Helena was too busy calling for help out the window to notice. As she yelled for help, I spotted yellow gas spewing from a firehouse. All of the destruction was coming to pass. *Everything* Aisely said came true.

Helena continued to scream for help. I didn't bother to join her because I knew there was too much chaos for anyone to help us. I had no abilities that could save Helena while I was in Aurick's body. I would be able to leave Aurick's body for safety, but that would mean leaving Helena behind. Her voice got hoarse, so she stopped shouting. We both stood in the room, trying to think of ways to escape. Helena stripped her jacket and shirt off, leaving only her black bra on. She used her clothes to block the spaces at the sides of the door. She then told me to do the same and block the bottom of the door. I ended up stripping down to white briefs with a tomato print. I felt slightly embarrassed.

"We're not getting out of here, are we?" Helena said, calmly looking to me. It pained me to look at her and not say anything. Helena said that gas rises to the top first, so we both got down to the floor and sat in a corner of the room. "I'm so sorry I got you into this. I feel like an idiot saying those stupid things at lunch about living for this kind of life. You must think I'm so weird."

"You're not weird. Humans naturally thrive for excitement and even chaos. They were never meant to have totally peaceful lives. If that were the case, they would be miserable living their routine lives. At least I think so."

"You speak like you're an alien."

"Oh, yes, I'm an alien."

Helena smiled and looked at me. "Is that so? Where are you from then?"

"Mexico."

Helena laughed and leaned on me. We both watched on as the yellow death leaked through our clothes that we'd blocked the spaces of the door with and started rising to the top of the room, just as Helena said.

"Let me ask you a question. How did you know to come for me?"

I was quiet for a while and then said, "I had a hunch."

"A hunch?"

"Yeah." The yellow gas slowly filled the room. "Do you really like Derek?"

Helena looked up and smiled. "You don't?"

"No. You deserve better."

The gas got thicker.

"I'm not sure about that."

"Why do you say that?"

"I've been weird all my life. No one ever wanted to be around me. They judged me. They said there was no way I would ever belong if I stayed the way I am. I worked myself to a skeleton trying to prove them wrong. I pushed everyone close to me away so that I wouldn't be held back. I pretended I didn't care about anyone, so in return, no one cared about me. When I needed help, no one came for me. I even sucked my pride up and prayed. I guess I was too lost to be heard." Helena gazed deeply into my eyes and grabbed hold of my arm. "You came back for me. It's as if you were my—" She abruptly stopped as if she caught her words. "I'll thank you if we make it through this."

The thickness of the yellow death was far too apparent now. There was nowhere to run. There was no one to pray to. It was my time to leave for safety. I stroked Helena's hair. That long godlike hair. I grabbed hold of Helena and touched lips with her.

"Good-bye, Helena."

I began to separate myself from Aurick's body.

But for some strange reason, Aurick's body wouldn't let me go. I concentrated harder, but it didn't work. It was as if his human will were stronger than mine. But that would be impossible. We could now smell the yellow death. All hope was lost.

As Helena and I drew our last breath, the undamaged part

of the window began to crack. The crack grew outward as if it were a spiderweb. The room started to vibrate as if we were being hit by an earthquake. Then a great vacuum blew into the room, sucking up the yellow death and pulling Helena and me closer to the window. We helplessly clawed on to the floor for dear life. I took hold of one of Helena's hands and smashed my fist through the floor to hold on tighter. Her hand slipped from mine. Helena grabbed the ledge of the window and dangled above the New York City pavement. Helena wanted to be on top of the world, but not like this.

The wind abruptly stopped. I took my opportunity and rushed over to grab Helena's arms, pulling her to safety. We both lay on the floor, breathing hard, as if we hadn't breathed in years. Helena asked if I was okay. I told her to wait for me by the elevator. I lay there on the floor trying to recuperate. What was going on?

A screeching scream sliced through the air. It was Helena's voice. I got up and began to make my way out of the room. My body suddenly felt heavier. At first, I thought it was because I was exhausted. Each leg felt as if it weighed a ton. It caused them to move slower and slower until I couldn't take another step. I then knew this wasn't natural exhaustion. Some type of pressure was pushing me down.

I fell to the floor and rolled over on my back. I tried getting up but it was no use. I felt like a gimp. A man wearing a black business suit walked into the room. He was one of the men that had lain dead in the other office when I was in search of Helena. I didn't understand what was going on. I asked him, "Who are you? What did you do to Helena?" He didn't reply. He got down and picked up Helena's purse, which she'd left on the floor. I asked again who he was, but he ignored me. He went into the purse and took out lipstick. He then took off the cap and rubbed the lipstick with his finger. The red lipstick turned green. It was the same type of lipstick one of the four Adilah members wore.

"Wow, babe, you mean to tell me you don't recognize my presence? You truly are a dog." He put lipstick on his lips. "It's me, Lofie."

Lofie?! My brother Lofie from way before the Eden Incident? We'd stopped communicating a long time ago. For my safety. For his. For that of everyone around us.

"How have you been, Lofie?"

"Don't give me that 'How have you been, Lofie?' crap," he said, getting on top of me and grabbing my collar. "You abandoned me. I don't believe I can ever forgive you for that!" Lofie stared deep into my eyes. His glare was so harsh it made my eyes sore. "Ah, what the death. I'll forgive you. I never was the type of person to hold grudges."

Lofie moved in to kiss my lips, but I turned my face away. "What's this? You deny a kiss from a dear old friend?" yelled Lofie at the top of his voice. He got off of me and stepped back.

"What did you do with Helena?"

An expression of even more irritation wrinkled his face. "She . . . is just peachy. I pushed her in the elevator and let her leave. I didn't want that slut ruining our special reunion."

"Why are you with Adilah?" I said mild-temperedly.

"You have the nerve to change the subject after what you did to me? I sacrificed my status for you. Two times. I searched every corner on earth to find you. And when I finally find you, this is what you talk about with me?"

"You almost killed me. Me and her . . ."

"And who? You and that whore?" Lofie paced back and forth, holding his arms behind his back. "I saw you risking your life for that slut. You never did that for me. What does she have that I don't have?" His steps got harder and louder. He ranted on and on some more about how long it took to find me.

"Helena isn't a threat. She's just a stupid journalist who's in way over her head. Why would you go this far just to get to her?"

"Oh, please. Her workplace just happens to be one of the easiest places to set those chemical weapons."

"Then why did you get it set up at the restaurant?"

"Those were the humans of Adilah. They're all average Joes and mental patients. They may act tough but they're really cowards. They're too scared to kill her up front in fear of getting caught and being thrown in jail, so they just try to sabotage her appointments. It's so hard to find good help these days. I basically have to do everything around here. Can you believe I had to weld some of the doors shut myself because they couldn't even chain the doors properly? Oh boy," he said, slapping himself on the forehead with his palm.

"When are you and Adilah going to stop this, Lofie? It's getting real boring."

He abruptly stopped moving and started laughing. "Boring? It's only just begun, sugarplum. We're going to paint the town red, red with the blood of every human here, starting with your little girlfriend, Helena."

"If you try to hurt Helena again, I'll—"

"You'll what?" Lofie said, intensifying his voice. "You may be vastly stronger than me in spirit form, but while you're in that meat-bag, I could crush you instantly. And it looks like you won't be able to leave it anytime soon."

A gust of wind blew through the room. Two dark figures stood by the window. One was holding Aisely to his knees, preventing him from moving. Aisely was crying like a baby.

"How are you able to use a corpse as a vessel?" I asked Lofie.

"I'm not. All I am doing is moving this body's parts like a puppet, using air to communicate with you. It's hard, like death. Maybe I should kill and mutilate your host so that you'll be stuck in that body for ages."

Lofie picked up a pen and held it over me as if he were going to stab me. "Naw, I don't want to go to the Null for what's going to happen next." He looked down at my crotch. "So maybe I should just castrate you?" He pondered it. "Naw, I wouldn't want to lose that tool of yours . . . not yet anyways."

"What are you planning to do?"

"That's none of your business!" Lofie screamed. "I'll tell you if you join me." He lowered his voice again. I stayed quiet. "All right, I'll tell you if you kiss me."

"I'm not stupid enough to trust you, so you can forget it. I'm not dealing with the likes of you."

"Don't try to sound like Daddy, 'cause you're not, even if you'd like to be. You're on our side. You are us."

"I'm nothing like any of you."

"Daddy judged us to definite destruction. That includes *you,* love muffin. Saving her won't save yourself. You're on *our* side whether you like it or not." Lofie got on top of me. He sat on me in a way where his "junk" touched mine. He leaned forward, remaining inches from my face. "What if I told you there was a way to escape Daddy's execution? What if I told you there's a way we could start over? What if I told you there is a way to live forever? What if I told you there was a way out of this fantasy world?"

Lofie's words surrounded me. Lofie was always nuts but this time he was really losing it. How could we ever escape Father's wrath?

"Think about that, sweetie. I saved you this time. I'll even call off the headhunt on that slut. But if you ever, I mean ever, try to pull a stunt like getting in our way again, she and every human you've ever met will be slaughtered like little piggies."

"Helena is a news reporter. She's fixed on exposing your clan. There's nothing that I can do."

Lofie gave a cruel smile. "If we catch Helena getting into

our business again, she *will* die." Lofie moved in, dragged his wet tongue down my chin and up across my face. "Good-bye, sweetie."

A powerful gust of wind blew through the room. The corpse fell to the floor. Lofie and the two dark figures vanished without a trace. I was able to move my body again. I got up and wiped Lofie's saliva off my face. Aisely ran over to me, still crying. He frantically told me that he was beaten up.

"Shut up, you big baby."

VIII

SUNNY BEACH

I spent the next week inside Aurick's apartment. I didn't talk to anyone, not even Aisely. I didn't answer the phone or the door. The phone rang constantly. I got messages from the band and from the job. They wondered where I was. Jamie made the most phone calls. She constantly knocked on the door and called for me, but I didn't answer. I thought about everything Lofie had told me. I thought about that silly, impossible hope of escaping Father's punishment. Father's justice. How would anyone be able to do that? Once Father says something, it becomes. Just as His name means.

I thought about many things. But most of all, I thought about Helena. The Fallen always bring trouble to any human who is around them. I was a prime example. If I wanted Helena to be safe, I knew I couldn't stay in this obstructing body any longer. I needed to find a way to rip myself from this meat-bag. The phone rang again. It was Angry Kid. He left a message saying to meet him at Dead Man's Pub, that he had some good news. This was one of the first times I'd ever heard Kid say something positive. I couldn't pass up this chance.

It was about seven in the evening. It was dark and chilly. It seemed as if it were always dark and chilly in this godforsaken area of town. I walked in Dead Man's Pub and sat down at the bar. The bartender noticed me. Her eyes welled up in surprise. She stopped pouring whiskey for a male customer and went over to me, which made him heated. He told her to get back over there, but the bartender just told him to shut up and wait. She grinned from ear to ear and said, "Hey, Aurick. Where on earth have you been, darling?" She spoke with a Southern accent.

"Oh, I kicked the habit of drinking so there was no need to come back here."

"Well, I guess you haven't kicked the habit completely since you're here. The Lord's good drink called ya back, huh?"

She chuckled and I chuckled to be friendly and said, "Naw, I'm just here to meet up with a friend. That's all."

The bartender giggled. "I'm just messing with you, darling."

She poured a glass of water and served it to me. "You must be really brave to be gone for so long and come round this neck of the woods again."

"Why?"

"Since you left, folks have been looking for you. It was always about you owing them money. Especially that guy Samson who they say you beat up some years back. They stopped looking for you for some time now, but still, it's mighty dangerous to be round here."

I laughed. "Thank you for looking out for me. But I'll be okay."

She smiled and leaned over the counter and gave me a peck on the cheek and a hug. "Just be careful, honey."

I waited for what felt like two hours. The first hour, I felt annoyed. But by the second, my body got a little nervous. People that had known Aurick had started coming in. They would notice me and start whispering to others. I asked the bartender for a shot of liquor. I needed to dull this stupid body's nerves. Just when I got up to leave, an arm grabbed my shoulder. I quickly turned to see it was Kid.

"Where do you think you're going?" Kid was smiling as if he'd won the lottery.

"I was about to leave, stupid. What took you so long?"

Kid kissed the rabbit foot he was wearing around his neck. He never let that thing out of his sight.

"A black cat crossed my path so I decided to take the longer route." Kid always said that kind of crap when he was late. Kid didn't hesitate and asked the bartender for some shots of liquor.

"How did you get here before me anyway? You took the train?"

"No, I took the sidewalk." Kid looked confused so I helped him out and said, "I walked."

"Damn, all the way out here? Do you walk *everywhere*?" I ignored his question and watched him as he swallowed his shots. He gulped three down and ordered some more. I told him to hurry up and share his news.

"Christ, Aurick; take a chill pill. Usually I'm the one with a short fuse." Kid held one shot glass in each hand. He chugged them one at a time, gargled, then swallowed. "I got a record company to sign our band."

I forced a smile. "Wow, that's cool."

"All we have to do is play for some music producer in a few days." I wanted to tell Kid that I wasn't going to be in the band anymore, but I didn't want to hear his whining. I asked for some shots from the bartender.

"Now I know you've been flaking out on us, Aurick. But I'm willing to forgive." The alcohol was causing his speech to slur. "My life is going to hit a turning point. I think I even found someone I love. Someone who's been close to me for a long time and I didn't even know it."

"Lucky you." The woman isn't so lucky, I thought.

"Isn't it funny how someone could spend their entire lives looking for something when it has been right there the whole time? This world's full of irony. Though at times that irony could be cruel."

His eyes couldn't find a focal point on my face. I don't know how he drives in these conditions all the time. He has talent.

"I just don't need you messing this up for us this time, man."

Some thugs started to gather. They were looking at me, trying to match my face.

The bartender walked over to us. "Aurick, I suggest you guys skedaddle the hell out of here. Those guys over there are Samson's friends. You're bringing too much attention."

"All right. That's enough drinking. We need to get out of here."

"What's the rush, Aurick? Enjoy the night while it's young," Kid said, downing another shot.

"If you don't want to die young, then let's get out of here. Now."

"All right, just one more." Kid gestured to the bartender for two more shots. I grabbed his arm and forced him to get up.

"Good night, Aurick. Be careful." The bartender handed me a card with her phone number. I took it and put it in my pocket. I didn't want to make the same mistake Aurick had made the night he almost got killed by Samson, so I went through the front door this time. People were smoking outside. They were all bundled up together to ward off the chilly wind. Some stared at me. We excused ourselves through the groups of people. Kid went over to the driver's side of the car, and just when he was about to get in, I said, "You're going to drive in that condition?"

"Yeah, why not?"

I rolled my eyes and stared at him in a way to get him to figure it out himself.

"Then why don't you drive?"

"I don't have a license." Amid all of my accomplishments as a human, I'd never bothered making a trip to the DMV.

"You don't have a license? What do you live in, the eighteenth century?" We both got in, with Kid driving as usual.

"Don't worry, Aurick." Kid held his rabbit's foot in his hand. "With lucky foot right here, nothing bad can happen to me. Well, maybe you, but not me." Kid kissed the rabbit foot. He always brought that foot wherever he went. He trusted that nasty thing with his life. Little did he know that pagan objects attract bad spirits.

"Well, that makes me feel a lot better," I said sarcastically. People outside the pub were still staring at me, trying to match my face. *At least we're out of that death trap,* I thought. I was worried about Kid's driving intoxicated, as he made little swerves left to right and had one near collision. Still, we arrived at my building alive. My head started to pain me. When I opened my car door, Kid said, "Remember, Aurick, don't screw this up for me."

I gestured to him to get lost. Right after I slammed the door shut, I started to get extremely dizzy. My headache suddenly got twenty times worse. I moaned, grabbed my head in pain, and collapsed to the ground.

Kid rushed to my aid. "Whoa. You are hammered, Aurick." Kid laughed his head off. "You should really take it easy on the Jesus juice. This could escalate into a real drinking problem."

The pain gradually dulled. I still couldn't walk on my own so I had to use the drunken fool as a crutch to get into the building. The cruddy elevator wasn't working as usual so we had to go up the stairs. We occasionally almost tumbled down the stairs together but managed to get into my apartment alive.

"I'm just going to rest my eyes here for a while. Wake me up in four minutes," Kid said, collapsing onto the couch.

My head was still banging with pain. I went into the bathroom and splashed cold water on my face. I looked into the mirror (which I hadn't done in months) and saw that I had deep and dark bags under my eyes. I stared into the mirror for a few more minutes until it seemed the walls started to vibrate and twist. I saw Helena's reflection through the mirror. Her head swelled. Her eyes shed tears. Her tears then turned into blood. She got closer and closer to me. Her hand grabbed my shoulder. Her hand was icy cold. Her eyes turned entirely black. My stomach suddenly started to churn. When I looked up into the mirror, Helena was gone. The effects of possessing a human were getting more frequent. I had to leave this body as soon as possible. I walked back to Kid and shook him.

"All right, it's been four minutes. Get out."

Kid replied with a deep, loud snore. I threw a blanket over him and walked into my bedroom. Sephirot was sleeping on my bed. When I got closer, I saw that the cat smelled me. His eyes were still closed but his ears were wiggling around. "Trying to catch me by surprise again, Sephirot?" I jumped onto the bed and grabbed him. He meowed loudly to tell me he was hungry. I gasped. "Did I forget to feed you again? I deeply apologize."

I cooked him a small steak and a little bit of mashed potatoes, his favorite meal. He was munching it down as if he hadn't eaten in days. Probably hadn't. But he's a survivor.

I went back to my bedroom, lay down, and closed my eyes. Sephirot jumped on the bed and lay on my chest. "You're my best friend, Seph. I hope you know that." Sephirot purred and fell soundly asleep. "In a few days, Seph, I'm going to be leaving you." Aurick's body let out a tear. I closed my eyes and fell asleep.

I woke up the next morning to find that Angry Kid was gone. I got undressed and went into the bathroom to take a shower. I slid the shower curtain over to see Angry Kid coming out of the shower naked. "Aw," Kid said. I shielded my eyes, backed up, slipped on some water, and hit my head on the floor. Kid aided me but I kicked him out right afterward. The indignity of it all.

I went to the hospital to visit Doughy's mother, Shelia. I came in with a bouquet of dandelions. She was sound asleep. I placed the flowers carefully on the countertop near her bed so I wouldn't wake her. I didn't have a card saying whom the flowers were from but I didn't worry. I visited her from time to time and I always brought her dandelions, so she would know it was me. Shelia and I had gotten quite close, and she saw me as a confidant. If she weren't in her condition, I would take her out somewhere special.

I spent time thinking about Helena. I thought about what I was going to say. This would be our last psychological appointment, so these final words had to count.

Helena was 6.423 minutes late. I checked my watch repeatedly. Each minute that passed by felt like a separate eternity. The sweat glands under Aurick's skin secreted hot sweat. I had to focus and keep his temperature under control. Helena finally strolled in. She was wearing her usual black sweatpants and sweatshirt look.

"Hey, Superman, how's the crime fighting?" Helena said, grinning.

"If I'm Superman, then you must be my damsel in distress."

Helena grinned some more. She leaned forward slightly and said, "I'm no one's damsel in distress." She reached into her bag and threw photos onto the desk. I picked them up. They were pictures of people in yellow raincoats and bunny masks. "I took these after the attack." I stared at them and then stared at her. "I'm getting closer and closer to finding out their location. It's just a matter of time before—"

"You're still investigating them?"

"Yeah, why not?"

"They tried to kill you."

"So?"

"So I want you to stop." I wanted to tell her just how much she was in over her head. I wanted to tell her just how much danger she was in if even one Fallen saw her getting close to them again. "This investigation is going to get you killed."

"That's never stopped me before."

"No, Helena. This time it's different."

"Different? How would you know?" She paused and stared into my eyes. "Do you know something about this case that I don't know?"

I looked down. "I just don't want anything to happen to you."

Helena said that she was going to be just fine. But I knew for sure that if she continued, she was sure to be dead and there was nothing I could do to stop it.

"You're not going to be fine. You're in way over your head."

Helena's eyes widened. "Who do you think you are to tell me how I should live my life?"

"Uhh, your psychologist, perhaps?"

Helena got up and snatched the pictures from me. She grabbed her bag off the floor and walked toward the door.

"Helena, I apologize. Don't—" Helena slammed the door before I could finish. I sat there feeling stupid. I put my head down and massaged my temples. I thought about how wrong that conversation went. Was this how I was going to end my relationship with Helena?

My last patient came in. He began speaking about his new set of problems. I cut him off and said in a soft, tempered voice, "I don't care. Get out."

"Excuse me?"

I raised my voice. "Get out!"

The next day, it was time for me to end my last chapter with the band. I was going to get this record deal done. I wore my best suit and practiced my instrument before I left. As I was walking down the stairs, I bumped into Jamie. She was carrying groceries. I could see one of the bags contained cans of cookie dough. She looked concerned. "Aurick, where have you been? I thought maybe something had happened to you after I left you behind in Times Square." She dropped her bags and gave me a hug and a kiss.

"I'm okay. I was just sick."

"Oh, that's good to hear." Jamie smiled. "I had a great time last week. I'm going to a skiing resort next weekend. I was wondering if you wanted to come."

"I'm sorry. I can't."

Jamie looked down and then looked up into my eyes. "Oh, that's okay. I know a busy person like you wouldn't have the time for a stupid skiing trip. How about we just go out to eat again? How about tomorrow night?"

"I'm sorry, Jamie. I won't be available then either."

Jamie looked to the floor again in disappointment. Then she looked up at me again. "Yeah, busy, busy, busy Aurick. How about I just make you some cookies? We could eat them together. Tonight perhaps?" I turned her down again. "Okay, it's fine. Well, I don't want to keep you here so I'll get out of your way."

"Good-bye, Jamie."

She waved at me and picked up her bags. Her face was red. On her way up, she stopped abruptly and said, "You don't like me much, do you?" Her question caught me off guard. Jamie didn't make eye contact with me this time.

"Of course I like you." There was a long silence between us.

"It's because I act so needy, isn't it?"

"No, no, it's not that." I started fumbling my words. "I like you . . . as a friend." After another long silence, Jamie continued her way up the stairs. I didn't mean to hurt her feelings. I really did like her. Just not in a romantic way. I liked her as a pet. A pet that you could pet, hug, feed, and take it outside from time to time. Even though I didn't mean to hurt Jamie's feelings, I still did. Aurick's skin turned red and his eyes got moist.

I entered the record studio with my head down. I was still bummed about my last encounter with Helena. I blew it. I blew it all to death. A veil of shame and discomfort wrapped me up. It felt as if I were underwater.

Doughy was in the recording booth tuning his guitar. Terra was fumbling in a desk for something. Kid was speaking with a chubby man in a plain black suit. I would describe him as "shapes." Sweet-talking him most likely.

"Hey, Aurick," Terra called out to me. She came over and gave me a hug.

"Is this the last member?" the man in the suit said.

"Yeah, that's him," Kid said, speaking in a soft tone. This was the first time I'd ever heard Angry Kid speak so nicely to a person.

"You're late, Mr. Pantera. I've been waiting for over an hour." The man was full of crap. I was exactly 2.75 minutes late.

"This is Mr. Eric Fisher." This was the first time I'd ever heard Kid say *Mr.* in front of someone's name. "He's a music producer from Dark Soul records, which is a partner with Lucifer records."

I stretched my hand out for a handshake. Eric Fisher hesitated but then shook my hand. He looked pissed off.

"I'm sorry. A black cat crossed my path so I took the longer route," I said, copying Angry to annoy him. It made me sick apologizing to a snake like this guy.

"You should've been wearing one of these babies," Kid said, flashing his rabbit-foot necklace.

"All right, let's get this show on the road and stop wasting time. Time means money," the producer said, walking off. It took everything I had not to break Fisher's face. I just needed to get through this and impress this pig. If I could get this deal done, the band would be happy and I could leave Aurick's body with some sense of accomplishment. Kind of.

We were all in the booth with Fisher outside, peering through the window.

"This is the first chapter of our riches and fortune. So don't screw this up." Kid leaned over to me. "This means you, Aurick."

"Oh, shut up, Kid," Terra said. "Aurick is the best out of all of us."

Doughy laughed and said, "Yeah, you're just mad 'cause he's better than you."

"Shut up, Doughy," Kid responded, getting red.

"Hey, hey, hey," Fisher said. "What's going on in there?"

"Sorry, Mr. Fisher," Angry Kid said. He glared at me and looked back at his guitar. "All right, kick it off."

We began playing. A few minutes in, we were doing all right. Terra was fine on drums. Kid, for the first time, looked happy playing his guitar. Happy Kid is what we should call him. Doughy on bass messed up initially, but he got it together and played well. And, of course, I was great on guitar.

All was well until I suddenly started to get dizzy. I missed a note, which messed up others on the floor. The band briefly glanced at me. I resumed playing. The effects of the possession were getting worse. I started losing control of my fingers as they violently strummed guitar strings randomly, screwing up the song. These damn ten fingers. It was like the fingers had a mind of their own. The band looked at me with concern. Kid made eye and mouth gestures, telling me to stop messing up. I gained control of the Fantastic Ten again.

Just when I felt a little better, my hand violently struck the guitar strings so hard that three of them popped. My body started to spasm as if I were having a seizure and I fell backward against the drum set. I heard yelling and screaming. Eventually, everything faded to black darkness.

❖   ❖   ❖

I awoke on a sandy beach. It was bright and sunny. Not a cloud was in sight. The seagulls cawed and swooped down to the sand. I could see them dragging out baby crabs from sand holes and then lofting them away to the sky. The sweet salt from the seawater was fresh and crisp. It was a perfect day. I was still in my suit. I sat there for a few minutes, wondering just what had happened and where I was. I rubbed my head in pain.

"Your head hurts?" a voice said.

I turned around to see a familiar face behind me. I was confused because there was no way this person could be standing near me, talking to me. It was a woman. She was wearing a bright red silk dress. The dress was loose, and air flowed through its folds. She had light brown skin with a reddish tint. Her hair was light brown. It reached past her knees. The sun's rays bounced off her locks, making her look like a messiah. She smiled. She came closer.

"Impossible," I said, standing up and backing off in astonishment.

"What's impossible?" She came up to me and kissed my lips. "What's wrong with you? Sit down." I did. She sat down and placed her arms around me. I stared at her as if she were an alien from outer space. She smiled. "What is it?"

"Is it really *you*?"

She laughed. "Of course it's me. Who else would I be?"

She leaned against me and rested her cheek against my cheek. Her skin was as smooth as butter. Her long hair entangled me like a fly in a spiderweb. I didn't mind. It smelled of cinnamon and cocoa butter. I thought I would never feel her embrace again. I was wrong. We both laughed in unison. We looked into the sunset. It was so quiet. It was so peaceful. I wanted this to last forever.

After a few minutes, the sky grew darker. I thought maybe a cloud was blocking the sun. I was in too much peaceful bliss to pay it any mind. The sky gradually got darker and darker. I looked up. It started to drizzle. The drizzle turned into rain and the rain turned into a downpour. Finally, the downpour turned into a full-blown storm. The woman still had her face pressed up against mine. She was smiling as if nothing were going on. Wind blew sand all around us. The waves crashed into crags on the beach. Lightning crashed onto the beach, turning spots into fields of glass.

"What's going on?" I ripped myself from the woman's grasp.

"What do you mean?" She tilted her head in confusion. The ground vibrated and rumbled. She grabbed on to me again and hugged me with passion.

"Tell me, what's going on?"

She peered deep into my eyes. "We're going to die, silly." She embraced herself tightly. A great wall of water gushed from the horizon, creating an almost pitch-black shadow. The woman's beautiful, bright face was the only thing I could see. I rubbed my forehead against hers. I wanted to feel her sweat, her heat, one more time.

"Good-bye, once more," I said.

The black wall of water swept across the beach and swallowed us.

IX

SEIZURE OF PROPERTY

It's a game. A game of insecurity, and you were dealt the most terrible hand in the world. Flipping the positive into the negative is essential. In this game, life and death align themselves against you to defeat you. You can't do it alone. False confidence and individualism will sink you with their weight of wishful mantra. Hymning affects nothing. Assemble everything you need to win the battle. To slay the beast. You can do it. I know you can.

Wow. I haven't seen that red face in a very long time.

My eyes opened. I looked around and saw I was back at the apartment. I was on the floor on my back. I tried to get up but I couldn't move. It was as if I were paralyzed. After a few minutes of trying, I got on my feet, except it wasn't *me* who got on my feet.

"Aw, man. My head is killing me." It was Aurick. He stretched his arms and legs. I was still in Aurick's body, but Aurick was in full possession of his body! How could this have happened? I was confused. This had never before happened to me. I tried desynchronizing myself, but it wouldn't work. I started to feel panic, which I had felt only a few times in millions of years. I strained harder but all I managed to do was generate strong electrical pulses that made the apartment lights flicker. "I thought I changed the lightbulb yesterday," Aurick said, looking off in confusion. He brought over a stool and used it to get up higher to change the lightbulb.

I was still in awe. How could a human regain consciousness during a possession against *my* will? This was embarrassing. I was stuck in this meat-bag against my will. I knew for damn sure this would surely tickle Aisely's side.

Aurick walked around the apartment in a daze. "I never bought these curtains." Aurick tugged on them while still holding his head. "These are so gay."

How dare Aurick say that after I brought some class into this dump!

"Why am I dressed in this tacky suit?"

If I could, I would've controlled Aurick and shot him in the head. Aurick went into his room. "I never bought these sheets," Aurick said, feeling the covers on the bed. "Is this really my place?" He looked around. He saw pictures of himself and his friends, which confirmed to him that this really was his place. He fumbled around on the dresser and saw pictures of Helena Way. I felt so stupid for forgetting to throw them out. He picked the pictures up and brought them really close to his face. "Who is this lady?" It showed him with his arm around Helena smiling. He picked up other pictures that were scattered on the dresser, pictures of him and the band in a group shot playing our instruments. Aurick left the room a little more quickly this time, almost in a panic. He looked at himself in the mirror. "When did I start getting all of these white hairs?"

Sephirot ran over to see what was going on. Aurick and Sephirot made eye contact. "When did I get a cat?" Sephirot arched his back and fiercely hissed. Aurick shooed him away, but that just made Sephirot fiercer. Aurick chased Sephirot under the bed. Aurick reached for him. Sephirot scratched his hand, causing a bloody three-clawed mark. Aurick backed off. His head began to throb.

Flashes of memories I had these past seven years enveloped him. He couldn't understand where these images were coming from. He began to sweat. He walked into the kitchen. He opened the fridge and pulled out a can of beer and began to drink. (Aurick never had trouble drinking during the morning.) He closed the fridge when he saw a calendar on the door. He looked at it casually at first. But when he saw what year it was, he freaked. "It can't be!" Aurick said, coughing up the beer. He ran down the stairs without changing his suit. He bumped into Jamie.

"Hey, Aurick!"

Aurick stopped.

"I just wanted to apologize about how I acted yesterday. I was way out of line."

"What are you talking about?"

"Remember last night?"

"No," Aurick said bluntly. Jamie explained while Aurick grew more agitated. "Jamie, what year is this?"

Jamie looked at Aurick as if he were a psycho. "Are you high, dude?"

Aurick grabbed both of Jamie's shoulders. Jamie looked afraid and concerned.

"Just tell me what year it is." She did. Aurick's eyes widened as if he were indeed high. "It can't be."

Aurick ran down the rest of the stairs. He went to the corner store. He picked up a magazine and looked at the front cover. Some man who worked there yelled at him to pay for it. Aurick ignored him and looked at the date. Aurick gagged as if he were going to throw up. He backed up and knocked over a basket of oranges. Aurick ran, with the workers yelling at him. Aurick went back up the stairs to his apartment. He played all of the messages on the answering machine. The first message was from Terra.

"Aurick, what the hell happened to you? You freaked out on us, man. We've been looking all night for you."

The next message was from Doughy. "You need to get back to us quick, man. Kid is freakin' out after what you did. When you do get back to me, we need to talk. My mom has been asking crazy things from me."

The next was from Angry Kid. "What the hell is wrong with you, Aurick?" Kid's voice was fierce and slurred as if he'd been drinking. "You blew it for us, you bastard."

The next message said it was from Helena. The message just played silence as if someone was thinking of something to say. There was a short breath right before the message ended.

Aurick backed off and almost collapsed on the floor. "This is way freaky, man. What the hell is going on?" More flashes of memories from the last seven years rapidly flickered in his mind. Memories of all the people I had met. All the problems I went through. All the life-threatening situations I barely survived. It hurt his head and eyes. I had enough of this. I made my entrance.

"You're possessed. That's what the death is going on."

Aurick got up and looked around. "Who said that?"

"I did."

Aurick spun around. If he'd spun his neck around any harsher, he would probably have gotten whiplash. Aurick took a deep gulp of spit and said, "Who's there?" Aurick got a kitchen knife from the sink and walked around in a creeping catlike manner. Aurick toppled against the wall. "Aw, my head. Why does it hurt so damn much?" Aurick gripped his head with both hands as hard as he could.

"Look, you have to listen to me. If you don't do what I say, the effects will get worse."

"Who are you?" Aurick said, his voice cracking from the pain.

"I'm a being who has been using your body for the last seven years."

"What the hell are you talking about?"

"You don't remember much because you were unconscious the whole time. I lived a life as a human. I stayed in your body so long that I'm somehow stuck. If we don't do something quickly, we'll be in trouble."

Aurick was quiet. He'd sweated so much that my suit was wet.

"That's impossible." The throbbing in his head stopped. He got up and walked toward the door. "I've been drinking way too much. It's just a voice in my head, that's all." Aurick opened the door. "I just need some fresh New York air." Aurick began walking through the busy streets of New York. His hand was still stinging from Sephirot's scratch. He went to the store to buy Band-Aids and headache medicine. He was still sweating hard. The clerk and the people behind him on line were staring at him as if he were crazy. He took out some dollars I'd left in his pocket.

"It's not in your head. Why do you think you have all of that strange furniture? You never bought that. You never could even afford that stuff." Aurick ignored me, counting the change he'd gotten back. "You never had a cat. You hate animals, especially cats. His name is Sephirot. I've been taking care of him for seven years."

"Shut up! You're not real." The clerk looked at Aurick as if he were crazy. Aurick rushed out of the store and swallowed two of the pills. His hands were trembling so he dropped a couple more on the ground. He put the Band-Aid on his hand.

"If I'm not real, then why does the newspaper agree with me?"

Aurick ignored me, but I could tell he was thinking about what I was saying. Aurick shifted his eyes from side to side.

"Why would the newspaper lie to you about the date? It's been three years. Ask that old lady passing us."

Aurick abruptly stopped the old lady, which startled her. He asked her what the date was. She told him, which freaked him out again.

"I must be going crazy. That's it. Those drugs and alcohol must be taking a toll on my brain. That's it. Where's the phone book? I'll get some professional help. That's what I'll do. Nothing to worry about."

Aurick got back to his apartment and went into his drawers, shifting through all the notes and documents I'd been storing for these seven years. Aurick peered into each of them, trying to recall the unrecallable. "Why don't I remember *any* of this?" He saw my doctor notes. "A number and address to a therapist's office?"

The next day, Aurick set up an appointment with a therapist who was a coworker of mine in the same building. "Aurick Pantera? You're really my patient?"

"Do I know you?"

"Of course I know you. It's me, Samantha. We went to graduate school together."

"I did?"

"Yeah, you were a genius. I was years ahead of you in that school yet you managed to flash past me in just a few years."

"I did?"

"We even went out on a couple dates. You really don't remember any of this?" Aurick freaked out again. He jerked back in his chair too hard and fell backward and rolled. He got up and walked out her door. "Hey. What about our session?" Samantha said, calling out to Aurick.

On his way out of the building, Aurick bumped into Helena, who was entering for her session with me.

"Hi, Aurick. I've been trying to call you." Aurick looked confused. "I'm sorry that I yelled at you. It was stupid for me not to expect you to get upset after I sprang out my investigation on you like that. I know you were just looking out for me." Helena kissed a side of my cheek and gave me a tight, warm hug. Aurick said nothing, hurried off, and went back home.

"Now do you believe me?" I said, dragging my voice.

"So you're a ghost?"

"No, not a ghost."

"A demon?" Under divine law, the Fallen and angels alike cannot directly reveal who they are. That would spoil the existence of the metaphysical universe and obstruct some of Father's purposes.

"I cannot tell you directly who I am under divine law. You would have to figure it out on your own."

"So you're a demon?"

"I prefer that you not call me that."

"What, a *demon*?"

"Yes, that! Stop saying it," I said, raising my voice.

"Oh." There was pure silence for a few seconds. Aurick suddenly let out a burst of screaming. He ran all around the house yelling, "Oh my God. Oh my God. Oh my God. Oh my God." I told him to shut it but he continued running around. He went on for a few more minutes. I used all of my strength to get control of his foot and trip him. Aurick fell on his stomach and chin. He bit his lower lip. "Ouch."

"Can you stop messing around and listen to me?"

"Get out of my body!" Aurick ran out the door once again and flagged down a taxi. He got in and gave the driver an address.

"Where are you going now?"

"Somewhere that an evil demon like you could never enter." It was raining outside. The driver stopped across the street from a medium-size cathedral. Aurick ran out of the car without paying.

"Hey, give me my money!" the taxidriver said, yelling and forming a fist. Aurick ignored him and ran across the street. Cars sounded their horns as they swerved to avoid hitting Aurick. He ran into the church.

"Ha! Consider yourself exorcised, demon," Aurick said, approaching the church door. "I've known Father Daniel since I was a kid. He's one of the holiest men I've ever met. You don't stand a chance."

"This isn't going to work." Aurick ignored me and went inside the cathedral. It had been decades since I'd been inside any church. I usually visit a random church when I want amusement from the lies the ignorant public are fed. Some people were sitting in the seats with their heads bowed and hands together. All of them were praying. Some were crying while they prayed. Aurick ran up to a man wearing regular street clothes. The man looked as if he was headed out the door to go home.

"Father Daniel, Father Daniel!" Aurick said, grabbing the priest's jacket. Danny was alarmed with surprise.

"Why, Aurick, I haven't seen you in years."

"There's no time for that. I need your help." Aurick asked Daniel what year it was. Danny looked at him as if he were crazy but told him anyway. "If you're saying it, then it's the truth. Then that means I'm not crazy." Aurick looked relieved but, after a few seconds of thinking, said, "Wait a minute. That must mean I really am . . ." He coughed and looked as if he were going to pass out. Danny was frightened by this crazed man in front of him.

Aurick explained to Danny everything that had happened. Danny asked Aurick if he had sought mental counseling. Aurick said yes and explained further. Aurick then asked Danny for an exorcism and Danny agreed. He didn't actually believe Aurick, but he agreed to appease him. He also wanted to investigate his old friend's issue.

"Okay, I need to prepare. Give me your address and meet me

at your home in a couple of hours." We were soon back at the apartment sitting on the couch waiting for Danny Boy.

"I'm telling you, this isn't going to work. All you're doing is wasting Father Daniel's time."

Aurick ignored me, but he was still sweating and shivering from fear. There was a knock on the door. Aurick ran over and opened it. It was Danny, wearing his priest clothes and a brown jacket and a hat. He was wet from the rain. He kind of looked like the priest from that 1973 exorcism movie. It was humorous. I could hear the theme music already.

Danny Boy told Aurick to lie down on his bed, and he did just so. Sephirot hissed at Danny when he passed by. Danny pulled out a Bible, some beaded necklaces, capsules of water, and a miniature wooden cross. He did a cross gesture with his hands across his body and Aurick's body. He wrapped the beaded necklace around his palm and wrist. He started reading something from the Bible. Danny held up the miniature cross to Aurick. Aurick was into it so much that he actually believed that it was working, flailing around on the bed as if he were crazy. Danny's reading got louder and more intense. He opened the capsules of "holy water" and sprinkled them on Aurick. It didn't burn a bit the way they show in the movies. He waved the cross more rapidly. Aurick flailed even more. I wanted to puke.

The exorcism went on for more than forty minutes. It was dreadfully boring. The only thing I worried about was Danny using God's real name. If Danny used God's real name and asked him to help Aurick on top of that, then I was done for. Fallen are contracted with God to follow certain rules on earth. If a Fallen pestered a human and that human used God's real name to save himself, that Fallen had to leave the human and premises right away. If that Fallen didn't obey that law, then marooners would be sent to drag that Fallen away. The Fallen would probably be sent to the Null for disobedience.

I was going to pretend that Danny's exorcism was working

just to get it done with as quickly as possible, but as long as stupid Aurick was being dramatic, the exorcism was to continue, and Danny would be closer to using God's name. Still, I wouldn't be surprised if he didn't know it. Thank God most people are too superstitious and/or ignorant to use it. Aurick calmed down finally. He relaxed on the bed peacefully. Both men were panting.

"I believe my work here is done. This victory belongs to God," Danny said with a proud smile. I couldn't stand that a human believed that he defeated me. *Sigh.* People and their religions. Aurick thanked Danny with all his might. Danny finally left. A few minutes later, there was a knock on the door. We both thought it was Danny coming back. Aurick opened the door to find Jamie standing there before him. Aurick looked nervous and embarrassed.

"What was all that commotion?"

"What do you mean?" Beads of sweat were rolling off Aurick's forehead.

"I heard someone saying something like 'Let the power of God repel you,' over and over again. Are you okay?" Aurick said he was. After a few more seconds of Jamie's trying to examine Aurick's nervous expressions, she continued, "Well, anyways, I brought you a snack to eat." Jamie handed him a bag of her fresh-baked cookies.

"Aw, man, I haven't had these in a long time!" Aurick said, rudely snatching them away from Jamie and munching them down. "Man, these are delicious. Jamie, you really should consider doing a cookie-baking business."

"Are they really that good?"

"Yup. I bet these are good enough to commercialize. You could be making millions." For once, Aurick was being genuine. He had always loved Jamie's cookies. "We should go into business together."

"Wow, you look happier."

"I *am* happier. I decided to turn over a new leaf and live the rest of my life honestly." Yeah, right. I felt as if I could puke. "Look out, world. Aurick Pantera is a brand-new person!" Jamie looked at him with a raised eyebrow before she left, but Aurick didn't care.

He picked out his outfit for the day: sweat clothes. He sang, whistled, and hummed in the shower, which was something I thought he would never do. He was different. He was jolly. He couldn't stand still while he was shaving, which caused him to cut himself. Even then, he maintained his jolly attitude.

X

ΠEW LEAF

Once a sinner, always a sinner. You have the unique gift of proving it wrong where I could not. Prove it wrong. Rise from the dirt that you were born in and don't settle for the clouds. But be wary. They will fear you.

Aurick woke up at six in the morning. This was unusual because Aurick hated getting up in the morning. He didn't even have anything that he had to do so early. I hadn't been surprised this much in centuries.

Aurick got up and stood on his bed. He did a big stretch. He got off the bed and went into the kitchen. He opened the fridge. He went in and took out a can of beer. Ha! Some things never change.

Aurick held the can close to his face. "Oh, no, no, no, Aurick. It's a brand-new life here on out."

He then poured the beer down the drain of the sink. This was a shocker. He took out the rest of the beers and poured them out too. "Aurick Pantera is high on life and tomato juice from now on," Aurick said, then drank *my* tomato juice. He left and went to the Brooklyn Bridge. He jogged across. It took him a while, but still, this was Aurick, so this was impressive. While waiting for a light to change, Aurick jogged in place.

A lad was walking a cat on a leash, which was weird. The cat was actually calm. A flock of pigeons flew onto the street to scavenge for scraps of bread left behind. The birds wildly flapped their wings, which attracted the cat. The leash slipped from the young lad's hand and the cat ran across the street after the pigeons. The boy ran after the cat across the street, incoming cars coming at him. The boy grabbed the leash and yanked the cat back toward him. It was too late for the boy, I thought. Aurick dashed across, scooped the boy up, and dodged the oncoming cars, which were honking wildly. People nearby clapped in applause for Aurick. He did a fancy gentlemanly bow for the crowd. What a show-off. When I did these heroic things, no one applauded for me.

Aurick continued his jog. He bumped into an old flame. They exchanged greetings, which was different because the old Aurick would have walked right past her without a thought or care. What am I saying? This *was* the old Aurick. Wasn't it?

Meeting her seemed to spark something for him. Aurick went back home and started calling as many old flames as he could. Aurick went through women like toilet paper. He apologized to each one that he called. I was really shocked.

After he was done, he went over to his closet. He reached deep into its dark corners and pulled out a dull and dusty black Bible. Aurick coughed and his eyes watered. "Let's try this again," Aurick said, cracking it open. He began reading from it. Bwah, what a phony.

He read that thing all day. He even fell asleep with it on his chest. Aww, how cute. I felt as if I could puke.

Aurick woke up bright and early the next day. Two times in a row?! He immediately got to the side of the bed and started praying with his hands folded together. "Dear Lord. This is Aurick Pantera. Thank you for saving my life."

How insulting. *I* was the one who saved his miserable hide in the first place and got him to turn his life around. I do all this for him and God takes all the credit. Typical.

"I'm dedicating the rest of my life to you. Please show me the way. Amen." Aurick then went to Father Daniel's cathedral. He wore his jacket because it was chilly out. He said hello to Father Danny.

"How're you doing Aurick?"

"I'm great! I feel like a new person."

"Wow, I haven't seen that smile since you were a boy."

"Things have changed. Thanks to you, I start a new life."

"No, no, Aurick. It is not because of me. It is because of God you have your newfound appreciation for life that He has given you." There goes God again, yanking the credit away from me.

"I feel like it's not enough. I want to actually *do* something for the Lord."

"Well, if you want to, you can volunteer. They're fixing up some free food and free clothes later on in the afternoon at a shelter."

"Wow, Father Daniel. That's a great idea." Ugh! Aurick was making me sick with his phony manner.

He went down to the shelter and volunteered just as Danny Boy advised. The merciless New York winter was arriving soon so many of the poor and homeless had made sure they were down there for some coats. The shelter was packed. Reporters from many different networks were here to get a bite out of the story, hoping to shine a light on the wonderful side of New York and giving a breath of fresh air to its citizens. After all, we were heading toward the holy holidays.

The volunteers handed out coats, hats, scarves, socks, underwear, pants, and other items. Yet a few scumbag volunteers were stealing and keeping some of the items for themselves.

Aurick was handing out the sweaters and looked as if he was enjoying himself. I was still skeptical though. Soon, the shelter ran out of clothing. Many people were left empty-handed. Shelter staff asked the downtrodden to leave so they could close down. As Aurick headed out, two men wearing tattered clothing stopped him in front of the building.

"'Scuse me, mister. My name is Rocco and this is my companion Bolo. I was wonderin' if you would be so kind and give me and my associate of mine some spare change." Rocco was just less than six feet tall, and Bolo was about two inches shorter than him. Bolo was standing a few feet away with a metal golden shopping cart. He was quiet. His left eye was gray and damaged, as if it was blinded. He stared at us with that dead, cold eye of his.

Aurick checked his pockets for money. He pulled the insides of his pockets out and said, "I'm sorry, Rocco. I don't have change on me right—"

"Please, mister, I don't ask for much. Winter's gonna be a witch this year. I'm trying to get up money for the coats they're selling right over there." Aurick looked over to see whom Rocco was pointing at. The scumbags who had stolen the clothes from the shelter were selling them for profit. Aurick walked over to the corrupt volunteers. They were all small and weak looking.

"Hey, didn't I see you at the shelter?" Aurick asked the forefront man.

"Yeah, and?"

Aurick smiled and said, "I was just thinking this was a clever scheme you got there."

The forefront man smiled and laughed. "Yeah, I do this all the time. Whether it's free cans of food or free clothes, I get 'em all for myself and turn it into a hefty profit."

"Wow, that's smart. I don't think I could do that. I think I would be too scared and guilty."

The man laughed. "Ha, not me. It's every man for himself in this world. There's no more room or help for poor folk anymore. They're kicking all of us out. I got kids to feed. And I don't think God is comin' down to put food on my plate."

Aurick's face reddened and he clenched his fists. He overturned the bins of clothes and started tossing them out to the crowd. The crowd cheered and scrambled for the clothes. The forefronter, steamed, lunged toward Aurick and swung his fist at Aurick's face. Just before Aurick was hit, another fist smashed into the corrupt volunteer's face. He tumbled to the ground. Aurick turned around and saw it was Bolo who took him down. An officer driving nearby saw what happened and came over. He asked what was going on and Rocco told him everything. The officer called for more officers to come over. They arrested all the corrupt volunteers and also handcuffed them and put Bolo into the police cruiser for disorderly conduct.

"Don't worry 'bout him. It's warmer and they got good food where he's going. Lucky bastard," Rocco said.

"Why did he help me?" Aurick said.

"Probably because that man pissed him off. And he took a likin' to you."

"To me? But I didn't even say two words to him."

"Ha! I know. Crazy bastard believed that you were going to do good things in the future. You or your friend that is."

"Me or my friend?"

"Don't worry 'bout it. Bolo's schizophrenic."

The crowd had scavenged the area for every scrap of clothing they could find. There was nothing left for Rocco.

Aurick took off his jacket. "Here, man."

Rocco's face lit up in surprise. "No way. You're giving me this nice coat?" I didn't know what he was talking about. The coat was cheap like death.

"You need this more than I do."

"Oh my goodness, thank you." Rocco gave Aurick a quick kiss on the cheek and a big hug. Rocco smelled like liquor, soup, and urine. Aurick squirmed a little, then they said their farewells. For a moment, I considered that just maybe Aurick had changed.

As he walked away, someone called out to him. It was Helena, once again.

She held a microphone to his face and Timmy followed suit with his camera. Aurick was surprised and freaked out. Helena asked Aurick what had just happened and he responded, trying to sound educated and collected. (It came off amateurish.) Helena closed the segment saying, "This is a rare specimen of New York City. A selfless man who fights for justice. A man who is truly a hero. A hero needed in such dangerous times"— Aurick felt awkward being called all of these grandiose titles — "as if he is answering a cry of help like an angel sent by God. Back to you, Kevin."

Helena ended and Timmy put down his camera. Helena punched Timmy in his arm.

"Ouch!" Timmy said.

"I told you to stop shaking the camera!"

"I'm sorry, Ms. Way."

"Sorry for the weird angel-sent-by-God crap. I had to be as dramatic as possible." Aurick looked at Helena as if she were crazy. "What's wrong?" Aurick hastily walked away as if he were scared of Helena. Helena was confused.

Aurick didn't want anything to do with anyone I had associated with for the past few years. How pathetic.

Aurick spent the evening alone in his apartment. His head started to hurt him once again. Dizziness came and went just as fast. Aurick was still freaked out about being possessed and having seven years of his life stolen . . . I mean, borrowed. He was just dying for a drink. He stared at the walls as if they were television. He was worried about being possessed again. How weak. He said a short prayer. I was tired of this charade. I wanted to get out of this body.

I wondered where the heck Aisely was. He usually pestered me every other day. Just when I needed him, he goes missing. All I could do was wait.

Aurick spent hours resisting the urge to obey the calling. That's right, give in, you prick, I thought. "Grr, I need a drink," he said, standing up abruptly and grabbing his head. He put on a warm hooded sweater and went out the door. It was almost midnight. There was only one place Aurick would go at this hour. Dead Man's Pub.

He took the front entrance this time around. He didn't ever want to go near the back entrance again. He was learning. He sat down on a stool at the bar. He called over the bartender.

"Hey, Aurick, back again so soon?"

Aurick looked at the bartender in confusion. "I was here recently?"

The bartender returned his look. "Of course you were, darlin'. You came a few nights ago, remember? You were waiting for a friend."

"Oh, yeah," Aurick said, lying.

"Waiting for someone again, babe?"

"Ah, no."

"Oh, couldn't resist the callin', huh? What would you like to drink?"

"An Angel Marriage please."

Aurick stared at his drink for minutes. The bartender looked at him as if he were crazy. She remembered seeing him wolf his drinks down one after the other. Now he was as scared as a virgin child. Thugs in the bar were looking at Aurick, trying to match his face. Aurick didn't notice at all. A female was sitting a couple of stools over. She was exchanging looks with Aurick. She was his type, well filled out in all the right places. She was wearing a blazing red-hot dress that screamed, "Bam! I'm here everyone."

The odd thing about her was that she was wearing green lipstick, which I found tacky and annoying. It clearly clashed with her dress, but no man would care because she was so attractive. I found it annoying. Her legs were posted in the direction Aurick was sitting. He was trying not to look up her dress, but kept failing over and over, and the female knew it. Various men from the bar were trying to pick her up, but they failed, one after the other. She was particularly interested in Aurick tonight.

"You're cute."

Aurick turned around and faced her. He looked over his shoulder a few times to check if she was talking to someone else. "You're talking to me?" Aurick pointed to his chest.

The female giggled. "Of course, silly. Who else would I be talking to? The invisible man behind you?" I chuckled because that could've been taken quite literally. "What's your name?" The female moved to the seat next to Aurick. She leaned close.

"Do you really need to know my name?" Aurick got too excited and tipped his drink over. A bit dropped into his lap. The female took a napkin and wiped Aurick's lap, which thrilled him.

"Come on, I'll drive you," she said. Aurick and the female got up. She proposed to leave through the back door. Aurick quickly refused, almost in a panic. On their way out the front, men in the bar glared at Aurick in raw wrathful jealousy.

The female drove to Aurick's building. When they got out front, she pressed Aurick up against the door. She forced her tongue down Aurick's throat. Aurick's eyes widened in surprise. She kissed so hard that it hurt. It was difficult for Aurick to even breathe. She started unzipping and unbuckling his pants. "Right out here?" he whispered.

Just when it was getting good for Aurick, the female was yanked away. Aurick opened his eyes to see a flying metal pipe. The pipe hit Aurick in the stomach. Another struck him in the ribs. Aurick was on his knees when another swing struck his back, which forced him to his stomach. He moaned in pain.

"Long time no see, buddy." Aurick slowly raised his head. Samson stood over him, wearing a long black jacket with one of his hands in his pocket. Some of his goons were with him. One was holding the fiery female to the wall. She was oddly calm. Almost as if she enjoyed it. "I looked all over for you, Dwayne." Samson chuckled. "It was so hard because Dwayne wasn't even your real name. I wonder how many other people you screwed over. There was shakes and rumbles about you being at the bar. I was excited to reunite with you again."

Samson pulled his hand out of his pocket. Aurick squeezed his eyes shut, fearful it was a gun. Samson had nothing in his hand but was wearing a black glove.

"I wanted to reunite with you ever since you turned me into a freak." Samson angrily tugged off the glove to reveal that his thumb and index finger were missing. He shoved his freak hand in Aurick's face. "God must've cared deeply about you to have backfired the gun like that." Again, God stealing credit from me. What a thief! I'm getting real sick of this.

A headache suddenly came on. For some strange reason, I felt the pain also. It was excruciating, so severe that Aurick and I almost forgot that Samson was even there.

"You won't have anyone to save you this time. Say your prayers." Samson pulled out a black instrument of death. He used his good hand. He aimed the gun and held the trigger firmly. I couldn't do much of anything in this condition. I tried manipulating the air around his hand to knock away the gun, but it didn't work. I tried leaving Aurick's body, but that didn't work either. I would be in the worst condition if this host died. *The* worst. Aurick squeezed his eyes shut. Samson pulled the trigger.

Oddly, the gun didn't blow Aurick's head off. Samson checked if the safety was off, which it was. He squeezed the trigger over and over but nothing happened. Samson gave the trigger one last squeeze, and the gun suddenly backfired and exploded. Shards and bullets hit each of Samson's goons. They ran off, crying in pain. Samson looked down to see all of his fingers blown off on his good hand. The fiery female was gone, as if she were cigarette smoke in a hurricane. Aurick got up and punched Samson in his stomach. The force of the punch was so hard that Samson spit up blood. It surprised Aurick himself. He must've caused some internal bleeding. Samson, doubled over, screamed while Aurick repeatedly kicked him on the ground. Samson leaped up and pushed Aurick into the wall, choking him with his forearm. Aurick then grabbed Samson's hand and squeezed it tightly. He gave it a quick, hard twist and broke his forearm in half. A flap of skin was the only thing that held his bloody arm together. Aurick stumbled back in disbelief over what he had just done. Samson screamed like a little girl and ran away. Aurick also ran away, going inside and up the stairs. He bumped into Jamie. Jamie asked what had happened, but Aurick ignored her and ran up the stairs in a blind panic. He ran into the apartment and collapsed on the floor. He vomited on the floor and then passed out. What a drama queen.

XI

AURICK CHRIST

You are the peak of unlikelihood. Yes, you are. Out of nothing and into something. How is that possible? I do not know but it happened anyway. You are irrational like the rest of your kind. You are unpredictable because you do not know what will happen next. That's the difference between us. I know the future but you do not. I do not know if that's for the best or not. I leave you this to be your guide. I lived my life for you. You are the woman I love. I just hope this reaches you.

Aurick awoke a few hours later. He was exhausted. He wasn't even sure if he'd dreamed what he'd gone through last night. He filled up a glass with water, grabbed some headache medicine, and gulped down the pills. He rubbed his temples and sat down on the couch and let off a big sigh. "Did that really just happen?" Aurick said, tilting his head back on the couch and closing his eyes.

"No, you dreamed the whole thing," I said in a sarcastic tone. His eyes ripped wide-open. He leaped off the couch and looked around. He spun around a few times to see the source of the voice.

"Who said that?" Aurick backed into a wall.

I sighed because I didn't want to explain this all over again. "Do I really have to explain this to you again?"

"Father Daniel exorcised you. How are you still here?" Aurick looked from side to side.

"He failed. All of those unnecessary theatrics for nothing. Religious leaders are so incompetent these days."

"Did you do that to Samson?"

"No, *you* did. I was there the whole time though. Sorry I couldn't help you out sooner."

"You mean . . . I broke that guy's arm like that on my own?"

"I was surprised too. But I realized because of my presence, you were able to release the restraints your brain had over your maximum strength on your own."

Aurick got on his knees and bowed his head down. "Please, Mr. Demon, sir. Don't feed on my soul. I'm sorry for trying to exorcise you."

I sighed in exasperation. "Didn't I tell you not to call me that? You can call me Mr. Spirit Being or Lord."

"Yes, Mr. Spirit Being Lord."

"You watch too much television. I'm not going to feast on your nasty soul. There's no such thing as the kind of soul you speak of, anyways. The only soul that exists is the meat-bag you embody. You humans should read the Bible more."

Aurick raised his head. He was sweating buckets. He was shivering pathetically like a coward. "Okay, what do you want from me then, Mr. Spirit?"

"As you found out from the last few days, I lived your life for seven years, suppressing your consciousness. Using my abilities and using your body for so long fused our selves very tightly together. It would be very hard for us to separate, so we are going to need help."

Aurick tightened his fist. His shivering wasn't from fear anymore. He suddenly lifted his head up. "You mean to tell me you stole seven years of my life?" The windows cracked. He was accidentally releasing residual power from my presence. He looked around in surprise.

"Yes, for that I apologize. But we must not waste time. We have—"

"I want those seven years back!"

I was offended that he even dared talk to me in such a manner. "You're not going to have *any* years left if—"

Aurick's eyes lit up with an epiphany as if he'd remembered something just now. He ran over to his closet and opened the door. He looked on, astonished, to find the stacks of money laid out on folded towels and blankets.

"I remember this."

"What are you doing? You need to listen to—"

Aurick looked at the stacks of money as if God himself were before him. "Where did you get all this money from? What do you do with it?"

"I have written books and I am a psychologist. I don't need much so I save a lot. I use it to purchase clothes and food. The rest I just give away."

"And you still lived in this dump? What a waste."

"I don't need much. I am above petty human desires."

"Yeah, right, like you were above paying for all those fancy suits and curtains."

I tried to think of something clever to say but I just ended up stuttering.

"There's tens of thousands of dollars here. Think of the power I could have!" Aurick said with his mouth and eyes watering.

Aurick spent the next two hours counting the bills over and over. It was quite annoying. After he stopped drooling over the money, literally, he took a fistful of cash and stuffed it into his pocket. Probably about $3,000. Such an Aurick move. He put his jacket on and swooshed out of the door. "Where're you going?"

Aurick walked up the stairs. "I'm doing a little shopping." Aurick went to Jamie's apartment and asked her if he could borrow her car. She agreed without hesitation, as usual. Aurick left the building and went to Handsome Mephisto, the clothing store where I buy all of my suits. I guess some of my urges, thoughts, and memories had rubbed off on him. He submerged himself into Handsome Mephisto as if he'd dived into an Olympic-size pool.

The guy who worked there dumped one of his customers and came to Aurick. "Oh hey, honey, back already?" he said, putting one hand on his waist. I keep telling Reggie to stop doing that, that he looks like such a stereotype. Just because I'm a demon, do I go around haunting people's houses or kill people? No. But I should cut him some slack. He listens to my advice and tries his best. Once I commented on his blond highlights, that they looked tacky. He dyed his hair completely blond.

"You must be ballin', huh?" Reggie said.

Aurick flinched a bit and then peered into the man's face, trying to recognize him. "I know you?"

"It's me, Reggie. Wow. I guess Botox does make a difference, huh?"

Aurick grabbed armfuls of suits and tried them all on. Aurick giggled and Reggie giggled and they laughed together like two kindergarten girls playing tea party. Aurick picked out all sorts of colors. Pepper red, misty blue, lime green, banana yellow—it didn't matter. He just wanted to show off.

Aurick walked in and out of the clothing booth constantly asking Reggie's opinion. Reggie smiled if yes and frowned if no. This was hard for him because he had difficulty controlling his facial muscles after the Botox job. Reggie hated frowning anyway. He said that frowning caused ugly wrinkles. After Aurick picked out his suits, he thanked Reggie. That was heartwarming to Reggie since I never showed any type of affection to him.

Aurick headed to Jamie's car. He had to walk down the street a ways and turn the corner. It wasn't really crowded. For some strange reason, I felt tired. I didn't understand why. Beings such as me don't need to sleep. I guess I was still synchronized enough to feel certain human feelings. Aurick was still wide-awake though. I drifted off and everything faded to black.

I awoke some days later. I couldn't recall any dreams I may have had. It was night. Aurick was driving through the city. I could see Aurick's reflection through the rearview mirror. He was wearing a blazing-red suit with his short hair gelled back. A woman was sitting in the passenger seat next to him. She was Aurick's kind of woman, the double-D type. She was a good-looking black chick wearing a white drape that showed how big her cans were. She had on white lipstick, I guess to match her attire, and wore her hair up in a swirly noodle style. Just from this I knew Aurick had been using his money to get whatever he wanted and all the women he wanted. Yes, these past days he had been bringing women in and out of his apartment, surely demolishing the reputation I had built up for him. *Years* of respectable service crumbled in a few short days.

Aurick parked outside some club. He used the valet parking. The valet scurried over to Aurick's car like a puppy and opened the door for him. He stepped out of the car with his lady friend stepping valiantly to him. I was stunned and at the same time annoyed when I saw the vehicle. It was a shiny black Ferrari. The most recent model. Aurick must've used the money in the closet. I found myself fighting for calm, feeling something that perhaps humans would call . . . rage.

"If I see just one scratch, consider yourself deported." Aurick tossed the keys to the valet, intentionally missing so that the man would pick them up from the ground. Aurick held out his arm without looking, and like a trained dog, the lady grabbed hold of it and walked with him toward the door of the club. Black women usually intimidated Aurick. I guess since he had all this money, he felt as if he could do anything.

Bouncers were at the door. They checked a list and saw that Aurick's name wasn't there. Aurick flashed a few hundred bucks and slipped it in one of the bouncer's pockets. They opened and held the door for Aurick and his lady. The female, impressed, gave him a slight nibble on the ear. Aurick replied by putting his arm around her waist. I felt his pulse speeding up. He tried but couldn't hold back the smug grin splitting his face.

He felt good. He felt unstoppable. He felt like a king. He felt like an immortal. He felt like . . . a god.

He made me sick.

"What are you doing here?" I said, startling Aurick, causing him to hop. His lady friend asked him what was wrong.

"Nothing, babe. Wait for me over there." Aurick went into the bathroom. He looked around and took out a cell phone and put it to his ear. "What does it look like I'm doing? I'm having fun."

"All you're doing is wasting my time."

"Hypocrite. You wasted three years of *my* time. Three years of *my* life." Aurick stopped to let people wash their hands and leave.

"What is this place?"

"This is Club Eden." Club Eden was a club Aurick always used to go to. Trust me, it wasn't because he liked to dance. He came here for one sole purpose—to gamble. All types of people came from all over the city for illegal gambling here. Club Eden had the nickname Club Good or Bad: you either walked away with money beyond your wildest dreams or lost absolutely everything with the possibility loan sharks would be after you. You needed two thousand bucks just to get into a game. Aurick had exactly that. "Just let me get through this in peace."

"Ha, you're going to get through this in pieces if you do this."

The club was bombarded with flashing blue, red, yellow, and white lights—clearly not for the epileptic. The couple walked through the dancing crowd. They went to a dark corner to a dark door. It was guarded by another couple of bouncers.

Aurick made a head gesture, which told the bouncer to let him through. The couple walked through the door and went down a staircase to a big room. The walls were black. Thick, white cigarette smoke filled the air. There were about thirty men and women, mostly men. They all wore black. Aurick was the only person wearing red. Doofus. He stuck out like a sore thumb. A red and bloody sore thumb.

I felt embarrassed but Aurick loved it all. He sat down and joined the game. His lady couldn't stay unless she was playing. Aurick smacked her on the bottom and told her to have some drinks upstairs. About three minutes in, he tilted his chin down and whispered, "Hey, Mr. Spirit, I need your help."

I sighed in exasperation. "What is it?"

"I was superstrong and kicked Samson's ass the other night. Do you influence other things?"

"Yes. So?"

"Well, a couple days ago, I got nonstop flashes of people's thoughts. I was going crazy. I thought it was you just pestering me at first, but you didn't say anything for days. It was something different." I was really sick of Aurick's talking to me like this. "The voices stopped after a while. I thought maybe if I concentrated enough, I could win thousands playing at this club easily. It's not working."

"Two words. Death no!"

"Aw, come on. I could wrap this game up real quick and we'll be out of here."

"Are you talking to me?" a player two seats down from him said. Other players stared at him, wondering if he was a bit loopy or if the whispering was all part of his game-playing.

"Oh, no, I'm not. I was just . . . talking to myself, thinking about something funny that happened yesterday." Aurick smiled and nodded once and looked around to the others. Others had their eyebrows arched. Aurick nervously had his grin still stapled on. These players were thugs. Whether Aurick was getting help from supernatural means or not, if he was caught cheating, he would be in a mess of trouble.

Aurick kept pestering me. I ignored him for a few minutes. Aurick was sweating pretty hard under the pressure of the game. He had always been a lousy gambler. "All right, I'll cut a deal with you," he whispered. What could any human offer me? "I promise I'll help you leave if you help me win this. After this game, I'll be filthy stinkin' rich. We'll both win either way." I thought about it for a few minutes. "Come on. You owe me seven years of my life. I swear to God that I won't screw you over."

This felt depressingly familiar. First Aisely's shenanigans, and now this fool's. When would my suffering cease?

I sighed. "All right. I'll help you." I read all the humans' minds at the poker table. I wasn't perfect at it but it was sufficient enough to clean out everyone's pockets. This was Aurick's lucky night. The players looked absolutely angry and cheated. Couldn't blame them. They had been.

"Sorry, boys. Tonight's just my lucky night." Aurick swept all the chips toward himself with his arms as if he were hugging them. The players gave Aurick suitcases of money that wouldn't be traced back to the club. The losers stared down Aurick as he began to walk to the exit. "Good night, gentlemen. Don't hate the player. Hate the odds." Aurick always loved rubbing victory into his opponents' faces. He called over his bimbo and squeezed her into him, giving her a hard, painful kiss. She said ouch and laughed. It was all awkward and mortifying for me to witness.

They walked out of the club. He bossed the valet around and rudely told him to get his ride over here. A black van pulled up in front of Aurick and his female. It stayed there for a while. "Hey, moron, this isn't my—" A white cloth wrapped across Aurick's face. It smelled strong and intoxicating. Aurick reached into his pants for his gun. Someone grabbed his arm and stopped him before he could grasp it. Aurick passed out and was thrown into the black van.

Aurick awoke in the back of the van. He was handcuffed, gagged, and blindfolded. He tried to stand up but couldn't because his feet were also shackled. He wiggled around and desperately tried to scream, but a man in the back knocked the daylights out of him. He lay calm for a while. I told him in his mind, "We can still communicate mentally. Just think about what you want to say to me."

"Oh, thank God. Get me out of here," Aurick said in his thoughts.

"Didn't I tell you this wasn't a good idea? You failed to obey my wisdom. This is one of the many problems with you humans. You think you know everything but you don't know anything."

"Okay, okay, you were right. I'm sorry. Just help me get out of here."

"I can't do anything right now. You're in a moving van with a man in the back and two in the front. All are Russians. The one in the back and the one in the front are armed so I can't do anything."

"Oh, please, Mr. Spirit. You have to help me." If I weren't stuck in Aurick's body, I would've ditched this disobedient idiot and let him die. But we had to work together.

I read their thoughts. "They're driving us to some type of bridge. They're going to shoot and dump us in the water below."

"Oh, God, that's horrible." Aurick started to sob and shed tears, which soaked through the blindfold. The man in the back told him to shut up. Aurick didn't stop. The man threatened with a louder voice. Aurick quieted down in fear of being hit again.

"Oh, shut up. They're not going to kill us. *Yet*. They're going to wait till we get to the bridge. That's where we'll make our escape."

"Our escape?" Aurick thought soberly.

"Yes, escape."

We came to a stop at a small bridge. It was dark and cold like a corpse. Aurick was nervous. A bit of urine trickled down his pants. I could feel it. It was repugnant. The man in the back with Aurick literally threw him out of the back of the van and gave him a nice kick to the stomach. This time I could also feel it a bit. The two others lifted Aurick to his feet and walked him over to the side of the bridge. One of the men took off the blindfold to reveal a crying, sobbing man. Jeez, Aurick was almost as bad as Aisely.

"Okay, Aurick. This is our chance. Concentrate force to your feet."

"What the hell? This isn't *Star Wars* you know. I have no idea what you're talking about."

"They're going to shoot and throw us over. You have to imagine yourself landing firmly on water."

"What the hell?" Aurick turned around and looked over the barricade to see the watery depths below. "There's no way we're going to survive that splash."

"I know we wouldn't. That's why we're not going to splash at all."

"What are you talking about?"

"Just trust me. Remember. Imagine yourself landing on your feet. Without fear. Don't worry. I'll help." All three men stood a few feet away from us, I guess so they wouldn't get Aurick's brains on their beautiful suits. One pulled out a gun from the inside of his jacket. He raised the instrument of death and aimed between Aurick's eyes.

"On the count of three, jump."

"Jump?"

"One." One of the men asked Aurick if he had any last words. Aurick was silent. "Two." Aurick licked the sour sweat trickling down his lips. He released all the urine he was saving up at full force this time. The armed man squinted his eyes to maximize his vision for the perfect kill shot. He gradually pulled the trigger. "Three!" Aurick turned around and jumped over the barricade. A loud bang and a hiss buzzed just past Aurick's ear while airborne. Aurick chomped down on his lower lip as he dipped down through the air. To Aurick's surprise, he landed safely on his feet. Aurick panted and coughed in relief.

"Oh, thank God." There went God again, stealing my thunder. After Aurick collected his breath and mind, he gained back his reasoning. "Wait a minute. How could I be standing if . . ." Aurick looked down to see if he was standing on water. He panicked and started to tumble.

"Stop panicking, Aurick. You're going to fall and drown."

He balanced himself, looking as if he were walking on a tightrope at the circus. His body shook with uncontrolled fear. He started crying again.

"Stop crying, Aurick. It's okay. You're still alive."

"It's not that."

"What then?"

Aurick sobbed. "My money!"

We could hear the van's tires screeching as it sped off. We were finally safe. Well, for now anyway.

XII

MY NAMELESS FRIEND'S FRIEND

Aurick spent the next day sulking about the money that was stolen from him. He was angry, and the only thing that dwarfed his rage was that he'd walked on water. He walked back and forth through the apartment repeating, "I walked on frickin' water!" Yes, indeed. "Am I the new Messiah, Mr. Spirit?"

"No, Aurick. You're just a regular human who happened to stumble upon things greater than your understanding."

"Ha! It seems like you're the one who stumbled upon me. What made you choose me to possess, anyway?"

"You didn't have many people who knew you. No real friends, no family, no steady job. If you were gone, no one would miss you."

Aurick looked a bit heartbroken. I'd pretty much told him that he was a loser. He quickly fixed his face from hurt to curiosity. "I guess you and I are the same then," Aurick said, throwing himself back on his bed.

"You and I could never be the same."

"No real friends, no family, no purpose." Aurick threw both his arms behind his head and used his hands as a pillow. "Sounds like we have that in common." He sat up on the bed and folded his legs in. "So how did you turn into a de . . . I mean a . . . what should I call you?"

"Fallen."

"Right. How did you turn into a *Fallen*?" Aurick said in a giddy voice.

"That's none of your concern."

"Did you do something evil?" I silently ignored him. Aurick rested his chin on his fist, trying to come up with something. "Did you backstab God?"

At that moment, a wind blew through the room. It was strange because the window and door were closed. There was absolutely no source. Aurick looked around. He shrugged his shoulders and continued his prying.

"Nah, he just couldn't keep his hands off the ladies," a mysterious voice said.

Aurick looked around. "Did you say that?"

I ignored him and waited for a certain someone to make his dramatic appearance. Sephirot jumped on the bed and sat in front of Aurick. It startled him.

"You didn't say that, did you, Mr. Kitty?" Aurick said, petting Sephirot's head and combing his fur with his fingers.

"His name isn't Mr. Kitty. It's Sephirot," I said, quickly correcting Aurick.

"Ha, what a stupid name for a cat. I'm calling him Spike."

What a stupid commoner's name, I thought to myself.

The cat opened his mouth and said, "I think its name should be Garfield."

Aurick's eyelids peeled open. He leaned forward and stared into the cat's face. Everything was silent.

"Are you making me see things, Mr. Spirit?" I didn't say anything. Aurick continued to rudely stare into Sephirot's face.

"Didn't your mama ever teach you that it's impolite to stare?" the cat said. Aurick jerked back and flipped off the bed accidentally. He quickly got back up. He had a lump on his head.

"You are such a stereotype," I said, dragging my voice while speaking telepathically.

"Am not!" Aisely said, still possessing Sephirot. He jumped off the bed and ran up to Aurick's feet. "How am I a stereotype?" Aurick backed up against the wall. He was deathly scared. He started to pant and sweat heavily.

"It's because you're being dramatic. Why can't you be collected like me? You give us Fallen a bad name. Get out of Sephirot's body."

"Isn't being collected and cold a stereotype too? And for your information, I'm not doing this to be dramatic. You haven't been able to see me in days." I was confused because I thought Aisely wasn't around at all. "I decided to take over this cat's body so that I could communicate with you."

"How long have you been watching my torment?"

"Since you were being exorcised by that freaky priest. That was funny as death."

Aurick was freaked out the whole time, eyes bulging wildly. Aisely and I just carried on the conversation as if he weren't there.

"I must be losing my spiritual awareness. It must be the side effects of being attached to this meat-bag. It's getting worse." Aisely told me to open the refrigerator door. I didn't have control so I told Aurick to open the door for him. Aurick hesitated but he eventually crept over and did just so. What a good boy. Aisely went inside. He pushed some leftover red gelatin on the floor and ate it.

"Oh my Lord! I haven't tasted this in decades," Aisely said, smashing his snout into it. Aurick stared at Aisely's cat form without a word. Aisely noticed and said, "What is it? Didn't I tell you it was rude to stare?" Aisely put his face back into the meal. "Humans have no manners these days."

Aurick made a step forward. "Did God leave the gate in hell open for you things to escape or something?" Aisely ignored him. Aurick sighed, moaned, and put his hands over his face. "Oh, man, I'm definitely going to hell for associating with you things, aren't I?"

"The hell you speak of doesn't exist," Aisely said, not looking up. He was too fixated on his meal to focus properly. Aisely went back into the fridge and pushed a glass jar of mayonnaise on the floor, cracking it open and spilling it. He began to lick it up as if it were pudding.

Aisely's answer had Aurick confused. I decided to explain more thoroughly. "*Hell* is the English word for the Hebrew word *Sheol*. The literal meaning for *Sheol* is 'the common grave.' A grave for man and animal. A common grave for men and women. A common grave for cats and dogs. A common grave for Catholics and Muslims. You're all going to the same place. So in a way, you are right. You are going to hell."

Aurick had a dim-witted look on his face. "So I'm going to be tortured in the grave then?"

I sighed in annoyance. Why must I clean up his religious leaders' messes? "No, Aurick. The Bible says that there is no consciousness after death. If there is no consciousness after death, then there is no soul to be tortured. When you're dead, you're dead. Like a candle flame vanishing with the wind. Simple as that." Aurick looked astonished. "To assure you, Jesus said himself he went to Sheol when he died."

"So . . . you're saying Jesus went to hell?"

"Exactly. The only difference is that JC was brought back to life in *another* place. Therefore, he is no longer in hell."

"Then what about all the fiery torment stuff if you're bad?"

"Scare tactics. Scare tactics spun by your world's religious leaders to strike deathly fear into the ignorant masses for absolute control of economics and governmental rule and policy. Poor saps."

"Wow, a *demon* giving me a lecture about the Bible. That's ridiculous."

Aisely quickly swung his head and directed his full attention to Aurick. "Hey, watch the racial slurs round here!" Aisely's voice was as deep as a lion's roar.

Aurick stepped back against the wall and took a big, hard gulp.

"That's a word that's very offensive to us. *Fallen, meteors, spacemen,* and maybe *Kryptonians* are acceptable. And besides, I'm nobody's minion."

"Careful, Aisely, not to directly say that we are actually that D-word," I said telepathically, keeping Aurick out of the conversation. "We don't want to break that certain divine law."

"Oh, right, sorry," Aisely said. "Not that I'm saying I am this D-word you speak of, Aurick, but don't call us that."

"Sorry."

The three of us spent the next few hours watching television. Aurick stayed just because he was scared. What he really wanted to do initially was run out of there screaming. But the more time he spent with Aisely, the more comfortable he got. They talked about football. Aurick said that he liked the New England Patriots, while Aisely said he liked the New York Giants. That surprised Aurick greatly.

"Hey, Mr. Spirit. What's your favorite football team?" The question took me off guard. I didn't really watch sports. They're all the same to me. They all lack suspense and interest. No matter who wins, all the players get millions, so what's the point? After a team has won a season, the cycle repeats itself over again the next year.

Still, I didn't want to feel left out so I said, "The Devil Rays."

There was a silence in the room. Suddenly, there was a burst of laughter between Aurick and Aisely.

"Jesus Christ, man. The Devil Rays are a baseball team. How could you not know that?" Aisely said with his chest and back moving up and down from laughing. This made it funnier for Aurick so Aisely started coughing up. "And the Devil Rays isn't even the name of that team anymore. It's the Rays now! Man, you suck." Aisely coughed and choked. Aurick patted his back to help him spit out the hair ball that was stuck in his throat. "Thanks, Aurick."

I didn't want to seem foolish again so I stayed silent for a while.

Aurick went down to the store and got three six-packs of beers. Dan Jackals. Aurick's favorite brand of beer. He popped one open and began guzzling it down. I could also taste it so I had to deal with the disgusting flavor. Aisely looked on as the beer foam dripped from Aurick's lips. He licked his lips with his spiky cat tongue in lust for a taste. Aurick turned and noticed Aisely's desire. Aisely quickly turned his attention back to the television.

"It's okay, dude. You can have some."

"No, it's okay. I don't want to impose."

"No, really, man. You're a cool dude. Here you go." Aurick snapped a can from one of the plastic rings and handed it to Aisely.

"Wow. For me? A human has never offered anything to me."

Aurick smiled and said, "You had me at death to all humans." Aurick's stomach growled from me wanting to puke.

Aisely's eyes watered. He tipped over the can, let the liquid pour out, and drank. Aurick got drunk off seven beers. Aisely got drunk off just one. His speech slurred right along with Aurick's. They played together. They laughed together. They danced together. They sang together. Their favorite song was "99 Bottles of Beer." I was mad that they actually sung the whole song. Aurick stripped to his boxer shorts, saying he gets hot when he's drunk. Then he played several games of chess with Aisely. Aisely beat Aurick every time.

"Wow, you are like . . . unbeatable at this."

Aisely moved a pawn up a square. "Yeah, I've been playing this since it came out a few thousand years ago."

"I thought chess came out in the fifteenth century."

"For humans it did."

Aurick turned to Aisely. "Wait a minute. You're telling me this game was invented by you people?"

"Spirit creatures like me have a lot of time on their hands." Aisely was right. We do have a lot on our hands being immortal and all. Aisely went as far as to make a deal with the German human chess player Emanuel Lasker. Aisely dictated to Lasker moves during games. Aisely was so good that Lasker remained world champion for twenty-seven years. "There are a lot of things you humans got from us."

"Like what?"

"The atomic bomb."

"You people did that too?"

"Yeah. Some pissed-off Fallen wanted to get the world blown up so they inspired some human scientists to come up with the blueprints and ingredients for it. Though they didn't get what they wanted, there's still hope for it happening in the future."

"Wow. It's like you're opening up all the secrets of the universe."

"More like opening Pandora's box." Aisley cleared his throat. "I was the one who invented the story of Pandora's box by the way."

"Wow."

"Yep. Plus I killed the dinosaurs too."

"No, you didn't, Aisley," I said.

They shared each other's thoughts all through the night.

"You're the coolest human I've ever met." Aisely's voice was slurring more than ever.

"Aww, shucks Aisely."

"No, I'm serious. We should be like . . . best friends."

"Really? Me?"

They eventually got tired. Aisely fell asleep on Aurick's lap, curled up in a cute way. Aurick's head leaned back over the couch with his face facing the ceiling. They both snored loudly and in rhythm, so much so that it almost sounded like a song. My being began to synchronize itself with Aurick's some more. I could feel the drowsiness of his being asleep. I tried to fight it. Eventually, everything faded to black.

I awoke. It was morning and Aurick was driving Jamie's car. Jamie must've lent it to him. Jamie would do anything for this man. Aurick was nervous. His hands were heavily shaking.

"Don't be nervous Aurick," Aisely said, jumping to the front by the gearshift.

"Nervous about what?"

"Oh, you're awake, Aurick Two. A host getting up earlier than the possessor; that's embarrassing."

"Aurick Two?"

"Since you're going to be stuck in that body for a while, and you can't stick to a name on your own, I'll just call you Aurick Two."

"Why do I have to be Aurick Two?"

"Well, that's a stupid question." Aisely paused and looked at me as if expecting me to answer. I didn't, so he said, "It's because Aurick One woke up before you, silly." That was downright ridiculous to me.

"Why are you nervous?"

Aurick didn't answer me.

"Aurick One can't talk right now. He's meditating his vengeance." Aisely scooted over to the other front seat. "We're headed to one of those Russians who robbed him the other night." Aurick stopped at a red light. "One of them is staying at a hotel a few minutes away. He still has the suitcase of money." I could see Aurick's face through the rearview mirror. He kept looking into it. It was as if our eyes were focused on each other.

"No, Aurick. You don't want to do this. This guy is way too dangerous."

"Nope, you're wrong, Aurick Two. He doesn't have weapons

on him at the moment. I checked. Right now he's sleeping on his nice comfy hotel bed. He won't expect a thing."

As soon as the red light turned green, Aurick planted his foot on the gas. He was really pumped and ready to do this.

"This is a bad idea."

"This is the best time to do it. The guy is going to take a plane back to Russia later on in the day. This is the only chance we've got unless you feel like following him all the way out there. I don't know about you but . . . if I was a human, I would never take a plane anywhere the way foreign relations are going."

"That's not what I meant. I don't want anything to happen to this body while I'm here."

"If you mean physical violence, Aurick One has your influence. With Aurick One's strength amplified by you, there's no way he'll lose. And on top of that, I'll be there just in case anything goes wrong. It's a sure thing."

"Gee. I feel *much* better," I said.

It was about five in the morning so traffic was light. It was easy finding a parking space. Aurick parked across the street from Athena Towers, one of the most prestigious hotels in New York City.

"Go through the back door. You don't want your face shown. I'm going to leave Mr. Kitty's body so that I can watch over you. I'll help you along the way." Sephirot's body dropped, and he closed his eyes and curled into a ball as Aisely left his body.

Aurick got out of the car and left the door unlocked. He went to the back entrance of the hotel. A security camera was above the door, actively monitoring the perimeter. Aurick hid around the corner.

"This isn't a wise idea, Aurick."

"Don't worry, this'll be quick. Aisely said the money is right upstairs. With you, I could take down an elephant with my bare hands."

"You have a mirror?"

"No. Why?" I told Aurick to go back to the car and get one from Jamie's car. Women always carry mirrors with them everywhere. Aurick did just so and returned to the back side of the hotel. "Why do you need this?"

I told him to raise the mirror up. "I'm losing contact with my kind. The mirror will amplify my vision."

"What are you talking about? I don't see a thing."

"You're just a regular human. Only my kind or humans with high awareness can sense spirit beings. Humans like psychics."

Aurick looked astonished. "How does a human acquire higher-spirit awareness?"

"A spirit being must be around that person so much that the person's body gets used to its presence." Usually the only way for a human to acquire this is with the help of a spirit being.

"Used to its presence?"

"The human's five senses will be able to keep up with the molecular vibrational pace of that spirit being. Every spirit being has a unique frequency. We spirit beings use this to identify each other, just as an animal identifies others by its sense of smell."

Aurick looked dumbstruck. I decided not to go further. I looked into the mirror. I could see Aisely screwing with the wiring of the security camera above the door. Aisely put up a hand, notifying me that the camera was down. I told Aurick to move. The door was locked. Aisely was annoyed that he had to do more. The lazy lout. We heard the door unlock. Aurick quickly moved in. He took the stairs up.

"What floor is this guy on?" Aurick said, stopping halfway up the first flight of stairs. Aurick held up the mirror for me to look through. Aisely held seventeen fingers up. Aisely can make himself appear with as many thumbs as he wants.

Aurick sighed with disappointment. He was about as lazy

as Aisely. These guys were meant for each other. Aurick began his journey up the seventeen flights of stairs. I guess we weren't properly synced again because by the third floor Aurick was panting and sweating. Aurick stopped running when he got to the sixth floor and began to walk. By the twelfth floor, Aurick's walking turned into creeping. By the fourteenth, his creeping turned into limping. By the seventeenth, Aurick was on all fours. His lungs were burning and he had a little bit of a blood taste on his saliva glands. After a while, even *I* could feel his exhaustion. I guessed that meant we were well fused again.

After a couple of minutes, Aurick took his first step down that long hallway. I had a feeling he was going to have to make a choice. A choice to benefit off someone's loss, stirring up a stew of vengeance. A choice to risk it all and delve deeper into darkness and hope to uncover some form of light to justify it. Aurick pulled out a black ski mask and wore it on his face. Aisely smiled as he unlocked the man's hotel door.

As soon as the red light turned green on the card-key lock, Aurick crept into the room. It was a two-room suite, like a nice small apartment. The Uzbekistani man who'd robbed Aurick was in bed with his wife. That was unexpected. Aisely shrugged his shoulders as I glared at him for not telling us that there were other people were involved. Aurick stood there. He was shaking. His sweat started to soak through his clothes. Aurick thought about the fear he'd endured the night when those Uzbekistanis tried to kill him. Aurick squeezed his fist so tightly that it crackled.

"You have a choice, Aurick. Get your vengeance and your money at the cost of a destroyed family"—Aurick ground his teeth so hard that a couple cracked slightly—"or you can walk away."

The wind pushed the door closed, causing noise. The Uzbekistani inched his head up and gradually opened his eyes in a daze. Aurick was frightened out of his mind. "Don't worry," Aisely said to me, "I'm blinding him from the sight of you. You're invisible to him." I relayed that to Aurick, which made him sigh in relief. The man slowly tore himself out of bed and crept his way to the bathroom. "Now's your chance, Aurick One. Go get 'em."

Aurick got over his nervousness and went over to the bathroom door. We could hear the sound of the man urinating into the toilet water. Aurick swung the door open and ran behind the man. Aurick yanked the man's hair and dumped his face into the toilet water. The man struggled with all his might, flailing his arms around. Yellow bubbles rose to the top of the surface of the water. The man became motionless. That's when Aurick flushed the toilet and swung the man to the cold tiled bathroom floor. He coughed, gagged, and spit up the yellow toilet water. He was in a daze, barely opening his eyes to Aurick. The man opened his mouth to yell to his female to wake up. His mouth opened but nothing came out. Aisely held back the air and sound waves from leaving his throat. There was nothing he could do.

"What do you want from me?" The pitiful urine-drenched man said. Aisely was now letting him speak softly for some questioning.

"Where's the money you took from me?" The man started to sob a bit. "Where's my money?" Aurick said in a loud voice this time.

"The other two men—" The man stopped and coughed up some more water.

"What about them?" I'd never seen Aurick this serious.

"They robbed me."

"What? You're lying."

The man crawled backward until his back touched the wall of the tub. "They took it. Knowing them, they probably ate each other for it by now."

Aurick backed up. He looked as if he wanted to puke. I could feel the anger boiling over. His face turned red as a beet dressed in hot sauce. Aurick reached into his pants and pulled out a black object. An instrument of death. The man gasped and pressed against the wall of the tub, clinging to it for sheer life with his back.

"Where are they?"

"I don't know where they are."

Aurick raised the black death and aimed it. "I'm going to ask you one more time." Aurick cocked the gun. That evil, unforgiving sound sent shivers down the man's back.

"Oh, God, no. I don't have it. I swear. It could be anywhere in the world right now."

Aurick ground his upper and bottom teeth together so hard that some of the bone crumbled. I could see Aisely's ecstatic expression through the medicine-cabinet mirror.

"He's telling the truth, Aurick. He doesn't know where your money is. Let's get out of here," I said.

"Ha, you're unbelievable, Aurick Two. This guy tried to blow your head off at the bridge and you're going to let him go? That's ridiculous."

"Yes, that is correct, Aisely," I said calmly. "We're going to do the smart thing and go now. Right, Aurick?"

Aurick's vengeful expression didn't budge an inch.

"Looks like you don't care about Aurick so much after all, Aurick Two. If you let this guy go, he's going to find you. And I'm not going to be there to save the day."

"Ha, you couldn't save a termite if you tried to."

"You have nothing to lose, Aurick One. I'm making sure the lady outside is sound asleep. No one is watching. You're home free."

I couldn't believe I was acting as Aurick's good conscience. It was like a television show where an angel and a demon rest

on each side of the character's shoulders and try to persuade
the person to follow a particular path. Aurick struggled with his
angel's and demon's arguments.

His fingers squeezed harder on the trigger. Aisely licked his
"lips" in anticipation. I wanted to cover my ears but I didn't
have any. Suddenly a splitting pain struck Aurick. I could feel
his pain too. It was as if his head were splitting in two. Aurick
backed up and dropped the gun on the floor. He clasped his
head. He almost slipped on the urine-water and backed into the
wall. Another horribly familiar pain gripped Aurick's chest. He
was having a heart attack. The same kind of heart attack I had
a while back when I was in control. We felt sick. We felt dizzy.
We felt disoriented. We felt as if we were going to die.

Aurick opened his eyes and looked up. He saw his own
instrument of death breathing down his nostrils. Breathing the
lead breath of death into Aurick's lungs. The man had turned
the tables on his assailant. Aurick was done for.

Just as the man tightened his grip on the trigger, the
bathroom door creaked open. "What the . . . ," Aisely gasped.
"The wife is sleeping." The door opened all the way to reveal
a little girl in a long white T-shirt. She looked about four years
of age. She must've been occupying the second room. She was
standing there, trying to decipher the situation. The father
jerked his attention away from Aurick and looked to her.

"Hailey. Get out of here."

Aurick took this chance and pushed the father so hard he
flew back. The father's neck landed on the edge of the bathtub.
A loud crack echoed off the tiled bathroom walls and beat
down against Hailey's small ears. Aurick took a long, hard
gulp and looked down at the dead Russian. The dead man.
The dead husband. The dead father. Aurick's body shook like a
washing machine. He then turned to Hailey. She wasn't crying.
She didn't shed a tear. She didn't look scared. She didn't look
heartbroken. She didn't look furious or anything. Her face was

a blank slate. Though she didn't have a facial expression, I saw what she felt. Though she didn't say a word, I knew what she said inside.

Hailey looked up at Aurick. She stepped around him and walked to her fallen father. She stood over him. Aurick's stomach started to churn. He ran out of there. He ran to the staircase. He leaped multiple stacks of stairs at a time. He ran and ran. He ran till his tongue tasted like copper and his kidneys felt like bags of needle stacks. And then he ran some more. He screeched Jamie's car tires out of the space and barely missed ramming a pickup truck on the way home.

XIII

MY NAMELESS FRIEND'S GIRLFRIEND

Aurick was a wreck. He was emotionally, psychologically, and physically drained. I allowed him to rest. We didn't speak at all. Aisely didn't talk either. In fact, I don't even think he was anywhere around us for miles. I didn't know whether it was out of shame or that he wanted something better to do. We saw these things all the time. Whether it's the abusive mother of three getting beaten to death by an abusive alcoholic husband, or a child murdering his own parents for the life-insurance sums. How could creatures like these be given so many opportunities for redemption and we, the firsts, are left to die for just one misstep? Aurick spent the next morning playing solitaire. He sucked at it. He kept cheating; looking at the facedown cards when he was stuck. He stopped playing after a card gave him a paper cut under one of his fingernails. He sucked on the wound. I could taste it. Disgusting. Suddenly, Aurick started to choke. He started shivering and getting dizzy. After a few minutes, the side effects went away. "What was that?" Aurick said, still panting hard.

"It's time, Aurick."

"Time for what?"

"It is time for us to separate." Aurick's eyes widened and he took a deep swallow. He got up and walked to the window. He looked into the sky. His eyes drifted from cloud to cloud.

"No."

I was stunned by his response. So much that I think I influenced his heart to skip a beat.

"What did you just say to me?" I said, deepening my voice in all dead seriousness.

Aurick looked nervous. "No." He licked his lips, stared down at his hands. "I've never won a fight in my life. The way I broke Samson's arm. He was twice my size and I broke it like a twig. The way I flung that man across the bathroom. Before you came along, I was barely able to fling a bowling ball, let alone a whole man." Aurick stepped back and sat on the couch. "I even . . . walked on water." Aurick looked up to the ceiling. "I'm not done with this yet. The power you've given me, it's too grand to pass up this easily."

"This power got a man killed."

"For that, I'm sorry. But I can't let you go just for that."

"It is too much for you." I deepened my voice again. "We are not even supposed to be talking so directly right now. We're both in danger."

"It'll just be for a little while." Aurick gritted his teeth for a few seconds. His expression gradually turned into a smile as if he'd just thought of something. "The way I see it, you still owe me for living in my body for free. There's no way I would let anyone get away without paying for that."

"I'm warning you, Aurick."

"Ha! Or what?" Aurick said with confidence in his voice. "You could've hurt me or forced me to do whatever you wanted whenever you wanted but ya didn't. The truth is . . . you don't have any power over me. Do ya?" Aurick waited for a response as if he wanted to test something. I didn't say anything. There was nothing I could say. He had discovered my weakness.

The phone rang. Aurick let it ring about four more times before he got annoyed and went to pick it up. It was Helena.

She asked if I was going to be at the office today. "Wait, you're Helena Way?"

"Yes?"

"Helena Way? One of the greatest news reporters that New York City has ever had?"

"Uuuuuuh . . . are you okay, Aurick?"

I tried my absolute best to take control for at least a little bit to slam that phone down before Aurick said anything else. I failed. Aurick happily agreed to their next appointment. "See you there, Ms. Way." He made a kissing noise to Helena and hung up the phone. "Well, I'm going to get some action today." I felt as if I were on fire. On fire with the flames of Jah.

"If you go there, I will kill you."

Aurick laughed. "Ha! What's your problem? I'm just meeting up with the hottest topic in New York City. The new muckraker of this generation." I didn't answer. Aurick looked as if he'd just realized something. "Oh, wait a minute. Aaaaaw, don't tell me you had a thing for Ms. Way? Was that the reason why you stayed in my body for that long?" Aurick waited for a reply but I didn't answer. "Oh, that's cute." Aurick stood up. "Hey, I don't see a problem here. We're sharing the same body so when I'm making love to her, you'll be making love to her also, right?"

There was nothing I could do and he knew it. Whether I was going to get an opportunity to fight back, I did not know. All I could do was to wait and see.

Aurick spent hours trying to decide which of his many suits to wear. He showered, brushed his teeth, and gelled his black hair back. He put on his favorite cologne, Legion Scent. He finally decided on a dark-blue, pin-striped suit with a matching tie. He looked into the mirror with overwhelming pride. He looked tacky to my tastes.

He went to the office and patiently sat down. Aurick smirked the whole time. He was doing this to get back at me.

Helena walked into the room. She was wearing her usual sweat clothing. Aurick was surprised, thinking Helena chose to look nice all the time. Helena looked surprised too to see him wearing his ugly clothes.

"Wow, you look handsome!" Helena lied. "You going on a date?"

Aurick quickly changed his surprised expression. "Every visit with you feels like a date, Ms. Way."

Helena's cute little mouth smiled. "I guess so." She sat down and began venting her problems and opinions for the week. Aurick followed along. As she kept going on and on, it became harder for Aurick to follow. It may have been tiresome for him, but it sounded lovely to me. It had been a while since I'd heard her sweet voice. Her weird, witty sense of humor.

He sighed in exhaustion. "How could you handle this every day?" Aurick said to me under his breath. I didn't reply.

"You said something?" Helena said.

"Oh, nothing. Go on."

Helena did so. Aurick rubbed his head and his eyes.

"What's wrong? Am I boring you or something?"

Aurick slightly leaned over the desk and looked into Helena's eyes. She leaned her head back in discomfort at his stare.

"Have I ever told you that you look beautiful?" Oh, boy. Here came the Aurick Swagger, as I like to call it. Aurick swore he was a master of seduction. My Helena wouldn't fall for such tricks. Her eyes widened in surprise. I for one was more angry than surprised. She looked away to the left corner of the room.

"No. Actually, you hardly ever say anything to me during our sessions," Helena said, switching her vision to the right corner of the room, trying to avoid eye contact. Aurick followed her eyes as they went across the room.

"From now on, I'm going to do all the talking," he said. Helena fixed her eyes on Aurick in curiosity but somewhat out of focus. I guess she wouldn't ever have believed that I would come on to her like this. I had played my character well. Too well.

"You know, Helena, you may not have noticed but"—Aurick wheeled his chair over to Helena's side. I'd never even noticed that that chair had wheels—"I have admired you for a very"—Aurick leaned his head forward to Helena's neck, taking a deep breath of her sweat—"very long time." Aurick may have not known, but I knew it was the kind of sweat that she got from working out before she got here. It was mixed with perfume. Angel Tear perfume to be exact. Compared to her natural scent, Angel Tear smelled like a wet diaper.

"Wow. This is unlike you, Aurick. You're usually so reserved. I kind of figured"—Aurick's lips touched Helena's neck—"you were gay or something." Helena closed her eyes in pleasure.

There was nothing I could do. It was so awkward. It was as awkward as watching your parents doing it. It was as awkward as sinning against God.

Helena abruptly stopped and pulled away.

"What's wrong?" Aurick said, moving a bit forward.

"I don't know. This feels"—Helena turned her head away. It was as if she was a bit ashamed. Thata girl. Resist this defiled temptation—"wrong."

She had her head down. He gently picked her chin up with his index finger. They both stared deep into each other's eyes. I wasn't sure, but I believed Aurick was inadvertently using some type of hypnosis. A small amount or a huge quantity, I wasn't sure. Then, in a burst of fire and desire, they smashed faces and ate each other's faces as if they were at a Chinese buffet. As they twisted and swirled, Helena fell back on the desk with Aurick falling with her. I could feel the pinching pain of Aurick's lips pressing against hers. I wasn't about to give up all hope. I concentrated with all of my might and forced Aurick's teeth to chomp down on his lower lip.

He yelped in pain. "What happened?" Some blood dripped from Aurick's lips. He touched the blood with his finger and looked at it. He looked back to Helena with Helena looking back. They resumed cannibalizing each other, not caring about the copper taste of Aurick's blood. Sick. Two sick people.

Just when things were getting bad, thankfully, my messiah rescued me. Dr. Samantha Fisherman opened the door to see Aurick over Helena on the desk. Aurick stopped and looked at Samantha. Samantha, shocked, quickly closed the door. Helena pushed Aurick off her and picked up her bag to leave.

"Sorry about that," Aurick said, sucking the blood from his lower lip. "Well, not really."

After Helena and Aurick said their good-byes to each other, Aurick took his black Ferrari out for a drive. "I can't believe all this time you've been with that hot piece you've never gotten a taste. Are you gay or something?" I didn't want to dignify his question with a response. "Well, I guess if you did like men, it wouldn't be considered homo. Bestiality?" Aurick said, actually trying to figure out the correct term. "Well, whatever it is, you have to indulge yourself in this world." It was ironic that a human was trying to teach *me,* a demon, about living a demonic lifestyle. "You gotta grab life by the horns and break its freaking neck! You know what I mean?" I didn't answer again. "That woman is mine. There's something odd about her. In a cool way I mean."

Aurick parked his car. The elevator was broken as usual, so Aurick had to walk up the stairs. There was a loud banging, a banging on a door. My door. Well, Aurick's door for the moment. It was Angry Kid and some of his friends. Not any that I knew of. Kid turned to see Aurick.

"There you are, you bastard! Where the hell have you been?" Angry Kid angrily walked over to Aurick. Aurick backed up a bit in discomfort. I could tell Kid was high.

"Do I know you?" Aurick said.

"Was that supposed to be a joke? You think this is funny? You ruined the deal. You've ruined us."

"What are you talking about?"

I had to intervene and say to Aurick privately, "He's talking about our band."

"You have a band?" Aurick said mentally so that only I could hear.

"Yes. During one of our body's violent reactions, we somehow ruined our band's deal with some big-time music producer. Just go along with it."

"I've got a better idea," Aurick thought with a grin on his face.

"You think this is funny? Wipe that stupid grin off your face." Aurick ignored Kid and continued grinning. "We need to get to a club right now. We're late for a show." Kid grabbed Aurick's arm and pulled him in the direction of the stairs. Aurick stopped Kid from moving any more. Kid yanked his arm more and more, but Aurick's new strength was superior to Kid's. "Stop messin' around." Kid punched Aurick in the chest. Aurick responded by punching Kid in the stomach. Kid stumbled to the ground. He coughed and moaned. Aurick led Kid to the banister and sent him tumbling down the stairs. Kid's friends rushed over to him. They were weak and scared. They didn't dare to try anything. Aurick smiled on triumphantly as they helped Kid up and walked him down the stairs. Aurick felt like a true alpha male. A feeling he'd never known since he rescued a girl he liked from a gang of bullies when he was a boy.

Aurick continued through the week getting that alpha-male feeling by beating on people. Some were people whom Aurick owed huge debts to. Pride. Some were people who'd bullied him in the past. Payback. Some were people who'd tried to push him around. Defense. Some were people who'd stepped on his toe. Rage. Some were people whom he just didn't like. Jerk.

He was high on power. So high he could spit on all those who'd wronged him from the heights of Olympus. He won countless bets at gambling tables all over town. He no longer needed me to use my mind-reading abilities, though he used it to a much lesser degree. He planned to use the money to start businesses. We were playing dangerously against the rules. Careful now, Aurick. Your wax wings are melting.

I was able to manipulate Aurick's body parts from time to time. At first I was only able to move them a bit when Aurick was sleeping. After more practice, I could move them a bit against Aurick's will while he was awake. My ability came and went.

One day, Aurick called up Helena Way. I tried desperately to yank the phone cord from that wall, but I couldn't. He invited Helena to go to dinner with him at Athena's Fortune restaurant. It's the five-star cousin of Neptune's Garden. Helena agreed, though with a bit of hesitation in her voice. What about her "significant other"? I thought. Is Aurick smooth enough to get her to forget about Derek? Annoying but impressive.

Aurick put on a black suit. He started fixing his tie in the bathroom mirror. He stopped and stared into it. "I hope you're not mad at me. I'm only living my life. Am I right or am I wrong?" I didn't answer. "Look, you had your chance with her. It's time for me to show you how it's done. Don't you have any girlfriends in demon world or wherever you said you come from?"

God created us with just one gender, I thought to myself. Neither male nor female. When angels were able to come to the human's material realm, we could only manifest ourselves as men.

"Wow, that sucks. No action for all eternity." I was startled that Aurick had heard my thoughts, though from time to time we could hear each other's thoughts and see each other's memories. "Does that ever get boring? Do you get lonely?" He didn't hear my next thought.

Aurick drove down to Helena's home. She lived in a pristine building. It had twenty-four-hour security, beautiful chandeliers, clean windows, clean floors, clean walls, clean smells, clean people. Every brick on the thing was clean. It had everything.

Helena walked out the front door. She wore a hot red, strapless silk drape with a white faux-fur coat slightly open. She even wore makeup. The best part was her hair. That long, radiant hair was tied into a single, extravagant braid. It was beautiful. She looked absolutely radiant. So radiant she melted her ice-cold surroundings. She made Aurick's Ferrari look like an ugly, cheap, diseased prostitute.

Aurick's pants tightened as soon as she stepped into the car. She smiled with nervousness, which I'd never seen Helena express before. It was exotic. It was beautiful. I had to figure out a way to stop this from happening. I vowed to myself on my life that I would stop this from happening. Aurick struck up small talk with her. I concentrated with all of my life force and managed to violently jerk Aurick's hand. The car swerved a little. This gave me an idea.

"Are you okay?" Helena said. Aurick looked at his hand as if it were an alien.

I wanted to stop this date by any means necessary. I felt like a prophet sent by God on a mission. I felt like Malcolm X. I thought about slamming the gas pedal so hard that the car would smash into something, ending the date. But that would risk Helena's life. So I decided to slam the brake pedal so that the car behind us would hit the back. I thought this was safer, not for the other driver, but, oh, well. I did just as I'd planned, but the car behind us stopped just short of an inch from us. Helena screamed and Aurick screamed louder. The driver behind us yelled some vulgarities at us.

Aurick safely got to Athena's Fortune. "If I see just one dent, you're going to be working at my sweatshop, pal," Aurick said to the valet, tossing him the keys. Helena looked bothered by his comment. Aurick grabbed hold of Helena's waist as he confidently walked with her to the entrance. Then he grabbed her behind tightly. She looked bothered again. I would know. I'd heard all of Helena Way's dos and don'ts on dates at our sessions. Most of them were the "give me room" rules, "don't obnoxiously brag about yourself" rules, "don't talk on your cell phone while on a date with me" rules, and "never, ever, *ever* slurp the spaghetti" rules. Aurick didn't hold any doors for Helena. I felt that was rude. When they got to their reserved table, Aurick didn't bother sliding back the chair for Helena, which I also felt was rude. We got a decent table with a big red tablecloth and nicely laid out utensils. A timid-looking man came over with a pen and pad of paper in his hands.

"Ms. Way, may I have your autograph?" Helena looked a bit annoyed but she smiled and took the pad.

Aurick looked irritated. "You've got to be kiddin' me. You're going to interrupt us when we're trying to eat?"

"No, it's okay, Aurick," Helena said.

"No, it's not okay. Get out of here!" The man walked away in embarrassment. Aurick apologized for overreacting, though he didn't mean it.

We got a tall, brooding Russian waiter who startled Aurick at first. He didn't want to see another Russian ever again after what had happened not that long ago

Aurick ordered his meal first, cutting off Helena from ordering hers. "Man, I have a weird craving for tomatoes. Waiter, get me a plate of tomatoes." Aurick saw that Helena and the brooding waiter were looking at him in a funny way, so he changed his meal to pasta and chicken.

"Just give me broccoli," Helena said.

Aurick in turn looked at Helena in a funny way. "Just broccoli?"

"I'm on a diet. I'm in the public's eye, remember?"

"Oh, yes, you must maintain that gorgeous body of yours."

That stupid line didn't impress me. He was lying anyway, as human males do. Aurick liked women with big breasts. Enormous breasts. And Helena did not have enormous breasts. His infatuation with big breasts ended his four-year relationship with a woman he tried to coax nonstop into getting breast implants. Helena tried to hold in her smile but failed. She blushed in a cute, demure way.

When Helena's broccoli came, she gobbled it down without Aurick's even getting his order of pasta. She was still hungry so she ordered more. "You know, Helena, you should go for a ride on my yacht sometime."

"You have a yacht?"

Aurick gave a quick, loud fake laugh. "Yeah." Aurick took a deep breath, stretched out his arms, and placed the back of his elbow over his chair. It was full-throttle boasting from here on out. "I try to keep things modest. I have plenty of money. I try not to show off my fancy clothes and my dough." Aurick was losing the cool points that he'd earlier earned. "You should take a ride on my yacht."

"No can do."

"Why not?" Because you don't have a yacht, I thought to myself.

"I'm not too fond of water."

Aurick titled his head.

"When I was a kid, I loved to swim," Helena said in a jolly tone. "My parents always used to force me to do things that I didn't want to do, like playing the violin, piano, chess, and they never let me play with the other kids."

"That ain't so bad," Aurick said in a dismissive voice. "I wish my folks had got me into that stuff."

"They made me read all of Shakespeare's plays by the time I was ten."

"Oh."

"There was one thing that I did like that my parents allowed me to do."

"What was that?"

"I loved to swim. I swam so much I always looked like a prune." Helena giggled and Aurick fake-smiled along. "When I swam in my pool, all of my pressures washed away. One day I went swimming in my pool and my cousin Victoria came along. We swam and swam together. Victoria was younger than me and wasn't nearly as good a swimmer as I was." Helena's jolly tone and swift speech gradually turned slow and low. "My mother called me into the house for something. I don't remember what, but she was such a strict hard-ass that I just had to come in fear of her yelling at me. I left Victoria alone in that pool."

"What happened?"

Helena stopped chewing her broccoli and was silent. Then she said, "I came back to find Victoria dead. She must've cramped up and drowned. My parents cried and cried for months. My mother blamed me for leaving her there alone."

Aurick's face was serious for the first time that night. "But you were only ten."

"She didn't care. She told me that I killed Victoria. Ever since then, I've never stepped into a body of water besides a bathtub." Helena abruptly munched into her broccoli.

"Wow. A normal person would've been really screwed up by that."

Helena made a loud single crunch into her food and stopped. "That sounds funny coming from my freaking psychologist." Ha, he forgot that he was her psychologist. Idiot.

"It doesn't matter that I didn't remember that I was her psychologist. Your little girlfriend is mine." I was sharing my thoughts with Aurick but he was also sharing his. He had the full intention of taking her to his bed tonight. I didn't have to read his mind to know that.

And he was grumpy. He repeatedly asked the waiter for his meal. He'd been waiting for more than half an hour. He fidgeted around and tapped his fork on the table repeatedly. He tapped all the way through Helena's talk. He wasn't a good listener, and Helena was a good talker. Helena saw that Aurick was aggravated and wasn't listening. She gave him a deep sigh and got up from her chair and walked away. Aurick asked where she was going, but she didn't answer. Helena marched into the kitchen of the restaurant. I could hear Helena mumbling something. She was too far away for me to hear everything. The next thing I knew, I could hear Helena. Half the restaurant heard.

"Do you know who I am? I'm Helena Way, the journalist for the *Daily Universe.* If I don't have this man's meal in five minutes, I'm going to report these health violations. Such as these cockroaches crawling on the walls."

The people who heard got grossed out and left. Helena waltzed out of the kitchen and came back to her table. Aurick looked impressed. Sure enough, his pasta came right away. Four minutes.

"Whoa. How did you do that?"

"When you're famous, people are such ass-kissers." Aurick laughed but Helena was serious.

Aurick immediately gorged into his plate. He made slurping sounds, which broke the "never, ever, *ever* slurp the spaghetti" rule.

"And it also helps when you have the power to shut their business down."

A jingle rang out. It was Helena's cell phone. She put it to her ear. I couldn't believe she was breaking her own "don't talk on your cell phone while on a date with me" rule. She lost eleven cool points for that. Helena initially tried to cut the conversation short, but then her annoyed and embarrassed facial expression turned serious and excited. "You've got to be kidding!"

Aurick looked concerned, but not as concerned as he was when he was waiting for his pasta.

"All right, I'll be there right away. Don't go anywhere." Helena closed the cell and jammed it into her purse quickly. "Come on, we have to go."

"What? What happened?" Aurick said quizzically with a string of spaghetti dangling from his mouth.

"I got a call from Timmy. He thinks he's found the whereabouts of Adilah."

"Adilah?"

"Yeah. I'm sorry but I can't let this opportunity pass me by. Are you going to take me?"

"No way. I haven't even had a chance to eat my entrée. Sorry, but you're just going to have to wait."

"I'll pay you."

"Let's go."

XIV

NAMELESS FELLOWSHIP

Be careful not to stare at love for too long. Your heart will turn to stone. The harder of a stone you are, the easier it is to crumble. Everyone misses the mark at some point, but do not be misled. Don't give up on the art of romance because you will die. There is only one that I know of to not have. For the sake of sanctity and sanity, that must remain true.

Helena hurried ahead of Aurick. Aurick lazily followed her lead. She ran back and grabbed his arm and pulled him to move faster. Aurick started up the engine and waited so that the engine would warm up properly. Helena told Aurick to forget about the stupid car, and he drove off without warming it up. Aurick was pretty confident that he was going to get repaid by Helena either via money or sex. Or even both.

Helena was going to meet up with Timmy at Reese Pier, where he thought Adilah was using an abandoned warehouse. Helena, with no forcefulness behind her words, told Timmy to wait until she got there before making any moves. She was thrilled that she was going to get one step closer to Adilah, possibly ending their string of terror. This would be her greatest accomplishment.

If we catch Helena getting into our business again, she will die. Lofie's words about Helena echoed through my mind. If any Fallen were around, they would definitely find out. It was a miracle that Lofie had kept his word. If Lofie weren't obsessed with me, Helena would have been dead by now.

"Aurick, I have to tell you something."

Aurick looked surprised to hear from me. "Oh, now you're talking to me. I thought you were giving me the silent treatment."

"Look, I don't have time for this. We don't have time for this. I've managed to keep her safe this far. If she gets spotted by just one of them, she's dead." Aurick looked over to Helena. He looked back into the rearview mirror. "If anything happens to Helena Way, I promise you, I will hold you accountable." I put all seriousness into my voice. "That is of course if *they* don't get to you first."

"*They?*"

"Fallen."

"Fallen? Fallen like you?"

"Not like me. Much meaner. Much more psychopathic. Helena's been trying to expose some cult. It's being run by Fallen. I don't know how many. They've already tried to kill her. I've managed to keep her safe this far. If she gets spotted interfering again by just one of them, she's dead."

Helena saw that Aurick was distressed. She asked if he was all right. He replied that he was fine. They got to their destination. Possibly their *final* destination.

She got out of the car. She poked her head back in. "Thank you, Aurick. You helped me out big-time. You can leave now. Timmy will drive me back home."

Aurick gritted his teeth tight and swallowed hard.

"What's wrong? You're acting like you're holding a dirty little secret," Helena said, smiling.

Aurick forced a smile back. "Maybe you should forget about this. Let me take you back home."

"Don't worry about me. I'll be just fine." Helena crawled back in the car and pecked Aurick on the mouth. "I had a great time." She slammed the door and walked away.

Aurick started the car. He looked into the rearview mirror. An immense wave of rage leaked out of me. The rearview mirror cracked. Aurick jumped. "There's nothing I could do. Why should I get involved in dangerous crap like this?"

"You wanted to get involved. Now you have to make a choice. A choice that may change your life forever."

Aurick pretended that he was warming up the car, but he was really thinking about what he should do. He would be risking his life for someone he didn't care about, for no money. He thought about driving away and never messing with my associates ever again. He knew there was a large possibility that Helena would get hurt. He knew he had power over me for now, but also knew I would eventually break free. He would be a zookeeper letting out a caged lion. I put that into his mind. I caused his lungs to contract, his muscles to tighten, and his heart to beat more quickly, augmenting his natural fear. Aurick fell for it. He got out and locked his car. He called out to Helena. She wasn't in sight.

It was freezing outside. Aurick could see the white clouds of breath that came out of his mouth. It had that crisp, cold scent of snow in the clouds. Aurick ran around in circles, calling out to Helena. Then he saw a man in a yellow raincoat. He walked toward the entrance of the abandoned warehouse. I told Aurick that the man was a member of Adilah. At that moment, Aurick ran around the corner of the warehouse to avoid being spotted by the member. Aurick panted hard in relief. "God, I hope I don't get pneumonia."

"Aurick, what're you doing here?" Aurick swiftly turned his neck, almost breaking it. It was Helena, crouching with Timmy on huge metal crates stacked one story up near one of the warehouse's fire escapes.

"I'm here to help you," Aurick said, whispering in a way that sounded as if he were yelling at the same time.

"Why?" Helena said, whispering the same way.

Aurick didn't know what to say.

"Just tell her that you need to be there to experience and understand her line of work to help you understand her better," I said to Aurick. Aurick told Helena just so.

"Okay. Just don't screw up."

Aurick climbed up the crates. Helena was the first one to get to the fire escape. She tried to open up a window, but it was too heavy. "Would you hurry the hell up, Timmy. Stop wasting my time."

"Yes, Ms. Way." Timmy scurried up to her like a little puppy. Timmy and Helena used all of their strength but still couldn't open the window. We could see people inside the warehouse.

"Can you help us out here, Aurick?"

Aurick scampered over and opened the window by himself with ease. Some glass and part of the frame cracked.

"Whoa. You're strong, Aurick," Timmy said, looking on in admiration.

They stepped onto a metal platform, being careful not to make any noise. They stepped over to the rail and looked down below.

"Get down," Helena whispered.

They got down with their stomachs hugging the platform. Helena and Timmy took out their cameras and zoomed in to see what was going on more clearly. It looked as if they were readying themselves for an assassination.

"What the hell? It looks like they're having some type of . . . party."

Eighty-eight people were down there. Many were huddled together, casually conversing with each other. Some were talking about TV shows that they'd seen the previous night, while others were speaking about the new restaurant they'd been to called Eve's Castle. Some looked kind of strange. Some sat on the floor

rocking back and forth, biting their fingernails. Some were talking and laughing to themselves. Some walked around in circles.
If I didn't know any better, I would have thought they all had
escaped from a madhouse. Sodas, fruit punch, potato chips, pret-
zels, popcorn, and cake were on long, cheap tables on the floor's
periphery. A podium was at the center of the floor.

"What the hell, Timmy? I thought you said Adilah was
supposed to be here," Helena said angrily.

"But it has to be them. Look, they're wearing those yellow
raincoats and I saw some wearing masks." Timmy's eyes got
watery red.

"Well, that's a relief," Aurick said. "Come on. Let's get out of
here now."

"Wait, look," Helena suddenly said, looking horribly shocked.
"What is Derek doing here?" Derek was in a yellow raincoat
just like the rest. "He knows these people?"

It was apparently so as Derek, jolly, greeted and shook
everyone's hand. He smiled and they smiled back. He walked
over to the podium. Derek raised his arms and said, "It is time,
my brothers, to begin." His "brothers" immediately stopped
whatever they were doing and directed their attention to Derek.
Derek put on a bunny mask and everyone else did the same. "It
is time for our brotherhood to strike again."

"I told you, Ms. Way," Timmy said, wiping his eyes.

"Shut up, Tim, and get your camera ready," Helena said,
getting closer to the edge, getting her own camera ready.

"We managed to cause massive damage to this city. Our last
targets were a firehouse, a police station, and a restaurant."

"I just wanted to say . . . " one of the members among the
crowd said, "I just wanted to say that I'm very proud of how
everyone handled those attacks. I was damned impressed with
you guys." There was giggling through the crowd and some
patted the man on his shoulders.

"Yes, I am very proud also, but this is only the beginning. We shall strike fear into the world that wronged us. We shall saw the pillars of corruption. We shall rust the foundations of oppression. We shall gnaw on the establishment of destruction. We shall laugh in the face of damnation in which in turn we shall sleep in the belly of redemption." Derek's speech went on about vengeance and the evils in the world. I'd never heard so many words ending with *tion* in my entire existence. And that's a very long time. "We shall—"

"Yeah, whatever," a man said, cutting off Derek. "We've been at this for years and we still haven't gotten our rewards yet. Why in the world should we even continue?"

"You must have faith, brother. *We* must have faith. Our God will reward us in due time. We just need to endure for her. We need to—"

"I'm tired of this crap," the man said, cutting Derek off again. He ripped off his mask and tossed it to the floor. "We've been risking our necks for this God for years and she still hasn't shown herself to us. How do we know this God is even real?"

After a loud gasp a hushed silence came over the crowd.

"But she *has* shown herself, my brother. She revealed herself to a select few of us."

"Just a few?" The man laughed. "You *few* probably fabricated all of that just to manipulate us to do whatever you want."

"Blasphemy! I would hold my tongue if I were you, Brother Tex."

"Don't call me your brother anymore, *brother*. You and this invisible pink unicorn are frauds. We have all been lied to. I am—" Brother Tex let out a loud grunt.

The crowd made a complete circle around the man, facing him. A knife was sticking from Tex's back. He dropped to his knees.

"Destroy the traitor," Derek said, thrusting his hand toward the man. The crowd closed in on him and started punching and kicking all over the traitor's body. Some actually started biting his hands as if they were trying to eat him.

When the crowd finally stopped the vicious assault, they directed their attention back to Derek, ignoring those that were still standing on top of the traitor's body.

"This is what happens when you blaspheme against Adilah. Against God. Against Justice. We shall move forward and shall not look back."

Timmy was leaning against the rusty railing, trying not to miss one moment with the camera. A piece of the rusty railing broke, sending Timmy over it. At the last second, Helena grabbed Timmy with one arm. Somehow, Helena with her small frame managed to keep a firm hold of Timmy and started yanking him up. Timmy yelled and cried in fear.

"Shut up, Timmy. You're going to blow our cover."

"Too late," Aurick said. The members rushed over each other to get to the stairwell that led to us. Aurick helped Helena and yanked Timmy over onto the platform. "Let's get the hell out of here!"

The window mysteriously slammed shut.

"I can't get it open," Helena said.

Aurick, Timmy, and Helena tried with all of their strength to lift it, but it mysteriously wouldn't budge. Helena tightly gripped her camera and smashed the window. Timmy jumped through the opening and onto the fire escape. Aurick shoved Helena out of the way. He got one of his legs outside, then one of the cult members yanked him back in and restrained him. It took four men to restrain Helena. They brought us down to the floor before Derek. They forced us to kneel before him, almost breaking our arms.

"What do we have here? A couple of rats," Derek said.

"You're the one who set me up, aren't you, Derek?" Helena said, struggling to get up.

"My name isn't really Derek. My real name is Brother Dex. I am sorry for toying with you the way we did. We wanted to just walk up to you and blow your head off, but no one here wanted to risk going to prison." Brother Dex smiled, then laughed softly. "To tell you the truth, I could have ended you a long time ago."

"You didn't have the balls."

"That's just it. I wanted a few licks off before we killed you."

Helena smiled and said, "And I wanted a few licks off of you before dumping your sorry ass. That little pecker of yours couldn't satisfy me long enough to stay." Dex's soft smile turned into an angry fit. I was disappointed that Helena picked me over him because of that, but, oh, well. "The truth is *honey*, the only reason I went out with you was because I *knew* you were associated with Adilah. But I never dreamed you were the big fish." Helena knew he was part of Adilah? She's brilliant. "But then again, being the head of a deadly terrorist organization would make sense. Trying to make up for something, *honey*. I mean a plastic garden gnome could've pleasured me more than you. Not that I need a garden gnome. Aurick here is ten times the man you'll *ever* be. Ten! In more ways than one too."

Some of the members giggled, enraging Dex even more. "Shut up, all of you. It's not funny. You're going to pay for making fun of me." They still laughed. "Damn it, in the name of Adilah, be silent!" They finally hushed themselves. "God will soon fix that small problem after I do her bidding. Adilah will provide for all."

"Small problem is right. But it'll take a miracle to fix that thing."

Adilah members laughed again. When Dex turned to them, they fixed their smiles immediately.

"You're right," Aurick said. "It's not funny. Many men have erectile dysfunction. I do sometimes too."

"Really?" Dex said hopefully.

"No, not really, but I know you're having a big problem—"

"Small problem," Helena said.

"—but this isn't the way to solve it. Let us go. Well . . . at least let me go. I don't have anything to do with this. I don't even know Helena."

Helena looked shocked for a moment.

"I hope you and your new boyfriend will enjoy your new lives in hell." Aurick jerked away from a member's grip and ran, leaving Helena behind. It was in vain though. They quickly caught him and brought him back.

"God commanded us to let you live, but you just had to push it. You just couldn't give up." An Adilah member handed Dex Helena's camera and her cell phone. "Now all of your meddling will be in vain." Dex smashed the camera on the ground and then the cell phone.

A piece of lens fell to the floor before Aurick. When I looked into it, I saw Lofie. He was leaning on Dex with his "arm" around his neck. He was smiling with satisfaction. He waved and blew a kiss to me.

"I can help you out if you ask, you know," Lofie said casually.

"Help me then," I said plainly.

"Wow," Lofie said, laughing out loud. "That was quick. I've never seen you so desperate for help. Do you really like this human that much?"

"Stop playing around. If you're going to help, then help."

Lofie walked over to Helena and crouched down to her level. "I bet the only reason you want to save Helena is to taste that sweet, sweet body of hers, right?" Lofie traced his "tongue" just over Helena's cheek. "You want her treasure box? Her . . . forbidden fruit?" Lofie's voice deepened. "Her Venus flytrap!" Lofie's voice grew light again. "I've always found sex absolutely fascinating. The way the two bodies melt into each other. The way their hearts seemingly beat at the same time at the high point of their explosion of crimson passion. Daddy never gave us the privilege to show each other love like he's given humans. Sex is the ultimate display of affection. The epiphany of emotion and triumph. The reason to love. The reason to hate. The reason to live. The reason to die. The reason to disobey."

"What's your point, Lofie?"

Lofie smiled. "All these millennia we've known each other and I could never express just how much I loved you. Lucky for us we can use human bodies as a gateway to our eternal love."

"You mean *your* eternal love."

"Oh, sugar muffin, you're so shy. But that doesn't matter. The point is that I want to share such immense passion with you."

"The answer to that is no."

Lofie just smiled. "I guess you don't like her after all. I guess I wouldn't too if I had been fooled by a female in the past. I guess Helena dies then." Lofie turned his back to me. "Just like *she* did."

I had no choice but to give in. Lofie had me by the testicles. Or should I say *will* have my testicles. I knew what I had to do. I had to put away my pride for now for my sake. For *her* sake.

"Yes."

Lofie nodded. He whispered something into Dex's ear. Dex looked blank for a moment. He came back to reality as if someone had turned on Dex's on switch.

"I suddenly feel that I don't need to kill you, sweetums," Dex said, kissing Helena on the cheek. "I already destroyed all the evidence that can harm us. You may go."

Adilah members looked at each other in surprise. Some were frustrated while others were terrified. If they wanted to keep their own lives, they would have to obey their *God*. Helena yanked her arm away from a member in a final act of defiance and pride. The members cleared a path for us to walk through. It was a hallway of human walls with eyes staring at our every step. We went on through the front while Adilah went through the back exit.

We managed to escape. Or should I say, we were let go of. More important, we were let go of *alive*. Aurick went straight to the car. Helena went after him. He was shaking like crazy. Helena wasn't shaking at all. That's my girl, nerves made of orichalcum. Helena looked angry. Losing a chance to finish off Adilah must've crushed her. And finding out that your boyfriend was the leader of a murderous cult didn't help much either. She opened the window on her side and breathed in the fresh air. The wind flushed out the old stuffy air like a toilet. It was refreshing. Helena's jet-black hair fluttered all around, messed up. But it was a nice kind of mess-up. I could smell the mixture of her natural scalp oils and strawberry-scented hair gel. It was nice. Aurick kept looking to Helena to see how she was holding up. Helena didn't look at him at all. Her eyes were on the road more than Aurick's were.

"How are you holding up?" Aurick said, giving a slight jab to her arm. Helena painfully rolled her eyes. Aurick turned his attention back to the road.

"I can't believe you were about to leave me there to die," she said, abruptly turning to Aurick.

"I can't believe I even *came* with you in the first place. You almost got *me* killed," Aurick snapped back.

"I thought you cared enough to watch my back."

"This was supposed to be a normal date. Not a war on terrorism." Aurick stopped at a red light. "And didn't I come with you?" Yeah. For the money. "You're crazy to think that I didn't care about you." Yeah; he just cared about getting paid.

"I don't need you to care about me."

"You're not making sense. You're crazy!"

Aurick and Helena stared down each other with angry daggers. I could feel the gravity of their energy. At that moment,

Helena lunged at Aurick and gave him a long, passionate kiss. I felt their conflict. I felt their anger. I felt their desire. Sometimes I felt that Aurick and I were the same person. Aurick grabbed her and kissed with equal passion. I couldn't believe they were doing this at a streetlight holding up traffic. The cars behind us beeped their horns. Aurick and Helena didn't care. They let them wait. Aurick offered to spend the night at Helena's place but she said she had to meet up with Timmy. When Timmy left us, he took the video footage with him. Helena had a video voice recorder in her bra. I wondered why she would have that when she didn't know this was going to happen. Helena told Aurick that she never leaves home without it. It was Helena's plan all along.

Aurick skipped into his apartment. He was ecstatic that he'd just made out with Helena Way, the greatest reporter of New York City. I was ecstatic also. Not in the way or why Aurick was. But in the way that I knew what was going to happen next. Not to me of course.

Aurick lay on his bed. He wanted to eat but he was too tired to eat. Aurick felt someone on top of him. Ha. Lofie just couldn't wait long, could he? Aurick opened his eyes to find Brother Dex on top of him.

XV

SPIRITUAL HARASSMENT

Lofie was controlling him. Aurick tried to scream, but mysteriously his mouth couldn't open. Lofie wrapped his glossy green lips around Aurick's. Aurick tried to struggle but Lofie wouldn't let him move. Lofie held Aurick down with air pressure while he used his hands to take off his own pants. He had pink boxers with green hearts on them. Lofie then took off Aurick's pants. All Aurick could do was scream for help in his thoughts. Lofie wanted to mess with my friends, so that's just what he was going to get. Lofie slobbered on Aurick.

Suddenly, Lofie stopped. He looked into Aurick's face. Lofie took another long, slimy lick and examined the taste as if he were testing out a new wine. He gazed deep into Aurick's eyes. "You're not my sweet," Lofie said with a confused face. "You're a fraud. What's the meaning of this?" Lofie connected with my mind. "Get into control now!"

"I can't."

"Why not?"

"Aurick is in full control. I've been in this condition for weeks."

Lofie's face filled with bewilderment. "A demon getting possessed by a human? That's unheard of. How did that happen?"

"I suppose because I've been in his body for too long. I've been trying to get out but I can't."

Lofie bit his lip. He tried to hold his laughter, causing himself to snort. He let go and burst out into full, unfiltered laughter.

Then he abruptly stopped. Then he got angry. Aurick's eyes bulged with terror.

"That means I won't be able to make true love to you. You knew this would happen. You fooled me!"

Indeed I did. But I wasn't going to let him know that. "It's out of my control. I'm still in the body, so if you want, go right ahead and do whatever you please."

"But it won't be the same if you're not in control!" Lofie said loudly. "It's not the same if you don't feel me."

"Promise me nothing will happen to Helena."

Lofie laughed out loud. "I guess we have something in common hot lips, babe. I don't have control over that either."

I felt a naked feeling in the pit of my stomach. And it wasn't because of Lofie. Lofie abruptly turned around. He stared deep into Aurick's eyes. Aurick was still struggling to scream, letting out slight mumbles. Lofie snapped his fingers. At that moment, Aurick became unconscious, ending the mumbling. His eyes were still open.

"What do you mean?"

Lofie laughed out loud again. "It is *his* call. The truth is I work for someone. Or should I say, I'm working to work for someone. I'm sort of a right hand of justice." Lofie got off Aurick and backed away from the bed. "Someone who will deliver us. Someone who will save us. Someone who will bring us back to life. Someone who will give us one more chance. That's something not even Daddy would ever do for us."

I was silent. I couldn't think of anything to say.

Lofie walked around the room, casually looking around, admiring the new drapes. "I have to do one last favor for him and I am in. This will decide whether I am worthy or not. You should too." Lofie came over and crawled onto the foot of the bed, eagerly waiting for my response.

"I am so sick of this."

"Aren't we all?" Lofie smiled.

"I am sick of *all* of this. There's a reason why I'm living as a human. I just want to live the rest of my death sentence out in peace, and you bastards come and ruin it all. I just want to be left alone!"

Lofie laughed out loud again. He crawled up on all fours like a hyena and moved over to Aurick. "We both know that's not true. Deep down at the back of your throat," Lofie said, leaning toward my face, looking into my lips, hinting at something, "you want to at least go down in a blaze of glory. Not retire like an old fart in an elderly home. Truth is, you want to prove Him wrong." Lofie kissed the bridge of Aurick's nose. "I *will* have you, love bunny. There is no doubt in my mind that you will be *mine*. *All* mine." Lofie hopped off Aurick and opened the door. "I will let you know when Adilah will strike again. I will find you. This will be your last chance to be reborn. Don't screw this up."

Lofie was gone. I was a mess. I felt emotions I hadn't felt in centuries. I felt fear. I felt excitement. I felt doom. I felt hope.

Aurick awoke the next morning. He had a crushing headache as if someone had bashed his forehead with a sledgehammer. He tiredly stumbled through the apartment over to the refrigerator. He pulled out a can of tomato juice and gulped it down. Suddenly, Aurick's eyes widened as if he realized something. He spit up the juice, leaving a spray of red mist in the air. "Was that a dream?"

I had to take advantage of this opportunity. "No, it wasn't."

Aurick hopped up a bit in surprise. I guess he forgot that a Fallen occupied his body. "You mean to tell me that weird guy was in my room last night"—Aurick paused and swallowed—"and kissed me?"

"More than just kissed you." I hated lying but I was desperate. "He went all the way to third base and scored a touchdown." I didn't know whether I was talking about baseball or some other sport.

Aurick looked sick all of a sudden. He collapsed but held himself up against the refrigerator door. He ran to the bathroom and spewed his insides up into the toilet. A few droplets splattered up, touching the tip of Aurick's nose.

I told him that a Fallen had possessed and raped him. I also told him the Fallen was going to keep harassing him and raping him every night.

Aurick vomited again. Aurick wondered if this made him gay. Homophobe. "How do we stop that freak?"

"You can't. *I* can. But the only way *I* can is *if* I regain control. And the only way for me to regain control is to see that doctor." I wasn't truly sure. I didn't know if Dr. Doctor could even help at all.

"But I need you. I won't let you go."

"I can't leave even if I tried. I have unfinished business with your body. But if you'd rather make love to a Fallen every night, that's fine by me."

"I'm not taking that chance! I'll run somewhere he'll never find me."

"You can never escape from him. He will find you."

"I'll take the risk." Aurick got dressed in a hurry. I didn't know what Aurick was planning. It would all be in vain anyway.

He ran out of the apartment. The elevator was broken . . . again. Aurick hurried to the steps, then suddenly everything got fuzzy. Aurick's head throbbed with pain. A couple seconds later, his chest started to throb in pain also. His heart was beating so fast it felt as if it could burst at any moment. He slammed against the dirty wall. I shared his agony. Blood trickled down his nose. We needed to go to the hospital. I needed to think of a way to get there. How? Duh. Get hurt. I mustered all of my focus and strength and jerked Aurick's leg backward. Aurick flipped and tumbled down the stairs. Payback for Angry Kid. Aurick lay there unconscious.

※   ※   ※

Aurick woke up at around five. He was in a daze. He was too tired to speak. It was a busy day at St. Peter's Hospital. But then again, *every day* is a busy day. What hospital isn't? Dr. Doctor could be anywhere. Or anyone. I thought it was strange that we weren't in an emergency room but in a regular hospital room. I also found it strange that we were in a room by ourselves. Usually there were two to a room. We even had a bed near the window. A nurse came into the room. Aurick's vision was blurry but not blurry enough to miss the nurse's enormous breasts.

Aurick was half awake thanks to the hospital drugs. Something else was half awake also when the nurse came over to his side. She plumped his pillow. Aurick mumbled, "Thanks." She smiled and brushed his hair back with her fingers. The nurse pulled out a syringe. I found it weird. I didn't think we would need anesthesia. I went into her mind, which was filled with confusion and conflict. It was forcing me out, which was unusual. It was as if she had two minds. She *did* have two minds.

She squeezed the liquid to the top of the needle. She slowly moved the deadly instrument to Aurick's arm. I told Aurick not to let her inject him. Aurick was too drugged up to react. Just as the needle touched Aurick's skin, I jerked Aurick's arm and grabbed the nurse's hand at the last moment. She jerked back. Her face was filled with confusion and fear as if she herself had no idea what was going on. She dropped the syringe and ran away.

Five minutes later, a doctor came in, the one with that freaky crescent-shaped smile.

"What's the big idea? You trying to kill me or something?" Aurick said groggily.

"My apologies, Mr. Pantera. I mixed you up with someone else," he said, keeping that smile on his face. This was definitely Dr. Doctor. "Can't stay out of hospitals can you?"

I connected with Dr. Doctor's mind. "The side effects are getting worse. Though I am still in this human's body, I am not in control. This body continues to get hallucinations and painful headaches. It also had another heart attack. Worst of all, I'm stuck." My words seemed not to faze Dr. Doctor, as if he had seen this before. Then again nothing seemed to faze Dr. Doctor.

"Oh, that is unfortunate. At this rate, you're going to go insane."

Dr. Doctor's words shocked Aurick so much that some of the anesthesia wore off at that moment. "What do you mean go insane?"

"That's if you don't die first."

"Die?"

"Your mind is ripping itself apart trying to separate the two entities. The problem is that you've been fused together for so long you're solidly embedded together."

"How are you going to fix it?" Aurick and I said at the same time.

"I can't fix anything." At that moment, Aurick's heart dropped. Sweat spewed forth. "If you're lucky, your bodies will separate themselves after some time."

Aurick and I thought the same thing: that was a lazy response. "There has to be something you can do," Aurick said. "I can't die like this." And I can't live like this, I thought.

Dr. Doctor paced around the room for a few seconds. "Maybe there's something I can do."

"What is it?" Aurick said quickly. He sat up and looked on eagerly for Dr. Doctor's response.

"I can allow your other half to take control of your body."

What a crappy solution. Fix the symptom but not the illness itself. What a typical doctor.

"Hell no."

"Hell yes," I said a second after Aurick.

"I don't want him controlling my body anymore. He already has done enough damage to my life as it is."

Oh, yeah, blame me for your miserable life. Typical human.

"I'm sorry but that's the best I can do." Dr. Doctor walked over to Aurick. He placed his thumb on Aurick's forehead and gazed deep into his eyes and spit a glob of saliva into them. Aurick fell unconscious.

Aurick got up moments later, only this time, I was in control. I had that feeling of being in a wet bag of meat again.

"Thanks, Dr. Doctor. That knocks out one of my problems."

"Glad I could help."

"Too bad it's not enough. There has to be some way of getting free of this monkey." Dr. Doctor sat down at my bedside. "How much time do I have left?" It was annoying watching that smile while I was in so much pain.

"It can happen at any time. Ten years from now, next month, next week, tonight. It depends. All I can say for sure is that the more you use your abilities, the faster you both will be ripped apart. Fighting for dominance also speeds up your degeneration. The side effects will get much more severe and much more frequent." Didn't I ask this guy for an actual solution? "The only other thing I can think of is—"

"Hold that thought," I said. I hadn't seen Shelia in a while, and since I was already at the hospital, I might as well see how she was doing. I hopped out of bed. As I walked through the hallway, being followed by Dr. Doctor, I felt a mysterious draft. I forgot I was wearing a hospital gown. I immediately felt embarrassed.

I walked into Shelia's room. She was alone. The other bed in her room was empty. She was smelling a flower. I believe it was a dandelion. She looked as if she was thinking of something. She seemed depressed.

"Hello, Shelia. How are you feeling?"

I startled her a bit but she seemed to be relieved and happy that I was there. "Hello, my dear. You got hurt again? What happened this time?"

"I had a little fall."

"Oh my God. Are you all right?"

"Yes, I am fine."

"I'll pray for you anyway. What brings you here?"

"To see you of course. I've missed you."

Shelia smiled. Her eyes swelled up with tears. "You always know just what to say to cheer me up."

Out of all the humans I knew, I could say Shelia was one of my favorites. I felt that she needed some fresh air. She wasn't supposed to leave her room, but Dr. Doctor allowed it. She was in no shape to walk. I took her to the roof by wheelchair. Though it was a bit chilly outside, it wasn't windy at all. It was quite refreshing. I wheeled her over to the edge by the barrier. Shelia's eyes wandered through the milky clouds. It was quite . . . pretty.

"Can I ask you a question, Aurick?"

"Yes, ma'am."

Shelia didn't say anything for a few seconds. She seemed scared to speak. "What do you think . . . heaven is like?"

Aurick's gut wrenched. I felt my heart skip a beat. "I don't . . . remember."

"What do you mean you don't remember?"

"I mean . . . I don't know."

Shelia laughed. "That would have made sense if you were an angel."

I smiled and gave a short, genuine laugh. "I am not good enough to be an angel."

We stayed up on the roof for about fifteen minutes.

"Can I ask you a favor?"

I smiled. "Anything you want, friend."

"I want you to kill me."

Aurick's blood pressure shot up. I gripped the handle of the wheelchair tightly. The sweat on Aurick's palms wet the handles. I came over in front of Shelia to face her. I knelt down so that I could be on eye level with her. I gazed into her cheerless, tearful eyes. They looked like a dog's eyes after its master has died.

"That's something I cannot do, friend. I am sorry."

She sniffled and wiped away a tear, which was rolling down her cheek. "No. I am sorry for asking you that. I asked my son to do it but he didn't have the heart to. I must've put him in so much distress because of that." Shelia lowered her head. "I've been in so much pain lately. None of the medications are working anymore. I'm sick. I'm old. My hair is falling out. I'm ugly." She lowered her head even lower.

I leaned in closer. I lifted her chin up with my finger to make eye contact with her. "No. You're beautiful, Shelia." That didn't seem to cheer her up a bit. "Even when you're facing death, you should fight to the end, even if it may be futile." I wasn't sure what I was saying. I wasn't sure if I believed it myself.

"One day, I will be forgotten. Even by my own . . . son."

I didn't know what to say to that. I leaned toward her. My lips slowly met hers. I put Shelia into a deep trance. I absorbed all of her emotions and she absorbed all of mine. I felt her pain and suffering and she felt mine. I made her see herself as she was when she was young. Young, agile, healthy, cheerful. She played jump rope. She cooked. She fished. She partied. She ran a marathon. She was at bliss. Within the dream, I made love to her. It was as real as the real thing. When the trance was over, Shelia was fast asleep. I rested my forehead on hers. I heard gravel crunching as someone's footsteps approached.

"This world is filled with so much pain and suffering. It's such a shame," Dr. Doctor said. He still had that smile on. "No matter how much she did in her lifetime, she will fall short against the final companion." I didn't move from my position. I wanted to feel Shelia's warmth. "She will soon find eternal bliss. She will soon be released from this fantasy world. How beautiful."

I didn't want to hear any more of Dr. Doctor's romanticizing. "Did you think of any way I could get free of this body?"

"You could set your body on fire and burn it to a crisp, freeing yourself."

That wasn't the answer I was looking for. "No thank you, Doc. Murder would get me sent to the Null. Not to mention the excruciating pain I would have to go through dying like that."

Dr. Doctor sighed. His eyes wandered over the endless sky. It was dark enough to see some of the stars. "The things us Fallen must go through to achieve everlasting peace. For humans, it takes a journey through hell to find their God." Dr. Doctor laughed. "For us, it takes a journey through hell to find . . . slumbering death."

Dr. Doctor had always been a philosopher. His ideas had got him in trouble back in the days before man. I myself always found him to be weird. But in a way, I also found his strange ideals to be a breath of fresh air. His individuality often gave me . . . peace of mind.

But not today. I was done with my treatment so I found no reason to stay any longer. I took Shelia's sleeping body back to her room. I picked her up from her wheelchair and gently placed her on her bed. I kissed her forehead.

I went back to my room and put on my clothes. As I headed toward the exit of the hospital, Dr. Doctor came running at full speed after me. He looked troubled. He stopped before me. He was panting and coughing like crazy. "Oh my goodness, Mr. Pantera!"

"What? What happened?" I said, alarmed.

Dr. Doctor stretched out his arm, his hand clenched. He was

still panting. He opened his hand. "I almost forgot to give you your reward. You've been such a good boy."

It was a lollipop. I took it and put it into my pocket.

The next few days were intense. I felt nothing but paranoia. I had no protection. Lofie could come at any moment. I stayed awake as long as I could. I kept Sephirot with me while I slept. If Lofie tried to sneak up on me, he would spook Sephirot, which would alert me. I couldn't even see Lofie if I was awake anyway, so I set mirrors up all around the apartment and kept a small one with me in my pocket at all times. This would enhance my vision, allowing me to see spiritual beings from Nameless. Shopping for bed comforters didn't even clear my head anymore. I was jumpy every time I saw a shadow. I couldn't believe it, but I even wanted Aisely around to guard me. And I began to realize that I missed him. Sephirot wasn't enough. I needed company.

I went down to Terra's home. Walked of course. She was there. Her eyes widened in surprise. "Holy Christ, speak of the devil. I was just talking on the phone about you."

"Hopefully not everything."

She pulled my arm eagerly. "Make yourself at home." She guided me to her couch. "I'll make you a cup of coffee."

"I'd rather have tea. Oh, and grape jelly in it please." She took my order and walked toward the kitchen. "And a tomato please." I looked around her apartment. It was a mess. Pizza boxes were piled up in a corner sheltering roaches. Magazines dated months ago were on the floor. Empty soda bottles littered the table. The floor was sticky from dried juice. I need to help this dear girl clean up.

"Coming right up." She came back and gave me my desirables. She got the order right. I could always count on Terra to do things for me. I patted her on her head. She sat next to me on the couch. She rested her feet on the table in front of us and turned the television on with the remote control. The news was on. At first I wasn't paying any attention. I just wanted another presence, but then there was a segment about a cult.

"We bring you tragic news. A reported two hundred and eight people have been found dead. It seems to be a mass suicide. Resources say these victims were part of an underground cult that has been launching deadly attacks throughout the city for some time now. . . ."

"What is this world coming to?" Terra said, covering her mouth in disgust. "Why in the world would they kill themselves like that?"

I pinned some of the tomato on the rim of the mug like a lemon and sipped it. It was quite yummy.

The reporter went on. "This case is being intensely investigated. There is also an issue being raised about forcing all religious leaders and cultlike organizations to consult the government about all activities and beliefs they are practicing. This would put all establishments of religion under close surveillance and would leave little room for privacy. This is surely kicking up a storm.

"Our next story is about a woman who was eaten alive by a hammerhead shark in Coney Island. Back to you, Tom."

I wondered if Helena was yanking her hair out right about now. She wanted to be the first to expose them. She was investigating for weeks to expose them and now *everybody* knew about it. At least she would be safe now. I couldn't figure out why Adilah would finish themselves off like that. Did Lofie do this? Why would he after he told me he would need to do one last attack? Did I somehow cause this to happen? I looked to Terra. She was so focused and still broken up by the news. I couldn't remember the last time I felt hurt for another person. I couldn't remember the last time I felt at all.

"Terra?"

"Mmhmm?" Terra said, still locked to the television.

"Do you think I'm a bad person?"

Terra quickly tore herself from the television and focused on me. "What makes you ask that?"

I couldn't bear looking at her. I looked forward and sipped my tea. "I just feel like . . . I made Kid's, Doughy's, and your life worse."

Terra smiled gently. She moved closer to my side. I didn't look at her and kept my focus forward at the television.

"That's just silly, Aurick. Of course you haven't made our lives worse. In fact, I think you made it better. What's wrong?"

"Sometimes I believe I bring pain to everyone I meet."

"Oh, Aurick." Terra moved to my side and put her arm around my shoulder. "You're the nicest guy I've ever met. And trust me, I've been through many to know that. Before you entered into my life, my life was a hell. I felt like I could never live on my own. I was a parasite." Terra's eyes got a bit watery. She still maintained a warm smile. "Remember that time that jerk laid a hand on me?"

"Which one?"

Terra gave a quick laugh.

"The one that gave me a black eye. You came in the middle of the night in your pajamas. You beat the crap of that bastard and hung him over the balcony by his ankles in his boxer shorts."

Terra and I laughed.

"Yes, I gave him two black eyes for touching you."

"Exactly. You spent the night with me telling me that everything was going to be okay. You even slept in the same bed with me not expecting anything in return." Terra brushed my hair back. I felt okay to look at her now. "Even after that happened to me, I still fell for the same thing over and over again. And you know what? You came back for me every time.

For the first time in my life, I feel alive. Take a look at this."
Terra held out her hand. A ring was on her ring finger. The
diamond was small but pretty.

"You're getting married?"

She nodded her head slowly.

"Seriously?"

Terra laughed. She shook her head up and down rapidly this
time.

"Oh, wow, that's just great. Who's the lucky fellow?"

"A lucky fellow that I stayed celibate for."

"And he actually waited? That's a rare find."

"Yep. An endangered species." She leaned over and kissed
my forehead. "Thank you, Aurick."

She always made me feel better. Even though it was
temporary, it helped a lot. I thanked her.

XVI

THE GOOD, THE BAD, AND THE NAMELESS

You didn't choose it, but whether you like it or not, you have great respon-
sibility on your shoulders. Show the world that you are worth it, my dear,
just as I . . . attempted. Yes, show the seraphs and the cherubs that you
were not a mistake. You are my only nonmistake.

I agreed with Terra that I would perform with the band. I felt
up to it. We were going to play at the Maya. It was a medium-
size theater. Sponsors sure do love our music. (A little hypnosis
helps.) Maya had huge paintings and profanities written on
its dome-shaped roof. Angry Kid, Terra, Doughy, and I were
backstage getting ready. Terra and Kid drank water. I was
surprised. I didn't think they ever did a show sober. Terra was
trying her best to stop doing heroin. I was quite proud of her.
Doughy was the only one who was drinking alcohol.

I sat at one of the dressing room mirrors. I spent hours
staring at myself. The bags under my eyes were darkening
more rapidly. Even though I had, it looked as if I hadn't slept
in days. More and more white hairs were growing on my head,
particularly from my temples down to the sideburns.

Kid entered my room looking for something. He pulled a can
of beer out with one hand. So much for sobriety. He brought
over a stool with the other and sat next to me. He spent minutes
looking into the right side of my face while I looked forward. I
could see his studying look from the mirror.

"I never did like you, Aurick. I'll admit that. But I know you never really liked me either." I didn't change my facial expression a bit. "Even though I don't like you, I still respect you." Wow. That was the nicest thing Angry Kid ever told me. "Since childhood my mother always told me that I was crap. That I would never amount to anything. She spat at my dreams of playing." Kid snapped the lid of his beer open. "For a time I believed her. I believed her and I wound up going to prison for armed robbery. When I got out, I was still a loser. Didn't learn my lesson. I hit rock bottom." Kidd took a few gulps of his beer. "That's when you came along. You brought back my passion for playing and kept me out of trouble. Though barely." Kidd offered me a sip of beer. I shook my head no. He sipped some more. It seemed he wanted to tell me something but couldn't spit it out. As if he was embarrassed to say something. "You've always looked like you were searching for something. As if something was missing in your life. Like you didn't belong with us. I think that's why I couldn't stand you. I felt like you believed that you were above us. But now I see you really don't belong here." Kid leaned just a bit closer to me. "You helped me find my way. I hope you find yours." Kid finished his beer. He got up. "We've been given another chance. Some music producers are going to be at the show. There're going to be crawling at our feet in no time. My life is turning around for the better. Here, I want you to have this." Kidd pulled off his rabbit-foot necklace and handed it to me.

"Your rabbit foot? You want me to have it?"

"Yeah."

"But it's your most prized possession."

"I don't need it anymore. I want you to have it." I took it and put it in my pocket. Kid crumpled up his can of beer and tossed it to the ground. "We're finally going to be gods of this world, so don't screw this up, loser!"

Wow. That was nicest thing Kid ever said to me. Probably the nicest thing he'd said to *anyone*.

I walked around backstage, anxious to get this show over with. I went inside one of the rooms. Doughy was there. He was cramming all sorts of alcohol down his throat. It looked as if he was nervous about something. "What are you worried about? Haven't you gotten used to performing?"

Doughy turned to me in surprise. "Oh, it's you, Aurick. I'm okay. I'm just a bit nervous about getting onstage."

"You're not worried about the show at all, are you? You're worried about something else."

"What do you mean?" Doughy took a shot of liquor. His trembling hands were shaking the cup slightly.

"I visited your mother, Shelia, in the hospital the other day."

"You did?"

"Yes. She asked you to kill her, didn't she?"

Doughy hopped up a bit and turned to me. "No. What are you talking about?"

I walked over and sat on a chair beside him. "Don't lie to me. I know she asked you because she asked me to kill her too."

Doughy turned forward. He looked into the mirror. He seemed to get angrier and at the same time distressed at the sight of his reflection in the mirror.

"I'm such a coward. My mother has done so much for me." Doughy rubbed his eyes to help hold back the tears. "I'm not her biological son. Even though I'm adopted, she's sacrificed everything for me. The one thing she asks me and I can't even do that." He wept with more force. I got up and rested my hand on his shoulder. He couldn't bear to look at me. He kept his attention on his palms.

"You are her son. Her legacy. Her rebirth. This is something only *you* can do. Sometimes we must do the most painful things for the ones we love. Even if that means not being able to see them ever again." I rubbed his left shoulder with my hand for reassurance. "I believe whatever you choose, Shelia will understand. You decide."

Doughy didn't say anything. It looked as if he felt a bit better. I felt better.

An hour later, it was ten minutes before showtime. The band was pumped and ready to go. I was ready to go. I sat in my room sipping tomato juice. I closed my eyes and took deep breaths. When I opened my eyelids, I fell back over my chair. Helena was in my room in front of me. Was I hallucinating? Did Angry Kid slip LSD in my tomato juice?

Helena laughed. "Surprised to see me?"

I painfully got back on my feet and quickly changed my surprised expression. I couldn't allow her to think she had caught me off guard. She was wearing a fiery-red spaghetti-strap dress. It was tight enough to show off every curve on her body. She wore red lipstick to match and makeup that made her skin look toasty.

"Helena. What on earth are you doing here?"

"I'm here to see you, silly." She seemed not to believe she needed to explain more.

"How did you know I was here?"

"I didn't. It was a slow day for journalism so I decided to check out Nameless. And what do I find? You of all people!" Helena smiled with her head tilted slightly. She looked like a character from a children's educational television show. Helena seemed excited about something other than true journalism. Which was odd. She also didn't seem to care that her work on Adilah was going down the toilet. Which was odd. Well, if she didn't care, I didn't either. She seemed to be fidgeting a bit and tapping her fingers on the table. It looked as if she were holding back from doing something. "You didn't tell me you were a big rock star. Why didn't you tell me?"

I shrugged my shoulders. "I guess I felt a bit embarrassed about it."

"Why? I think it's cool."

I don't know how, but it seemed as if Helena had anticipated this. "Come on. Therapist by day and rock star by night. That seems a bit odd to me."

"Nonsense. I could think of things stranger than that."

"Like what?"

Helena got off the table and slowly moved to me. She stood before me in voluptuous beauty. She lunged forward against my mouth, clamping on it with hers. It was so hard it hurt my front teeth. I didn't mind the pain though. She didn't either. I grabbed her waist and moved forward. I lifted her onto the table, knocking over all of the perfumes, makeups, and various knickknacks. (Knick knack, give the dog a bone!) She clamped her legs around me and gripped tightly. I lifted up her dress. Its straps loosened and dropped off her shoulders. She ripped my tie off. She was strong. So strong she seemed to overpower me. She grabbed harder and harder. Something seemed off. Helena's body wasn't giving off that natural scent I recognized. It wasn't her signature. I pulled back from her mouth. Her legs were so tightly clamped I couldn't break free.

"You bastard."

Helena smiled at her fraud. Except it wasn't Helena. Helena was just a vehicle. Lofie was the driver.

"Why are you here?"

Lofie passed his hand over his mouth, changing the lipstick from red to green. Lofie glanced at the door, causing it to lock. "I told you, I came to see Nameless perform. Now perform!"

Lofie pulled me in to him and began sucking my face off. I pulled back only for him to pull me back in. I tried to be careful with Helena's body, but Lofie wasn't leaving me any choice. I pressed Lofie back with my forearm so hard, the mirror behind him cracked. He became semidocile.

"Stop playing around, Lofie. Get out of Helena now!"

Lofie smiled. "From the looks of things, it looks like you're the one who needs to get out of Helena." Lofie lifted his chin and busted into full-fledged laughter. I pressed even harder to stop his maniacal laugh but it was in vain. "Come on. You'll get what you want and I'll get what I want."

I slapped him this time. But not with too much force. I didn't want to break a bone on Helena.

"Ouchy. Careful now, babe. You don't want to wind up being sent to the Null." Lofie continued laughing.

It hurt me so much to witness this madness. I didn't know what to do. "Shut up." I slapped Lofie across the face again, with more force this time.

A bit of blood trickled from the corner of his mouth. He touched some of it with his finger. "How could you hit the slut you love?" Lofie kicked me back. I hit the floor. I mysteriously couldn't get off my back. He got on top of me. "Domestic violence is illegal, you know." He licked the blood from the corner of his mouth. He looked as if he'd tasted a new pie. He spit it out to the side.

"Yucky. This woman tastes like crap. Women taste like crap." Lofie chomped down into the flesh of my shoulder. I opened my mouth to yell. Nothing came out. Lofie wasn't allowing sound to leave my mouth. "Now that's more like it." I struggled to push him off but he was too strong. He was less synchronized with his host so he had more access to his natural strength.

"What happened to Adilah?"

"There were way too much of them. All I needed was a few."

"Murderer."

Lofie laughed it off. "Hypocrite. You're the coldest one of us all. I at least feel sorry for my little soldiers. Almost."

"What did you promise them?"

"Every one of them had unbearable mental problems. I

promised to heal them after they served a cause. It's amazing what people would do for a prize and a cause." Lofie was a bat. Just like bats, they masquerade as birds. Like most of this world, a creature of darkness would look like a creature of light from afar. They convince humans that they want to help them and get them to serve them. Any reward is good to most, no matter where this reward comes from. "It's the living proof that anyone would do anything when they have nothing."

"So you fooled them then?"

"Fooled them?" Lofie said, smirking. "Deep down, they knew that they were getting nothing. Humans naturally believe in false hope just to make them feel better. I didn't have to do much but give them hope."

Even though I knew it was in vain, I tried with all of my being to push him off. His face grew red with anger. "Why do you fight against it? Do you not love me? Or is it that you want to keep this woman sacred? Huh!?" I didn't answer. I stopped struggling. Lofie's facial expression turned from angry to smiling. He sat straight up and leaned his head away from mine. "You go through all this trouble to defend her. You won't get anything in return you know. Just ask Adam. Oh, I forgot. You can't. He's dead, because of *her*."

"I don't want anything from anyone."

"Adam was the first human on the earth. Daddy gave Adam the sole duty of naming everything on the planet." Lofie licked his lips like a cat about to eat a helpless mouse. "Do you know how long that assignment took? Adam spent decades all alone trying to fulfill that assignment. Human beings are social animals. Can you imagine a human being spending decades in solitude? Just when Adam was on the brink of insanity, Eve came along. He was thrilled to see another person like him. He loved her dearly and wanted to give her the world. He trusted her with all of his soul. That's when Eve tempted him with the forbidden fruit. Eve was born with a loving companion while Adam had to work to get to his reward. She knew she had absolute power over him. Adam loved his Father but he loved Eve as well. Adam was faced with a moral dilemma. He didn't want to disobey his Father that created him, but he didn't want to distance himself from his only true love. Fearing he would be alone for all eternity, he took a big good bite of that juicy fruit."

"What's your point?"

"In return, Eve destroyed not only the human race, but our race also. So who is truly the liar and deceiver of the story now? Daddy created man to rule woman. And He created angels to be over man and woman just over animals. Men were here to guide them to perfection. To guide them to eternal life. To think nowadays a woman can be president." Lofie snorted. "Do you know the difference between men and women?" He waited even though he knew that I wouldn't answer. "The driving force men have for the money, the cars, the houses, the gold, the jewels, is for women. They don't care for any of that crap. The driving force women have for the money, the cars, the houses, the gold, the jewels, is for *themselves*." Lofie leaned his face toward mine. "Even with this knowledge, you still protect this daughter of Eve? This deceiver? This murderer? This daughter of genocide?"

"Lofie . . ." I dragged out my voice. "You're insane."

Lofie smiled. He got so close my lips slightly touched his. "I am disappointed in you. You of all people should know what I am saying is true. They have led you to your demise just as you led me to mine. The only difference is that you were deceived while I was not." Lofie raised me up with one arm by my collar. My feet were dangling over the floor. "I want you to be delivered with me, so I am using Helena as insurance. To think, *this* would be your weakness."

There was a knock on the door. It was Terra.

"Come on, Aurick. The show's about to start in a few minutes." She gave another loud kick.

"Tell her you'll be right out," Lofie said quietly. "Do it or I'll kill her."

"I'll be right out. I'm just putting on my makeup," I said calmly.

"Well, hurry up. The crowd is going crazy." I heard Terra's footsteps as she walked away.

Lofie flung me back against the wall. I crumpled down into a seated position. "As long as you don't mess this up, Helena will be all right. If not, she shares the same fate as her 'mother.' All you have to do is keep the audience busy with the knowledge of their . . . impending doom."

Lofie walked out of the room with conviction in his step. I didn't know what to do. If I went along with it, Helena would be safe at the cost of the entire theater. Though I didn't really care about these people, it would be disgusting for others to get in trouble because of me. I had a decision to make. My companion Helena or my loyal fans.

"You can't be serious about going out there," a voice said. I looked around. I didn't see anyone. "This brings back memories. The shoes on the other foot now, huh, Mr. Softy?" It was Aurick. He was able to take back control of his body and now he was able to communicate with me under control. He kept amazing me every time.

"I am and I will."

"You're going to get me killed. Not that you care. You can't get harmed either way."

"That's not true."

"What do you mean? You're an immortal spirit being!"

"If a Fallen's host dies, that Fallen is stuck in that body for good. The only way a Fallen can be released is if the carcass rots away to ash. Until then, the Fallen must endure the almost unbearable pain of being immobile and rotting. So in a way, I'd rather be in your shoes right now."

I got my clothes fixed up and put on my stage mask. The show must go on.

Even without drugs, performing was intoxicating on its own, and nothing was more intoxicating than being on the edge of failure. To absorb all of the glory. The crowd thundered with applause and shouting. I could smell the literal aroma of excitement. These people were going to get the show of their lives. Nameless played with all of their soul. The crowd yelled with all of their own souls. We played so loud the vibrating could be felt blocks away. Car alarms could be heard outside. Nameless was having a blast. They shifted from one side of the stage to the other. Angry Kid jumped into the sea of cheering people, which sent the crowd into a primal frenzy. He "swam" all the way back to the stage. Doughy showed no excitement at all. This false sense of security pained me. It was like the party the night the mighty *Titanic* sank to the watery depths. Like the monotonous morning before the Twin Towers had fallen. Like the evening meal before the Son of God was unjustly executed. Except this time, no one would be redeemed.

I ran over to the sound equipment and unplugged all of the instruments and the amplifiers. The only thing I left on was a single microphone. "Hey, what the hell are you doing?" Angry Kid yelled. That's the angry Angry Kid I knew. I ignored him and walked to the front of the stage.

"Everyone needs to leave through any nearest exit immediately," I yelled.

Terra rushed over to my side. "What's wrong, Aurick?" The crowd was confused. No one knew what was going on. Instead of obeying me, they stood there dumbfounded. I had to do something that convinced them that this was serious. I yanked my mask off and threw it aside. The crowd gasped. Their faces immediately grew concerned.

"The show is over! Everyone needs to leave now!" The gasps and silence turned into whispering. Kid ran over to me and snatched the microphone out of my hand.

"He's just kidding you guys," Kid said, smiling. "This guy's such a jerk." Kid forced himself to laugh to calm the crowd. It seemed to work. They started to smile. I yanked the microphone back. I told them that it wasn't a joke. Kid struggled to take the microphone away again. "Give me the mike, Aurick." I pulled back and he tried to pull back with greater force. Suddenly, there was a loud hissing noise. The crowd quieted once again. They looked around nervously. Kid and I stopped fighting and looked through the audience. A yellow mist was flowing through the crowd of people. After a few seconds, there was a lot of coughing and thumping noises. Then one by one, people started dropping to the floor. It was like flies being picked off. Then a surge of panic flooded through the theater. The people ran to the nearest exits, only to find them all locked. They tried ramming and kicking the doors open. It was in vain. Before they were dropping one by one; now they were dropping dead in groups. A vast number of them rushed to the stage. It was like a sea flooding toward us. And behind that sea was an ocean of yellow gas rushing. Terra, Doughy, Kid, and I dropped everything we had and ran for our lives. We ran backstage with the flood of fans and gas after us. The door mysteriously closed after we got through. The people were trapped at the main stage. I tried opening the door but it wouldn't budge. Yellow gas crept through the spaces of the door. I could hear cries and screams that turned to thumps and silence. Terra pulled me along. We were on the edge of death.

Gas was spewing through the rooms through the vents. Doughy suggested we run up the stairs to the roof. We ran up as fast as our bodies would allow. The door to the roof was stuck. Yellow gas crept along the stairs after us. I could smell that strawberry scent. Each of us yanked on and kicked the door. We then kicked it all at once and the door flew open. We ran along the roof. We panted and gasped for air.

"What the hell was that?" Terra said. Her eyes were dilated from fear. There was a loud pop. Everyone was still. Terra was the stillest among us. It was as if she were a standing statue. She collapsed to the ground.

"Stop asking questions," a man with a bunny mask said. He was holding a black instrument of death in his hand. It was smoking and pointing at me. Terra stared up to the sky motionless. Doughy was so shocked that he was motionless as well. Angry ran to Terra's side. He shook her over and over. He slapped her across the face a couple of times to wake her, but it didn't work. He grabbed Terra's hand. He rubbed her engagement ring. He began to weep. "No one move." Kid looked up at the masked man. He screamed at the top of his lungs and rushed toward him. I called for Kid to stop. The man fired a couple of shots but he was too scared to aim properly. Kid tackled him to the ground, sending his mask flying off. Kid swung with everything he had. Then came another pop. The man and Kid were still as stone. Kid keeled over to the side onto the roof. He rolled around and moaned in pain.

I ran toward the grounded man, but he got up too quickly and got the draw on me. "I said to stay back!" He fired, hitting me in the shoulder, stopping me in my tracks. I hardly felt anything.

I looked into his face. It was Brother Dex. He looked as frightened as we were. "You don't have to do this, Dex. You're just being tricked by your leader." He seemed to be surprised that I knew he was being led by someone else. Doughy was looking over the ledge trying to find a safe way down. I needed to at least buy him time to get to safety. "Yes. I know about your leader. She is a fraud that will only bring despair."

"Don't disrespect my God!"

Doughy stumbled over the ledge. He didn't hit the pavement because I could hear him crying. He must've been holding on to the ledge.

"She's only using you for her own purposes. After she is done using you, she will forsake you."

"You're a blasphemer. Adilah has already shown us miracles. She will heal me."

"She has lied to you. She's already annihilated the rest of Adilah. What do you think she will do with you after you've outlived your usefulness?"

Dex seemed confused. He looked all around. He didn't know what to do. "Adilah said I was special. That I was different from the others. That I had the most faith." He looked somewhat disappointed. His disappointment turned to an anger. "Faith has got me here and faith will get me out. There's nothing you can say to trick me." He pointed the gun at me with stern conviction. "You've only brought this onto yourself."

There was a loud thump. Dex looked dazed. He wobbled and fell to the ground. Behind him was Helena. Except it wasn't Helena. It was Lofie, saving *me*. He took away Dex's weapon. Lofie had a blank expression.

"Thank you, Lofie." I sighed in relief.

At that moment, Lofie aimed the gun at me. Lofie looked angrier than I had ever before seen him. "You are absolutely unbelievable." Lofie walked slowly up to me. I didn't move. All throughout human time, Lofie's mind had been unstable. He was the only being in history, including Father, that I could never predict. I stood absolutely still, staring into his eyes. "I told you not to get in the way of this and you still did. All for the likes of these swine. You tossed away your only chance of freedom." Lofie walked over to me. He put the gun into my mouth. Lofie started crying. "I didn't want to have to do this to you, but you left me no choice. I wanted you to be rescued along with me. You'd rather help *them* than be with me. I see now you never truly loved me. *Never.*" Lofie pulled the gun out of my mouth and replaced it with his tongue. He then kissed me gently with his lips. "You'll regret not loving me." He put the gun to his own head. Helena's head. A loud bang rang out. Except it wasn't from Lofie's gun. Lofie collapsed to the ground. Dex was standing a few feet away holding another weapon. He then pointed it at me. Suddenly, Lofie got up and ran with all his might and punched a bloody, chunky hole through Dex. Dex fell to the roof. Dead this time. Lofie fell along with him.

Lofie had killed him! For *my* sake. I ran over, almost tumbling, to Lofie's side. Lofie was on his back.

"Why did you do it? Why?!"

He was in a daze. He said nothing.

"I thought you wanted me to feel pain. Why did you do this for my sake? Answer me!" I lifted his head up.

"You're my honey bun. I need to protect my honey bun. I couldn't let a mere man take you away from me." Lofie smiled.

"Why are you smiling? This is no laughing matter. Look at you, buddy. You're hurt."

"That's the smile I know and love." I didn't realize I was smiling. I felt my face. "I haven't seen that smile in thousands of years. Since back when everything was all right. To see that smile, it was worth it."

Lofie was one of the last angels born. The first person he ever saw was me. Ever since that day he was my constant shadow like a newly hatched chick and its mother. Just like a kid brother, he wanted to be just like me. He followed everything I did. That always bugged me so I used to always tell him to get lost, but he shrugged it off and continued anyway. Others found it unhealthy and counseled him for it, but he didn't listen. The only person he listened to in those days was me. And that's what brought him his demise. The day I turned into a meteor, he was heartbroken. He turned himself into a meteor just to show that he loved me. To him, I was his brother. His lover. His mother. His God. I didn't cry. I was too used to this. My tears dried up long ago. My poor little brother.

The air twisted all around us. I looked up to see an obnoxious old owl. The refraction from Aurick's tears allowed me to see them. Morning Owl, Condor, and a couple others were standing over us. Condor presented himself as a soldier in golden armor with broad silver wings. What a show-off jerk.

Lofie gave a light laugh at the sight of them. I asked them to step back. Morning Owl nodded his head and they all stepped back a few feet.

"Oh, looky here. Daddy's little fairies have arrived." Lofie coughed in pain, looking to Morning Owl.

"Lofie. You have directly killed a human being. We're taking you to trial and then to the Null," Morning Owl said.

Lofie switched his eyes back to me. "Good-bye, baby. I'm going on a sweet vacation. The trip will be bearable if you are with me, you know. Want to come with me?"

"I have unfinished business," I said.

Lofie smiled. "Can't blame an old fool in love for trying." I smiled. Lofie closed his eyes, unconscious. Owl and his unit were expressionless. Did they feel happy or saddened by Lofie's condition? How will they feel when *I* bite the cold steel of punishment?

I leaned my head over and kissed Lofie's forehead. "Good-bye, brother."

Owl looked over and nodded to his unit. They pulled Lofie out of Helena and disappeared with him.

"Is the Null a painful place?" I said.

"I do not know. Only our Lord knows," Owl said.

I snorted. "What about you? I think you know a lot about what has gone down tonight. You were here the whole time watching, weren't you? You could've stopped this from going down."

"It was not my place to intervene."

"You put your pride before other people's lives?"

"I think before I act. That is the difference between us stars and you meteors. That's what got you here."

"No. It is *thinking* that got us here."

Owl silently looked over me. He eventually faded away.

I sat there at Helena's side. I didn't know what to do. I examined her wound closely. And what do I find? I found that the bullet that Dex shot off barely grazed Helena's side, causing a minor scratch. Unbelievable. Lofie was so dramatic.

I ran over to Kid. He was unconscious but still breathing. I took off his rabbit's foot necklace and put it around his neck. I heard cries for help. I almost forgot that Doughy was hanging from the ledge of the roof. I ran over there and helped him up. After he caught his breath, he ran over to Terra. After a few moments, I heard him wail, like a wolf howling to the moon for help.

ΠAMELESS ALLEGIAΠCE

I spent the night with Helena at the hospital. She was fine until hours later, when she experienced uncontrollable seizures. The doctors had no idea what was going on, and none of their medicines or machinery worked for long. Every time Helena stabilized, her body would again explode into powerful fits of tremors. That's when Dr. Doctor came along with that sly curved smile, as usual. Soon after being treated by Dr. Doctor, Helena was in peace. I asked him what was wrong with her. He told me he needed to examine her more. He shooed me and the other doctors and nurses away so he could work in peace. I trusted him. Dr. Doctor's abilities would allow him to scan Helena's deficiencies more accurately than any human or machine could.

I visited Kid. Doughy was with him. We didn't say a word. Kid, fast asleep, was in terrible shape. They'd stabilized him, but the gunshot wound had hit his spine. The doctors said that he might never walk again. I unbuttoned the top buttons on my shirt and loosened my tie.

Dr. Doctor called me back in the room with Helena. "She has a brain tumor. It seems to be getting bigger at an abnormal speed."

"Abnormal? What could be the cause?"

"I don't know. What happened to her tonight?" I thought of everything that had happened. There was so much pain and fear it was difficult to sort through the madness.

"Helena was taken control of by Lofie."

Dr. Doctor shook his head up and down as if he was absolutely sure what the problem was. "When a spirit being takes control of a host, all of the host's body functions at an accelerated rate. Like regenerating lost tissue, growing fingernails, growing hair, growing new teeth, etc., all gets a boost of speed."

"Then shouldn't Helena be able to heal faster?"

"Not necessarily. A host's health problems can also be accelerated and even shorten the person's life span itself."

"Since you know the problem now, fix her."

"That may be extremely difficult."

"Why?"

"The tumor is wedged severely close to vital points of her brain. Not only that, but peculiarly, more tumors seem to be sprouting around. I have never seen something like this before. Quite frankly, I don't think she will live long."

My heart sank. I felt sick. In vertigo. Before I realized it, I was biting a hole through the inside of my lower lip. I could taste the blood.

"I am sorry, Aurick." It was hard to believe him with that unchanging grin on his face.

I sat down beside Helena. I brushed the hair away from her beautiful face. I brushed along her cheek and neck with my hand.

"There is still one thing I can do for her." My heart leaped. I quickly turned to him. "It's the best medicine that anyone could ever offer."

"What? What is it?"

"Death."

I swallowed hard and thought maybe I misheard with this body's failing hearing. "What?"

"Death." Dr. Doctor's smile didn't change a bit in speaking the words that countered it. "She would drift away in a never-ending peace."

"No thank you."

"Think about it. She would never feel pain ever again. No more pain, no more fear, no more fighting, no more suffering, no more—"

"Enough."

"That's such a shame. It looks like she won't take the final step toward peace . . . like your other dear friend Shelia has."

I bit another hole in the inside of my lip. This time I felt the pain. I didn't care. Before I knew it, my arm was already pressed up against Dr. Doctor's throat. He stayed calm.

"What did you do to her?" He didn't say anything so I pressed harder. His smile made it seem as if it had no effect.

"Shelia was in pain. She was having thoughts of committing suicide so I gave her a gentle push," Dr. Doctor said calmly.

"You bastard. You killed her."

Doctor started laughing in a casual way. Almost as if I'd told him a knock-knock joke. "You're such a hypocrite. I knew what you were thinking. You wanted to euthanize her that day Shelia asked you. You were tempted. The only reason you didn't go through with it was not because you felt it was wrong, but you were scared and wanted as much time as possible with her. Such a display of selfishness is disgusting."

I lifted my hand. I wanted to hit him with all of my force. He took Shelia away from me. That poor, sweet old woman. One of the best people in the universe and he took her away.

"You know it's true. That's why you're so boiled up right now." Dr. Doctor laughed again. "How ludicrous, a grand demon such as yourself resorting to violence. The humans' hot temper has rubbed off on you."

"You're part of Adilah, aren't you? That's how you knew everything about Vex. You even persuaded that psycho into harming Helena when she came here. You killed Vex before she could leak any information to Helena when she was interrogating her."

"Well, I didn't kill her. Don't be silly. One of my human nurses did it for me."

"You think this is a game? You think this is funny?"

"You don't want to harm me, Mr. Pantera. I *promise* you that you don't want to harm me."

I balled my hand into a tight fist. Just when I decided, there was a gust of wind. I looked through a window behind Dr. Doctor. Aisely was standing behind me. I let Dr. Doctor go.

"Don't think even for a second you're getting a lollipop from me."

Aisely told me to come with him. I asked why but he wouldn't tell me. He didn't say a word. This was tremendously odd. This was serious. He remained ahead of me. He was slow enough to follow around corners and into the elevator. An old woman in a wheelchair asked me to push the floor she wanted. I did so. Memories of Shelia surfaced. She didn't deserve to die like that. With no one to say good-bye. With no one to remember her. Alone. No one does. Death isn't natural whether it's due to an accident, aging, or deliberate intention. Because it's all of those three in one. No. Death isn't natural.

It was snowing, for the first time of the year. The streets were filled with people getting their last-minute Christmas shopping done. I kept bumping into people, knocking over their bags and boxes. I didn't care. My thoughts were still on Helena. Guilt washed away all concern for me or others. I felt responsible.

Aisely and I walked for hours. We left the city and entered the suburbs. "Where on earth are we going?"

Aisely didn't answer. Today must've been Shut-Up Aisely Day. This could be my favorite holiday.

He brought me to a bone-white mansion. We walked to the front gate. It was golden and massive with the letters *J* and *A* on the front. There were no cameras. The building itself was three floors high. The gate was open and we walked through.

Massive bushes were sculpted in amazing detail to resemble rabbits in different poses, positions, and actions. The snow that fell on them made them even more beautiful. I wanted to have a closer look. I walked over to one. A man was trimming some of the leaves. He was in his midfifties, wearing a green-and-gray gardening outfit. He had pale skin with all-white hair. He didn't seem to mind the cold.

"Are you responsible for these beauties?"

He turned around. He had tired-looking eyes. He put on a bright, friendly smile. "Oh, no, I simply do maintenance for the master."

"Wow, these are really beautiful."

He smiled even more. "I know. The master is quite fond of rabbits. Shall I show you to him?"

"Yes. That would be nice."

"Come this way." His smile made me feel welcome.

We got closer to the front. I noticed children playing around in the yard, laughing and having fun. Rabbits were running around everywhere. One child chased one toward us. He fell over and scraped his knee. The gardener went to the young boy and knelt before him. He helped him up. The boy was crying. "It's all right. Don't cry," the gardener said with a warm smile. The boy stopped crying immediately. "Come on. Let's clean that wound." We went inside.

The inside was equally as beautiful as the outside. There were large paintings of rabbits, some realistically detailed while others were more abstract. If the art weren't so beautiful, I would have started to think the master was a little obsessed. We went to the staircase. At the top of the first case, there was a massive painting. It was of a woman. A beautiful woman smiling. We continued up the stairs. Each few steps showcased another picture of that same woman on the wall.

"Can you wait here a sec?"

The man cleaned the boy's wound in the bathroom. He dabbed some alcohol on the wound with tissue. The boy cried from the burning sting. "Now, now, hush. Sometimes you have to hurt yourself more to heal the wound." The man's words comforted the boy once more. After thoroughly cleaning and dressing the wound, he sent the boy back down the stairs. "Careful not to fall down the stairs." The boy didn't listen and ran anyway.

"Children will be children," I said.

"Yes, yes, I know. It's only when they hurt themselves severely that they truly grow up."

"Most of the time."

We went to a big door. It was painted pink. The big pink door. It had a golden doorknob. The doorknob had the word TRAITOR on it. We went inside. The room was dark. Clocks were on every wall in the room. Lit candles were on a long dining table at the center, giving the room a shadowy texture. Bibles were placed at every single seating section. No one was in the depressing room but Aisely, me, and the gardener.

"I thought you said the master was in here."

The gardener went to the other end of the dining table. The short end. "He is here," the gardener said with a colorless tone. "You have to look closer. Look beyond. Beyond deception." The gardener's smile turned expressionless. I looked closer. It was him. The gardener was the master. I didn't know if the kindness he'd showed was the gardener or him the whole time.

"Sit."

His voice was plain, clean, and cut. The way he spoke made me not want to complain or ask questions. I sat across from him. Aisely sat next to me.

"You've done a great service for me, Aurick. Or should I say Aurick *Two*." I couldn't tell if he wanted to crack a joke or was asking a question. Aisely seemed to enjoy the remark as he held back laughter. "I am the master of this ranch."

"I haven't done anything for you."

"You haven't? But Aisely tells me you helped destroy the theater last night."

"Aurick Two is quite shy," Aisely said. "He's too modest to take any credit. Ain't that right, Aurick?" I couldn't believe Aisely was a part of Adilah. This is why he brought me here. To see the head honcho. The master stared a hole into Aisely that told him that he was a moron. Aisely looked down in embarrassment.

"Whatever may be the case, you are now a part of this."

"I am not a part of this and I don't *want* to be a part of this."

There was a long silence in the room. The candles flickered. The master faded and reappeared just as fast.

"Yes, you do," the master said in a smooth, plain voice. As if he knew the future for sure. I was enthralled to listen more. "What if I told you we had another chance? What if I told you meteors can become stars once more? What if I told you we could *restart*?" This was Lofie's rant.

"I would tell you that would be impossible. I would tell you that you're crazy."

The master didn't say anything. Aisely paid full attention, which was strange. His focus made me focus.

"As you know, we spirit beings have all sorts of abilities. We have had billions of years to develop them just as God developed His own abilities. What if I told you one of us meteors has finally developed an ability that can actually restart our lives? What if I told you one of us had the ability to erase our sins?"

The master and I stared into each other's eyes, lost in our own world, a world that not even Father was able to enter.

"Go on."

"A few of us have the ability to see into the future. Impressive." He rolled his eyes. "But useless if an all-powerful being wants you dead. All these years we've been trying to figure out a way to change the future. This was foolish and we were fools."

"You got that right."

"Our eyes were so focused on the future, we didn't realize that the past was the most important." My eyes were entranced. He leaned forward slightly. "We have found someone who can actually pass through time itself."

Ridiculous. "That seems far-fetched. What proof do you have that this person's ability is reliable?"

"You and Aisely have the proof."

"What do you mean?"

"Remember the time we were trying to save humans throughout the city from dying?" Aisely said.

"Yes. People died anyway."

"Yes, but they died in a different way. Some didn't die at all while others did. You changed their fate. Even if it was slightly."

"So?"

"This shows it *is* possible to change events in time," Aisely said, turning to me in excitement and hitting his knee on the table. "We changed their fate. We can change ours."

"Once a meteor crashes down to earth, they can never rise to the stars again," the master said, leaning on his folded hands. "But there is one thing we *can* do." The master unfolded his hands. "We can stop ourselves from ever falling in the first place."

Aurick's heartbeat quickened. It was hard to breathe. I didn't know it was because of the side effects of the joining or the effects of what the master said. This all sounded so . . .

"If you are so sure of this theory, why haven't you done so yourself already?"

The master sat upright in his chair. "For a long time Aisely knew of this person's abilities. He goes by the name of Zero. He did not realize Zero's potential and squandered it on trivial tasks such as helping humans." Aisely immediately put his head down in shame again. "We recruited Zero. He has spent time practicing the big jump. I have spent the last few months trying to find more meteors who I felt deserved to be saved, those who I felt would be great leaders."

"So you made them join that organization Adilah?"

"Yes."

"For?"

"We needed to get the winged ones off our backs. We needed distractions to stay under the radar. And some flies still hold on to their feelings to serve their God. I wanted to make sure everyone cut those ties to Him so that no one would bail out or compromise our goals. I wanted to make sure everyone was ready."

"What happened to all of them?"

"They were"—he paused for a great number of seconds—"unsuitable for great responsibility."

"So you kicked them out?"

"Yes. They are *somewhere* where they can't reveal my plans for the future. The only loyal ones that remain are Zero, Lofie, and I."

He was hiding something from me. Why would these Fallen give up on this opportunity for another chance?

"Aisely wasn't with you?"

"We let him join later. Just when everything was almost set up to perfection, Zero fled."

"Why?"

"I do not know for certain. He said that he felt that we shouldn't go against God. That we should accept the consequences of our actions. And that this defiance would make our punishment even more severe."

"Where is he?"

"We've spent months looking for him to no avail. Then Aisely came along. Aisely had been using Zero's associate's precognition abilities for his . . . heroics. Aisely had been very close to Zero and his associate."

"Associate?"

"He is someone who has been spending time with Zero.

They have been helping each other with their abilities. That is where you come in, Aurick. Aisely knows exactly where Zero's associate is. You must go with Aisely and find this associate. They've spent years together so he must know where Zero is hiding. There's a chance Zero told his associate to keep his mouth shut, so it may be up to you to rip it open."

"I won't be of any use then. I'm trapped in this body. I'm too weak to force anyone to do anything at anytime." The master smiled and laughed softly. "Why don't you do it?"

"I am also trapped inside this body. But you have an ability that I do not. Aisely told me of your mind-reading capabilities. Use that to your advantage." The master stared a hole into me. It felt as if gravity were pulling me closer to him. "Are you ready to forsake our Father completely like He has forsaken us?"

In all of my time, no one had ever asked me that question. I was persecuted and prosecuted for betraying Father, but I never actually admitted that I had. I never *felt* as if I did either.

I didn't know what to do. "This seems impossible to me. This is all too . . . unreal."

At that moment, a young boy burst open the door. He ran to the master crying. The master turned his chair to face the little boy. His forehead was bleeding. The boy stood before the master. The master had a calm smile and rubbed the boy's shoulder. "I told you to be careful."

The master turned and looked to me. "Everything is possible when you lose everything." He turned and rubbed the wound on the boy's forehead. The wound and the blood vanished. He smiled and patted the boy's head and told him to go. The boy smiled in return and ran out.

"I hear that you are quite fond of a woman named Helena Way. She had been getting too close to us and was messing up our goals. Because of her meddling we lost a few Fallen. I hear she is in the hospital right now because of Lofie."

"So what about her?"

The master smiled softly again. He leaned back and looked up to the ceiling. "I know a thing or two about love. I know that a person would attempt impossible things for it. I know that people use love as a crutch for an excuse for the greater good." He focused on me again. "Did you see the way I healed that boy? If you do this favor for me, I will heal Ms. Way just as easily as I healed that boy. Not that I would have to. If we stopped ourselves from ever falling, Helena most likely wouldn't have gotten into that situation. You can also come along on our journey. If we fail, you will still have Ms. Way to have for yourself. You have nothing to lose except your justice. Do you accept my offer?"

We left the mansion. The master offered to fly us home by the helicopter he owned, but I declined. I told Aisely to meet me at my home some other time. He amazingly agreed and didn't complain, which was a blessing. He was just ecstatic. I wanted to use the long walk home to meditate on what had just occurred. I thought about everything the master had told me. Even though most of it made sense, I still felt that something was . . . missing. Even so, I felt excited. I wanted to know if this would actually work. She was my responsibility.

XVIII

†HE ÎNNOCEN† AND
†HE NAMELESS

I fixed Sephirot the last meal that I might ever I cook for him, beef stew and steamed snails. He absolutely loved it. I sat at the table next to Sephirot watching him eat. I petted his body. I wanted a good final feel of his warm fur. He purred and vibrated in pleasure. He's still nice and plump. I still remember when I first met Sephirot on that cold night on the roof when he was a scrawny weakling. He was nothing but a forgotten soul left behind in the dirty slums of the world. Forgotten like me.

Speaking of forgotten souls, Aurick hadn't said anything for a while. I wondered if he was secretly planning something. Whatever might be the case, I had peace of mind as I played with Sephirot.

Just when I was enjoying my time, destruction took my peace away. The noise was coming from upstairs. I tried to ignore it but the screams of a young, desperate, defenseless woman irresistibly beckoned me. Micky and Jamie trouble again. Sephirot captured the string I was dangling when I was distracted by the noise. I was angry now. I stomped up the stairs and over to Jamie's apartment door. The yelling got louder. I heard a slap. I knocked on the door. Not a regular knock, but the type of knock policemen use on strangers' doors. The yelling ceased. Everything eventually went quiet. I could hear the occasional sniffling and footstep. I knocked hard again. "Jamie, open up. I know you're in there."

"I can't come to the door right now, Aurick," Jamie said, sounding as if she was trying to stop herself from crying.

"Then what's all that noise in there?" There was a long silence.

"It's the TV. Everything's fine. Really."

I rolled my eyes. I kicked the door open. Micky was there with Jamie in the living room. Micky had a belt in his hand and was wearing only underwear. He had his arm around Jamie. I could tell Micky was drunk. I could smell his alcoholic stench. Jamie looked petrified. I stood there with a blank expression. Micky knew what was coming to him. He pulled out a knife. I rolled my eyes. I walked up to him. He swung the knife at me. I slapped him down. This made him angrier. He swung with more ferocity but I slapped him again. I knocked the knife away and grabbed hold of his neck in an armlock.

I dragged Micky to Jamie's bedroom and toward the window. Over he went out the window. The only thing that was keeping him from his demise was my grip. A grip that could give out at any moment. I dangled Micky outside Jamie's window by his ankle. "Aurick stop! You're going to kill him!" Jamie said, crying as she pulled my arm. He cried for mercy. While I was enjoying the scene, Micky's ankle slipped from my grasp. I caught him by his shoe. That was a close call. It would've been a shame to be sent to the Null without seeing things through. I decided that was enough, so I sent him home in his underwear crying.

I spent the next few hours consoling Jamie. She told me everything that had happened. Micky had asked Jamie to marry him but she had refused. He had a few drinks too many, which led to the situation we were in just now. Jamie kept crying. Every time it seemed I had helped her to feel better, she would break down and cry again. I held her in my arms in an older-brother kind of way. I remembered having to do this with

Lofie after someone would hurt his feelings and he would come over crying to me. Like him, I told Jamie to toughen up. To be independent. "Didn't I tell you to stay away from pigs like that? Didn't I tell you to stay away from *that* pig?"

Jamie suddenly looked appalled. I didn't know why. I thought I was giving exceptional advice.

"Oh, please. You are such a hypocrite." Jamie tugged free from me. "I've seen what kind of women you bring inside and out of your apartment." After Aurick took back his body, he went on a binge of debauchery. Any woman that looked his way, he seduced her. Well, I shouldn't say *he* did, but his money and material possessions did. "All this month you've went through them like toilet paper, so don't act so high-and-mighty." She crossed her arms in a fit of anger.

"That wasn't my fault." My rep that I had worked on for so long was destroyed by that idiot.

Jamie looked at me as if I were stupid and there was nothing I could say. "Not your fault? How in the world isn't it your fault?"

I wasn't sure what to say. What could I tell her? That I'm really a demon taking residence in a human's body and the human somehow took back control and had sex with countless women?

"What I meant was, I don't want you to be like me. I just care about you, that's all."

Jamie stepped close to me. "If you care about me so much, kiss me."

"What?"

"If you truly meant what you said, kiss me."

"No, Jamie. I don't like you like that. You're like a—" Suddenly, my body jerked forward and kissed Jamie. My arms clamped Jamie's body and squeezed her against mine. My body wasn't mine anymore. It was Aurick's again. He was doing this on purpose. To mess with my mind and relationship with her. She was surprised at first but then gave in. I meant what I said, but I didn't like Jamie like this. It took a bit of effort but I finally released myself from Aurick's control and pulled free of Jamie. Jamie went forward and grabbed me again. I pulled free again. "Stop it, Jamie! You're just a child. A confused child."

"It looks like you're the only one confused here. I know what I want." She tried locking lips with me again but I pulled back again.

"Good-bye, Jamie."

"Where are you going?"

"I'm taking a shower."

"Take a shower with me."

"Stop it, Jamie."

I went back to my apartment but I stopped at the door. Jamie would be planning to pay me an unannounced visit later. I knew I couldn't stop Aurick from taking advantage so I decided to visit Helena and Angry Kid at St. Peter's. I hoped that they were still breathing.

St. Peter's was busy as usual. Death is always busy. I bought some green dandelions for Helena. Shelia would've loved them.

I walked into Helena's room. I dropped the flowers to the floor. Helena wasn't there. Her bed was empty. I felt naked. What had happened to her? Did she move to another room? Was she . . . alive? I ran up to a nearby nurse. I frightened her but I didn't care. I asked her where Helena Way was. The nurse told me that she had mysteriously felt better. They had tried to convince her to stay for observation, but she left. The nurse said that Helena looked upset. I was relieved. I thanked and hugged the nurse. The nurse was confused but she went along with it.

I went to Kid's room. He was by himself. He lay on the bed motionless but awake. His rabbit foot was lying on the counter near him. It was dirty. He usually kept it clean as if his life depended on it. He was watching television. It didn't look as if he was actually watching the show though. It looked as if he was *staring* at the television. Like when a person hears someone but doesn't actually *listen*. I knocked on the already open door to announce that I was there. It didn't seem to move Kid a bit. It looked as if he were in another world. I went to Kid's side. "How are you holding up?" Kid didn't answer. His eyes were on the television. It was a show about some superhero. Kid was twirling something in his hand. It was a ring. Terra's engagement ring.

"Moth Man was the most powerful being in the universe. He came down to earth to save the world. Best job in the world. He had the cars, the money, the jewels, the adoring fans, the fame and glory. He was a god. And you know what?" Kid waited a while as if he was expecting me to answer. "Answer me!" Kid said, yelling so loud everyone could hear him outside.

"I don't know, Kid. I don't watch this show," I said, closing the door.

"He gave it all up just to be with the woman he loved. Isn't that beautiful?"

"Why don't you change the channel? There must be something less corny on."

"I would, Aurick. I really would. But if I were to switch the channel, it would be a breaking-news broadcast of the little incident at the concert. This is one of the only channels left untouched by pain."

I'd become too desensitized to be bothered by these kinds of tragedies. Similarly to what reporters become when working in their field for so long. Such as Helena. We'd seen it all. We were alike. I don't know if that made us stronger or weaker.

"I'm sorry about what happened to Terra."

"Don't give me that crap! I heard what that murdering bastard said. He said that *you* brought this on yourself. You brought this down on all of us."

"Listen to yourself, Kid. You believe the word of a psychotic terrorist?"

Angry Kid was silent. It felt as if the silence were crushing me under its weight.

"Moth Man and I have things in common. I was going to give up everything for her. Drinking, smoking, shooting dope, no more, all for her. The only difference is that when Moth Man gave up everything, he lived with the woman he loved happily ever after, while I lost everything and received nothing at all in return." Kid grabbed the rabbit foot off the counter. "Well, where the hell is my happy ending?!" Kid chucked the rabbit foot at me. I caught it before it hit my face. Kid gave a slight laugh. "Women sure could make a fellow do anything for them."

I left the room. Kid's mind was driven to madness. There was nothing I could say or do. I called Helena's apartment but there was no answer. Just my luck. Terra is dead, Angry Kid is hospitalized, and Helena is missing.

I wondered how Doughy was doing. I walked to his apartment. It took about three hours. His door was halfway open. Music was blasting through the halls. I thought maybe something was wrong. I went through the door softly and crept through the apartment, trying not to make any noise. I checked through his room and bathroom. No one was there. I was getting a headache so I turned off the blasting music. I wanted to drink some tomato juice, so I went to the kitchen to see if there was any in the refrigerator. Doughy was on the kitchen floor passed out. He was sitting down with his head against the counter with a bottle of wine in his hand. I opened up the fridge. I was relieved to see Doughy had enough taste to store tomato juice. I pulled out the bottle of V8 juice, opened it, and put it to my lips.

"Hey, Aurick." I dropped the glass. The juice traveled over the tiles and reached Doughy's jeans. "Don't worry about the spill." He sounded drunk. "My maid will clean it up eventually." He was definitely drunk.

I got a broom and swept the glass up. The broom got wet. I hate it when the broom gets wet. Doughy didn't bother to get up. I ignored him. I switched to a mop and started cleaning up the juice. "Get up, Doughy. You're in the way."

Doughy ignored me and took a gulp of wine. "Look, Aurick. I moved up to wine. Aren't I classy?" He started laughing.

"Come on, Doughy. Let's get you cleaned up."

He didn't move an inch. He took another drink of the wine. I started pulling it away and he pulled it back. We struggled for a few seconds until it smashed to pieces on the counter behind him. Wine flew all over Doughy. He didn't care.

"Aw, look what you did. The maid's going to get pissed off when she sees this mess." A small bottle fell out of Doughy's pocket. I picked it up. "Hey, that's mine," Doughy said lazily. The bottle said ProteX. Doughy takes these for his chronic depression. The bottle was empty.

"How many did you take?"

Doughy drunkenly looked up at me. His head was wobbly. "Take what?"

"ProteX. How many pills of ProteX did you take?"

Doughy looked down. He looked at his fingers. He picked up his hands and showed me all of his fingers. "This much."

"Come on. Get up."

Doughy didn't obey me so I yanked him up to his feet. He was so dizzy he fell back down. I dragged him through the apartment leaving a trail of glass, wine, and vegetable juice. I dragged him all the way to the bathroom and put him in the tub. I turned on the shower. The cold water seemed to sober Doughy up. He sat up.

"Why did you do this?" He rubbed his face and smoothed out his hair. He was holding back tears. "It's not fair, man. I let my mom die like that. She died in pain. She asked me one simple thing and I couldn't do it. I was such a coward and I couldn't do it. She was fast asleep and I had the pillow in my hand. I had all the time in the world but I couldn't do it. The next day I come back and I find her dead." He couldn't hold back the levees anymore and a flood of tears broke loose. "Terra's dead. I loved her. More than a friend. I always wanted to ask her out, but I was scared that she would reject me. I passed the opportunity just like the way I let her get shot. I stood there frozen. I saw that masked freak coming with the gun but I stood there helpless, just like with my mom. Kid's never going to walk again. My career's finished. Everything went to hell. I just want to die!"

I plugged the drain and let the water rise. Doug was too drunk to notice. The water almost went all the way up the rim. I turned the shower off. Doug tried to get up but I forced him back down. He tried again but again I forced him back down. He swung a fist at me but I dunked him underwater. Water splashed all over the place, drenching my beautiful suit and flooding the bathroom floor. Doughy clawed at my hands, cutting them. After a minute passed, Doughy was motionless. Just as the last air bubbles went to the surface, I lifted his head up for air. Doug jerked around and gasped for air. He still didn't have any strength to move so he lay there motionless. I sat on the floor next to the tub.

"You think you have it bad, Doughy? Let me tell you something. You don't even know the meaning of bad. I know what bad is. At least you have a second chance. At least you have a chance at happiness. True happiness. I on the other hand haven't seen sunlight for years. Never will again. I've seen countless nations destroyed. I've seen women raped and beaten by soldiers. I've seen babies bathed in flame for gods that didn't even exist. I've seen armies mutilate defenseless villagers and decorate the land with their carcasses like Christmas ornaments. I've seen lives

thrown away for disillusioned countries and their ridiculous beliefs. You don't know how many human friends I've seen either
murdered or stolen away from me. I don't even know the number. I've had one-third of my brothers die in one day. Now most
of them are either murdering psychopaths or lost wanderers.
One-third of my brothers died and you know what?"

"What?"

"No one cried. In the entire universe, no one cried for us. Not
even once. I figured that if no one cried for me, I wouldn't cry
either. Or for anyone else. Devils don't deserve to cry."

"You sound like you aren't human or something. Are you an
alien?"

"Yeah. You could say I'm an alien." I splashed water on his
face.

"Hey, Aurick. If I fall asleep, I'll die."

"So?"

"I don't want to die anymore. Can you stay with me so I
won't fall asleep?"

I smiled. "Yes. I'll stay with you."

"Thanks, Aurick. You're my best friend." Doughy kept
nodding off so I had to keep slapping him over and over to keep
him awake. "I forgot to tell you something, Aurick."

"What?"

"I want to tell you but I forgot what it was." How annoying.
"All I can remember is that it involved some lady named Helena
Way. I don't even know how she got my number or knew
who I even was to begin with." Helena's investigation and
tracking skills were sharp. Doughy spent a few minutes trying
to remember to no avail. I "opened" his mind up to the truth.
"Oh, I remember! She said she had been trying to reach you
today but you didn't answer. She wanted to meet you at the
psychiatric center for her appointment tomorrow." I wasn't sure
why Helena wanted to meet me tomorrow. We didn't have an

appointment tomorrow. "I didn't know you needed psychiatric help, Aurick. I think I may see one of those brain doctors."

It was just a few days before Christmas. I was down. Fallen get really depressed during this time of year. Just the sight of Christmas trees and presents angers us. Most of us hide underground until New Year's Eve. That's the time of year that Fallen party and even blend in with humans. Demon and human are one and the same on that day. I don't know why they like it so much.

I was in my office waiting for Helena. Every second I looked at the watches on my wrists. I checked both of them in case one was a little off. I counted the number of times the skinny hand touched twelve on the clock. I had the jitters.

"Why are you obsessed with this lady?" Aurick was awake and about.

"Quiet, Aurick. I am trying to concentrate."

"Let me guess. You're thinking about what you're going to say to her when she gets here. Aren't you? A demon in love. How cute!"

"I'm thinking about the punishment you are going to receive if you force me onto Helena like you did Jamie. Don't ever do that again!"

"Was that me or was it really you?"

"It was you! A flea-bitten pig like you doesn't have any class whatsoever."

"I can't believe a demon is lecturing me on how to treat a lady. You're the only bad guy around here. You said it yourself. God is going to annihilate you things, and us humans are going to live. I might as well put you to use before you die and enjoy the ride."

"You're in dangerous territory. There's still a limit on forgiveness from God, you know. If you're not careful, you'll be just as damned as I am."

"I'll take the risk. I'm having the time of my life! For the first time in my miserable life, I'm on the level of gods such as yourself."

Footsteps could be heard from the hall. They got louder as they came closer. They were Helena's footsteps. I recognized her pattern of walking. "Just stay out of my way."

The door opened. I was correct. It was Helena. "Hello."

"Hello, Aurick." She wore a smile that could brighten the room by itself if I turned off the light switch. "I need you to come with me."

This unexpected request made me nervous. I asked what was wrong. She gave me a reassuring smile and said everything was okay. I went with her. I never liked surprises, but in this case, I let it slide. What was Helena going to show me? Was she going to give me something? I was excited. I thought she had something for me right outside the building. She led me to her car and drove us away, so apparently I was wrong. I had a couple of patients after Helena, but I didn't care. She smiled at me and I smiled back.

"I thought you were sick," I said. "Now you're hopping all about. What happened?"

"I don't know. I felt like I was dying a thousand deaths. That's when some weird, happy doctor shot me with a dose of something and I was more energetic than I've been in my whole life."

"Doctors sure are handy."

"Handy if the side effects aren't too bad. I might wake up with an extra pair of breasts in the morning. Not that men would mind . . . I think."

The drive was two to three hours long. Oh, what could the surprise be? What could it be? She took me to a river. It was dark and the stars were visible. She stopped at a secluded area. She told me to come with her. She left the car on. I walked with her over to a railing. No one but us was in sight. Helena reached into her inside jacket pocket.

Helena's expression changed from smiling to serious. She

pulled out a death instrument. It was pointed at me. I felt naked inside.

"How long were you planning to keep up this charade, Aurick?"

I was confused. What was going on? Why was she doing this? "What's the meaning of this? What are you doing?" I stepped closer to her. She nervously backed up.

"Don't take another step! I mean it!" She was shaking. She kept biting her lower lip. I looked deep into her. Was she possessed?

"What's going on, Helena?"

"Don't act stupid. I know you're a terrorist. I know you're with Adilah."

"What are you talking about?"

She reached into her pocket, fumbling with the gun and her jacket. She pulled out pictures and threw them on the floor. The pictures were of me entering the mansion where Aisely had taken me.

"Tim took these. My investigation led me to Mr. Jacques Powers. He's a multimillionaire who owns that mansion. One of his remaining retards led me to him. Apparently he's the leader." I knelt down and looked at the pictures more closely. "He's the head of a terrorist organization, and who do I see going to his house? You, Aurick!"

I had no idea how to explain this. What was I to tell her? *I am an ancient old demon who just wanted to have a reunion with another demon who just happened to be the leader of the same terrorist cult who just happened to want to kill you.*

"It's not what it looks like." That's the only thing I could think of at the time.

"What a load of crap! You've always acted weird. It makes sense now. That's how you knew Adilah was going to attack me at my office. That's why every time there's an attack, you're around. That's why you always discouraged me from investigating Adilah."

"That doesn't make sense. I've been close to you for a long time. If I wanted you dead, I would have succeeded a long time ago. I've even saved your life. Twice. The only reason I discouraged you from getting close to them was because I care about you! Why would I ever hurt you?"

"Maybe because you just didn't have the balls to do it. Needed someone else to do it for you. Just like Derek." We stared at each other as if neither of us knew what to do next. "Then what were you doing at that Jacques Powers's mansion, huh?"

I hated lying but I had to get out of this mess. "I am an FBI agent." I know it sounded stupid but that's the only thing I could think of.

Helena's hand was shaking so much the gun could fire at me at any moment. "You think I'm that stupid? I should shoot you right now."

"It's true. I have been investigating Adilah for years now. I almost have everything I need to sink Adilah once and for all." Dr. Doctor warned me about using any type of abilities from my true self but I had no choice. I used hypnosis to make her more gullible. I wasn't absolutely positive that it was going to work with all her anger and fear, but I didn't want to hurt her. *I* didn't want to get hurt either. I continued my lies to try to convince her. I disgusted myself.

"It's true?" It *was* working. "You're not here to hurt me?" Helena was so scared. So confused. She didn't know what to do.

"Of course not. I-I-I . . ." I wasn't sure if I meant it, but it would increase my chances of living. "I like you!"

At that moment, Helena's scared, innocent face turned sour and angry. "*Like?* You *like* me?" I think I may have made her angrier. I could hear Aurick's laughter.

"Yes. What's wrong?"

"Even in the face of a gun, you're afraid to say that you love me? You don't really care about me! You really are with Adilah!" She got closer and squeezed the gun as if she were going to shoot at any moment. "I should splatter your brains right now!"

"What are you waiting for? Use your superdemon powers and take her out!" Aurick said. I told him to shut up in my thoughts. I would never hurt Helena. Even if I had to risk my own being, I would not hurt her. I moved closer to Helena.

"Step back!" Helena said. I took another step. "I said get back! I'm warning you." Her whole body was shaking. I'd never seen her so frightened. She was always strong and willing to risk herself for her job. Her duty. Her justice. I took two more steps forward. Her arm and hand seemed to relax.

"You know I'm not part of Adilah. I know you're not going to shoot. I know you don't have the heart for it. You're not a killer. You're a wonderful person. A wonderful journalist who just wants justice." I got closer and closer. "I *like* you a lot. I *like* the way you obsessively talk about your job. I *like* your loose conduct. I *like* your passion. I *like* the way you abuse Timmy. I *like* the way you share your perverted thoughts. I *like* your weird sense of humor. You know I really do *like* you. I know you *like* me."

Before I knew it, I was face-to-face with Helena. Her eyes were like deep black voids. If her eyes were the Null, I would do a million crimes against humanity to vanish into them. I leaned my head forward and tasted her lips. Those cherry-flavored lips. This was the first time I'd ever legitimately kissed her. She was so scared she didn't realize she was still holding up the gun. I pulled down her hand. She pulled herself into me as hard as she could. It hurt. Only one other woman had made me feel this way. Made me feel naked inside. It was so long ago. She kissed like *her*. She smelled like *her*. She tasted like *her*. Just like her, our love wasn't allowed in this world. I picked her up.

She used her legs as an anchor to hold herself on my waist. I walked with her over to the car all the while kissing her. She pulled my hair back so much it stung. I slammed her back on the hood. Our lips were locked. She wrapped her arms around my neck and squeezed her legs tightly around me. She was like an octopus. I was her trapped prey. I started peeling her clothes off, starting with her tight blue jeans. She unbuckled my belt.

"Thata boy, Aurick Two!"

I yanked free and backed off.

"What's wrong, Aurick?" Helena said, sitting up in alarm

"Yeah. What's wrong, Mr. Spirit?"

I realized if I did this, Aurick would feel the pleasure of Helena's skin. I dreaded the thought of his filthy hands touching her. "Nothing. It's nothing. We need to get out of here."

"Is it because we're outdoors?" Helena looked embarrassed.

"No. It's not that. It's just I need to get home."

She looked at me quizzically for a few moments. She pulled her jeans up and got into the car. I sat down next to her. There was an awkward silence. Helena was obviously wondering what was wrong with her. I read her thoughts. Her mind was in a flurry. *Was my deodorant working? Did I come on too strong? I knew Aurick was classy! But he's the one who came on to me. Well, I did put a gun to his head. Duh. Maybe that's what freaked him out.*

Without a word, we were on our way home. I occasionally looked over at Helena. She didn't look back. She kept her focus forward so she wouldn't feel even more embarrassed by looking at me. I looked again, and to my dismay, Aurick was sitting there next to me. I jumped to the side in alarm, hitting my shoulder against the window. The car jerked and swerved about.

Helena regained control quickly. "What? What the hell happened?"

I didn't say anything. I looked at Aurick. He was sitting on the gearshift looking forward with a smile on his face.

"Hello? Hello, Aurick! Are you high?"

I shook my head no and looked forward. Awkward silence replaced the excitement. I rubbed my eyes to see if they were playing tricks on me. I looked again and this time Aurick was staring at me. My eyes weren't playing tricks on me after all. Was it a demon messing with me? An angel? Was it God?

"No, God isn't playing tricks on you, Aurick. *I* am," Aurick said, putting his arm around my shoulder. I didn't want to scare Helena again and cause an accident, so I tried to act normal. I couldn't believe Aurick had tapped into such a capability. "Surprised?" I kept my eyes forward, watching the yellow and white stripes in the middle of the road. I wondered how long it must've taken to finish painting them all. "I can't believe you're wondering about stupid traffic lines. You should be wondering about how hard you're going to nail Ms. Way all night long, baby." I connected with Aurick mentally so I wouldn't have to speak verbally. I didn't want Helena to think I was crazier than she already did. "Forget about Helena thinking you're crazy! You're an almighty demon for Christ's sake. You should be more confident about yourself." I decided to ignore him. That's all Aurick wanted, attention. If I denied him that, he'd go away. "Don't ignore me. I could do this forever. It's not like I have anything else to do but watch my own body live my own life." It was as if Aurick knew everything I was thinking. "Yes, I do know everything you're thinking." I finally turned and looked at him face-to-face. I wanted to look the devil in the eye. "I not only know what you're thinking, but I also have access to your memories. Well, most of them."

I was stunned. "Lying is a sin you know."

"Then I guess I'm still safe from a confession session. Don't believe me?" Aurick said as if he was absolutely in control. "I know that you're scared. Scared because of your past. Scared of your future. I even know that even though you are a damned demon fly, you still have loyalties to your God. Or should I say ex-God. You don't want to displease Him by having any type of relationship with Helena." Aurick laughed. "For a demon you sure are no stereotype. I thought all of you were sadistic, shadowy creeps who liked sticking guinea pigs in microwaves. Guess I was wrong."

Aurick turned and put his arm around Helena. It seemed Helena couldn't feel it. Of course she couldn't feel it. This was just an illusion. This human had not only accessed my mind but now he was able to use some of my capabilities. "You shouldn't underestimate a human. Though we are just slabs of meat, we can overcome any obstacle. And you just happen to be one of my obstacles, Mr. *Fly*. When I get free, I am going to cage you and never let go."

"That will be the day when God is killed skydiving." I concentrated with all of my strength to seal Aurick away. Aurick started to disappear. I didn't know how long he would stay away. My nose started bleeding heavily. A headache started to ensue. I covered my nose and remained stoic so that I wouldn't attract more attention from Helena. That felt impossible since my skull felt as if it had been hit with the Holy Grail. The bleeding eventually stopped and I wiped away the blood with my shirt. Yet the pain was getting worse.

Helena woke me up. I guess the pain had knocked me unconscious. She asked me why there was blood on my shirt. I told her I must've had a nosebleed while I slept. I opened the door. When I looked out, I realized we weren't in front of my building. We were in front of *Helena's* building. I closed the door. "I have to go home, Helena."

"You can stay with me for the night."

"I can't."

"Why not?"

I was silent. I didn't want to have this conversation. I didn't want . . . *temptation*. "I just can't. This is wrong."

"Is it because of entering into an improper relationship with a patient?" she said, sliding her finger to and fro on my chest. "You know statistics of violation of this sort of medical ethics says that about eight percent of doctors do it at some point over the course of their career. I covered the story. And now I *am* the story."

"No, it isn't that."

"Why are you so secretive?" The truth is I didn't want to be secretive. For thousands of years, I was invisible to the world. And the world I did know couldn't associate with me. I was tired. Tired of hiding. "Whatever it is, I can handle it." I wanted to believe her but I couldn't. She wouldn't handle it. Just as *she* hadn't. Even if she did handle it, that would be even worse. If a human were ever befriended by a demon with the full knowledge of who he was and actually continued to associate with him, that person most likely wouldn't be forgiven. Or at least it would make it a heck of a lot harder to be.

"It's not that. I just can't be with you."

"Why? We're both human, so what are you so scared of?"

"I come from a totally different world than you. A deep, dark, dangerous world. If you stepped into that world, there's no telling what would happen to you."

Helena put on a hardened expression. "You kiss me, and then you dismiss me. You love me, and then you shove me. You save my life, and then you try to kill me." Helena paused for a second to think. "Well, you didn't try to kill me . . . I think, but that's beside the point . . . I think . . ." I thought she was starting to believe me.

"You slam me on top of the hood of my car with my pants down, and then you have me zip them back up. And then when I finally give in, you're afraid to go further?"

I couldn't bear to look at her so I looked forward. I filled Helena's life with hurt and confusion just as I did Jamie's. And Doughy's. And Terra's. And especially Angry Kid's. I felt as if

I were a virus moving from one host to another at the expense of their lives. I felt Helena's hand. It was warm. I looked at the hand's owner. Helena's face was no longer angry or confused. It was warm and sure. She had a reassuring smile that told me everything was going to be okay.

"It's okay, Aurick. You can trust me."

I followed her upstairs. Her building had twenty-four-hour security. It was safe. Safe from everything but beings like me. We went into her apartment. It was dark. She didn't bother to turn the lights on. She pulled me into her. I felt that warm, tenderized, moisturized skin. It reminded me of my first time with a woman. *Her*. The woman who led me to my death. My tragedy. This time it felt different. No, it *was* different. It wasn't I who was being led to destruction. I was leading Helena to *her* destruction. I was a guideless meteor to her gravity. There was no room on either heaven or earth for our love. We would make our own world. Like the fly to the flame, I couldn't tear myself away. The fire would burn us both alive. And so it went. We played with fire all night.

Everything went back to darkness. I awoke on a sunny beach. I was wearing a suit. It was hot outside. I looked around. I remembered this beach from somewhere. Helena was sitting by my side. She was in a long silk dress. The sun was shining right through it. She was smiling. How did I end up here? I didn't know. The touch of her lips melted away all of the questions that constantly raced through my mind. It felt good to return to quiet, ignorant darkness. I remembered this feeling. This forever feeling. Everything was back to the way it was. Before the flood of anger and resentment. Before the lust. Before the envy. Before the great infanticide. She was my mate. She was my master. She was my substitute God. Was it this I wanted? Was it this my brothers longed for? To serve another person?

I gazed upon Helena's body as she lay asleep. She was perfect in every way. Her belly suddenly started to enlarge. I rubbed my eyes to see if my mind was playing tricks on me. It swelled larger and larger every second that passed. No matter how much I shook Helena, she wouldn't wake up. Something was going to bust through her body. The once blue sky turned black. My suit disappeared, revealing my naked body. I called out to her but it didn't do a thing. Water suddenly gushed out between her legs. The entire area flooded. Helena and I were swept away by ocean currents.

I woke up. Was I dreaming? Did I imagine sleeping with Helena? I was in the bed next to Helena's sleeping body. I was relieved I wasn't crazy. We were in stylish crimson sheets of slick material that kissed my skin. Helena was under the sheets in a cute sort of way. I snuggled next to her. I wanted to wake her up. I wanted to know what she was thinking. I nudged her face with a kiss with my lips to wake her up. I nudged her again but she wouldn't wake up. Helena was always a deep sleeper. Don't ask how I know that. I flipped the covers off Helena's bare body to wake her up with the cool draft. I felt naked. It wasn't because I didn't have clothes on. Helena's bare body was trembling and she was drooling from her mouth. She was having a seizure. I hopped over and raised her head on my arm. "Helena?! Wake up!" Her body was alive but her soul was lifeless. I hopped out of bed and dialed an ambulance. I hopped back into bed and cradled her body in my arms again. She was sweating like mad. I put my finger in her mouth to take her temperature. She had a fever of exactly 104.3 degrees Fahrenheit. Suddenly, Helena's body stopped moving. I took deeper and more frequent breaths. Helena was dead.

I gave her the kiss of life and pounded on her heart. I wasn't sure it was working but I kissed her again and pounded her heart some more. I started to give her all of my air. I persisted.

I knew it would damage me but I had no choice. My abilities helped restart her breathing. I thanked God. (I couldn't believe I accidentally gave God credit for my own masterwork.) She was still unconscious. She could die again at any second. Aurick's eyes shed tears that landed in her mouth. I wished my tears would heal her. Memories of Shelia's words flashed into my mind. I remembered her telling me when things looked down, all you could do was pray. That was stupid. Father would never listen to the prayer of a dirty fly. A fallen meteor. An evil demon. God had abandoned me. Helena was abandoning me. I would return to being alone. I would return to the darkness. I fell into darkness.

I awoke in a bathroom. It was a public bathroom. It smelled like fried chicken boiled in urine. I was throwing up into the toilet. Except it didn't feel like me throwing up. It felt as if I were watching myself throwing up, not taking part in it. I had no idea what was going on. Was this a dream? Was this reality? My body was dizzy. It bumped into the walls as it went over to the sink. My throat gargled the faucet water a few times and spit it out; it had turned yellow. My head looked up and looked into its reflection. Except it wasn't my reflection. Aurick's face smiled and said, "I told ya I would be back!"

XIX

†IMELESS

Purity. Out of impurity came something as pure as love. You are the essence of my love itself. It was gone and now it was found through an unlikely vessel. I love you. Nothing will separate us. Nothing.

Aurick had regained control of his body. I asked him how long he had been in control. He didn't answer me. I asked him what had happened to Helena. He didn't answer. I could feel his facial muscles forming a smile. Aurick left the bathroom and went downstairs to the subway. There were crowds of people. They were all barely an inch from the yellow line of death. More and more subway deaths rose as the population of New York City rose dramatically in recent years. It was so crowded we had to pass up two trains because of the dangerous crowding. We waited at the end of the platform where it was less crowded. We finally boarded, and like vultures, New Yorkers lunged at any seat available. Aurick ended up standing. At least it was less crowded than the other cars.

Aurick wouldn't tell me what happened so I tried to read his memory. This wasn't an easy task. Reading surface thoughts is much easier than digging through complex structures of emotion, subconsciousness, past thoughts. It must've been easier this time around though as Aurick was able to scan through my memories.

This was just the morning after Helena and I had that fiery night. I remembered moving against her body as I entered her. I wasn't there yet. I searched more. I saw the image of our warm bodies moving together rhythmically in complete unison. It was like a boat dancing on the waves of the ocean. Waves and waves of aftershocks, one after the other going through us. This was the ultimate experience that deteriorated Lofie's sanity. The ultimate experience that cost the lives of many of my brothers long ago. The ultimate experience that killed *me*. I searched further. I could see Aurick waking up. I had sealed him so he didn't experience my pleasure of Helena. Aurick was in the same bed next to Helena under the crimson sheets. I could see Aurick shocked. His shock turned into lust. He shared his tongue with her and then thrust into her.

And then I looked further.

Aurick crossed the line. He utterly disrespected a god. I slammed Aurick's head into the pole he was holding on to. People around us looked at Aurick as if he were crazy. Aurick smiled and tried to play it off as if he'd accidentally bumped his head because of the train's jerky motions. He was going to pay. I made Aurick punch himself in the face. Aurick once again smiled and tried to ignore the pain. I used his own fist and tried to strike again, but this time he caught it with the other hand. People spread around us to get away from Aurick's seeming madness.

"It's cool, people. Coffee is bad for you, so this is how I wake myself up in the morning. You should try it too," Aurick said, smiling, pretending to punch himself in the face again. People seemed to slightly buy his idiotic excuse so I took it a step further. I choked Aurick with his own hand and pushed him backward. He made choking noises. He tried desperately to yank the possessed hand free but I had too much of a tight grip on him. I pushed him, scaring some out of their seats. I smashed his head through the glass. The whole train screamed in fear. His head was in the blackness of the tunnel. Some people tried to pull him back in but I kicked them away.

"Get off of me!"

An upcoming light was getting closer and closer by the second. I believed the impact would knock Aurick's head off. I pulled his head back, missing the incoming light. Then I put it back in the darkness. Aurick screamed in bloody terror. I didn't care. I enjoyed the fear. I enjoyed the tears. I felt myself returning to the old me.

"What's wrong? Don't you believe in the light at the end of the tunnel?"

"You're bluffing!"

"You're not going to be saying that when your head is sent flying through this abyss. Matter of fact, you won't be saying anything at all."

"Not my head, our head. If you kill me, you're going to be punished severely. So cut the crap!"

"Do you really think I care about the consequences? I am a god. You are my slave. You are my spoiled little bag of meat. I've already made my choice by betraying an omnipresent being. At this point, my fate is already sealed, so why should I wait any longer? When I think about it, it seems you have committed treason also by abusing an unnatural world. *God's* unnatural world. It seems you're going to be damned."

Another subway light was getting closer. People were screaming all over the place. Closer and closer our fate was going to be tied together. Aurick and me. Me and my best buddy.

"You're lying."

"If fact, if you died now, you probably would have no chance at redeeming yourself. But I am not sure though. Let's find out together, shall we?"

Aurick's face filled with panic. "Helena is fine. She's at the hospital." His whole body jerked in uncontrollable fear. "Oh, God, please no." Tears ran down his face but were sucked into the abyss.

"The only God you have now is me. Say your prayers."

"All right I get it. You win. I'm so sorry." I yanked Aurick back just in the nick of time, sending him tumbling to the dirty train floor. Aurick looked up to see everyone staring at him in astonishment. The train stopped at a platform. Aurick was so embarrassed, he ran out in tears. Some nosy people alerted the train conductor to what had happened but we were long gone.

We took a taxi home. Aurick pressed the elevator button to call it down, forgetting that it was broken . . . as usual. He sighed with exasperation and lugged his exhausted body up the stairs. I had to help move his limp legs. Every step he took raised his blood pressure higher and higher. It felt as if we could collapse any second. We slowly walked over to the apartment door. Aurick leaned his forehead on the door while trying to put the keys in the keyhole. Our vision got blurry. It was like sticking a thread through a needle. At the moment he put it in and unlocked the door, his entire body trembled violently. Aurick collapsed to the floor and shook like a washing machine. The left side of his body became numb and throbbed in pain. Everything faded to black.

Sometime later, something rubbed against our right cheek. It felt like wet sandpaper. I wasn't sure who was in control of the body. The body's eyelid's opened. Sephirot was scraping our face with his sharp tongue.

"Are you dead, Aurick? And what about you, Aurick Two?" It wasn't Sephirot but Aisely using his body.

"Didn't I tell you to never manipulate Sephirot's body?" My body moved on its own. It moaned and rubbed its head and chest. Aurick was still in control.

"I know, man. I tried reaching you all day and this morning but I wasn't able to communicate with you for some reason."

"It must be because of the side effects of the possession. This body isn't going to last too long."

Aurick moved into the apartment. He reached into the refrigerator and pulled out tomatoes. Before I was on the scene, Aurick hated tomatoes with a passion. Now he was munching on them like apples. Our minds were melding together. I could feel our psyches collapsing.

"Your teeth are getting sharper and whiter. Your nails are getting sharper and your hair is getting longer." Aurick went into the bathroom and looked into the mirror. He saw that Aisely was right. "We better get this done quick."

"Get what done quick?" Aurick said, rapidly turning around to face Aisely.

"I've found Sam."

At the same time, Aurick and I said, "Sam?"

"Zero's associate that knows where Zero is. I located him."

"What does this have to do with me?" Aurick said, keeping his eyes wide open.

"Everything," I said. "Where is he, Aisely?"

"He lives in some old, abandoned house upstate. I don't know the address but I know how to get there."

"You have to be crazy to think I'm going there." Aurick's pride was getting on my nerves. Again Aurick believed he was on the level of us to have some sort of say in the matter. I still had some control of his body. I turned his body around in front of the faucet and turned it on. I bent his head into the flooding sink. Aurick struggled against me but I successfully dunked his head under the water. Aisely was laughing hysterically. "All right, I give up! I'm sorry!"

I commanded Aurick to not say another word. I needed to see Helena. I needed to know for sure she was fine. I ordered him to go to St. Peter's. Aisely waited outside the hospital. Dr. Doctor wasn't in sight. I went into the emergency room and found her. She was asleep but breathing.

I gazed upon Helena's fragile body. She was extremely pale.

I wanted to touch her gentle lips with mine but I didn't want Aurick to get the satisfaction. I tore myself away from her and left the building.

"I don't think I will be going on this mission," I said to Aisely. He was still in his cat suit.

"Still having doubts?"

"No. Helena needs me. I have to stay by her side."

Aisely looked upset but he remained composed, which was unusual. "I really don't understand how you could be that attached to a human."

"I don't either," a mysterious voice said. It wasn't Aisely the cat and it wasn't Aurick the pig. Dr. Doctor was on my left. I didn't know how he snuck next to me so undetected. He had that trademark crescent smile. "I heard what you said."

"I know you did. You're a creepy stalker."

"That's not what I was talking about." Dr. Doctor raised his head to the sky. "I guarantee you will do this mission."

"You're going to force me?"

"Nope. I'm not going to make you do anything." Dr. Doctor gave a quick laugh. It was ominous, as if he were foreshadowing a storm. "The ruler of Adilah foresaw what decision you were going to make. He struck Ms. Helena Way with this plague of infirmities. He saw that you had deep affection for her so he decided to use her as a pawn."

I felt naked again. "What's the point? Helena will die anyway if I help."

Dr. Doctor laughed again. "He has the ability to heal. An ability that few of us have. An ability that I long for. Ah, the bite of irony. Disgusting."

Aurick was shaking. He didn't know what was going on. He took a cigarette out of his pocket. A habit I frown upon. Dr. Doctor snatched the cigarette from Aurick's mouth. "Smoking is so unhealthy. Smoking is so . . . dangerous."

"What does he really want from me?"

Dr. Doctor laughed again. "Mr. Pantera, you're such a paranoid person. All you have to do is find the time-manipulator. After you've completed the task, your dear Helena will be healed to perfect health. That is all."

"You do know if Helena dies, the one who struck her with the plague gets deported to the Null?"

"Of course I do. That's why I kept her alive. That's what I was told to do. I don't know how much longer my medicine will last though. The leader is so sure he will be freed he isn't even thinking about that."

The leader was so sure his plan would work that he was risking being sent to the Null? What could be his goal? Did he even have a goal? Was he just lying? I was engrossed in more curiosity. I told Aurick to leave.

I was in their clutches. I couldn't say I was surprised. These are the works of demons. These are the works of those who have no path to tread upon. The works of those who have no hope. I wanted to wait a day to rest but Aisely insisted on getting this done now before we missed our chance. We needed to start moving now.

Aurick complained that there was no way he could walk all the way to our destination. I was persuaded to listen to Aurick's plea so we went back home. (Just because I'm mighty doesn't mean I can't be reasoned with.) Aurick walked up to his vehicle. As he was opening the door, Jamie spotted him. I told Aurick to wait. He complained but I sternly commanded him to obey. I told him to call Jamie over. Jamie happily came over to us, skipping like a little girl. In my eyes, innocent blood flowed through Jamie's veins. To me, she was one of the last remaining pure humans on earth. Jamie was an endangered species.

She asked me where I was going. I told her I was going to a faraway place. For all I knew, I could be sent to the Null on this assignment. She persistently asked me what exact location I was going. I couldn't tell her. Knowing her innocence, Jamie would probably try to follow me. I couldn't let that happen. She asked me if I would come back. I told her I didn't know. Her eyes swelled up like strawberries. She didn't have any known family and not many friends. She feared to be alone again. Feared returning to the darkness. As I was. As I *am*. She said that she would be waiting for me. That she would prepare a hot plate of her cookies for my return. Aurick kissed her. Or was it me who kissed her? I no longer knew anymore. Jamie loved me like a lover. I loved her like a younger sibling. Just as I loved Lofie long ago.

We drove for a few hours. Something was going to happen. A dreadful feeling lingered. I wasn't sure why but I felt as if the entire world were going to change. I knew Aisely felt it too. His feline fur was falling out. Nightfall crushed the sun. As we drove farther away from the city, the stars were a bit more visible. I gazed upon those beautiful twinkles. Humans can't see through the clouds but I could. Not nearly as well as I used to though. I need to get out of this body and see the stars again. Aisely gazed upon them too. Snow fell. It eventually blocked out the cosmic lights.

We stopped in front of a house. We got out of the vehicle and got closer. Owls could be heard hooting. I could see one gazing upon me. I wasn't sure if some owls had the ability to fully see spirit creatures, but I still felt uneasy being in front of their gaze. I felt as if they were judging me. The stairs creaked as we stepped on the porch. It was a dump. Every plank of wood was moldy like bread. Every piece of metal was rusted. Parts of the roof had collapsed.

"Are you kidding me? No one has lived here for decades. Why are we here?"

I ignored Aurick and told him to open the door. The moment

he touched the doorknob, the entire door toppled over. We stepped in. A big, gaping hole in the roof was letting in all the snow. The only light in that house was the light that poured in from the hole. Light, darkness, and snow. The place was falling apart. Termites had been snacking on this edifice for years. Raccoons, cockroaches, and birds occasionally ran across our path. This house was a homeless shelter for vermin.

"We have to go down to the basement," Aisely said. He guided us up the stairs.

"The last time I checked, basements are downstairs, not up."

"The path to the basement collapsed a long time ago. Be careful. This house is like a maze so follow me closely."

Easy for Aisely to say. It was difficult following a cat with the same color of darkness as within this black hole. Up the creaky steps we went. Every step we took sounded like scratching a nail on a chalkboard. On one step, Aurick's foot plunged through the staircase. He panicked and screamed, which made Aisely panic and scream. We walked down a hallway. The walls had pictures of a family. A father, a mother, a son, a daughter, a grandmother, and a black Labrador retriever. They smiled in every picture. What was peculiar was that every inch of the house was obliterated except for the pictures and their frames, which were as good as new. We stepped into a room. It had paintings of the family in various styles of art. They were all perfectly fine.

"Is it just me or is this house really creepy?" Aurick said.

"It's not creepy. It's actually quite depressing. I've seen this many times, Aurick. Some Fallen long for the family that they've lost. We call them squatters. Squatters latch on to families to improve the quality of their lives and help them bear their death sentence. They protect the whole family and even bring fortune. In fact, you humans call them guardian angels."

"So you're telling me that guardian angels are actually guardian demons?"

"Exactly. Inevitably, the family eventually dies off, leaving the demon brokenhearted. Pictures are kept and sometimes monuments are built in their honor."

"That's sad. Can we leave now?"

"No."

We walked to the end of the room and stopped at a wall. The wall was covered by a long curtain stretching from one side of the room to the other. I pulled it down, revealing a giant hole. We stepped through, going into another room. And this room had another hole. This time the hole was in the ground. "We have to go down there," Aisely said.

"No way! My legs are going to break if I jump down there," Aurick One said. Aisely the cat jumped down and landed softly on his feet.

"See! Your legs aren't going to break, Aurick One. Your body has been enhanced by Aurick Two's influence." Aurick procrastinated for a while. He was scared.

"Well, I guess if I could walk on water, I could do this." Aurick jumped and landed on the ground without injury. He sighed in relief.

The basement was full of piled dirt, rock, wood, and more debris. Boulders blocked the entryway. We continued on our way. It was narrow and dark, almost like a tunnel. We treaded on until we saw a curtain. It was blue and slightly new. A bright lava lamp sat on a crate at the corner. The light revealed a shadow behind the curtain. Aurick's knees were shaking. His eyes swelled up like ripe tomatoes. He slowly reached for the curtain. He gulped down a good portion of saliva and whipped a bead of sweat off his eyebrow. Aurick clenched his teeth and snatched the blue curtain down. His eyes widened. A black Labrador retriever stood before us. It was the same Labrador retriever as in the family pictures. He was sitting down. "Hello . . . Aurick."

Aurick jumped backed and fell on his back. He panted heavily. I told him to get up, which he did. He was okay with a talking cat, but a talking dog was too much for him.

"How do you know my name?"

The dog looked around at Aisely and back at Aurick. "Who told the human to speak?" the dog said.

"Tell Aurick to kneel down," Aisely said, whispering under his breath. Aisely bowed his head before him also. Aurick knelt down just as he was told. For thousands of years, dogs took orders from man, and now the roles were reversed.

"I have been waiting for a long time," the dog said. He spoke with a deep, broad voice. "What took you so long, boy? You know how I hate to wait."

"What do you mean?" I said. "We have never made any prior engagement."

"Oh, that's right!" the dog said, clenching his eyes shut as if he remembered something. "I must've gotten you confused with my vision of the future. I apologize, my boy. Sometimes I mix up the future with the present." The dog seemed as if he was grinning. Aurick was creeped.

"So you know what we want."

"Yes. I do know what you want. Don't try it though. It won't work," the dog said as if he was certain of the future. "I've seen it already." I knew this was a stupid idea. The dog knew everything that was going to happen. How in the world would we force information out of him? But then again, why would he stay here if he knew we were coming?

"Are you Sam?"

The dog sucked his teeth as if I'd irritated him. "Please do not call me that."

"Then what shall I call you?"

Sam's stomach moved in and out as he sniggered quietly. "So you *are* losing your connection with us. Then that means you've been spending a lot of time in that body. Fell in love, boy?" I ignored his question. "The name is Harvey. Harvey Samuel Carr." Harvey licked his dark lips.

"If you knew that we were coming, then why did you stay?"

"Why wouldn't I? How could I leave and miss out on all the fun?" Harvey knew something about the future.

"What do you mean by *fun*?"

"I've been roaming this earth for thousands of years. Millennia of waiting for my execution. You know how extremely boring that can be? I pass the time by foretelling the future for people. Foretelling to change their lives. Just because I know the future doesn't mean I can't enjoy it when it comes around."

"Every time you sent Aisely to protect people's lives, it made things worse."

"Yep," Harvey said, chuckling again. "I saw the events after changing their fates and created even more chaos. It was just as I planned. Aisely fell for it too." Aisely switched his eyes around. He was embarrassed that he was manipulated . . . again.

Harvey was what we Fallen call a Tugboat. He was among the Fallen's most famous Tugboats. We all had heard of Harvey's murderous escapades. Had I known this associate was Harvey, I wouldn't ever have agreed to come here. The most talented of deceivers. Tugboats are Fallen who want to take down as many human lives as possible to send intense grief and panic to all who were close to that person. They know that their day is coming to an end so they tug as much life down with them as possible, just as the name suggests. This particular Tugboat had sent New York City into a panic. He took up residence in a black Labrador retriever. He abused a schizophrenic man named David Berkowitz. He plagued his mind with disturbing thoughts and dreams. He eventually told David to kill couples throughout the city. In fear, David obeyed and eventually wound up in prison. He told the police that his neighbor's dog made him do it, but who would believe that?

"But enough about me. You are after Zero. The one who taught me how to see into the future."

"Do you know where Zero is?"

"Yep."

"Where?"

"Don't you want to know what he will be used for?"

"I already know." Harvey laughed broadly.

"What then?"

"As impossible as it sounds, he's going to be used to manipulate time and stop ourselves from ever betraying Father. We will have a clean slate without anyone knowing." Harvey stared at me for a few seconds and then burst into laughter.

"What is so funny?"

"You're ignorance is so funny."

"I guess that means you've already seen that our plan will fail."

"No. Actually I haven't been able to see the future beyond New Year's Eve. No matter how much I try, I just can't. I thought maybe it has something to do with using Zero's time-manipulating ability."

"Then why the laughter?"

"You really think it's possible for a mere angel to reverse time? The only being with the power to successfully accomplish such a task is the Creator. It would lead to absolute disaster if anyone tried to distort time."

"Then what about you? You're successfully using time manipulation."

"You are incorrect. I am simply watching the momentum of the particle flow of objects beyond the subatomic level. Like watching an old lady walking into the path of a speeding car. There is no time distortion. Though I am using it on a much smaller scale, I am imitating the Creator."

"What happens if someone other than Father would try such a feat?"

Harvey made that grin again. "To reverse this type of motion safely, you would have to reverse every single particle in existence. The only one who can do that properly is the Creator. An angel can only control so many particles and then . . ." Harvey paused. He licked his bright white teeth.

"And then what?"

"The devastation of all life."

XX

JUDAS

We are acorns buried by the master seeder. You lie in darkness and ob-struction. You cannot see. You cannot hear. You cannot breathe. Without your arms. Without your legs. Do not give up. Never. Press on and claw your way out. You must be patient. You will grow. I know it. You will rise above the soil. You will go where I will not go. It's fine. You are me. They will fear your limitless ascension. Trees die before they grow too large. They are threats. But you will not have anything limiting you one day. Be careful not to grow large enough to snuff out the sun. Please prove them otherwise. Use the sun. I love you, Purity.

I didn't know what to make of Harvey's statements. All of this sounded impossible. For the first time, Aurick and I were in shock from a common thing. Was Harvey lying? Was he toying with me? Was he messing with my mind just as he had done with humans' for thousands of years? I needed to know more.

"You are lying!" Aisely hissed, getting on all fours. His tail stood straight up.

"Believe what you want. It's not like I care," Harvey snapped back quickly.

"If you have such a cold heart, then why have you been taking care of the memories of your human family?"

"That's not my family. This was Zero's. All of the pictures, that's Zero's. All of the paintings, Zero's too. In fact, this family is what led to all of this."

"What do you mean?" I said.

"Enough about me and Zero. You should really be worried

about yourself, Aurick. I have seen a great tragedy in your life."

I felt naked at that moment. I had a feeling Harvey was telling the truth.

"Something about Helena Way, I believe."

I had enough of him. At that moment, I took full control of Aurick's body. I lunged toward Harvey. My body mysteriously stopped. My legs buckled and I went down on both knees. I tried with all my strength to move, but I couldn't. Harvey was effortlessly holding me down with his mind and wagging his tail. I reached into his mind. All I could see was . . . happiness. Harvey pushed me out. I coughed and vomited.

"I'm more powerful than you can imagine. Do not try that again." Harvey licked his pure white teeth once more and stretched his neck around. "Don't worry. I am going to tell you where Zero is. He is hiding somewhere on Mount Everest. Must be enjoying the sights. I don't blame him. I might take a vacation too. If you don't hurry, someone will reach him first."

"Who?"

"A Judas."

"A Judas?"

"Someone that you've known for a very long time. Someone close to you. Someone so close he might as well be standing right next to you." I looked over to Aisely as Aisely looked at me. Harvey turned around, showing his hindquarters. "And also, Justice is going to have Helena in his palm right about now I think." Harvey walked toward the wall and then stopped as if he'd almost forgot to say something. He turned his head to me. He had an ominous grin. "And another thing, if you do not use the right protection, Helena will absolutely die. But I don't know, there's a chance I am wrong. I've learned nothing in this world is foolproof. *Nothing.* Have a merry Christmas!"

That naked feeling came back.

Harvey continued to the wall of rock and dirt, which melted away, giving him a path to walk through. Harvey was more powerful than I'd imagined. He had access to a lot of his abilities, even though he was using a host. Most spirit beings could only manipulate liquids or gases, but Harvey could manipulate solid matter.

Everything Harvey said flashed through my mind. What did he mean about not having the right protection? I knew she was dying, but what did having the right protection have to do with it? But that was just the tip of the iceberg. Harvey talked about the time-manipulator being able to destroy all life. But that's impossible. If all life on earth perished, God would simply snap his fingers and resurrect all life. Not only that, but Harvey also said that a Judas would get to Zero if I didn't hurry. Judas was a once-loyal servant of God who backstabbed the Messiah. I looked at Aisely and wondered. Was Harvey trying to say Aisely would betray me? I came to get one answer from Harvey but in return Harvey raised even more questions.

I was in full control of Aurick. I did not know why. Either Harvey did something or I overpowered Aurick in my distress. Aurick seemed not to be there either. He didn't speak at all, not that I was complaining. I had enough problems as it was. Aisely and I found our way out of the house and started walking away. I looked to Aisely and said, "We are not going any further with this."

"What? Why?"

"This is getting too dangerous."

"Danger is my middle name."

"I'm not kidding, Aisely. This whole situation feels . . . foul."

"Aw, come on! You weren't bothered by Sammy, were ya? He was just messing with our minds. Just as he likes to mess with humans."

"Harvey is a demon who can see into the future. He foretold finding the time-manipulator would end all life. *All* life. I'm not going any further with this search."

Aisely suddenly stopped. He had a grave look on his feline face. "And miss out on our only chance of being in Dad's grace once more? Are you kidding me?" Aisely exhibited a fierce determination that I had never before seen. "This is our chance to avoid being executed and you're having cold feet about it? This should be the happiest day of your life."

"Harvey's prophecies have always come true. What makes this any different from the other prophecies?"

"You're wrong! Harvey predicted the future and we changed fate. Some of those people were going to die in a certain way and we changed that. Though it was slight, we changed the future. If we changed the fate of humans, we can change ours. Like catching an egg before it hits the ground." Aisely continued walking forward, turning his back on me. Aisely had *never* done that before.

"Yes, and breaking the egg into a million pieces in the process. Harvey is manipulating us. If we continue this errand, we are either not going to make any change or just make the future worse like all the other times. Don't you get it?!"

Aisely stopped and swung around again. "For thousands of years we've been searching for a way to be forgiven for our transgressions. A way to get away from our eternal sin."

"We don't deserve it."

"Why don't we? Humans were given absolute perfection and a beautiful paradise. And what did they do? They threw it away for a chance to surpass their God. They backstabbed their Creator. And what does Dad do? He gives them a Messiah to erase all of their sins even after their betrayal. Did they appreciate their clean slate? Heavens no! Matter of fact, they *continue* to destroy this planet. They treat the environment like they treat each other." Aisely's anger leaked through his body. The trees and grass bent all around him. "We, on the other hand, slaved for Dad for billions of years. We all genuinely loved and shared the cosmic pains of living for eternity with our Father. We screwed up one time. One screwup! One little misstep and we get discarded out of the gates. We prayed for forgiveness. We *continue* to pray for forgiveness. I want to ask you a question. Since your original sin, have you ever just once heard a reply?"

I remembered when I sinned that fateful night. I prayed with all of my might hoping to get an answer. All I heard were the waves that swept the earth that night. I understood and felt everything Aisely said. I couldn't lash out at him for how he felt.

"We love the Creator more than the humans ever possibly could. Dad gave humans their way to salvation. Why can't we receive the same kindness? Why can't we receive the same justice? Does our Father not love us? Does He not feel any shred of sympathy for His first sons? Has He ever shed one single tear for us Fallen? I have. And I'm tired of the tears." Aisely turned his back on me again and started walking off. "This is our final chance to take back our honor. You can go back to the world of darkness with the other hopeless flies. Not me. I won't do it. I've paid my debt."

Aisely pounded each step forward. For him, there was no turning back. I had two options. Follow Aisely and possibly win our thrones back or be on the safe side by stopping him from reaching Zero. I didn't know whether it made me more of a coward if I escaped punishment or accepted it. Did I truly care about the possible chaos or was I just scared of being punished further? I honestly had no idea what to do. I stepped forward in a quick pace. "Stop, Aisely!" Suddenly, pain throbbed through my entire body. It felt as if gravity were crushing me into a pancake. I stopped in my tracks. Another kind of pain surged through my insides. Every bone and muscle stiffened. My fingers stiffened into a position that looked as if I were going to claw someone. My legs buckled and forced me down to my knees. "Aisely, wait." Aisely didn't turn back. Was he causing this? Was Aisely the Judas Harvey was speaking of? My stomach turned. I threw up pints of fluids onto the grass in front of me. Was this being caused by the side effects? I fell over to my side. My body stiffened even further. Everything turned blurry. Everything turned dark. Everything turned absolutely black.

My consciousness emerged from the darkness and into the light. Red light. I looked up into the heavens to see a crimson-red sky. Not a cloud was in sight. I looked down to see myself a few feet over black gravel. I was dangling from a wooden pole. My body was completely bare. My arms were straight over my head with my wrists pinned into the wood with sharp pieces of metal. My feet were pinned into the wood as well. Though I didn't feel much pain from the impalement, I found it extremely hard to breathe. I looked around to see others in the same position as I was. Some were moaning in pain while others were silent. I was dizzy. Where was I? Was any of this real? I passed out.

I woke up again. I was a bit less disoriented. I was able to see more clearly. Hundreds of Fallen were all around me. Many were chained in various positions to various objects. Some were hanging from their necks from poles. They were still breathing. None of them were crying. I sorted through my racing thoughts to soon realize I was located at a Styx port. Styx ports are prisons for Fallen such as me. Many Fallen band together and do various assignments according to their own factions. Assignments such as confusing people's emotions, starting false religions, tempting stressed humans, and taking advantage of the mentally unstable. Many enjoy this work. For many, it's a good way to vent their rage against humans. Others get fed up and stray away from their group. The other group members sometimes make a deal with Styx bailors to hold the renegade Fallen for punishment until that Fallen complies once more. Sometimes Fallen are kept there indefinitely. Styx ports are stationed all over the world. Many are stationed in Antarctica. Others are in deserted lands such as the Sahara. They are usually stationed wherever humans aren't. This is so Fallen can't use one as a host and cause chaos while running away from Styx bailors. I did not know which port I was in.

I waited and waited. More and more Fallen passed by being brought to their cells. I saw the sadness in their eyes. Many had betrayed their Fallen factions. Others were betrayed *by* their Fallen factions. Some were new Fallen. Stars that had turned into shooting stars and crashed into earth. They get the worst of the treatment. Pain gradually increased throughout my body. After a while, I fell asleep.

I awoke again. I had a nightmare just to awake into another nightmare. A nightmare within a nightmare. Time and more time passed. I was absolutely bored. The only entertainment was seeing other Fallen being tortured in various ways. Some had boulders chained to their backs as they walked. Others were repeatedly stabbed with spears. We were all once a happy, civilized brotherhood. Now we were torturing each other like cattle being processed at a slaughterhouse. This place is for gods being God over other gods. My thoughts eventually focused on what got me here in the first place. Aisely had betrayed me. My loyal companion. My *only* loyal companion.

After all of the Fallen were judged, many still tried serving Father. After some centuries passed, all of us lost our minds. We became vengeful animals that feasted on the red life that poured out of humans' veins. None of us retained honor anymore. Well, almost no one. Aisely and I banded together and maintained the sanity that so many of our brothers had lost. We believed keeping our sanity defied God. We believed it kept us alive. We were fools to not have realized that we were already dead. I didn't hate Aisely for it. I didn't *have* hate left. Pain grew once more. I fell asleep.

I felt pain. I felt pain on my face. I felt slaps across my face back and forth. It wasn't as much painful as it was annoying. I gradually opened my eyes. I saw a familiar face. I saw the face of a god. "What do you want, Zeus-face?"

"Hello, my homey! I never thought you'd be here at my crib." Zeus-face was sitting on a golden throne being carried on the backs of other Fallen. Another show-off. Zeus-face was wearing black sunglasses, choosing to appear as a male human in his late twenties. He was bare-chested and wore colorful floral swim trunks and pink flip-flops.

"Can you keep your voice down? You're ruining my beauty sleep," I said groggily.

Zeus-face laughed. "You never were the talkative type." I was sick and tired of people saying that about me. "Come on, my gangsta dogs. Laugh with me," he said to the slaves holding up the throne. They moaned. "I said laugh!" The slaves forced a greater effort. Zeus-face was the head Styx bailor of this port. He controlled every*thing*.

"Which Styx port is this?"

"You are now located in Styx port A88." This port was in New York City's underground. That was good as I wasn't far from my human home. Fallen have never lost our Father's sense of order. "That's not going to be the case anymore though. You're being transferred to H44." H44 was a Styx port far away. Very, *very* far away. H44 was on the moon. The dark side of the moon. H44 was a prison reserved for Fallen who have been especially disloyal to their faction. This port was cake compared to H44. Nothing but terror stories came from that location, gruesome brutalities beyond your wildest dreams. They even say you'd rather go to the Null than H44.

"For what reason?"

"The one who sent you here wanted you to be far away from New York City." That sealed it. Aisely was the Judas. Harvey's prophecy had come true. "You must've done something grimey for someone to request you there. What did you do, homey?"

"Thinking about those other than myself," I said, putting my head down.

Zeus-face smiled. "Yeah. That'll do it. In this world, you gotta look out for number one. Helping others will only get you a world of hurtin'." That's something I knew all too much. "Take me for example. Back in the day, I was a scrawny, little spirit. I loved our brothers so much that I wouldn't stand up for myself when they bullied me. Now I'm the king of the world." Zeus-face waved his hands and gestured to the slaves below. "And as you can see, those same bullies are under *my* rule. And under *my* feet."

Zeus-face was an overly compassionate spirit before he fell. The other birds would constantly harass him, beating him up, and making him feel bad about himself. Zeus-face got so sick of being picked on. He trained his powers so much that he lost sight of his relationship with Father. This eventually led to his death. During his new life he obtained the freedom to cast vengeance on his ancient bullies. He rose and became the head bailor of A88, the most well-maintained Styx port in existence. In the entire history of mankind, only one Fallen had ever escaped. Back home, Zeus-face was a pushover. At A88, Zeus-face was a god. A megalomaniac. This was his palace and he was its king.

"Why haven't I been sent to H44 yet?"

"You been welded pretty tightly to your human host, yo. My bailors and I are pretty good with extracting Fallen from their hosts, but in your case it's been mad tough. We've hired an extraction expert. A surgeon, if you will. He's doing something at the moment, but he'll be on his way eventually, my G."

"I want to leave this place, Zeus-face," I said, raising my head.

Zeus-face sighed and raised his eyebrows. "I'm sorry, friend. I truly am. But that's something I cannot do."

"I have unfinished business to take care of. I need to get out of here."

"I am the leader of this port. What example would I set if I were to let a prisoner free for free? I was appointed by a client. Breaking my client's contract would be dishonorable. And you're the one who taught me to always keep my word. No matter what." Zeus-face leaned back in his chair and stretched his arms. "Not only that, but business has been slow lately. Our fellow flies have been all breaking away from their factions, eliminating the need for Styx. Ever since the last Great War of the Flies." The war was a huge uprising among the Fallen. Some Fallen took it upon themselves to fight against angels. Fearing that they all would get punished, other Fallen fought against the Fallen renegades. It led to chaos all over the world for decades. There have been many of these wars.

"You forgot you owe me."

Zeus-face took off his glasses. His eyes were colored gray. He wiped his glasses with his trunks. "Yes, I do owe you. Back then, you defended and warded off those bullies. You gave me such a boost of pride. You're the one who inspired me to stand up for myself. I'll tell you what. I'll see what I can do." Zeus-face put his glasses back on. He clapped his hands together a couple times and said, "Chop-chop." His slaves carried him and his throne away.

It felt like days. There was no rotation of the sun and moon so there was no telling how long I was here. Styx ports aren't actually constructs. They're actually enormous complex networks of illusions generated by Styx bailors. This allows everyone inside to communicate with each other. Time moves slowly here. Depending on the skill of the Fallen who cast the illusions, Styx time can be a hundred times slower than real time. I thought that maybe I was here for eight Styx-days. Zeus-face returned. He had bad news. He had tried to contact the one who made the deal to imprison me, but the person wouldn't respond. Zeus-face apologized. I didn't say anything in return. I was stuck here. Stuck here until the end of my sentence. Death. All hope was lost.

My mind was tearing itself apart. I wanted to die. The pain was getting much worse. Every time I took a breath, agony shot from my impaled feet and hands. There was still no word from Aurick. Harvey must've knocked him unconscious. It was a good thing, for Aurick would never have been able to take this excruciating torment. I felt that I deserved this. I wanted to feel more pain. I was paying for everything I'd ever done. I thought about Helena and her lovely smile. That lovely smile that cracked open when she pretended to laugh at your jokes. Those were the best. It reminded me of *her*. I thought of my past life. I remembered the first human I ever met. She was a small girl. She was drowning in a lake. I swam after her and yanked her body from the water. And then I met the girl's mother. *Her*. She fiercely cried over the body. The girl wasn't breathing. She thought she had lost her forever. I breathed life into the girl's lungs. There wasn't any knowledge of cardiopulmonary resuscitation back then so the mother was frightened. But then her happiness for the girl's life eclipsed her fear. She had already lost the girl's father so losing her would have killed her. She invited me to supper to show her gratitude. She made the most delicious sweet cakes. I taught her how to make chocolate-chip cookies, which nobody had ever seen before then. She was fascinated with my advanced knowledge. She was drawn to me as I was drawn to her. She was drawn to my perfection as I was drawn to her imperfection. I felt a great deal of comfort. A different kind of comfort. Her appreciation and warmth melted the veil of flawless standards off my skin.

I started to wonder if I really liked Helena or if I just wanted to get close to the other woman I had lost long ago. I wondered if Helena even really cared about me. She was famous for getting close to men just to get information out of them. Just as she did with Brother Dex. Was I wasting my time with her?

I knew our relationship was doomed, but was it actually worth the ride? Yet I wanted to see her again. One last time.

The only thing that kept me sane was the excruciating pain. It kept me awake. It kept me focused. The surrounding area started to bend all around me. An object was forming. It was a wooden pole like mine. Was it all in my imagination? Had I entered another plateau of madness? Then I realized another Fallen was entering the port. I was right. A being materialized on the pole. I could only see his outline but none of his features. His wrists and feet were pinned to the wood just like mine. His features gradually materialized. Was it Aisely? From that moment on, every second felt like an eternity. The sheer anticipation forced me to forget about my injuries. His face finally materialized. My entire world came crashing in. Just how meteors crashed into the world. My former leader. My onetime icon. My best friend. Morning Owl.

I squeezed my eyes tightly to clear them. Was Morning Owl part of an illusion just meant to torment me more? He looked exhausted. I called out to him. I needed to be sure I wasn't mad. There was no response. I called out to him again. This time he slowly picked his head up. He looked at me. Our eyes met. His eyes were filled with desolation. That look was unmistakable. But it couldn't be true. Just when I thought he was going to say something, he dropped his head. I didn't say anything. I thought of all the possible scenarios. Was he kidnapped by Fallen? That sort of thing had happened before. Was he undercover? That had never happened before, but there's a first time for everything.

That look in Owl's eyes. All of us Fallen knew that look.

"I am glad to finally have some company in this hole," I said in a gloomy tone. "But I am not glad that *you* are the company." Owl's expression didn't change a bit. He didn't even look up at me. It was as if he was expecting this. "You might want to keep the legs and your breath steady. It hurts like death if they're not." Owl didn't move at all. He continued to breathe as he was. "Were you kidnapped?" Owl didn't answer. "No, you would be much too powerful for that to happen. Are you undercover?" There was no response. I put my head down. "I see." I couldn't bear to see his downfall. This was astronomical. Morning Owl would never crash. He was above all of us. One of the wisest and most powerful entities in the universe. All I could do was to keep my head down. "I know this is extremely rude to ask between Fallen, but I just need to know."

"Isn't it obvious?" he said, still keeping his head down. "I sent you here. I was the one who sent you to the Styx."

XXI

HUMANLESS

Boomerangs come back from the past. Keep your eyes focused. If you do not, you will miss the catch, sending it smashing into your future. While reassembling your future, you will wonder why the repairs are left to you if you weren't the one who flung the weapon. Don't worry about why. Just focus on the potential of your commitment to finish what you started. I love you.

Was this real? Was this an illusion? Was another Fallen forcing Morning Owl to say such foul words? I sorted out all of the possible reasons why none of them made any sense. Why would my best friend do this to me? Why would he fall away from the grace of Father just to torture me? Just coming up with those questions didn't make sense. My eyes spread open like a woman dilating, preparing to give birth. Morning Owl was going to give birth to truth that would rattle my senses. He didn't speak. "How? Why?" I asked. He kept his head down the whole time.

Is this how Father felt? Just as I knew Morning Owl since my birth is how Father knew me since mine. Morning Owl betrayed me just as I had betrayed Father. This was the taste of my own medicine. They say the more bitter the medicine, the better. This medicine was not sweet or healthy. The cycle continues.

"I haven't been through these parts of the woods in a long time. They're getting really sophisticated with these illusions."

Owl looked up to the sky. "The sky could use a bit touching up. I'm going to have to talk to Zeus-face-san about that." Owl put his head down.

"No matter how much you try to fix the skies, you can never fix the storm in your heart."

"And that is why I am going to soar above them."

"What is that supposed to mean?"

"I don't actually know. I've always liked poetry." Morning Owl was in the realm of madness. And I wasn't talking about the Styx. There was no turning back.

"Please, for the love of God, tell me, why have you transgressed against me? Why have you treaded against your brother, Morning Owl?"

"Don't call me that!" he shouted, raising his head. His eyes fired years of hidden anger into my soul. I trembled. The entire Styx seemed to recoil in fear. "I have no name."

"How long?"

"How long what?" My brother put his head down.

"How long have you been storing all of this malevolence?"

"I don't remember how long." My brother was lying. When Fallen lose their connection with God, their sanity and memories become imperfect. Angels on the other hand have absolute total recall. My brother wouldn't lose any memory in this short time, being in the darkness. "So this is how it feels to lie. Oh, if only Adam and Eve didn't lie to their Creator, none of this would've happened." My brother made a light smile. "Oh, I lied again. I think. Is this what they were talking about, that you lose your mind in this state? Or is it the feeling of the first fresh breath of freedom?"

We watched as some bailors passed by. I waited patiently for our privacy.

"From my birth, I looked up to this source of light. You were my idol. I wanted to be just like you. I engraved your personality into my spirit. I wanted to be incorruptible like you. I felt so ashamed when I fell short of your incorruption. I thought you would never speak to me again. But there you were comforting me as I wept after *she* died."

"I remember that. You wept and wept for her. You thought you were going to die from the misery of losing grace from Father and her."

"You never left my side until the tears dried. My understanding came from you. I remembered when I was fed up with Lofie's obsession with me. You reminded me to never forget Lofie and to help nurse his mind." I looked up into the sky. I hoped for some stars to appear. "Shooting stars break to pieces when they hit earth. You kept me in one piece." I looked back into my brother's eyes. "Thank you."

My brother smiled gently. I felt that I had repaid him for all the times he made me smile. He made me smile even when there was nothing to smile about. All the hate stored in my brother's heart seemed to melt away.

"An ark is being built. It is almost complete."

What did he mean by that? "Ark?"

"When my unit was first trailing Adilah for suspicious activity, I found myself alone with one Fallen of the group when I captured him. He revealed many things about the plan, but he himself did not know everything. He told me that the group was trying to find a power to go back in time. An ability that was able to erase the sins of the past. Such a concept intrigued me. It was unheard of. I didn't know anything about it until late into the plan. But I did know something special was brewing. I needed to know more. I wanted more than knowing more. I wanted to be part of it. But I could not allow the members of Adilah to know. They could eventually get caught by my unit and would reveal that I had helped them. So I had to help them secretly."

"How?"

"I tried my best to thwart my unit from catching members of Adilah. And I had been working on my own to find the time-manipulator, Zero, for some time, but his ability to see into the future made it impossible to catch him. I didn't even know where his close associate, Harvey, was. I couldn't use heaven's resources for such a disloyal task, so I didn't know what to do. That's when you and Aisely came along. You knew where Zero's personal associate was. Those with insight can only see into the future within their own domain. Any being such as us outside of that domain can disrupt the momentum of the flow of time if we tread upon it. It is like a foreign pebble falling into a pond changing the currents. I followed you and Aisely to Harvey's territory and listened to your conversation. That's when I heard where Zero was located. You were thinking of stopping everything I was working for, so I dragged you to this Styx port. Your power made it possible for an escape so I wanted you transferred to H44. The only problem was that you were stuck inside that human body so Zeus-face-san had to wait for a specialist to amputate you from that tumor."

"Wait. Why did you go so far into getting the ark? You were an angel, so why did you want to go back in time?"

"For thousands of years I have seen suffering, watching what my little brothers have gone through. I wanted to deliver them back into the light. If just one of you made it to salvation, I would die happy. I swooped in before Zero could react and captured him for the Frontier of Justice."

"The Frontier of Justice?"

"That is what he calls himself. He was the one who planned all of this. He is currently holding Zero and trying to force him to use his time-manipulating ability. He is going with or without you so you have to hurry." My brother closed his eyes. He was communicating with someone. The pole I was pinned against vanished. I fell to the ground.

"What's going on?"

"I signed a deal with Zeus-face-san to imprison you. I just messaged Zeus-face-san to let you go. There's no more time. Get to that ark and close the door behind you. And don't you ever look back."

"Why don't you come with me? You can return to your status!"

He smiled. There was a long silence. He looked to the crimson sky. Stars glimmered, turning it light blue. He was so strong, no illusion could hold him.

"I don't think that would work. People like me would only make the same mistake twice. The only way to find favor into my Father's heart is with my death." His eyes pierced me. "Please do not make the same mistake twice! And don't bring me back. Get on that ark that you once missed."

The air danced all around me. Various colors and images of all the inhabitants swirled. I passed out and awoke in darkness. Drops of water fell upon my scalp. I felt wooden planks and uneven rock under my feet. The air was cold and damp. It was an abandoned subway path. I ran. I ran and ran. I wasn't sure if I was running the right way, but I ran as if I was. I heard Zeus-face's voice call out to me, "Have a happy New Year, gangsta!" All that time in the Styx was just a few days in the real world.

"Make it your New Year's resolution to improve your hip-hop slang!"

"Don't be hatin' on my swagger, homey!"

I made it to the surface. I ran through the streets. My brother told me that there wasn't a lot of time left. I didn't have time to make it on foot. The ark was sailing without me so I had to figure out something. I saw an empty car. I had to face my fear. I waved my hand over the handle and unlocked the door. I jumped in. I waved my hand over the ignition and started the car. I took my first step. My first baby step onto the gas pedal.

I reversed and collided into the vehicle behind me. The alarms of the cars all around me went off, alerting people nearby. It wasn't pretty but I made it out of the parking space. I was on my way to my lifeboat.

That's when lightning struck me. If I did change time and returned to my original status, I would forget everything I'd learned in the human world. If this did work, I would never have met any of my human companions. I would never have met Jamie. Oh, my dear sister Jamie. Before I met her, I thought all humans were selfish, disloyal pigs. She was alone in this world. Her innocence led her to be hurt by so many people. But even though that was true, she never gave up her search for happiness.

Doughy. I remember the first time I met him. He was constantly abused by his boss at the restaurant he worked in, where I would eat from time to time. Finding work without graduating high school was hard, so he endured every beating. He felt trapped. He had lost his dream. The beatings added up until he couldn't hold the pressure one morning. I remembered that morning he brought a gun to work. He'd had enough. He was going to destroy the person who'd abused him for years. I knew what he was up to so I offered to help him reach his dream of playing music. He'd broken down and cried.

Shelia. As her age progressed, her health worsened. Society had forgotten about her. She tried her best to keep hope, but time gets the best of almost all. I let her know that she was still cared about. I let her know that she wouldn't be forgotten after her departure. Her pain would end.

Terra. Her parents constantly fought and put her through hell. She constantly ran away from home. At a young age she lived with men many years older than her. She wanted love that her parents never gave her. At least I knew how it felt to be loved. She never did. She never was independent. She felt like a parasite. She had been tired, tired of the running. Tired of the beatings. Tired of the desperation. I brought her under my wing. I remembered the night I let her stay at the apartment. Instinctively she undressed and came on to me. I told her to put her clothes back on. She was bewildered. Every man she'd ever been with demanded to sleep with her. Yet there I was, sleeping on the couch in the living room while she slept in my bed. She eventually found her independence. She vowed never to rely on someone else again. She vowed never to accept anything below genuine love again. Though she died, it brought me comfort that she would be brought back again to continue that vow.

Angry Kid. He was always raging. Angry at the injustices of this world. Angry at the hypocrisy. He was a hardworking citizen when he was laid off. His fiancée left him when he became homeless. He gave up his dream for promised security and was betrayed. He lost his trust for women. He lost everything but the clothes on his back and his old, run-down car. He robbed a small grocery store. The idiot was so frightened he didn't know that he was trying to push open a door that you had to pull. Police cornered him. I caught him a break by sending the two policemen into a deep sleep, allowing Kid to escape. And that's when I cornered him. I wanted him to join my band. He didn't know that I had saved him so he was reluctant to join me, but I threatened to turn him over to the authorities. He had pride. His pride never let him admit that he enjoyed the band and appreciated my help. He even found love again. Kid and Terra. I bet his child would've been named Angry Terra or maybe Terra Kid.

Helena . . .

We all had no family. We were all homeless. We were all invisible to the world. We were Nameless. We were drawn to each other. They had turned me back from doing something unbelievably wicked. They turned my face away from evil. I wondered if I could live on without their memories. The good *and* the bad. Once Morning Owl said to me that people like him would make the same mistake twice. Was I like him? Would I make the same mistake twice without their memories? If I prevented my fall from ever happening, how would I know I would appreciate my position in the light?

I reached my destination. The mansion owned by Mr. Jacques Powers. The man behind the man. I needed to know more. I needed to know what Harvey was talking about when he spoke of the destruction of all life. I had the feeling that everything would be revealed. Everything was going to change forever.

As I was parking, I crashed into a fire hydrant. I got out of the car and ran through the open gates of the mansion. I ran as fast as I could toward the mansion. I could see the beautiful sculpted bushes. As I passed a rabbit bush, a dark figure ran in front of me. It was dark so I didn't see exactly what it was. It looked feral and vicious. I had no time to investigate so I continued on my path. I suddenly tripped over an object. I looked down. It was a dead rabbit. Half eaten. I ran toward the door. A rabbit was ahead of me. I stopped. The rabbit looked side to side. It looked absolutely frightened. At that moment, a beast jumped through a bush nearby and slammed on top of him. It tore the rabbit to pieces with its claws. It mangled and munched on its skull and tore the flesh away. And that's when it noticed me. Lucky me. It dropped the rabbit to the ground. It moved toward me. It was on all fours. It crept cautiously like a lion. It was ready to pounce. The beast got closer. It got close enough for me to see its face. It was a man. It was once . . . human.

It had claws that were sharp like talons. The pupils of its eyes were dilated to the size of ashtrays. Hair covered its entire body but left a few bald patches on his face. He wore tattered clothing. He had bloody wounds all over his body.

His mouth was foaming. I couldn't even call it a man. It was a Nebuchadnezzar, the Fallen who are in a human host too long. It was the result of the Fallen's and the human's minds' total collapse into insanity. The mind reverts to its primal state and focuses on its most simple bodily needs, such as feeding and mating. The myth of werewolves was derived from stories of Nebuchadnezzar. I was in this hungry werewolf's sights. Its eyes were enraged with primal hunger and instinct. I twisted around and pounded the grass. The beast screeched. The sound pounded against the back of my head. The Nebuchadnezzar dashed after me. I swerved around one of the giant rabbit sculptures and ran back toward the mansion. The beast jumped through the bush and tackled me to the dirt, clawing at me. It viciously dug its talons into my flesh. Even though it was a Nebuchadnezzar, a human was still inside. If I killed it, I would be sent to the Null. I'd come too far just to get sent to the Null right at the doorstep of my ark so I had to endure. Its rancid screeches caused my left ear to bleed. My consciousness was slipping away. I shielded my face and chest with my arms, which were being torn to shreds.

There was a loud pop. The Nebuchadnezzar abruptly stopped. It twisted its head around. A dart was sticking out of its neck. Another pop rang out and a dart hit it in the chest. It stood up on two feet and started slowly walking toward the mansion. It stumbled from side to side. Another dart dug into its stomach. After a few more seconds, it collapsed to the ground. I clumsily got up and wobbled a few steps. I looked to the mansion. Mr. Jacques Powers was standing at the window with a rifle in his hand. He called out to me. I didn't hear exactly what he said but I ran.

I entered the mansion. Only a few lights were turned on. It was gloomy and depressing. I looked at one of Jacques's rabbit paintings. They were bashed and torn. I looked at the others. They were also destroyed. I went up the staircase. There she was. That magnificent painting of a woman at the top of the steps. The face of the woman was shredded. What had happened here? Why was a Nebuchadnezzar here? I ran up the rest of the steps. A voice called out to me again. It came from the room where I spoke to that Fallen the last time I was here. The big pink. It had that golden doorknob with the word TRAITOR still on it. I put my hand on the doorknob. The metal burned my flesh. I jerked my hand away. I didn't have time to think about why the doorknob was so hot. I went through hell coming here. I wasn't going to let a doorknob stop me now. I grabbed hold of that doorknob. My flesh sizzled. The knob was hard to twist. I had to turn it with all my strength. It was agonizing but I managed to force open the door. My skin was scorched and smoky. The burning knob left an imprint on my hand. I was marked TRAITOR.

The room hadn't changed at all since last time. The room was dim. The long dining table was still there. Burning candles were the only source of light. The Bibles that were once on the dining table were gone. There was no sound. I didn't know whether it was because my hearing was damaged or if the room was absolutely quiet. As I walked farther, I could hear a fire burning, making a crackling noise. The sound came from a fireplace at the end of the room. A big chair was in front of the fireplace. The chair's broad back was toward me, so I couldn't see if anyone was sitting there. I crept over little by little. And there he was. Mr. Jacques Powers. The man behind Jacques Powers. He seemed to be lost in the flames. He was holding a Bible in his hands. He looked at it and tossed it into the fire. He watched it as it was eaten by the flames. "You almost missed your cruise."

"Sorry I kept you waiting."

"You didn't. I was waiting for everything to be set up

properly. Everything will be ready in a few minutes." He waved his hand, sending a nearby chair to slide behind me. To do that, he must be extremely powerful.

"Sit." He spoke with that same clean and cut manner as before as if nothing fazed him. "Your clothes look terrible."

"If you remember, I was being torn to ribbons by a Nebuchadnezzar. Why was that thing there?"

"Oh, that was just one of my pets. Its name is Puddles."

"I thought you said every Fallen was sent to the Null."

"I apologize. I didn't give you accurate information. Some are trapped in human hosts. Just like you and I are."

"What else wasn't accurate information?"

The master switched his eyes to the upper-right corner of the room. He was sorting through the memories. "Everything else was accurate." Angels aren't allowed to tell lies. They must mimic the Creator's qualities in every way. When some of us were disconnected from Him, we were given the freedom to lie. Some Fallen maintain their sense of truth while others lie at will.

"That's not what I found out." The master seemed to breathe less when I said that. Nevertheless, his facial expression stayed the same. "As you know, I spoke to one of Zero's associates. A fortune-teller. And you know what he said?"

"What did he say?"

"'The destruction of all life.' Even as obvious as that sounded, I've been wondering what that could ever possibly mean."

"You do know that fortune-telling can be inaccurate?"

"That's what I thought. In fact, even Harvey said that he wasn't absolutely positive that he was correct."

The master's eyes slightly widened for half of a second, then returned to normal. "Harvey? Harvey Samuel Carr? The same Harvey who originated Baal worship, responsible for the masses of defenseless children sacrificed into religious flames? The great orchestrator of war leading to the deaths of millions?

The same Harvey responsible for the thousands of Fallen deported to the Null for the first Great War of the Flies? You're a madman to believe everything he has to say."

"That's what I thought. He manipulates anyone and anything. He not only uses humans but also uses fellow Fallen as pawns. I couldn't trust anything he said. But you know what? He told me that you were holding Helena captive. Is that true?"

The master stretched his neck from side to side. "Yes. Yes, it is true."

"I want to know everything." The master was silent. He folded his two hands together and put them in front of his face. He was thinking.

"Why are you holding Helena?"

He put his hands down. He told me to come with him. He got up and walked to the right side of the room. I followed him. He stopped at a wall. He began singing. "Words are flying out like endless rain into a paper cup." He wasn't singing enthusiastically at all. He just barely added melody to the words. I recognized the song as one performed by the Beatles. John Lennon had written it in 1968 and released in 1970. ". . . Jai guru deva . . ." He sang the song to its conclusion. He stood there motionless. "Step closer to me please." I did just so. "Om." At that moment, the floor sank down. The elevator took us all the way down to a sub-basement. From there, we walked through a hallway. We made many lefts and rights. We were in a maze

"Do I have to ask?" I said, looking at the master.

He looked back and looked forward. "I am extremely wealthy. I retrieved a metal that no human had discovered yet. I sell the metal for money. A lot of money." Years ago, a man had discovered new metal under the crust of the earth. He called it gomorium. It's the strongest metal known to mankind. Companies currently use gomorium to support buildings in zones prone to earthquakes. Because the metal is expensive, it's only used sparingly. "I paid some humans to build me this home and this underground basement. I designed the structure myself." I could tell that he wanted me to praise him. I saw his facial muscles turning into a slight smile. He was a philanthropist. He used his vast amounts of money to build schools and hospitals in third-world countries.

He led me to a window. It was covered with a purple drape. A pink door was nearby. "We fell away from light. We are locked inside a dark closet surrounded by hollow winter coats in the middle of summer. As a result, we hunger for another light. A substitute. We hunger for attention." The master looked as if he was reminiscing.

"What are you getting at?"

The master sighed. "Before I can let you on the ark, I have to make sure you have your life jacket on. I have to make sure you are ready. I must be sure you are deserving of a second chance." I was enthralled with what he had to show me. I pondered about the method he would use to find out if I was ready. "This will show if you deserve to be resurrected. Are you ready?" He grabbed hold of the purple drape. I gulped and nodded my head. At that moment, he snatched away the purple drape. And there it was. It was my substitute light he was talking about. My patient. My substitute god. My Helena.

I stepped forward to the glass window. She was in a brightly lit room. It looked like a room that police use to interrogate their suspects. She was sitting on a metal chair. Her mouth was taped shut. The rest of her body was bound by ropes to the chair. When I said the rest of her body was tied with ropes, I meant that from below her neck down to her toes was completely covered by rope. She was unconscious. "What is the meaning of this?"

"This is your trial." He went back a few steps. "We Fallen form attachments to the inhabitants of this realm. These people were a breath of fresh air for us. We breathed too much fresh air and suffocated to death. You and I know this better than anyone else. Now it's time to be resuscitated."

"She has nothing to do with this."

"Oh, yes, she does. More than one way too." I turned and looked at him. "Those other people you helped kill in that concert were just strangers to you." I wasn't sure if I was responsible for getting those people killed. I knew I'd tried to get them out at the last minute, but I was too late. It was because of my hesitation. Maybe I *was* responsible. "You didn't care about them anyway, so you deserved little merit for the job. But this will definitely seal the deal."

I went up to the glass and put my hand and head on it. "What's the point? When we change our fate, we are also changing Helena from ever being in this situation."

"Like I said, this is not about life and death. This is about your strength to choose the right path instead of going with what your heart wants. Choose temporary love or choose everlasting life."

"But this is so dishonorable."

"Oh, please. Don't feel that way. You think Helena Way cared about *you*? Helena has been dishonorable all her life. Before you even showed up, I found this woman snooping around my business. She even formed a romantic relationship with me. She would do anything for glory. She didn't believe you when you said you weren't part of Adilah. The only reason why she slept with you was to try and get closer to me."

Part of the glass cracked in front of me. Was he lying just to break my attachment with Helena? He had to be! Or at least he was genuinely wrong. She had to have affection for me. As our bodies merged together in bed, I felt her heartbeat quicken. I inhaled her breath and she inhaled my breath like smoking cigarettes. She shook just as I shook when the aftershocks flowed through us. She couldn't have faked that. Could she? Just as *she* did long ago.

"You involved her by forming a close relationship. This relationship led her into this situation."

"If you didn't care about the destruction I took part in back at the concert, why did you accept me? I know it wasn't just because Aisely asked you to, so why? Did you just want the satisfaction of spilling as much blood as possible?" I said, tightening my fists. He didn't flinch an inch.

"That was just a baby step. There are some of us that wouldn't even go that far. Other than that, everything Lofie ever talked about was you. He nearly talked my ear off. He was deeply in love with you. If fact, the only reason why he even participated was because he wanted to go back in time and try to woo you. He didn't even care for the Creator's favor. He just wanted to be with you as long as possible. You were his god. He was even willing to go back in time over and over again until you finally felt the same kind of love that he felt for you."

The master was telling the truth. When I fell into the flood, Lofie followed right after me. He even directly cursed Father for punishing me. Lofie knew that he would be damned for it, but he did it anyway just to be with me. I was the only god Lofie ever needed.

"Lofie gave his life to save you. Don't tell me you're going to turn Lofie's efforts in vain for the sake of a liar."

Could Helena really have done this to me? She didn't believe me. She didn't trust me. She didn't love me. At least Lofie truly loved me. Helena used me. I felt that I did owe Lofie for his sacrifice.

"What do I have to do?"

He told me to go inside. I did so. I walked over to Helena. A trapdoor was under her seat. A small coffee table was next to her with a device with a red button on it. A big, crimson-red button.

"As you can see, there's a trapdoor beneath Helena." A loud screeching and growling was coming from beneath the trapdoor. "The sound that you hear is coming from three Nebuchadnezzars beneath you. When you press that button on that remote, the trapdoor will open, sending Helena to her death. And don't worry. You won't be responsible enough to be sent to the Null for this. And even if you did, I have the power to bring you back home anyway."

He had it all figured out. There was no excuse not to go ahead with it. Even though there was a chance this plan to get back home wouldn't work, it was still the only chance I had. I had no choice. I cared about Helena. But I cared about going home more. The master was correct. It would be just a temporary love. What I wanted was everlasting life. I wanted to return to the heavens again. I wanted to go back to the light where I belong. I yearned for the brothers whom I hadn't seen since I fell. I wondered if they yearned to see me as well. I grasped the remote in my hand. I looked into it. Logic told me to press that button. Push that big crimson-red button. I heard the screeches and wet growls from the Nebuchadnezzars beneath us. I couldn't bear to imagine them ripping Helena apart. At least when *she* died, it would be peaceful and I wouldn't be the one who delivered the final blow.

I looked at Helena's body. Her annoying lovely, horrible, innocent, fierce, helpless body. I thought of all the times Helena and I shared. I remembered when it was a beautiful day outside so we decided to have our session in the park. We lay on the grass looking into the endless blue sky. I was such a lousy therapist. So unprofessional. At least when she was involved.

Other times we were both so charged we would burst into laughter for no reason at all. Could Helena fake that? Even if she did care about me, it would be a temporary love. I would die and then she would die. I held my finger over the button. Everything in the room started to get blurry. Every object started to twist and flux around. The air and surrounding area looked like water. "What's going on?"

"It's ready. Our ark is ready. This is your chance to show our Grand Creator that we don't need Him to live. This is your chance to finally have the freedom to make your own decision. This is your chance to obtain justice!"

I squeezed the remote. My hands were trembling. The ark was ready. It felt as if the world were closing in on me. I felt naked. I felt everything depended on me. I wanted to do this but I didn't. I'm a demon. Why should I care? I didn't have rules so why should I follow any?

"Don't do it, Aurick!" I swung around and looked to the master. I thought he'd spoken but it wasn't him. I looked around but there wasn't anyone in the room. I looked at Helena but she was still asleep. "Don't do it. It's a trick!" The voice was like an echo bouncing off the walls of a cave. "It's a trap!"

"Who are you?" My entire body shook even more. I had no idea what was going on.

"A brother. I am a fellow fly. I was tricked just like you are being tricked."

"What do you mean? And where are you?" I looked around. I then looked to Helena once more. There was no way it could be true.

"I am here. I've been occupying this woman's body for months now. A bit before you came to know her." Thoughts raced through my mind. It felt as if I were being yanked back and forth. "There is no time to talk. I don't how much more time I have left to communicate with you. All I can say is that I was working with Justice for years."

"Justice?"

"The Fallen who is occupying the body of Jacques Powers calls himself that. Do not be fooled. You are in danger. Helena is in danger. *Everyone* is in danger. Zero is being held against his will and is being forced to open the gates of time and matter." Everything seemed to slow down as if time were freezing in its tracks. I suddenly felt sick.

"All of this time, I've been talking to you?!"

"No. This is the first time in months I've been able to talk. Don't worry. You've been dealing with Helena Way the whole time. But enough of that. Justice is planning to take his vengeance. His mild temperament is just a mask for his insanity. He wants to use Zero to . . . aaaaaaaaaaaaaahhhh." Screaming and screeches tore through my mind. Then there was silence. The voice went away. And there he was. Justice had a calm yet irritated expression on his face.

XXII

JUSTICE

I've seen the wildest things in the universe. I've seen eternal stars explode and heavens rip apart. I've seen empires die and the earth scorched into mayhem. Eternity desensitizes all of us. No one can escape completeness. We constantly look for something new. Something shattering. Something absurd. Though it has become rare, every once in a while something disturbs our senses. Every once in a while something rips us apart. Every once in a while.

"I will ask you one last time," the master said with a calm, clean tone. "Push the button."

I knew there were missing pieces to the puzzle. A part of me wanted to turn the other cheek, but another part of me wanted the truth. The cold, dead truth. Die in ignorance or live in hell. I turned to him. I turned to Helena. I looked at the remote in my hand and looked to Helena again. I squeezed the remote and flung it. The remote smashed into pieces against the glass. The master's face seemed to wrinkle up. He slightly shook his head in disappointment. The door slammed shut. The only exit. I ran to Helena and started to tear away the binding ropes. The trapdoor swung open. I grabbed her before she fell down into the dark abyss. Nebuchadnezzars tore the chair into bits the moment it touched the ground. I looked down. A body was there. I looked closer to see that the body was of a young boy. I lugged Helena on my back. It was good to feel her warmth again. She still had some ropes tied to her, but there was no time to untie her now. The door was tightly shut. I pulled and pounded on the metal door but it didn't budge a bit. I lay Helena gently on her side. I kicked the glass but it wouldn't crack. It wasn't naturally that strong. The master was causing it to be firm. The Nebuchadnezzars were getting louder. They were jumping high and trying to grab the ledge of the trapdoor. It was just a matter of time before they got to us.

I couldn't believe I'd fallen for this stupid idea. I'd relied on blind hope instead of obeying the facts. Just like last time. I sat there with Helena, waiting to be torn to pieces. A Nebuchadnezzar finally managed to climb to our level. It was on all fours, oozing blood from its mouth. Its hair was as thick as a lion's mane. Its pupils were dilated. There was nothing human left. There was nothing angel left. It was just an empty shell to feast. I pressed Helena's head to my chest and put my own head down on her scalp. I closed my eyes and braced myself. Then, there was a grinding sound. I opened my eyes. There was a loud pop and click.

"I opened the door. Get out now!"

I obeyed the voice and lugged Helena with me. Just as the Nebuchadnezzar clawed its way after me, I slammed the door on its face. I looked around and there was no one. "Down here, genius." It was Aisely in my dear Sephirot. He had opened the door with air pressure. "What in the world happened? You were in the clear!"

"We've been duped. We were just used."

"What are you talking about?"

"He just wanted us to distract marooner units and locate Zero. Just like he used all the other Fallen before us."

"No. He told me that if any Fallen were harmed, he would bring them back."

"He lied. He never planned on bringing anyone back. He never planned on helping anyone in the first place. There was no way to go back home in the first place." Aisely looked around in uncertainty. "He even locked some that disagreed with him away into humans. He even locked one Fallen inside of Helena!"

"I can't believe you're losing sight of the goal, Aurick," Aisely said as if he were absolutely sure of himself. "We're almost there and you're losing faith. Come with me."

I glared at Aisely. He started to walk away trying to lead me somewhere. "No, Aisely. Can't you see? It's just been a personal selfish goal of a Fallen. We've been misled by an Angel of Light."

"No! It is you that cannot see," Aisely said, stomping on the ground. The ground vibrated. He turned around and faced me. Angels of Light were Fallen who hold out false hope for any listeners, and Aisely was deeply duped. "You're not making any sense. What gain would he get for this then? Why would he go through all of this trouble just to play with our minds?" That was something I didn't know. "If he wanted to destroy all life, Father would just bring everyone back to life anyway as if nothing happened. No one would even remember. It would just be a big waste of time. Now why would a smart Fallen waste his time with that?" I didn't say anything. Aisely sighed and shook his head. "Exactly. If you want more answers, why don't you come with me? I am sure you will be forgiven and given another chance to come with us."

It was true that I still wanted to learn more. I wanted to see this through to the end. I agreed to follow Aisely. I gently put Helena on the ground against the wall. I was nervous leaving her there unattended, but Aisely assured me that nothing would bring her harm. Aisely, despite his foolish ways, was actually one of the most powerful spirits in the universe, and I believed he could keep Helena safe even at a distance.

We ran. We made numerous rights and lefts through that

maze. The air around us bent. It was like being in a tidal wave as it falls around you. Even the walls and ground looked like water. The world still felt as if it were closing in on me. I felt like a buried kernel. I felt as if I were suffocating. I wanted to get out. I wanted to live. I wanted to die. The madness was taking over me. Aisely seemed to be able to bear it. A light was at the end of the hallway. I felt terror passing through that point of light. It felt like the end. Though I was terrified, I wanted to know more. I needed to know more. I leaped into the light, and then . . . nothing. Everything was pitch-black. It felt as if I were in the mouth of Tartarus itself.

All of my life I'd been able to understand what was going to happen next before it even happened. For the first time in my life, I honestly didn't know what was going to happen next.

Tartarus let me go. Out of Tartarus and into Justice. I stood before him. The master was at the center of the room, completely naked. He was looking into an empty space. Winds blew. I felt as if I were being drawn in, as if I were being sucked into a whirlpool. He was holding a chain in his hand. At the end of the chain was a Nebuchadnezzar, sitting like a docile puppy waiting for its master's command. Some blurry, wavy air was around it. It formed a ball. Justice looked as if he was absolutely enthralled with it. The first expression other than boredom. Utter amazement. It was as if he'd waited for this moment all of his life.

"Can you see it, Mr. Aisely? It's beautiful!" he said, forming a fist in sheer excitement. "I've waited for this for so long." The room sporadically turned light and dark. He looked over his shoulder. He became irritated at the sight of me. "Why did you let him go, Aisely?" His loyal Nebuchadnezzar arched his back like a lion and started to growl.

"Um, I think Aurick deserves another chance. I don't think he meant what he did."

"It's too late, Aisely. Aurick already made his decision and he failed."

"It's never too late. You said it yourself. Everyone deserves another chance."

The master turned around. He had both male and female genitals. The master blinked as if he were pondering Aisely's words. The Nebuchadnezzar seemed to calm down. "There is grand wisdom dormant inside of you, Aisely. I shall give Aurick another chance. I don't want to mimic what Father has done to us."

"Why did you stick that Fallen into Helena?" I said, taking a few steps forward. "He says that this whole thing is a trap."

The master slapped his forehead with his palm. "For death's sake. Will there ever be an end to these obstacles?" The master sighed as if he had run a mile. "He was a Fallen who was helping the cause at one point. Midway through the plan, he grew cold feet and turned against me. He was going to reveal to a marooner our plans, so I had to shut him up. I sealed him in a human host. That human host at the time happened to be Ms. Helena Way."

"Why her?"

"As I've told you before, she's a backstabber. She tried to form a fake romantic relationship with me, which I don't tolerate. I wanted her to feel pain and suffering so I chose to stick the Fallen inside her. The only problem was that she persisted in uncovering Adilah, which slowly unlocked the Fallen I had put into her. She was too much of a threat."

"And that's why you tried to have her killed. You wanted to immobilize the Fallen for good so he could never ruin your goal. But why did the Fallen want to do that in the first place?"

"The closer he got to the truth, the more cowardly he became. He feared being punished for his actions so he tried to stop me. He even convinced Zero to run away from me. He also believed that would return him into the Creator's light once more." The master smirked. "Hopeful thinking. The bastard wouldn't just accept the fact that he will never be loved again. Bollix." The air seemed to twist more and more violently as time passed. "Here comes your make-up exam."

I looked behind me. And there she was. Helena was walking into the room. Her eyes were closed. The master was manipulating her body to move. She entered the room and stood feet away from me. "This is your last chance to cut your attachments to lies. Go to him, Ginga!" The Nebuchadnezzar rushed over to me. I was startled but maintained my composure. It happily came to my side. I grabbed the leash. "The moment you let go of the leash, your sin will be covered." My hands were shivering. I needed to do this but I was still hesitating. "Remember, Lofie got sent to the abyss to give you this opportunity. Don't disappoint him."

And there it was. My time had come. It was my chance to make up for my error. It was my chance to live. My chance to return to my Father's winged embrace. It would be at the cost of a human whom I cared about, but it would be worth it. A human whom I'd shared laughs with. A human whom I'd connected with. A human that I'd made love to. A human heart that had calmed the dirges of tormenting hatred in *my* heart. She'd stopped me from myself.

Did I really feel more loyal to Helena than God? Do it! Do it! Show Him that you don't need Him! Show Him that you control your own fate. You won't even remember this day, so do it. I felt love. I felt hate. I wanted the light. I wanted the darkness. I was stuck between two masters and I had to choose one. The eternal master who gave me life or the temporary master who *returned* life to me. Oh my greatness, weakness seized me.

"Looks like you don't learn from your mistakes."

I let go of the leash. I used the little control of my spirit abilities I had left and caused the Nebuchadnezzar's mind to only see Justice in front of him so he would not go for Helena or anyone else. I watched as the beast tore up Justice. He scrambled on the floor, spinning around and rolling with the Nebuchadnezzar over and over. Every time he threw it off, it clamped right back on his flesh. He wrapped the beast with its own chain. He tightened the chain around its neck and didn't let go. It struggled and it tossed around. Then the fray stopped. The Nebuchadnezzar lay unconscious on the floor. The master got back up. His back was toward me. He was panting and sweating like the dog he'd knocked out. He panted and panted some more. He was bleeding. I was counting on Justice to kill the Nebuchadnezzar, alerting some marooners to come and arrest him. Justice was smarter than that.

"That was extremely stupid. That was stupid indeed." He dusted his clothes off. He turned around revealing his true self. Aisely cringed and looked away. The monster behind the mask was revealed. Nearly half of the flesh on his human face was ripped off in the Nebuchadnezzar attack. Blood gushed down from his face and splattered on the floor. Some of the bottom and top rows of teeth were showing. Meat and other stringy webs of flesh dangled from inside and outside his mouth. He seemed to feel no pain. "It doesn't matter. You're all going to be dead anyway. It is complete."

"What do you mean *dead*?" Aisely said.

"The truth is that I've been lying to you. Mostly."

Justice seemed calm and collected. He was in control of the entire situation and he knew it.

"So you're not going to save anyone."

"Well, no, that was somewhat true. Sort of."

"Then what is all of this?" Aisely said, pounding on the floor with his feline paws. His teeth and nails were fully extended.

"God loves to keep promises. If fact, he not only loves to

make promises, He is utterly obsessed with keeping them. His word is His bond. Forever being tied to them is His greatest weakness." My stomach was disturbed. I felt something bad was going to happen. I just didn't know exactly what. "God once said that He would never ever, *ever* allow the earth to be destroyed. That the earth would stand forever no matter what. What do you think would happen if someone proved Him wrong?" Aisely and I stood there silent. "Proving a god wrong would make that god turn out to be a fraud. He would be revealed as a liar. He would have to admit that He lost. It would prove that He was never what He said He was. His very name means 'causes to become.' Someone who would cause *Him* to become would wipe out His very name. It would void His very name and His very purpose in life."

"So what? So what if you proved that you could break one of God's words? What does that have do with everyone else?" The air around us started to push us backward and then forward. We were slowly being sucked in.

"Everything, you fool! Proving that He is a fraud would take away His honor and His meaning for existence. He would be on the same level as *us*. The meteors. The flies. The snakes. The vermin. The dissected butterflies. The walking dead. The Fallen. He judged us to be executed. Now you tell me, Aurick. I would ask Aisely, but he never was the brightest sun in the galaxy. If He was put on our level, what do you think God would have to do?"

I pondered it. I pondered and pondered some more. I already knew the answer but I didn't want to accept it. "Father judged us to be executed. If Father was then put on our level, that would mean He passed judgment on Himself."

"And then what?" Justice said, smiling slightly

I reached inside myself and pulled out the answer. I didn't want to but I had to. "Father would have to execute Himself."

"Ding! You have answered the thirty-three million pieces of silver question correctly. Your prize is the suicide of your Tormentor. Ironically, He was the first to use that same strategy on King David. Look it up."

The world seemed to squeeze me into a slipknot. I felt as if I were dying. "Father is what holds this universe together. If He dies, we *all* die."

"Well, if you want an omelet, you have to break a few eggs. We were once perfect but failed our duty. God is just as perfect as we once were, so what does that say about God? What makes Him so different from us? Just because He came into existence first doesn't mean He's better than we who came second. Do we not have the same rights to life as Him? The way I see it, we all deserve to die. No, better yet. We all *want* to die. Zero here is living proof." Justice pointed to the end of the room.

"You're bringing in others that have nothing to do with this. Keep your vengeance to yourself."

"This isn't revenge. Revenge is just a selfish grudge to no avail. This is for righting universal wrongs. We are all a part of this from the very beginning whether we like it or not. This is for the sake of balance. For fairness. For truth. For justice."

"Only one problem with your idea. How in the world are you going to manage to destroy the earth?"

"To go back in time you would have to reverse the flow of the very nature of space. The only being who could ever perform such a feat properly is our Heavenly Father. If anyone tried that, it would deteriorate the fabric of existence." It made sense now. That explained why Harvey couldn't see into the future past today. There was no future to see. But such a thing couldn't possibly happen.

Aisely connected with my mind mentally. Aisely was one of the strongest angels of the heavens. *Far* surpassing me. He could stop almost anyone. He told me he couldn't get out of Sephirot's body for some reason. I wondered if he'd used it as a host for too long.

"Sorry. But I'm preventing Aisely from leaving that host by force. You're practically the strongest spirit in existence. I can't have you messing everything up. It's a shame you could never solve anything with your brain. You let your talented brawn fill your heart with arrogance and immaturity. As a result, you never grew up. You mind was frozen in childhood. How ridiculous." The roof over Aisely cracked and shook. Rock, wood, and chunks of debris fell on top of him. I raced over to him. I lugged and tossed as much debris as fast as I could. My hands bled. I ignored the pain and dug. I dug and dug some more. And there they were, Aisely and Sephirot. They were lying motionless and breathless. My two friends. My loyal friends.

"Why are you doing this? Why are you doing this to your own kin?!" I said, grasping Sephirot's little head in my palm.

The monster gritted his teeth in utter frustration.

"I'm doing this *for* you! For all of us!" Justice rubbed his forehead. "He sentenced His own sons to be executed like ill-bred dogs. My own Father wants to kill me. It's time He gets a taste of His own medicine." I felt his loathing. "Don't look at me like that! You and I are exactly the same. You really think that you came here to save your precious Helena? Give me a break." He laughed. "Deep down you came here for vengeance just like me. Deep down you want to spit in the face of His death sentence. You want to prove you don't need Him to live. The only difference between me and you is that you're confused."

"What happened to you?"

"You released a dog and it bit off my face!" Justice knew what I was questioning but he wanted to annoy me. He smiled. "I was a marooner. I was a marooner who was in love. In love with a beautiful woman. Her name was Adilah." He turned his side to me. I saw the clean side of his face. "Adilah had such a beautiful smile. Her luminous lips would eat up the darkest black of the night." He started laughing. "She was so funny. She would keep me laughing the whole day. She was the kindest spirit. She reminded me of who I once was. I guess that's why I was drawn to her." He gazed up to the ceiling. I felt he was sorting through the memories. The good ones, the bad ones, and the really bad ones. "I was careful with our relationship. I didn't want to be turned into a Fallen so I looked for every loophole I could find. Angels aren't allowed to materialize into humans or possess humans, so I used a human male to say everything I wanted to say. I made him move the way I wanted to move. He was my puppet. That man was me and that woman was mine. When they made love, I connected with their minds to feel what they were feeling. The male didn't know what he was doing half the time. I brought her things from all over the globe. Do you know what her favorite animal was?" He laughed lightly. "Rabbits. Forest rabbits, marsh rabbits, swamp rabbits, arctic rabbits, Mexican cottontail, mountain cottontail, pygmy rabbits. I brought her rabbits from all over the world to make her happy. And I was successful. She loved them all. I even managed to bring her a kangaroo." He giggled. "She fainted the first time she saw that thing. She named it Jo-Jo. I remember Jo-Jo punched her once and gave her a black eye. She got rid of it after that."

"I guess that explains all of the paintings."

"Back then, especially in those lands, women were treated badly by men. They could hardly own anything nor do anything. She loved me just as I loved her. I wanted to be with her forever. But I knew better. I knew I could never be with a mist. I don't know why I defied logic but I did it anyway. I tried keeping the mist afloat over the vastness of the ocean. I promised to love and protect Adilah forever. We were in everlasting love. And then misfortune happened." His face grew colder suddenly. The surge of pain rushed through him. It rushed through me. "Marooners were ordered from home to get out of the area. Father was going to burn the wicked city to the ground. The city was warned by a prophet but no one had listened, including Adilah. I tried my best to convince her, but she wouldn't leave. I had no problem with that. I would just get my Adilah out and everything would be fine. That's when we were ordered not to save anyone from the city. We were to leave every single thing in that city to burn. This was a direct judgment from Father. That's when my entire world stopped. I felt trapped. I didn't know what to do. Logic told me to leave and to never look back. But I couldn't. I didn't understand but I couldn't. Maybe I did understand but I went with it anyway. I felt like a coward. I felt like a traitor. I was torn between two worlds. The temporary or the everlasting. That was when I made my choice. It was futile. We *both* died that day. We were two lifeless bodies. Ever since that day, I've felt nothing but hatred. It was so much suffering I felt like I was going to drown in it." It seemed as if he started to literally choke.

"I understand the feeling."

"Oh, God, I can still feel the pangs. I can still feel the irresolvable revulsion. It's eating me alive. It was so consuming that I became a scorpion." Scorpions are Fallen who try to kill themselves. Just like scorpions, when they're near intense heat, they stab themselves to death. It is futile for angels because the only being with the ability to destroy spirits is Father. "I got past that stage and continued to live on. My past and torment manifested itself physically. Everything I touched withered. Each time I possessed a human, my stress would turn its hair pure white in a matter of days. But that's enough of the past. The past, present, and future will become unified in one last bang in a couple more minutes. We both know you feel the same way as I do. Don't lie because I can see the white hairs on your host." He caught me. He knew every emotion I felt.

"He tortures us for amusement. Living for eons must get boring. Maybe that's why He watches the humans as they burn themselves alive. Maybe that's why He idly waits as we all eat each other alive. I defended and worshipped the throne. I held His name over mine."

"You were the most serious one of all of us."

"That's right. And then I fell in love and He kills me for it. Where's the justice in that?" He tightened his fists. "You know what it is? It took me centuries of obsessively replaying it in my mind but I finally figured it out. He's jealous. He's jealous that a human truly loved me more than she ever possibly could love Him. He did say He's a jealous God." I always wondered the same thing. "He gave the human's their Messiah, so I'll be the angels' messiah. A dark messiah. I will exact the same justice He exacted upon me." He started to break down. It was as if the tears were about to gush out but were too frozen to. "I loved her. I loved her so much. I loved her and He took her away from me. He took away my Adilah. My poor, sweet Adilah. I spent eons serving justice. I was always promised justice would come through for me. Well? Where in the world is *my* justice?" Justice covered his face in sheer anguish. I cringed to see him like that. "He broke my promise, so I'm going to break one of His."

"You're right, Justice. When I fell, I wanted the world to burn as much as you do. I wanted to leave a scar on Father that could never be wiped away. To tell you the truth, I really don't know the difference between you and me. I don't know what urge is stronger. Spend the rest of my life with Helena or take vengeance against my king. I don't know what to think anymore. Do whatever you want. I'm too damned tired of this. Whatever happens, happens."

"They will hold you back from life. They're the death of us all. Don't worry though. I shall fight for indiscriminate justice just as my body dictates." He thrust his arm out to Helena.

"Come here, my darling." Helena walked over to him. "No wonder you fell in love with her. She is absolutely beautiful. Absolutely independent." He swept his fingers through Helena's hair. Violating her hair was like violating my soul. He had finally taken all of our dignity. Not letting a second pass by, he plunged his tongue into her mouth. He was making her a bloody mess. I didn't feel anger for some reason. I didn't know what to be angry at anymore. Maybe this is what I really wanted anyway. Revenge. This was the end.

I knelt and put my head down. I felt hopeless. I felt truly lost. I could see his tongue through his gaping wound. He spun her and put his arm around her shoulder. He placed the other arm around her stomach. "What do we have here? It looks like Ms. Way is . . . pregnant." I lifted my head up at that moment. I gazed upon Helena's stomach. I also looked at Justice's reaction—surprise and other emotions that I couldn't read. He put his nose to her neck and sniffed her. "And it looks like it's . . . your baby. Congratulations. You are going to be a father."

At that moment, I felt . . . *things*. I didn't know how to describe it. I didn't know what it was. It was nothing I had ever felt before. It was like a surge of energy. An array of new. A heave of escape.

Though I didn't understand what I felt, I knew what Justice was feeling. His eyes filled with . . . jealousy. I had a sense of what I was supposed to do. I didn't want to feel hatred anymore. I didn't want vengeance anymore. I didn't want to fight anymore. I wanted . . . peace. I snatched up a sharp piece of metal debris that lay before me and dashed straight forward. I knew the consequences of my actions. I knew the severity of my crime. I knew the severity of my punishment. It was worth it. I didn't understand why but it was worth it. I plunged the sharp debris into the heart of Justice. He gasped and coughed clots of blood. He backed off. I sloppily yanked the metal out.

Blood spilled from his open mouth and from his open wound. He collapsed to the floor. His host was dead. Justice was immobile. Stabbed with his own gomorium.

At that moment, my fingers stiffened. Blood leaked from my mouth. My knees buckled, forcing me down. It was so painful. It was a different kind of pain. I felt cold. I felt . . . the end. I'd used this body for too long. My time was up. At least my Helena was safe. At least her child was safe. I closed my eyes. For some reason, when I closed my eyes, darkness didn't come. I opened my eyes. I could see everything. I could see Zero. I could even see the manifestation of his time manipulation. Waves of different colors surrounded him. He was unconscious. But then I wondered why I could see everything in the first place. Why was I even standing up? And then it hit me. Aurick had awoken. He had awoken to find Pandora's box in the palm of his hands.

All types of shapes swung around me. Circles, squares, triangles, hexagons, etc. I looked down to see that I wasn't standing on any kind of platform. I was standing upon nothing. The entire realm looked like an endless hole, like outer space without the darkness but of rainbows. I realized that I wasn't actually awake. I was just seeing Aurick's thoughts and what he was seeing. I was in his mind. And there he was. Aurick in his mental manifestation was standing before me. His back was turned to me while he stared into something. It was like an orb that was showing everything on the outside of our mind. I looked into it. Aurick's physical body was walking toward Zero. The real Zero. Aurick was going to attempt to tap in to the ability to change the past. I thought if I spoke to the mental manifestation of Aurick, it would stop our physical body. So I spoke.

"Don't do this, Aurick. This power is out of your league."

The physical Aurick stopped before Zero. "This is it. This is what I've been looking for all my life." Aurick was in absolute awe. "It's beautiful. I can change anything I want. All of the mistakes I've made in the past. All of the chances of greatness I missed. I can do whatever I want. I can have whatever I want. I can *be* whatever I want. I could be a football player. I could be an astronaut. I could be a trillionaire. I could be the president. I could be the ruler of the world. I could be . . . a god." Aurick must not have heard any of the truth I had learned from Justice. He must've heard only the lies. Only things that Aurick wanted to hear. I waited for a marooner to show up. I waited and waited but nothing.

"It's not what you think, Aurick. It'll bring nothing but strife. The sun is out of your reach, Aurick!"

"I've been told that all of my life. I've missed so many opportunities. And for what? To please a God who never once helped me? A God who never answered one of my prayers?" Suddenly, the empty realm showed me images of Aurick. It showed all the times he needed assistance and felt that he never got it. It showed him suffering and crying. "I obeyed Him and got nothing in return but ridicule." More images flashed. It showed people laughing at Aurick's humiliation. It showed him dwelling in filth and failure. "Studied myself half to death through school. Academic degrees with no job. Food stamps for income. Student loans as a medal. The American dream lived up to its title. Just a dream. Honesty caused me to get left behind in this world. I became scum." Aurick didn't understand that if he went through with this, he would truly be scum.

"Your reward will be greater if you pass this up. Please, Aurick. I don't know if you'll be forgiven for this."

"I prayed all my life and you know what? I don't feel like praying anymore. I feel like actually doing something. I'm taking back what I deserve." Aurick's physical self plunged his hands into the bubble of energy.

And at that, his entire body was electrocuted.

XXIII

ΠΟΤΗΙΠG LESS

Out of nothing came love.

Aurick lay dead on the ground. His wings had melted. I too was helplessly immobile. The only thing I could do was see through my eyes. I couldn't even move those either.

I felt nothing but guilt. I had brought Aurick into this and it had destroyed his life. I'd used him to better the little amount of life I had at the cost of his possible *eternal* life. He was in the same state as I was. Except that I continued to live on and feel the pain of being dead.

"Trying to call a marooner unit here to stop me? Sorry, but that won't work."

More bad news hit me. I didn't immobilize Justice. I didn't understand how. There was no way his host could survive what it had just experienced. Justice grabbed hold of the skin from his face. In a sloppy jerk, he peeled flesh away. Nothing but blood covered his face. Small pieces of flesh, cartilage, and bone remained. The only remnant of his face was the skin around his right eye, right cheek, and a bit of lip.

"I'm a corpser."

I could still connect with Justice's mind. I thought corpsers were only a myth, those Fallen whose hosts have died while they were occupying the body. Usually when the host dies, the Fallen is stuck and completely immobile until the body rots away to dust. I had no idea why Justice was able to move and talk.

"This isn't going according to plan. I wanted to show you something before the big implosion. I wanted to leave this body in a more . . . dignified way. I guess I'll have to leave this meat-bag . . . the hard way." Justice thrust his arm to Zero and grabbed hold of him. That moment, the ground, the walls, the entire house, began to quake. Justice screamed in misery. The skin of his arm was melting away. Thrusting and throbbing in his wallowing. The peeling and melting of his arm spread to the rest of his body. He wallowed in his pain but I knew this pain was nothing compared to the pain of the cut of emotional ties to his brothers and Father. He was going this far for what he believed in. Skin and muscle burned away like paper. Then finally the burning reached his very bones and marrow. The quaking stopped. All that was left was blood-soaked ash. I looked around. What had happened? Was it finally over?

"No, it is definitely not over. You rejected my offer twice before." Justice's voice bounced all across the room. I looked but I saw no one. Justice had left his body. He was in his all-powerful spirit form. "But now you will see the final piece of my offer. The ultimate offer that no one can refuse. Come with me. Come with me and see my offer for you will definitely not refuse it. I *promise* it."

I blacked out.

I awoke. I awoke in a floorless land. I awoke on a wall-less land. I awoke to nothingness. I was no longer in my host. I was in my own spirit self. I looked around. There was . . . nothing. Nothing to look at. There was no justice, no constructs, no humans, no angels. There was just . . . nothing. Even with my eons of experience, I did not recognize the land I stood on. This land of nothingness. "Where am I?"

"I was able to snatch you out of your flesh after I was able to get out of mine. I'm well rounded when it comes to abilities.

Usually it takes millions of years for a spirit being to learn some-thing. Yet because of my rage, it made me master almost every-thing in a few thousand. You still appear as you because your mind still believes you are in Aurick's body." I looked down at myself and saw he was right. I did still look like Aurick. "Have no fear, my brother. For we are in a place where no one can bring us harm. A place where no one can hear our shameful confessions. The land of nihilism. The land of nonexistence. Indeed, a landless land."

He was right. I looked to the farthest of which my eyes could go and I saw nothing. There was just . . . whiteness. Not the kind of whiteness that you see in the snow. No, not even the snow that you see in the coldest of places of Antarctica itself. It was whiter and deeper than that. I was . . . terrified.

"Why is everything so . . . white?"

"It's not white. It is actually pink, but you can't see this space's true color. There's a shell that is enclosed around us for light-years. The shell is bombarded by all the particles in the universe so it has a pink color." My spirit frequency became unstable. This happens when a spirit is unsure of what is going to happen. I'd never been in one of these regions of the cosmos. "You should be terrified, my brother. Don't worry though. It is only natural and healthy to become unstable when exposed to something you have never experienced before. This is something even our dear Creator cannot understand. But I understand, brother. I understand your shuddering."

"Where have you brought us? I have never laid eyes on such a place."

"This is the womb of purity, brother. This is the womb of safety. A womb of rebirth. Indeed, a womb that will set us free. Inside the womb of an invisible burning phoenix."

"You haven't answered my question."

"Yes, brother, I haven't. But I cannot. Everything in

existence must have a name. In *existence*. This place is a place of nonexistence, therefore it has no name. No noun can be assigned to it." I did not say anything back. All I did was try to find a focal point for my eyes to be on. But I could not because of the whiteness. The only thing my eyes could fix on was Justice. For he was the only thing here. Or the only thing . . . *nowhere*. "You can try to name it anyway if you want though. I've tried to come up with many names just for fun. Let's come up with a name ourselves. We have plenty of time. For time does not exist here." Justice chose to be in the form of his host. Except his appearance was a much more youthful version of the body. In his human thirties. "How about . . . Womb of Sanctification?" Justice said, stretching his hand out to me. "Don't like it, huh? Okay. So how about"—Justice paced about—"Ark of Renewal? No-God's Land? Oh, how about—"

"Nothing," I said, cutting him off.

Justice turned his back to me and stared off into the distance of no distance. "Nothing, huh? Simple but appropriately appropriate."

"Why have you brought us here?"

"I am glad you asked that. Before we move on, I just want to tell you not to dwell on the elementary science of this entire thing. I just want you to focus on the semantics. The dreams, the goals, the future, the potential, and the wisdom." The future? I thought Justice wanted to eliminate all possible futures from existence. "This is our ark. An ark that you failed to get you and your former lover on. I am giving you a second chance."

"How will this give me a second chance? If Father dies, everything in existence will melt away just like your host."

"Yes, you are correct. But we are not in existence anymore . . . are we?" I didn't reply. I felt that I wasn't educated enough to either defend or rebuke his statement. "I found this realm by accident, you know. My original plan years ago was to break another promise the Creator had made. After he kicked us freedom fighters out of Home, he told us that we could not enter ever again. I wanted to prove him wrong." Justice vanished. I looked around but could not see him. Only his voice returned. "I tried for years with all of my burning passionate might and resources to break the veil that Home was protected by. Indeed, an impenetrable wall. An impenetrable womb that belonged to the Creator himself. I knew I could not tear open the Creator's womb that was protecting Home, but I nevertheless tried anyway. I dug and dug through every physical and metaphysical dimension like digging a grave and I could find . . . nothing." The voice stopped. I looked around as hard as I could but couldn't even sense Justice's presence, even though I was in my own spirit self. "I thought I had found nothing, and when I finally gave up, I found this nothingness." Justice appeared next to me. His appeared as a young boy in his preteens. He was walking calmly away from me again. "This nothing was my key to my goal. It would've been selfish suicide if I merely wanted to destroy everything just to destroy one person without anything beneficial to show after. It would've been incomplete justice. This was my way into *perfect* justice." He disappeared again. After a few seconds of silence, he reappeared once more, as a teenager, sitting on a stool. "There are many zones of this nothingness throughout the universe."

"How can there be nothing when there are infinitely smaller particles that travel and flow through them? That's impossible. Everything is connected to something. And if that's the case, this won't work."

"No exacto. During the formation of the universe, there exist giant cosmic geodes. Similar to the geodes found in magma that I've been to on my trips for gomorium. Though you cannot see the ends of these realms, they are indeed finite. Well . . . for now they are finite."

"I don't understand."

"Think of these zones as giant eggshells. Shells are made up of every kind of particle in existence. They stick together like wax that form into a sphere. These shells block out every form of matter and energy. Sure, some matter makes its way through the shell sometimes, such as you, I, and some forms of radiation, but it still remains mostly pure. Indeed, pure enough to withstand the time bomb that awaits outside of this womb."

"To move around physically, you need leverage. On earth, you must push your feet off the ground to walk. There is no leverage here. So how is it that you can move about?"

"I am propelling myself with particles from my body like an elevator connecting between my spirit body and the shell. Another way you can move around is if you form strips or platforms as a ground or swing using strings of particles from the shell. Speed is also limitless here."

"It seems you've figured everything out about this realm."

"I am far from figuring out everything in this . . . special world. There are many things I do not understand. Some of the rules of physics and metaphysics are not consistent. I believe you can break all the rules I told you if you have enough time to figure it out. God started in a world like this before creation but seemed to figure out a way to create something out of . . . well . . . . nothing. Very interesting indeed."

"So you are planning to stay within this womb and ride out the upcoming storm outside?"

Justice got up from the stool. "Yes." Everything he said was making sense. Everything Justice said seemed so unreal but absolutely believable at the same time. I put my head down and tried to get my thoughts together. This was so much to absorb. I felt a tap on my shoulder. Justice was over me. "I still haven't given you your offer yet."

"I refuse," I said right away.

Justice stared at me for a few seconds. He slowly smiled, then gave a short burst of laughter. "You haven't even heard it yet."

"And I don't want to. For I already know what you want. You want someone to join you after this cataclysm. You want to be a god. But you want a helper. I don't want it."

Justice smiled again. This time it wasn't a smile. "No exacto, my brother. No exacto. I don't want anyone to join anything. Because I won't be part of it." He rested his hand on my shoulder. "I don't deserve becoming a god. I don't deserve surviving this flood. My hands will be bloodstained. Indeed, stained with the blood of our Father."

"And—and what about me?"

"You. It is you. It is you that will be the new god of the new world."

I slapped his hand away and jumped to an upright position. "What are you talking about? This is absurd."

"I know it is," Justice said, laughing a bit. "Absurdity is all we have left. You will be the sole survivor. You will carry on the Creator's legacy. You will carry mine and Adilah's legacy. You will carry everyone's legacy. For the Fallen *and* for the upright."

"Oh, and what, live on forever by myself? This is the justice you speak of?"

"No, my brother, no. You will have the rest of eternity to figure out what only the Creator claims to know how to do. Create sentient life. Sure you will be lonesome by yourself for a very, *very* long time. But I am sure you will figure out the secret to abiogenesis. The Creator didn't always have his creations around him. He did it, and so can you."

"Father said it's impossible unless He does it."

Justice sighed. "My brother. Are you still holding fast to that lie the Creator fed to us all these years? Not everything He says is true. I will prove this when I break one of His promises shortly. You must think. You must think long and hard."

And so I did. I thought. I thought and I thought. I thought of every possible thing I could do with this decision. I could do everything and anything I could possibly dream. I would spend time figuring out the secrets that Father had been hiding from us all this time. The secret of creating life, the secret of sustaining life, and even the secret of bringing back life. So much knowledge at my disposal. But what if it was truly impossible to find out? What if Father was right? Oh, listen to me. I'm still calling him Father. He is not my father. Not anymore. That's right. He plans on killing me. Even if I couldn't figure out the ultimate secrets, He was going to kill me anyway. I was searching for an answer. An answer that would set me free. An answer that would satisfy why *she* had to die. Well, wasn't this the answer I had been searching for? Was this meant to be? I can create my own government. No, not *my* government. The government of the people. We would have a democracy. A divine democracy.

"Yes, my brother. I know your every thought. You have so much to gain and nothing to lose. You've always been a calm, collected one. Listened to all sides no matter how twisted they may seem. Neutral indeed. But you cannot let your neutrality hold you back from this ultimate decision. Not this time, brother. I beg you. For I know that you know the ache of loss as I do."

Yes, it was an ache. I was in pain. I'd lost something that would never return to me. But . . . I did have one question. One last question to make this ultimate decision.

"After this cosmic meltdown, nothing will exist. This realm of nothingness will expand infinitely after everything is gone. In this realm of nothingness, things do not behave as they would normally. Absolutely everything. Including our very thoughts. More specifically, our memories. Wouldn't that mean my thinking patterns will be gone?"

Justice nodded his head as if to tell me my question was plausible. "Your thoughts will be safe. As for your memories, that is indeed another story."

"What do you mean?"

Justice sighed and stood up from the stool. He looked as if he didn't want me to ask it. "With everything gone, your memories will fade away. They will fade away just like my spirit particles are fading away when I use them to move around. Just like fuel in a tank. I have a finite amount. Your memories also."

"Then why is it that my thinking patterns will be safe but not memories?"

"When I said they would be safe, I meant that they will be safe *eventually*. Your ability to think and process information will fade away but will return spontaneously."

"That doesn't make sense. Something can't come out of nothing."

"No exacto. We know this doesn't *seem* to make sense, but the Creator was able to achieve it."

"But why not my memories?"

Justice looked away. He then turned to me again. It seemed painful for him. He really did not want me to be smart enough to ask this. "The ability of thinking will return, but not the same memories you had. They will be lost forever like shooting a bullet into outer space. Never to return."

Never to return? All of my memories, all of my experiences, all of my sorrow, all of my happiness, everyone whom I know, never to return?

"A small piece of yourself may remain. Your natural temperament. That will hopefully guide you into being a good king. But even if you're not, you will still have succeeded in restarting this system of things."

Yes. Restarting this system of things. Isn't that what is most important? Yes, it is sacrificing so much to do it, but isn't that what is necessary for the greater good? Father believes so. He believes He has to remove the rebels to protect the remaining loyal. When Aurick wanted to use this power, it was for selfish gain. But as for me, I was doing this for good. Wasn't this the right thing to do? But without Father, who invented the concept, would there be such a thing as "right" anymore? So many things. So many things that surrounded me. So many factors and decisions to sort out at the same time. Is this what making cosmic decisions felt like? Did Father feel this kind of pressure every millisecond that passed? I felt as if I could die from the crushing pressure. I had to make a decision. This was for the best. This would be my ultimate sacrifice. But it was for the greater good. I had to say good-bye to this world.

"I refuse."

Crushed, Justice had calculated that I would accept the offer, but I didn't. "I don't understand," Justice said, looking down, clenching his teeth.

"It is simple. You are offering no valid solution. Wiping everything off the map and restarting the universe won't solve anything. This is not justice. It is mere terrorism. Merely a false bottom."

"Terrorism?! This is the only solution that is available. This is to free us. To save us."

"Wrong," I said, just at the moment his words ended. The bones in Justice's fingers became severely defined as he clenched them as hard as he could. "This is not to save us. This is just to escape the consequences of what we've done."

"We haven't done anything."

"Yes, we have. We proved that we ourselves are unable to rule perfectly. We were under a system that we failed to live up to. How could I, who has failed under a system, rule over others and expect them to live up to mine? Not only that, knowing that I have destroyed a god, and me being the new god, wouldn't that give my new followers the right to do the same? Truly flawed. What you offer is like atheistic philosophy, but more disgusting. Nihilism."

"It is you that is wrong. Your Father failed us."

"No exacto, Justice. Father is the only being that has proven to be able to set rules and live up to them. Not just Him but two-thirds of our brothers are still faithful. This shows that His system can work as long as we choose to live under it. If not, we will fade away."

"But you can learn to be as flawless as God. It will just take some time."

"Flawless as God? If He were truly flawless, what would be the point in destroying Him and becoming Him soon after? Indeed, truly flawed." Justice's appearance shifted once more. This time he appeared to be an old human man in his late seventies. "But even if you were right, even if you were correct about having the right to remove everything for the greater good, I could never accept having to allow my memories to fade away."

"Your memories have brought you nothing but pain."

"Yes, they have. But they have also brought me joy. Joy that others will not make the same mistakes I have. Joy that others have a future with my example of sin. Not only that, Justice. For me to allow myself to forget the memories of all that would perish, Justice, is . . . truly evil. It is not merely my pain that would be forgotten. But all of the pain from human, demon, angel, and god alike. No, Justice. I cannot allow them to fade away. That's why you'd rather die than to act as the new god, isn't it?" Justice did not answer. He was silent without a slight whisper or attempt at whispering. "You felt guilty because you could allow yourself to forget your love, Adilah. Well, I can't do it either. Without the memories of the past, we are forever doomed to be recycled by it."

"You are making such a big mistake."

"I will live the rest of my life to the best that I can. I will live to change the negative and turn it into positive. I will live with my sorrow. I will live my own *life*. I will fight the sorrow. I will defeat the sorrow by paying my debt. Paying the consequences for the greater good. For you, for Morning Owl, for Lofie, for Aisely, for Terra, for Kid, for Doughy, for Shelia, for Aurick, for Helena. For Sephirot as well. And I will do it *without* this false justice. This false bottom."

Justice shook his head in disappointment. I had crushed his calculations of my accepting this offer that I couldn't refuse. He knew I had made up my mind.

Then he suddenly vanished. I looked around but saw nothing. I tried my best to sense his presence but came up with nothing. The next thing I knew, I was sitting on the stool. I could not move. The stool rumbled and jerked. It shifted and morphed. It became a throne. A large one. A large pink throne.

"I promised that you would accept my offer. I will make sure you *keep* that promise."

Impaled. Spikes impaled me throughout my body. Arms, hands, legs, feet, and torso pierced. Justice made sure that I would feel the fullest extent of pain I could from this. They were thorns. On each thorn were more miniature thorns to multiply the pain.

"You will not stop me from vanquishing this evil," Justice said. "The original evil. You *will* be the new god of the new system of things whether you like it or not. Now sit there and accept your crown." Sharp pincers dug into my head. It was a crown made of nails. "Don't try to move because you can't. You have not practiced moving about in this empty realm of ultimate nonleverage. I have prepared for this battle that you have—"

"*Not*," I said, cutting him off. I was behind Justice while he was still facing the throne. He was bewildered at my ability to free myself. "How was I able to move around without leverage, you're wondering? I didn't." Justice did not move. "Your first mistake was talking to me. Even to talk to me you must use a bridge for your thoughts to reach me. I used the same bridge to pull me over here. It's in the shape of a rope. And that rope has bound you." Justice tried to resist but he could do nothing. "Resisting?" Justice stopped to listen. "You failed to correctly estimate my own power. You believed that you grew in power because of your rage. My rage for Father is ten times more than yours. The only difference is that I have something to lose now. I must make it back home."

"Home? You can never go back home!"

"No, not heaven, my brother. New York City." Justice burst into laughter. "You are laughing like a child." Justice's appearance turned into that of a young toddler. Not of his own will, but because of *mine*.

"What? Impossible."

"I'm getting used to this world. Did you not notice that my spirit frequency has settled?"

Justice meditated on this, spewing.

"Do not get me wrong, Justice. It is not my rage that has delivered my victory. It is a certain other emotion I cannot bring myself to say that guides my rage."

"Ha! You haven't won yet."

"Oh, but I have, Justice. Did you not once think of why God himself hasn't intervened even though the universe is on the brink of collapse?" I allowed a few seconds to pass for Justice to think about it. "It is because He already knows how things will play out. He is a giant supercalculator that can figure out anything and everything. And you know what He calculated? Your failure. And I am probably the one to cause it."

"You've left me with no choice then. There won't be a new god or new system of things. There will be . . . nothing."

My body froze. I could not speak. I could not think.

Blacked out.

I was on the floor. I was motionless. I was in Aurick's body again. Justice must've had a line connecting us to earth, like a bungee cord to bring us back. I could still not move. But this time my eyes could detect spirit beings once again. Justice was before me. He was looking down as if he had won.

"You can't move inside of a corpse. You're going to be like that until the omnicide. You did this. Because of you, there won't be a legacy. There will be nothing. My fury and quest for true justice keeps me alive. This fantasy world will end."

I had lost. Justice clumsily stepped forward. He was going toward Zero. He looked at my corpse. He looked into my dead eyes. He seemed to be disturbed. He moved another step and then stopped. He looked over to me again. "Why? Why do you go so far for them? Why would you go so far for beings who despise our kind? For beings who even despise the Creator Himself?"

I could still connect to Justice's mind and speak mentally. Though I could, I wasn't sure what to say. I just felt I had to say something. That's when Shelia came up into my mind.

"I remember a human once telling me something. She felt at peace with her life ending. I asked her why. She told me that she felt comfort with being in someone's memory."

"Whose memory would that be?"

"Father's." Pain swept across Justice's disfigured face. It seemed that I had struck a blow. Justice stared at me. His look was pained and I knew it was painful for him to look at me. He turned around and walked toward Zero. It was over. No one would remember us now. We would truly be nameless. Just as Justice was about to touch Zero, he froze.

The reinforcements had arrived in the nick of time. Shining Condor and a couple of other marooners were holding Justice in place.

XXIV

ΠAMELESS

*They will fear you. They have seen that you have grown too much. You
were at first entertaining with your brethren's ambition and advance-
ment. But you have advanced uncontrollably. Out of love you came to be
chaos. They will misunderstand your ascension. You are the brightest
star at the corner of the universe. My wings were made of spirit. They
were made by Father. But your wings are even more beautiful. They were
wings made out of ambition and metal. You will rise. You are restored
hope. I love you, Purity.*

Justice seemed not to struggle. The chaos leaking from Zero
abruptly stopped. It was over. They laid Justice on the ground.
Condor was in shining armor as usual. Even when it's the end of
the world, he has to be stylish.

Condor said, "Dizzy Roadrunner and Lazy Flamingo, take
him away at once."

"Yes, sir," Dizzy Roadrunner and Lazy Flamingo said
boringly but in absolute unison. "This is such a burdensome
task," said Roadrunner.

I didn't want Justice to leave yet. I didn't understand why but
I just didn't want him to go. Something powerful was growing
inside me. A surge of animation went through me. I wondered if
Aurick was truly dead. I didn't feel his wave patterns.

"Stop complaining and get out of here!" Condor said.

"You've been working us to the bone. Morning Owl was
way easier to work for. Why can't you be like him?" Dizzy
Roadrunner said.

There was no way I was going to see Justice leave like this. And there I was, standing up before everyone's eyes. Everyone was in complete shock. Justice looked the most surprised . . . I think. I took a few steps forward. My arms and legs felt as if they weighed a thousand pounds each. I stopped.

It was as if they were before God Himself. "I don't understand," Justice said. "To be able to move around as a corpse, you would have to have overwhelming hatred and a huge motive. If you did have hatred in your heart, then why did you try to stop me? You could've had vengeance."

I smiled. "I don't think it's hatred. I do feel annoyance but I don't think it's hatred. All I know is that I have a reason to live again. I have to live for them," I said, pointing at Helena on the ground. They started to move away again. "Oh, and Justice." They stopped. "I'll cry for you." Justice smiled. It was the kind of smile that tried to hide something. Sadness. Sadness and rejection. Helena used to smile like that when I first met her. The weight of my body forced me to my knees.

"You won't have to. I'll have plenty of time to cry for myself in the Null. Don't feel sad. I've been waiting for this for a long time."

I didn't know what he meant by that. Did he know this would happen? Did he know he was going to ultimately fail from the very beginning? "Good-bye, my brother."

Roadrunner and Flamingo took Justice, Zero, and the Fallen inhabiting Helena's body away for trial. All that was left was Condor to take me away. I remembered him telling me that he was going to love sending me to the Null. I guess he finally was going to get his wish. I bet he even prayed for it too.

"I bet you're happy to finally send me to the Null yourself, aren't you?" I said.

Condor had a plain expression on his face. "The death of your host is what alerted my unit here. After a few seconds to evaluate the situation, I realized you didn't actually murder your host. You even tried to stop a catastrophe."

"So you're not going to take me to trial?"

"Even though I believe you're not going to be sentenced to the Null, it is not up to me to make that decision, so I will have to ask a higher-up what to do. If they tell me that you're innocent, I will not return for you." Condor started to leave.

"What about them?"

"Justice is definitely going to be sent to the Null. As for the others, they will be taken in for questioning. We have to find out if there are any others who have time-manipulating abilities."

"Shining Condor?" I said, stopping him. "Home will never be the same without Morning Owl. He was truly a good spirit."

"I know he was. Always will be."

It was over. It was finally over. Justice didn't prevail. Harvey Samuel Carr's prophecy was incorrect. Everything before me vanished. Vanished away into the light.

I awoke in a bed. It was covered in clean white sheets. Light pierced my eyelids when I tried to close them. The room smelled like old people. A long, ugly polyester curtain was around me. I was alone. That's when I knew where I was. Only one hospital would put me in a private room this quickly. I was being held at St. Peter's Hospital. I was in Dr. Doctor's territory. I was in danger. Helena was in danger. I tried lifting my body out of the bed but I fell back down. My entire body still felt as if it weighed a ton. I struggled to get up but couldn't. I had the will to fight but didn't have the physical strength. A doctor walked into the room. He closed the door behind him. I was doomed. I was a helpless fly trapped in his web. As he came closer, I soon realized that the doctor wasn't smiling. This one was frowning. This doctor definitely wasn't Dr. Doctor. I sighed in relief. Suddenly, the doctor wrapped his hands around my neck. He squeezed my neck with such intense strength that I gagged right away. Just when I was about to faint, the doctor released his grip and slapped me across my face. "Oh, no! You're not going to go that easy," he said, slapping me across my face again. "You just had to spoil everything, didn't you, Aurick?" His face had an angry grin. Was this really Dr. Doctor?

"Is this a new medical treatment?" I mumbled. "I do not think it is working."

The doctor pulled up a chair from the other side of the room and sat at my bedside. He reached in his pocket. He pulled out a death instrument. That's right. He pulled out a cigarette. He put it to his mouth. He lit the cigarette and drew a puff. He drew a really long puff as if he were making up for all the lost time when he'd quit smoking.

"Where's Helena Way?"

"She's dead," Dr. Doctor said, still frowning.

"Thank you for taking care of her."

"How did you know I was lying?"

"You're a demon. Demon's lie. And plus you're not smiling."

Doctor glared at me. He knew he wasn't in control anymore. It was amusing seeing him tear himself apart. "You took away freedom for so many of us," he said, blowing smoke into my face. I coughed. "*All* of us. We were so close to peaceful slumber."

"Oh, boy! Not this rant again."

"Zero is my proof. When he fell, he clung to a human family for comfort. It turned out to be false comfort. He looked out for this single lineage for generations. That's until they were struck with a plague. He was completely distraught over it. He even haunted the house to keep out anyone who wanted to live in their house." That explained all of those paintings and pictures Zero saved at that abandoned house. "I tried comforting him with words, but it didn't help. His first family shunned him and his second one had left him. He was such a fool for holding on to a temporary attachment. That's when I told him about my journey to true peace. True *eternal* peace. He was extremely receptive to it. Such a shame such a talented lad like him was wasted."

That's when it hit me. I didn't want to believe it, but all paths of logic pointed me in that direction. "It was *you*. You're the one who put all of this into his head. You're the one who helped him develop the ability to manipulate time." That's when Dr. Doctor's frown turned upside down.

"Not really. But it was a pleasant surprise. I simply tried to form some way to end our own existence ourselves. But that would be too selfish. Why should I end our project with ourselves? I wanted to spread it to all. Zero didn't really understand completely what I was trying to do, but he went along."

"So you wanted revenge just like Justice did?"

"Oh, dear me, no! I have no animosity to my lovely God. I love Him more than I love myself." The more Dr. Doctor spoke, the less I understood him. "Imagine an almighty being living for eternity. Someone unmatched in power and knowledge. He must've spent trillions upon trillions of years in solitude trying to hone such magnificent power. All of our life spans and pain combined is just a drop in the ocean compared to His. Imagine the pain of solitude, what that must've been like." You had to be patient when Dr. Doctor was trying to make a point. You could never be sure what he was going to say. "And then after He had finally created companions, they stab Him in the back. How discouraging that must've felt. Only I understand this. I did this not out of spite or revenge. I did this out of merciful love for my heavenly Father." I told you that you could never be sure. "He is the most miserable person in the universe. He will *continue* to be the most miserable person in the universe. Oh, how my heart constantly goes out to my poor Papa." Doctor finished his cigarette. He plunged the remaining flame down onto the counter near me.

"Why did you heal me? I should be an immobile corpse by now. And why did you let Helena live?"

"It wasn't I who healed you. It was Justice. He even saved

your dear cat and that other thing." I couldn't believe what Dr. Doctor had told me. Was he lying just to torture me? "As for me, I want you and Ms. Way to continue to live on. I want you to suffer life. That's why I gave that so-called rant. You will understand sure enough. No one remains happy. *No one*." Dr. Doctor got up from his seat and pulled back the chair. He came over and scratched my head. That crescent-moon-shaped smile completely resurfaced. He walked out and closed the door behind him. A few seconds later I heard, "Good heavens!" He reentered, unwrapped a lollipop, and stuck it into my mouth. "I almost forgot to give you your treat."

I regained maneuvering control of my body a few hours later. I think it was something in that lollipop Dr. Doctor gave me. Though I could walk, each step felt as if it would be my last. It was worth it. Nothing was going to stop me. And there she lay. A sleeping beauty. I went in the room and closed the door behind me. It was against the rules to do that, but I knew Dr. Doctor would allow it. Her paleness had completely disappeared. She was well again. Justice had healed her. Thank you, my brother.

I slipped into bed with her. I was careful not to wake her from her dream. I put my head to her neck and inhaled her aroma. It was definitely her. Except this time there was a new scent. I placed my hand on her soft belly. I rubbed her sleek skin in circular motions. Life was growing inside her. My heart betrayed itself. A part of me felt ecstatic. But then another part of me felt absolutely terrified.

Three weeks passed. My body had completely healed and was fully functional. So far, my new year hadn't been great. I hadn't spoken to Helena since we'd left the hospital. She didn't return any of my phone calls and didn't come to any of our therapy sessions. I grew depressed. Was Justice correct about Helena, about her only wanting to use me? But we were friends long before I even knew about Adilah. We were so comfortable with each other. She wouldn't just dump me like this. We cared about each other. Or was it just I who cared about her? The more I thought about it, the more sorrowful I became.

I was alone. I waited by the phone for days. I only got up from the couch to get more tomatoes or feed Sephirot. I looked into the mirror. I no longer sensed that my body was decaying into a Nebuchadnezzar. With Aurick gone, there was no struggle between our two minds, which stopped the dissension. I did not care though. After a while, I stopped eating even the tomatoes. I stopped eating period. Sorrow overwhelmed me. This was how I'd felt when I fell out of Father's light. Except this time, I didn't have Morning Owl to console me. I wondered how he was doing. I even wondered how Condor was doing. Owl was Condor's mentor just as he'd mentored me. Condor was always jealous that Owl favored me over him. What a brat. Now neither of us had Morning Owl and I didn't have Helena. Ms. Helena Way. I guess Justice was right. Helena didn't love me.

My wristwatches on each hand were gone. The small ticking drove me crazy. The mention of time itself was driving me crazy. Even though my danger of being a Nebuchadnezzar was gone, I still felt that I was running out of time. My thoughts drove me crazy. They didn't make sense. Was I human? Was Helena real? Did I imagine this entire thing? They kept me awake at night. I even started seeing things. Images of Aurick standing next to me frightened me. I felt as if he were still here. Was I even an angel in the first place? Was I Aurick the entire time? Before I showed up, Aurick had been on medication for hallucinations. Sometimes he imagined entire scenarios. Did I inherit his sickness?

There was a knock on the door. I hopped off the couch and ran to the door. I grabbed hold of the knob and swung open the door. "Helena!" I soon realized that it wasn't my Helena. My arms were around the landlord, hugging him. He'd been knocking on my door for days now but I'd never answered him. He told me to get off him and that I stunk. He yelled at me for not paying my rent. I'd been too lazy to pay the rent. I'd been too lazy to do anything. I hadn't taken a shower in days. I let the apartment go to death.

After the landlord collected his check, I went to the kitchen and lay down on the floor. I must've been there for hours. Sephirot licked my face. My dear friend wanted some steak to eat. I got up and headed out the door. And there she was. Her knuckles were positioned as if she was about to knock. We stood there motionless. We stood there silent. Her eyes said all that they had to. They were like mine, tired. I grabbed her and pressed her against my chest. I squeezed her as if my life depended on it. My chin pressed against her neck. I wanted to smell her. And then she spoke.

"You need a shower, Aurick."

Another month passed. I had moved in with Helena. This was the first time I had ever lived with someone other than Sephirot. It felt awkward at first. She had to get used to Sephirot and I had to get used to her curtains. It was working out fine though. I watched her as she stepped out of the shower. She walked around the apartment naked. She was looking for a towel. She headed for the closet. I blocked her from opening the closet door. "Looking for this?" I said, raising the towel. She quickly reached for it, but I snatched it away so she wouldn't get it. She smiled and said, "Stop, Aurick. I need to leave."

"You'll need to dry off first." I raised the towel over my head. She jumped for it but missed. She tried again and missed again.

"Come on, Aurick, stop!" she said, giggling. I watched in amusement as her breasts bounced up and down as she jumped for it. She got fed up and began pulling my arm down. I tried pushing her off, but she started grappling me. We both laughed. I lifted her legs and pushed her against the closed door of the closet. I wrapped my lips on her moist lips. She locked her bare legs around my hips. No matter how many times we did this, it still felt like the very first time. We breathed each other's air as we panted. "Oh, great, now I'll need another shower."

Every day, I earnestly waited for her return from work. It felt like an eternity waiting for her. I didn't really want her working in such a dangerous job as she had a knack for making people want to kill her. I not only feared for her but for the life that was growing inside her. She still didn't know she was pregnant. The only thing I could do was wait for her to notice that she didn't have her period. Pretending not to know she was pregnant was difficult and tiring. It would look odd if I found out she was pregnant before she did, so I had to endure it. A part of me feared something else. I wondered if Justice was lying about Helena's being pregnant. What if he was just toying with me? Maybe that's why I never asked Helena to take a pregnancy test. Because of fear. And then . . . there was yet something else that bothered me. Something I didn't want to think about.

We lay on the bed together watching television. I snuggled my face in her long hair. That long, prolific hair. I inhaled it. As there were myriad strands of hair, there were also myriad thoughts racing through my mind. Was I becoming more and more human as the days passed? Was this the happiness humans were willing to fight and sin for? All I knew was that I wanted this to last forever. I didn't want to think about my decisions anymore. I just wanted to jump into the pool. No more planning ahead. This was against divine law, but I didn't care. I wanted to know her thoughts on it. I wanted to know how she felt. I mustered my courage and said, "Do you think we should be talking about marriage?" There was a long silence. A long, awkward silence.

Helena raised her head up. "Marriage?" She looked absolutely blindsided.

I picked up the remote and turned the television off. "Yes. We've been living with each other for all this time."

"It hasn't been long at all."

"But we've known each other long enough."

Helena put her head down on my chest. I felt her listening to my heartbeat. "I don't know how to be married."

That was a stupid reply. We cared about each other deeply, so wouldn't marriage be the logical thing? I guess this is what it was to be . . . human.

She raised her head again and looked into my eyes. "But . . ." She placed her index finger over my mouth, stopping me from speaking. "Shut up and kiss me."

And there we were at it again. Every time we started to speak about something serious, this happened. We were so exhausted from sex, we fell asleep right away.

Motion on the bed woke me. Helena was getting up. She slipped into her purple silk robe that I had purchased for her. "Where are you going?"

She looked back at me in slight annoyance. "I have to pee. Do you mind?" She walked over to the dresser drawer. She pulled out a small box. I didn't pay it any mind and rolled over to sleep. I closed my eyes.

"Aaaaaaaaaaaaaaaaaaahh!!!"

A screech rang out ripping me from my slumber. I got up in nervous alertness. I ran over to the bathroom. There was silence.

"What happened?" No one replied. I twisted the knob but the door was locked. "What happened, Helena?" Did she fall? Was a Fallen attacking her? The silence tortured me. I couldn't wait any longer. I raised my foot to kick open the door. Then there was a clicking sound. She slowly opened the door. A dumbfounded expression was on her face with nothing but utter silence.

"I'm . . . I'm . . ." she said, her voice shaking like a washing machine. "I'm . . . I'm . . ." Her eyes swelled up like two watery tomatoes. "I'm pregnant."

ПАΜΕ

For the infinite, the circle of life is mere fantasy. For the finite, the circle of life is reality. To the finite, it means victory. For the infinite, it means defeat. There comes a time when every being has to make a choice between these two factions. Will the circle of life be fantasy or reality? It is now up to you.

Though I already knew she was pregnant, I still was as ecstatic as Helena was. Or *was* she as ecstatic as I was? She was more shocked than ecstatic. She looked like a zombie. I hugged her. She couldn't believe it. She bought two more pregnancy tests. Both came back positive. She still couldn't believe it. She went back downstairs and bought four more. They all came back positive. "Oh, God! I am going to be a mother," she said, sitting down on the bed. She held her hands over her face. I pried her hands apart to see her blushing face.

"Are you all right, Helena?" She tried closing her hands over her face but I continued to hold them.

"I can't be a mother."

"Of course you can!"

Helena still couldn't accept it. We went to take a sonogram the next day. And there it was. The life within Helena's womb was really there. I had created something that no other Fallen had ever created before. I had created . . . life. In the midst of the joy, reality struck me. And not in a good way.

The truth is, I wasn't the first Fallen to have impregnated a woman. Others have lived human lives and taken up women of their own. Even though some Fallen may use a human body and live a human life, they still are Fallen. Spirit beings constantly leak radiation from their bodies. It can be harmful to humans and other forms of life if exposure is lengthy. Radiation can spread through the entire body, including sperm cells. The radiated cell grows within the womb. That's when things go . . . wrong. The radiation deteriorates the growth. The child usually dies before it's even born. Even if the child does make it to birth, it comes out either disfigured or severely mentally ill. Or both. They're not Nephilim, which were the offspring of *materialized* angels. *Perfect* materialized angels. Nephilin grew to be healthy humans. Beyond human. It was not so for offspring of Fallen. I'd never heard of any Fallen offspring who'd lived long after birth. That's why even though I was happy about the pregnancy, I was also terrified.

Helena was still stunned. For the rest of the day she lay in bed staring up at the ceiling. I lay beside her trying to figure out what she was thinking. I had lost my ability to read thoughts. I was as average as the average human. Well, almost. "I can't be a mother. I'm so reckless. I'm the most reckless woman on the planet."

"And you're also the most bothersome too. And the most dangerous."

Helena switched her eyes to me and gave me a long glare. "Gee, Aurick. That makes me feel much better." She rolled her eyes and redirected them to the ceiling.

I grabbed her hand and kissed it. I sighed and looked at the exact point on the ceiling she was looking at. "You'll be a good mother. No. You are going to be a *terrific* mother."

Helena smiled and rolled over to me. She pecked me on my lips. She snuggled her forehead against mine. We felt each other's warmth.

"I quit my job," she said, whispering under her breath.

"What did you say?"

"I said I quit the business."

My goodness! "For how long? Until you have the baby?" I said with fear and concern in my voice.

She smiled. "No. I'm gone for good. No more Ms. Reckless. No more Ms. Muckraker. I'm just average Ms. Helena Way. Or should I say Mrs. Helena Pantera."

It felt as if my stomach hopped through my throat. My entire body shivered. I wasn't used to all of these sensations back-to-back like this. I still couldn't believe any of this was happening. I would never have dreamed in a trillion years that I would end up here. I had a woman and a child on the way. Was this all in my imagination? Some Fallen hallucinate and imagine themselves as humans or sometimes animals. They imagine entire worlds that aren't real. Entire scenarios. Was I one of them? At this point, I didn't care. I was at peace.

The only thing that was missing was Aurick. He was gone and I was here in his place. Did I steal his life? I gave him so many warnings, but he wouldn't listen. It didn't make me feel better that I'd warned him. I felt kind of dirty for it.

It was seven months into the pregnancy. I was working as a psychologist and Helena's belly was big as a school. She had severe mood swings. I had to keep reassuring her that she still was pretty. And she still wasn't . . . fat. She ran me ragged. I served her every need. Every single day I made countless trips to the store, so many trips that my calf muscles hardened from running back and forth. I constantly gave her back and foot massages. My hands were exhausted. I fed her plenty of food. I never worked so hard in my life. I needed that baby to be big and strong. We prepared everything for it. We had already bought reserves of bottles, diapers, a couple of baby carriages, a crib, and some clothes. We even started looking for elementary schools. I don't know if it was merely blind hopeful thinking, but at least it was something. Hope was new to me. I wanted to savor every moment of it.

I checked the clock. I no longer wore a wristwatch on each hand. I had no need to constantly check and keep track of every second. Checking clocks on the wall is much . . . calmer. It was nine o'clock at night. We were looking through photos of each other that had been snapped these past months. Pictures of us on the carousel at Central Park. This was when she got motion sickness and threw up over my lap. Another picture was of Helena and I wearing cowboy hats when we went horseback riding. Helena's horse was spooked by my spirit presence while she was on it, which sent him running away in a panic. We managed to get the horse to stop, but Helena threw up on me when we got off.

Another picture was of us making funny faces at a restaurant. Later that night when we were getting intimate, because of her feeling under the weather from the food she ate, Helena threw up on my lap. *Yeah*.

"Didn't Timothy do a good job?" I asked. Helena got Timmy to shoot most of the pictures

"Eh. I guess he did okay." Helena shrugged.

After I finished looking through the photos, I rested my head on Helena's stomach. My hearing was still good enough to hear the heartbeat of the child. I rubbed her stomach in a circular motion. I felt complete. I felt at peace. I felt purpose. I wanted this moment to last forever. "Thank you, Helena," I said, kissing her belly.

"For what?"

"You gave me purpose. Without you, I don't know what I would've done. I was thinking pretty crazy things before I met you."

Helena smiled. "No, Aurick. I'm the one who should be thanking you." Yeah, right, I thought. I'd brought her nothing but trouble. She almost wound up dead because of me. "I was a mess. Everyone thought I was some courageous saint who wanted to fight for justice. That was so far from the truth. I loved the thrill of the chase. It was merely a crutch. Merely a drug. No matter how much thrill I got out of it, I still couldn't fill that empty void my parents created. Now that I think about it, I didn't even enjoy the thrill. Not at all." Helena looked as if she were lost in her own world. "I took the most dangerous assignments in hopes that I would kill myself for a cause. I thought maybe that would fill that void. Thank you, Aurick, for filling that void."

"You tried to make a void in my head with a bullet," I said, increasing my voice the more I remembered that situation.

"Yeah, sorry about that," Helena said, smiling. I didn't think that was funny at all. "Aurick?"

"Hmmm?"

"Do you think this is going to last forever?" It was weird for Helena to ask a question like that. She has always been cut-and-dry like me. Something was deeply troubling her.

"Nothing lasts forever, Helena." She was filled with fear of the future. A side of Helena I'd never seen.

"I hope it does. Do you think . . . the baby will be okay?"

"Why do you ask that?"

"Please, Aurick. I need you to make me feel better. I need you to promise me my baby will be fine."

Her question tore me up inside. I myself didn't know if it would be fine. In fact, chances were high it wouldn't be. The doctors had already said that they thought there might be damage in the frontal lobe of its brain, but they weren't sure. I didn't want to lie to her. But I also didn't want Helena to worry. She didn't deserve to worry.

"Yes, Helena. Our baby will be fine. I promise."

I promised. I rocked back and forth in bed. It was no use. Those words haunted me all night.

My worst fears came true. I awoke to a nightmare one morning to find Helena having a seizure. I didn't understand what was going on. I pounded my foot to the gas pedal, sending us dashing through the streets. I brought the car to a screeching halt when I got across the street from the hospital. I didn't have time to wait in traffic to get to the parking lot. I dashed through the street cradling Helena's pregnant body in my arms. I carried my baby as my baby carried hers. "I need a doctor here!" I said, bursting into the emergency room.

Waiting in the waiting room was absolute torture. Numerous bleak possibilities echoed through my mind. I tried my best to think of the light, but it didn't seem reasonable. Whatever the case was, my wife and my unborn child were in jeopardy and I couldn't do anything. I was useless. I held all the power in the world and I was powerless. Is this how humans feel when trying to solve a problem? Powerless? Is this why they sinfully strive for power?

Three hours passed. I spent my time twirling my ring around my finger. I couldn't get married to Helena. It was against divine law to set up such a life with a human. It would be a mockery of Father's institution. Even so, I wanted to wear something that was close to a wedding band. I gave her one too. She didn't wear it on her finger the way I did though but as a necklace. The ring was made of gomorium. It would last for ages. Oh, how I wish Helena were as durable. That's all I could do. Wish. Prayer was out of the question. Fallen such as me don't get the privilege to ask for help. I remembered the promise I had made to her. It painfully echoed through my mind. I promised that our baby was going to be fine. I was selfish to promise her that. So stupid.

A doctor called me over. They had no idea what was wrong with her. Helena had developed a fever and occasional tremors. They couldn't figure out what was causing it. Her health seemed perfect. I didn't expect them to do anything. No matter how much the doctors tried, they would just come up empty-handed. No human could ever heal spirit radiation. The only ones with the power to heal were certain Fallen and angels. Healing abilities were rare among Fallen, so that would take forever to find. Angels weren't allowed to use healing for private reasons unless Father gave them permission. And there was no way Father was going to do that for me. There was still a chance that Helena's spirit sickness would pass. All I could do was hope.

Within hours, Helena's health got better. Her fever went away and her tremors stopped. The doctors said that she would be fine. Hope wasn't a bad thing after all. That's when out of nowhere the doctors told me she was going into premature labor. They gave me some time to spend with Helena before she had the baby. "But isn't it way too early to have the baby?" Helena said, shaking in fear.

"You're going into premature labor, Helena."

"But how? We were so careful."

"It's going to be fine. We're seven months in. Many babies are born six months in and they grow to be healthy. Sometimes only five months." It seemed to calm her down a bit. She was still worried though. I'd never seen her so worried.

"Will you be there? Will you be there when I give birth?"

"Of course I will," I said, smiling.

"Thank you, Aurick."

Pain shrieked throughout Helena's entire body. She kept screaming that she felt as if she were being cut in half. She called for more painkillers but the doctors said that giving her any more might complicate the birth. It was complicated enough. Something about her contractions not being good. Helena repeatedly asked if the baby was going to be okay. And we repeatedly told her that it was.

Watching Helena cry in agony was painful. She screamed as she squeezed my sweaty hand. She was in so much pain that she fell in and out of consciousness. Was she going to be fine? Was the baby all right? Was the baby all right? Was the baby all right? My unrelenting questions made the doctors so nervous that they had to remove me from the room.

I paced to and fro outside the door. I'd never felt so frightened. I couldn't stop myself from shaking. I counted the seconds. Was she okay? Sometimes it takes over twenty hours for women to give birth. Even more than that! And here I was not being able to endure a few minutes. Memories of the past resurfaced. Especially memories of *her*. I was an immortal being while she was a mere mortal. Though I knew our relationship couldn't possibly last, I still allowed a relationship between us to manifest anyway. I was careless. No matter how much I knew the facts, I still hoped that it would somehow work. And you know what? It didn't. Our love was swept away by the freezing currents of reality. This reality drove Zero into pursuing suicide. He latched on to a family. No matter how tightly he held on, they eventually slipped away. And Justice. He was in love with the woman of his life. A new experience. A new life. Love pushed him over the edge of insanity and turned him away from Father. So many mistakes we've made. So many illogical decisions. Unnatural love. Temporary love. I was starting to wonder. Did we choose it at the cost of death without realizing it? Was it worth living for? Was it worth dying for?

Whatever the case, I was desperate. Desperate times call for desperate measures. My pride would have to die. I no longer felt like an angel. I no longer felt like a mighty spirit. I was broken. I was weak. Oddly enough, I felt . . . light. I sat down. I clamped my hands together and folded them. I tilted my head.

Please. I know you owe me nothing. I know I brought myself into this situation. Please. Oh, God, please. Oh, Father, please. Just this once. Just this one time. Help me fulfill my promise.

It was desperate. I don't know why I did it. There was no chance it would be answered, but I did it anyway. Though it was futile, it felt . . . good.

A hand touched my shoulder. I swung around. It was a male doctor. "I have some bad news, Mr. Pantera." My heart sank. "You may have to sit down."

"No. I'd rather stand."

"I've done the best I can." Everything absolutely stopped. I felt as if I were in another realm. "The spirit radiation seems to grow and grow. There is nothing I can do about it. Helena is going to die."

At that moment, everything turned silent. I looked at the doctor closely. How would a human know about spirit radiation in the first place? Lollipops were sticking out of his shirt pocket. That's when I realized it. I slammed Dr. Doctor up against the wall.

"What did you do to her?" I said, squeezing my forearm against his throat.

"I didn't do anything but do my job. You know, I am tired of being in this position," he said with perfect composure. Dr. Doctor had a plain expression on his face. That was unusual.

"Liar! I went to a different hospital to avoid you. Why is it that you appear here? You followed me!" I said, grabbing attention from bystanders.

"I don't work just in St. Peter's. I move from hospital to hospital." I didn't believe him. This was too convenient. I glared into his eyes. "Now come on, Mr. Pantera. It's spirit radiation. You're the only one who could've harmed Helena in that way." I hated to admit it but Dr. Doctor was right. But he could've done something extra to seal Helena's fate. "Your time with the humans really has made you illogical."

"You know how I know your lying? You're not smiling."

Dr. Doctor rolled his eyes in annoyance. "Do you want to keep strangling me or do you want to see your newborn?" At that moment, my legs grew limp. It was hard to keep pressing against Dr. Doctor. My baby was born alive? Was he messing with my head again? I let go of him.

He brought me over to a room. The light was dim. Dr. Doctor said that he'd reserved a room just for my child. There was a small bed. It was in proportion for an infant. And there it was. My baby. My living thing. My creation. My sleeping beauty. It was beautiful. It was a beautiful little girl. It was a beautiful, unique little girl. Her skin was dark. It looked smooth as milk chocolate. Her irises were red. A vivid red color. They flamed with conviction, like deep dirges. Her hair was a silky platinum color. It had a slight tint of light blue and gray. I counted all of her fingers and toes. The left hand had five fingers while the right had six. The right foot had five toes while the left foot had six. She was absolutely . . . *perfect*. I got on my knees by her bed and uttered, *"She's perfect."* Dr. Doctor wasn't as joyful as I was. He maintained his blank face. "How is her health?"

"Nothing is good! You brought a child into a world of meaninglessness. Nothing but pain and suffering awaits her." I ignored what he said. "So far it's perfect except for a bit of frontal-lobe damage. It's small though. It shouldn't affect her when she gets older. She's a preemie so we're going to do some more tests to make sure all of her organs developed correctly."

I gazed upon her. Gazed upon her purity. "Thank you, Doctor," I said with all respect.

Dr. Doctor sighed and rolled his eyes. "I kicked all of the doctors out of Helena's room. They don't know she's going to die. You'll have a few minutes to say your good-byes."

Good-bye? Was Dr. Doctor serious? I didn't know how to say good-bye. Father never programmed any of his creations with the ability to say good-bye. I'd never said good-bye to anyone. How do you say it? How do you say good-bye?

Here we were. Reunited once more. We went through the obstacles of hell together. We made love to each other. We loved each other. We defied all of nature together. I sat in a chair next to Helena. She looked so peaceful. I combed her black hair back and brushed her cheek with my fingers. I kissed her soft lips. I rubbed her cheek once more and said, "You did it, Helena. You created a new life."

Helena looked disoriented. She'd had a lot of pain and painkillers. She'd gone through a lot. "People have kids all the time, Aurick. It's nothing special."

Helena couldn't be any further away from the truth. Birth was incredible to the angels of the heavens. Human beings were able to create self-conscious organisms. We angels were never given that ability. No matter how hard we try. No matter how much time we have. No matter how much power we gain. We could never match the power to create new life. It's the one thing that separated us from them. It's the one thing that ties them to Father. The truth is, we were jealous of it. Each and every one of us is jealous of humans. All I could do was to sit in awe before Helena's power. Her magnificence. Her godhood.

"Thank you, Aurick," Helena said.

"For what?" I raised my head up.

"You saved me from myself."

"What do you mean?"

Helena reached over and grabbed my hand. "All these years. All of these years, I lived off the rush of being a field journalist. I took on all of the most dangerous cases and broke them all. I took such risky cases in hopes of getting killed someday. I never had the guts to do it myself. I was a mess. That's until you saved me. You swooped down and rescued me just in time. It was as if . . . as if you were an angel."

My eyes began to swell. I tried my best to hold the tears back. "*Me*? An *angel*?"

Helena squeezed my hand. Her eyes faded in and out of focus. "Yes."

"But I'm the one who got you like this in the first place. It's my fault you're in pain. I'm a bad person. I'm such a bad person."

Helena closed her eyes and smiled. "No. No, you're not a bad person. You're . . . an angel."

I couldn't bear it any longer. I turned my face away from her. It was so hard to hold back. I looked back. Life was fading away from her for good.

I turned back to her. "Don't leave me, Helena! You have a little girl that needs you! She needs a mother to show her how to be a woman. You haven't even seen her yet. She's so beautiful, Helena. She's a unique little girl. She's absolutely perfect. You can't leave me with a child. I don't know how to be a father. *I love you*."

"*I . . . like . . . you . . . too*." She smiled.

Suddenly, there was a long, loud, drawn-out breath. I quickly looked away. I didn't want it to be true. I slowly turned my face back to her to look. And she wasn't there. Helena.

"No. Don't leave me! Don't you dare leave me!" There was no reply. "You can't do this to me. Helena! Helena! I hate you!!!" No matter what I said. No matter how loud I said it. She wouldn't come back. My angel wouldn't come back to me. She abandoned me just as Father had.

I cradled my child in my arms. She was so warm. I could hear her little heart beat. I kissed her little hands. I kissed her little toes. I kissed her little belly. I kissed her little mouth. She was so beautiful. This was the greatest gift I was ever given. "Thank you! Thank you so much." Tears dropped onto the baby's face. It wasn't Aurick. It was *me*. *I* was crying. I cried for Helena. I cried for Lofie. I cried for Morning Owl. I cried for Justice. I cried for everyone.

I looked up. There I saw Shining Condor. Condor wasn't wearing any fancy armor this time. He was wearing a plain, long, black trench coat. Two marooners accompanied him. "Dr. Doctor really did harm her. Tear him to pieces before you send him!"

The marooners stood there motionless staring at me. Their faces were absolutely blank.

"No, Aurick," Condor said. "You're the one who killed Helena. We've come for *you*."

Of course. I had sex with her and got her pregnant. She died from giving birth to my seed. I had ultimately killed her. I instantly remembered Harvey's words about Helena: *And another thing, if you do not use the right protection, Helena will absolutely die.* Was Harvey talking about not having the right protection as in . . . *contraceptives,* which would lead to Helena's demise? But Helena had taken my seed *before* Harvey warned me. But Harvey did say that he gets the past, present, and future mixed up sometimes. Did that lousy dog know this would all happen? Did he lie and manipulate things to make things worse just as before? Did he want us to suffer rather than just have the universe merely end? Harvey trapped me either way. I had poisoned Helena like how I was poisoned by someone long ago.

The marooners moved forward. "Wait," I said, bringing them to a halt. "This child needs a parent."

"You know there is nothing I can do about that, Aurick. I am here to simply bring you to trial. The child will go into foster care."

"I know. But she needs a *proper* parent. And I know just who would be perfect."

Condor stared at me. He contemplated what to do.

Dizzy Roadrunner stepped up and said, "Aw, come on, Condor. Just give the guy a break."

That angered Condor. "If you speak out of place again, I'm going to report you. Now hold your tongue!"

"Hey! Just because you are a single rank over me, doesn't mean you're—"

"Quiet, Dizzy," Lazy Flamingo said, stepping in. "You need to learn to obey your superiors." Lazy turned to Condor. "But it *would* be nice to give him just a little extra time. It's not like a couple hours will make much difference." Lazy sighed in exasperation. "And can you make your decision already? I want to get this over with."

Shining Condor gave me extra time. I didn't delay. I went to the apartment Helena and I lived in. I picked up Sephirot. I grabbed all of the money out of a safe in the wall. Tens of thousands. Most of it came from Aurick's gambling. Helena always complained that keeping the money in a safe wasn't a good idea. I didn't trust banks so I kept it in a safe anyway. I went all the way back to Aurick's old apartment building. The elevator was working. For the first time since I've been here, the elevator was finally working. I prayed that it wouldn't fall and crash. Yes. *Prayed*.

I stood before Jamie's door. Jamie, full of pure innocence. I know she would freak out at the sight of my baby, but she would definitely accept the responsibility. What I was going to give her would never leave her side. Mother is God in a child's eyes. Anything less than that wouldn't be good enough for Jamie. This was the greatest gift I could ever give her. *True* family.

I looked over my baby one last time. She was peacefully sleeping. Though she was my death, she was also my life. My rebirth. I kissed her little fingers. Her little toes. Her little belly button. Her little mouth. I looked into those gorgeous red eyes as I brushed her platinum hair one last time. Then I looked over to Sephirot. My trusty steed. "Take care of my daughter. She's your little sister," I said, rubbing his fur. "Keep fighting to survive, little guy."

"You say good-bye to a cat before you say good-bye to me?" I looked to see Aisely. I hadn't seen him since the world almost blew up.

"Nope," I said plainly.

"Well, I wasn't going to say good-bye back anyways," Aisely said, crossing his arms like a brat. He looked absolutely heartbroken. I placed my daughter back in the baby carriage. I placed Sephirot in with her. I then placed the carriage in front of the door. The money was in bags next to the carriage. The money was to start Jamie's bakery that Aurick had once recommended. I also put in a card containing the child's name. And now . . . for the journal. Without memories, you will repeat history. I couldn't reveal to my daughter what I was, but I could tell her how I felt about her. I began to write. I began to write my final entry. Though ambiguous, I know she would decipher it using her heart. Others will misinterpret it, but I know she will know what it all means.

Out of infinite astronomical odds you came from my errors. I won't be there but you are not alone. You are not a bastard. You will always have a father, just as mine never left me. The seraphs and cherubs will be watching over you. They will be proved mistaken. They will see that the negative will turn to positive. I was the star that set into the west. But you were the star that rose in the east. You were the one that allowed me to leave this life with no regrets. Well . . . no. I will have regrets. I will regret not being able to kiss you anymore. To hold you anymore. To see the expression on your face when pain and death on Earth is no more. But my smile returns to me knowing that you will find someone to hold you one day. Yes, you are my legacy. Not just my legacy. You are the legacy of the Nameless. You will be a pain. But even so, I love you and trust that you will make me proud. It will all make sense when you make it into paradise where there will never be Nameless again. There will no longer be roads that end. No, they will continue without end. Yes, that's how the story will end. And again . . . I love you. I love you.

I felt that I was forgetting something. I looked through my clothes. I felt something furry in my pocket. I pulled it out. It was Angry Kid's lucky rabbit foot with a string around it. I didn't even remember having that in my pocket. I placed the rabbit-foot necklace around her neck and kissed her forehead one last time.

"I'm appointing you," I said abruptly.

Aisely looked surprised. "Appointing whom for what?"

"You, you idiot. You're going to look after my daughter."

"What?! You're crazy." He was absolutely flabbergasted.

"Not another word out of you. Use air pressure to knock on the door in exactly 32.69 seconds after I leave to call out Jamie. I don't want any weird humans touching my daughter with their filthy hands."

"You're crazy to think I'm going to take care of a child that's not even mine. That's your responsibility." I walked past him without saying anything. "I'm not kidding. Don't think you can boss me around. I'm not going to do it. I mean it, you deadbeat!"

I irritated him further by not saying anything and not looking at him. I smiled. "Good-bye, old friend," I said.

I went to the roof. I wanted to smell the fresh polluted air. I gazed up at the stars. Oddly, the sky was completely clear. Either humans had solved air pollution or I was mad. I didn't know what it was like in the Null, but I prayed that there would at least be stars to count.

"It's time," Shining Condor said. He was alone.

"Hold on."

Condor maintained a straight face. "What are you doing up here?"

"Enjoying the planet." I closed my eyes, feeling the cold breeze hit me. "For some reason . . . it looks . . . pretty to me again."

"Well, hurry it up already. I could plummet for allowing this."

I opened my eyes. "I have a finite life span while you have an infinite one. I need you to do me this one favor." Condor looked puzzled. Angels aren't allowed to do anything for Fallen so he wondered what I was going to ask. "Keep Morning Owl in your memories forever. Always remember his name."

Condor smiled. "I promise." I walked in Condor's direction. I didn't fear the Null. I didn't fear death. I accepted it. It was inevitable. I felt no anger. I felt no vengeance. Condor abruptly stopped me. "There's a chance you'll be found innocent at the trial you know. Though it's a small one, there's still a chance."

"How?"

"After you had sex with Helena, that Aurick person had sex with her."

I felt as if a meteor had crashed into my forehead. *Of course.* After I made love with Helena, Aurick took back control of the body and made love with Helena *also.* If the emission of sperm during Aurick's intercourse caused Helena to be pregnant and die, it wouldn't be my fault. At least not totally. Even if this was true, I still wasn't sure the judge would let me go. But you never know. Funny. Looks as if Aurick may have saved me. I just may enjoy this fantasy world a little while longer.

"I'm curious."

"What?"

"That card you left with your offspring. It contained her name. What is it?"

Names are for those with masters. Therefore, we have no name. The day of the demon is coming to an end. We await our upcoming execution. Many of us look forward to this imminent judgment. I am just one of many. Mine is one of many stories. I have wandered the earth for millennia trying to find a way out. I realize now that we have already found a way out. We will always live on in His eternal memory. We do not truly fear death.

We fear losing our names. The truth was that my name was never to be forgotten. True peace. Until then I patiently wait. Waiting patiently for the reunion. Irony's judgment is ticklish. She is Purity. To her, I am *Nameless*.

Never forget . . .

ACKNOWLEDGMENTS

I thank the woman who birthed me and kept me breathing all these years. Your family also helped me keep focused in strange ways. Don't ask how.

I would like to acknowledge all the people who got me this far. Thank you, Nicole Duncan-Smith and Karen Hunter, for discovering me. If it weren't for you guys, this story that had to be told would still be in the refrigerator.

Thanks, Clarence Haynes, for the patience, hard work, and buying me hot chocolate.

Thanks, Julio Rivera, for reminding me to keep my path straight and reminding me to keep everything in proper perspective. Seriously, you mattered.

Thanks, Hubert Beatrice, for being the mirror for me to challenge my bizarro world self. In an odd way, you helped me better myself as a person and strengthen my convictions.

I thank Eddy Collazo for being the funniest guy I met in years. You cheered me up through those bad years.

Trevon Steele. That's all I got to say about you.

Thanks, Ms. Rosenthal. You helped me rediscover my passion for writing.

Thank you, Ms. Katz, for letting me talk your ear to death five days a week for two years. It was fun.

I have nothing to thank Forhad and Fawad for. Seriously.

I don't like Penna.

Thanks, Victor and Victoria, for being good people. Victor you are smart. Victoria, you are funny and pretty.

You won't be forgotten, Rey Penbiro.

But seriously, thanks, Trevon, for helping me not take things so seriously, like a certain someone. You helped out a lot.

And thank you, Vosharra Wooten. You have a lovely name.

If I forgot anyone, I don't care. It's probably because I don't like you.

I got one watermelon.